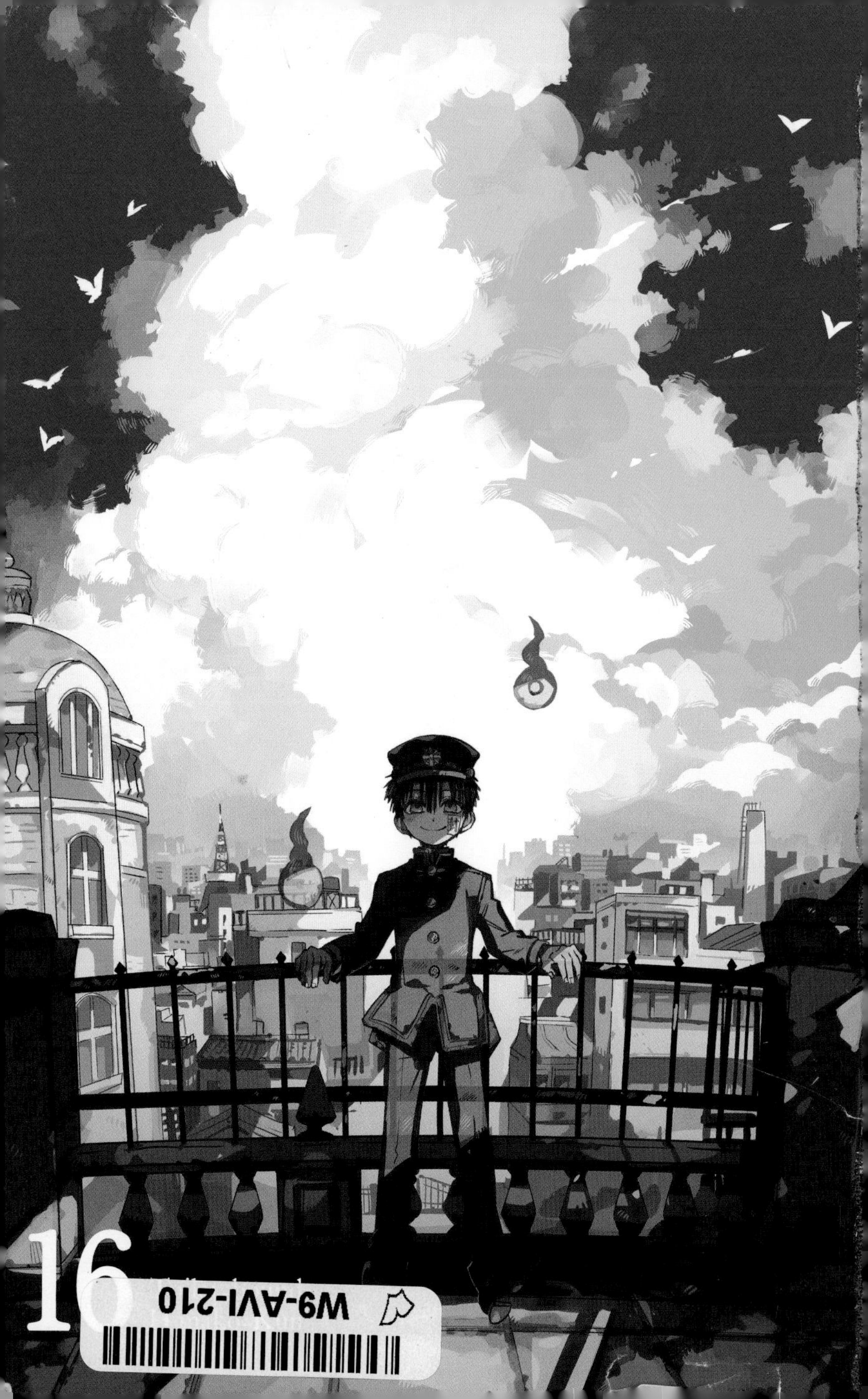
16

Contents

Spook 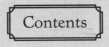76

The Red House (Part 1) ······· 003

Spook 77

The Red House (Part 2) ······· 031

Spook 78

The Red House (Part 3) ······· 071

Spook 79

The Red House (Part 4) ······· 099

Spook 80

The Red House (Part 5) ······· 137

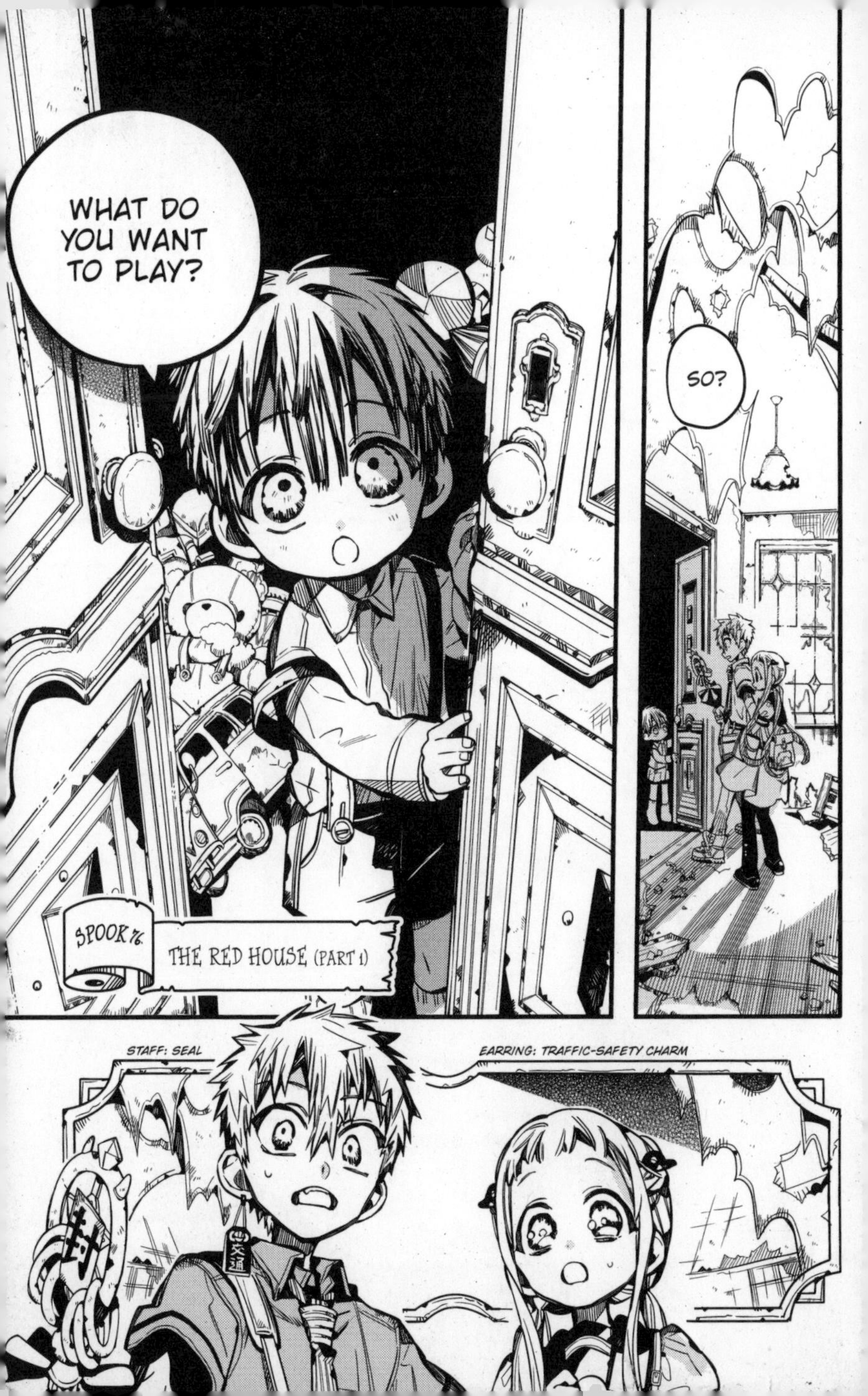
SO?
WHAT DO YOU WANT TO PLAY?
SPOOK 76.
THE RED HOUSE (PART 1)
EARRING: TRAFFIC-SAFETY CHARM
STAFF: SEAL

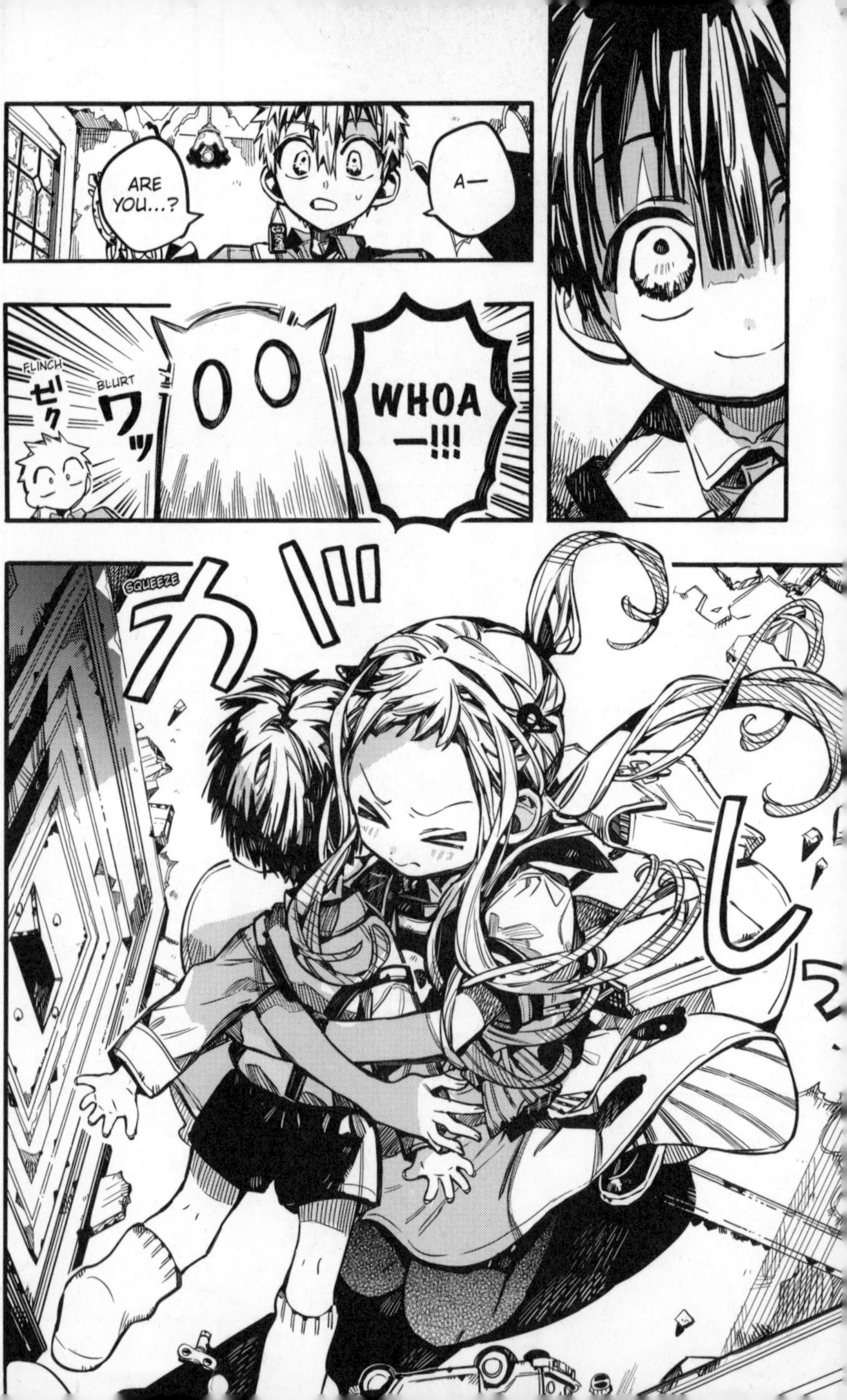
A—
ARE YOU...?
WHOA—!!!
BLURT
ワッ
FLINCH
ビク
SQUEEZE
しっ

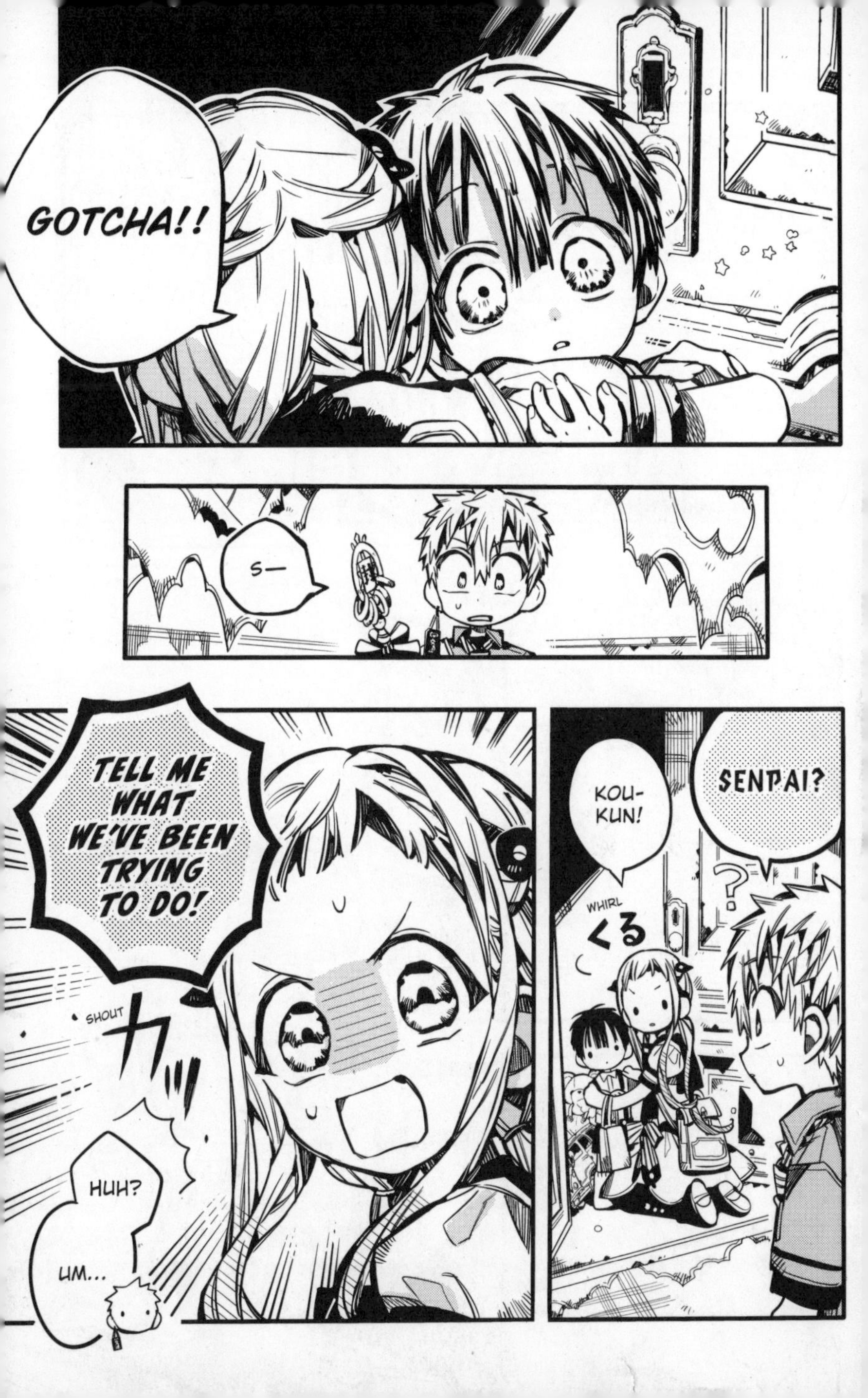
GOTCHA!!
S—
SENPAI?
KOU-KUN!
WHIRL
くる
TELL ME WHAT WE'VE BEEN TRYING TO DO!
SHOUT
カッ
HUH?
UM...

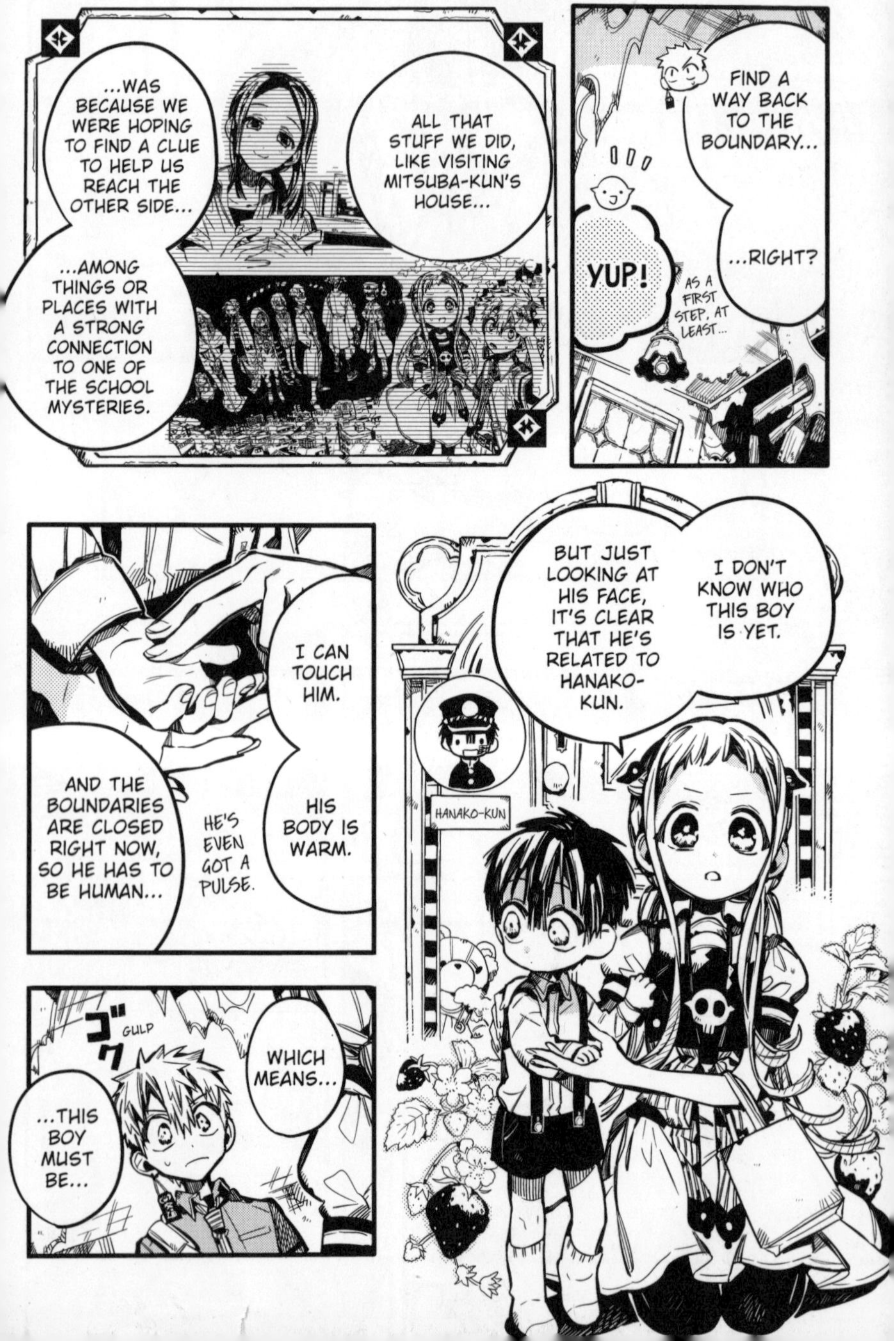
FIND A WAY BACK TO THE BOUNDARY...
...RIGHT?
YUP!
AS A FIRST STEP, AT LEAST...
ALL THAT STUFF WE DID, LIKE VISITING MITSUBA-KUN'S HOUSE...
...WAS BECAUSE WE WERE HOPING TO FIND A CLUE TO HELP US REACH THE OTHER SIDE...
...AMONG THINGS OR PLACES WITH A STRONG CONNECTION TO ONE OF THE SCHOOL MYSTERIES.
I DON'T KNOW WHO THIS BOY IS YET.
BUT JUST LOOKING AT HIS FACE, IT'S CLEAR THAT HE'S RELATED TO HANAKO-KUN.
HANAKO-KUN
I CAN TOUCH HIM.
HIS BODY IS WARM.
HE'S EVEN GOT A PULSE.
AND THE BOUNDARIES ARE CLOSED RIGHT NOW, SO HE HAS TO BE HUMAN...
WHICH MEANS...
ゴク GULP
...THIS BOY MUST BE...

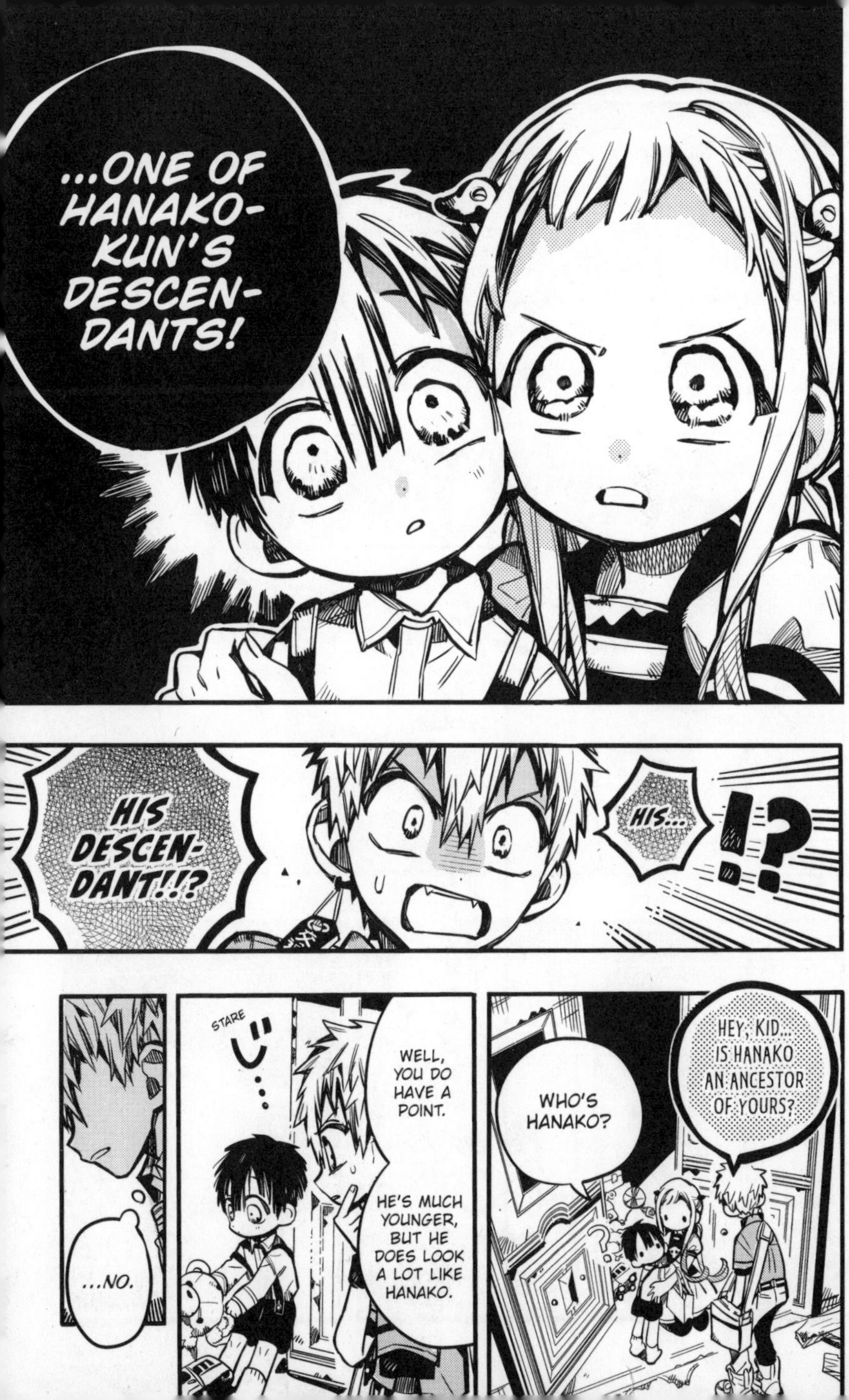
...ONE OF HANAKO-KUN'S DESCEN-DANTS!
HIS... !?
HIS DESCEN-DANT!!?
HEY, KID... IS HANAKO AN ANCESTOR OF YOURS?
WHO'S HANAKO?
WELL, YOU DO HAVE A POINT.
STARE
HE'S MUCH YOUNGER, BUT HE DOES LOOK A LOT LIKE HANAKO.
...NO.

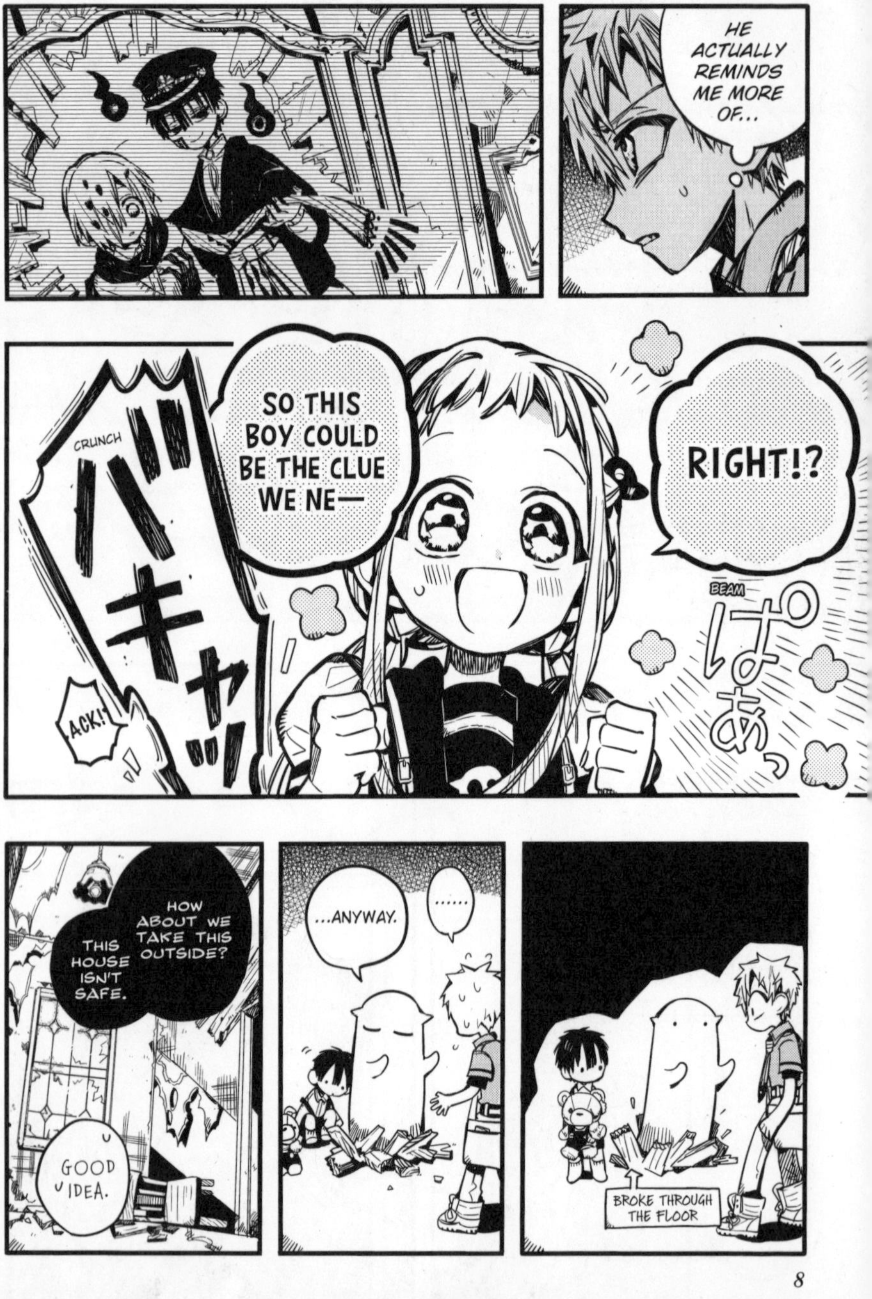
HE ACTUALLY REMINDS ME MORE OF...
RIGHT!?
BEAM
ぱあっ
SO THIS BOY COULD BE THE CLUE WE NE—
CRUNCH
バキャッ
ACK!
BROKE THROUGH THE FLOOR
......
...ANYWAY.
HOW ABOUT WE TAKE THIS OUTSIDE?
THIS HOUSE ISN'T SAFE.
GOOD IDEA.

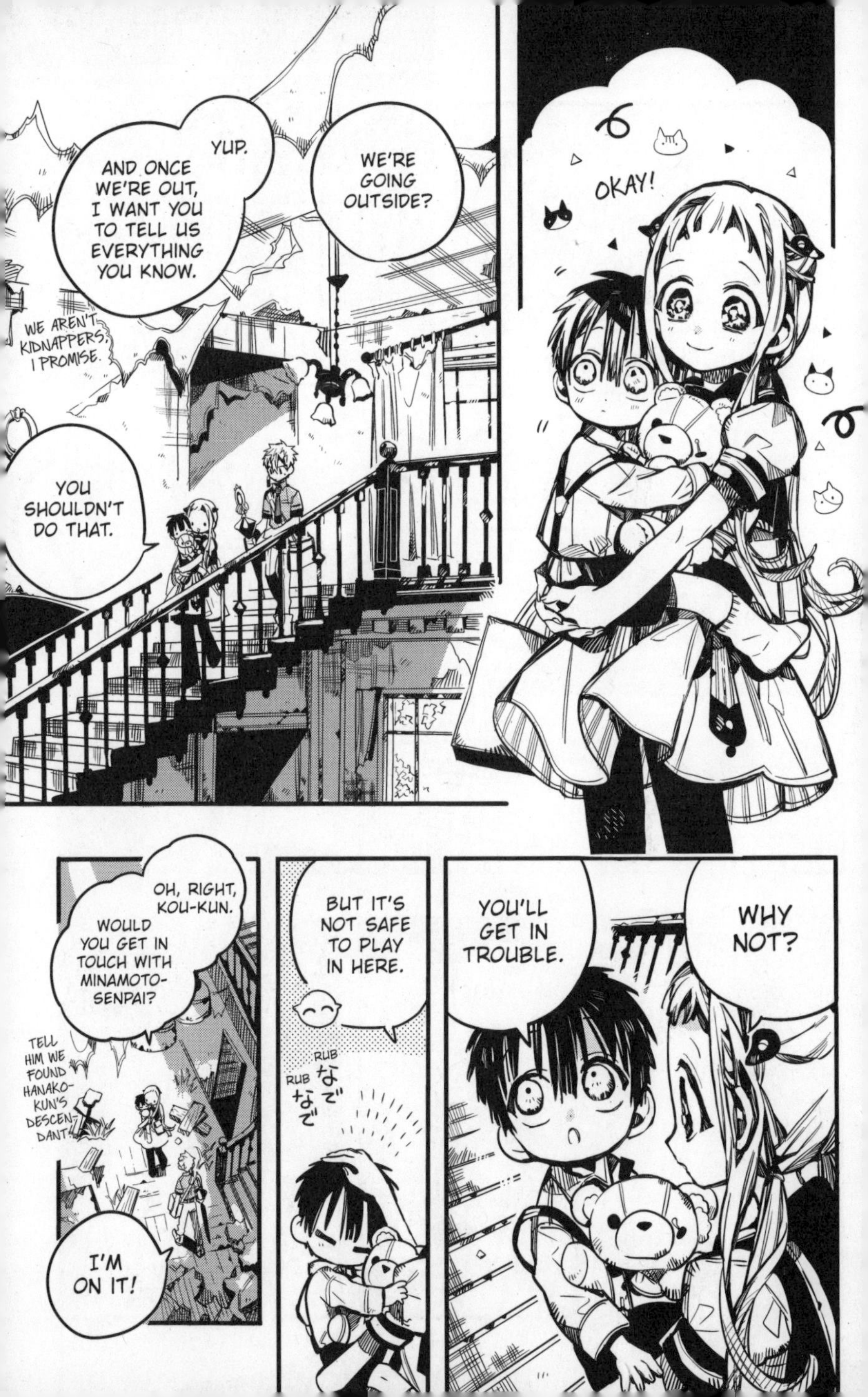
OKAY!
WE'RE GOING OUTSIDE?
YUP. AND ONCE WE'RE OUT, I WANT YOU TO TELL US EVERYTHING YOU KNOW.
WE AREN'T KIDNAPPERS, I PROMISE.
YOU SHOULDN'T DO THAT.
WHY NOT?
YOU'LL GET IN TROUBLE.
BUT IT'S NOT SAFE TO PLAY IN HERE.
RUB なで RUB なで
OH, RIGHT, KOU-KUN. WOULD YOU GET IN TOUCH WITH MINAMOTO-SENPAI?
TELL HIM WE FOUND HANAKO-KUN'S DESCENDANT!
I'M ON IT!

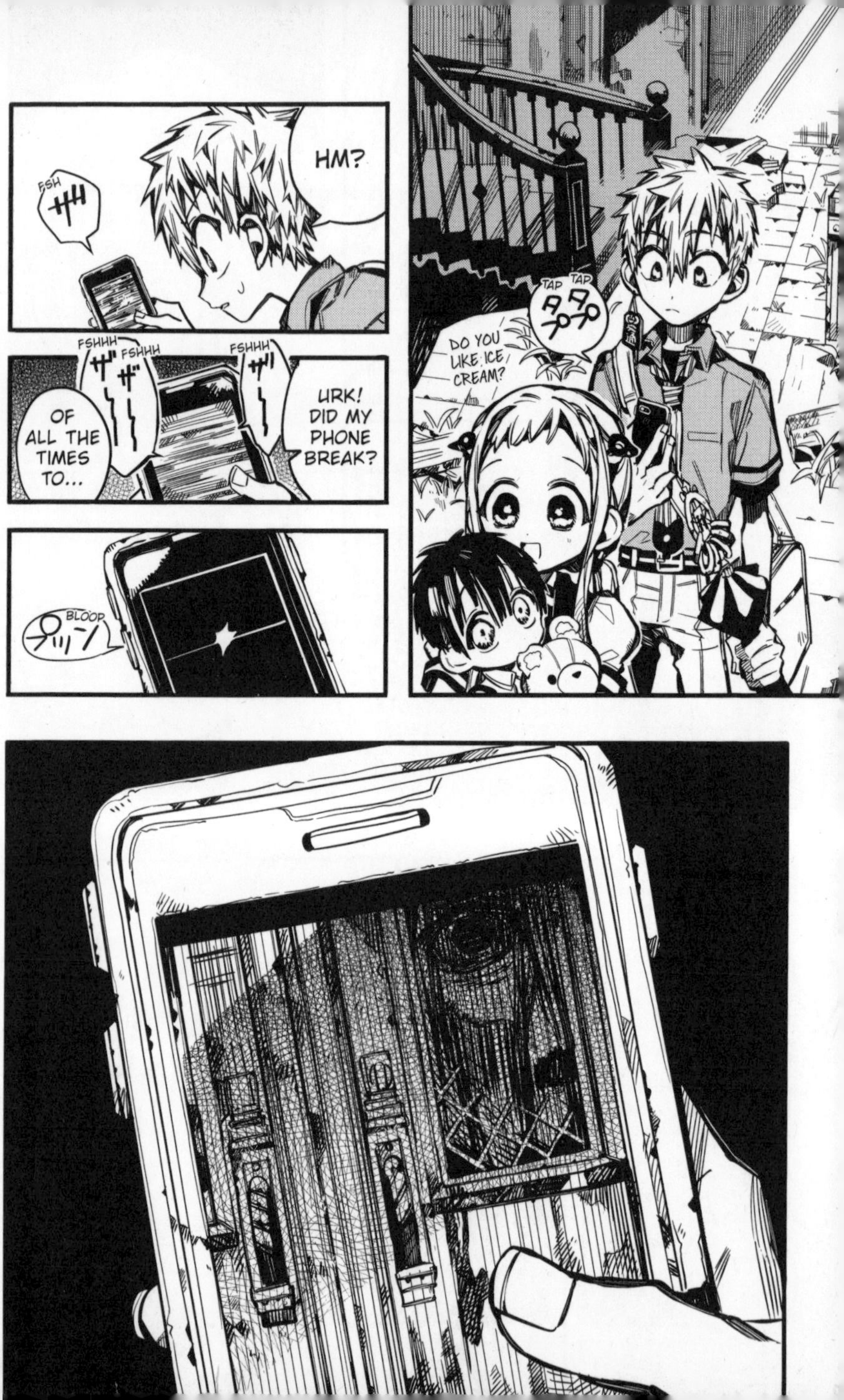
TAP TAP
DO YOU LIKE ICE CREAM?
FSH
HM?
FSHHH
URK! DID MY PHONE BREAK?
FSHHH FSHHH
OF ALL THE TIMES TO...
BLOOP

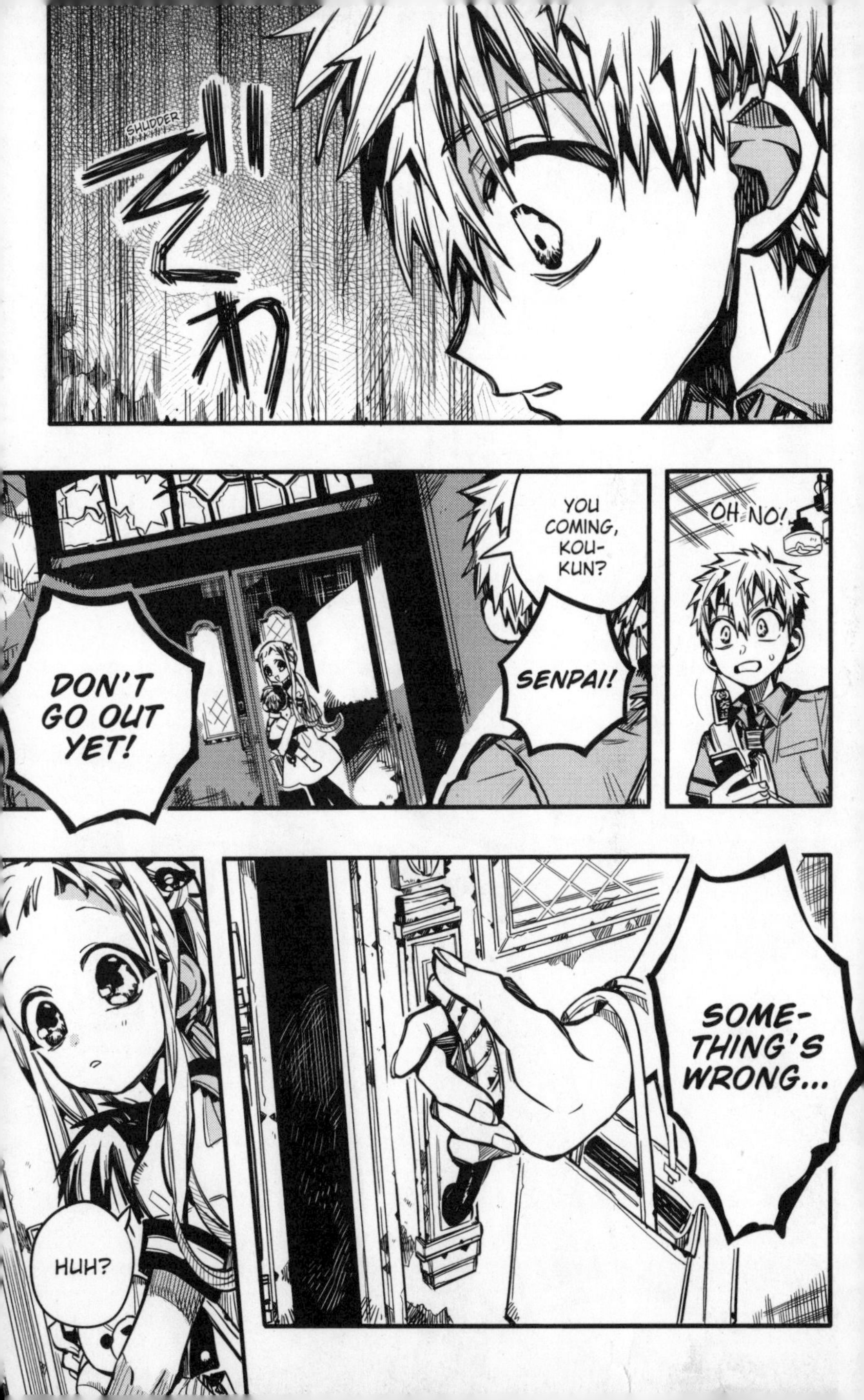
SHUDDER
OH NO!
YOU COMING, KOU-KUN?
SENPAI!
DON'T GO OUT YET!
SOME-THING'S WRONG...
HUH?

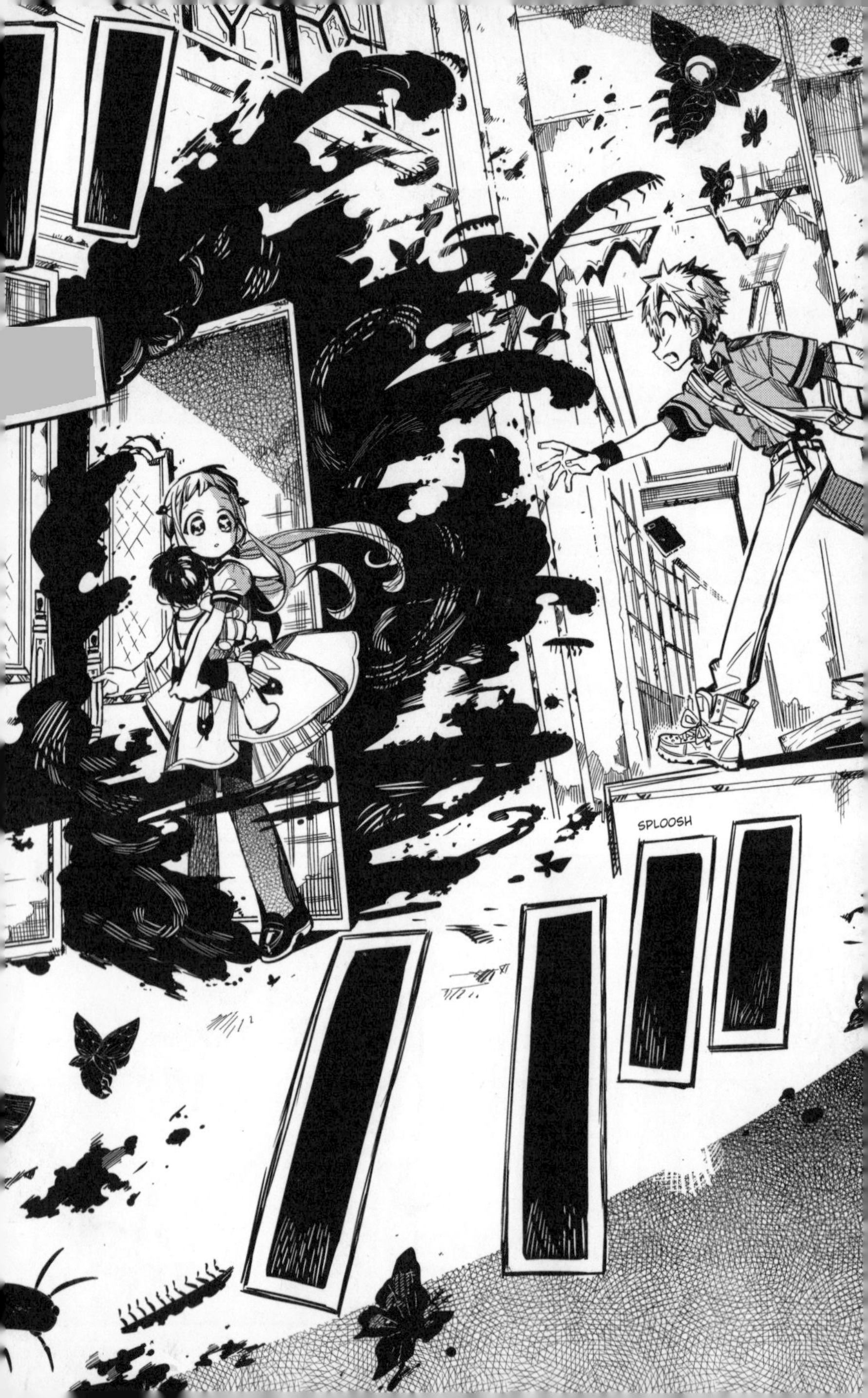
SPLOOSH

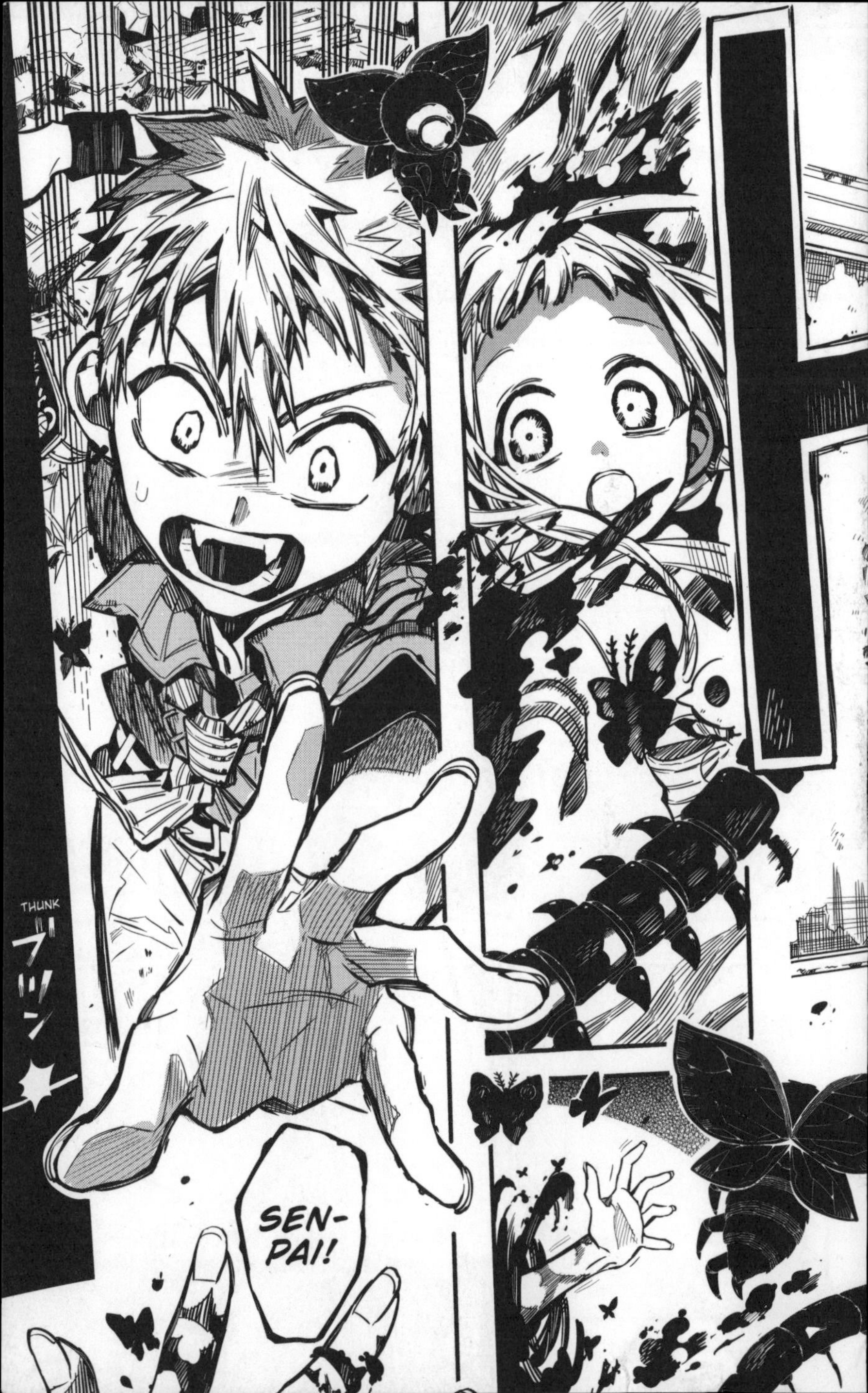
THUNK
ブッツン
SEN-PAI!

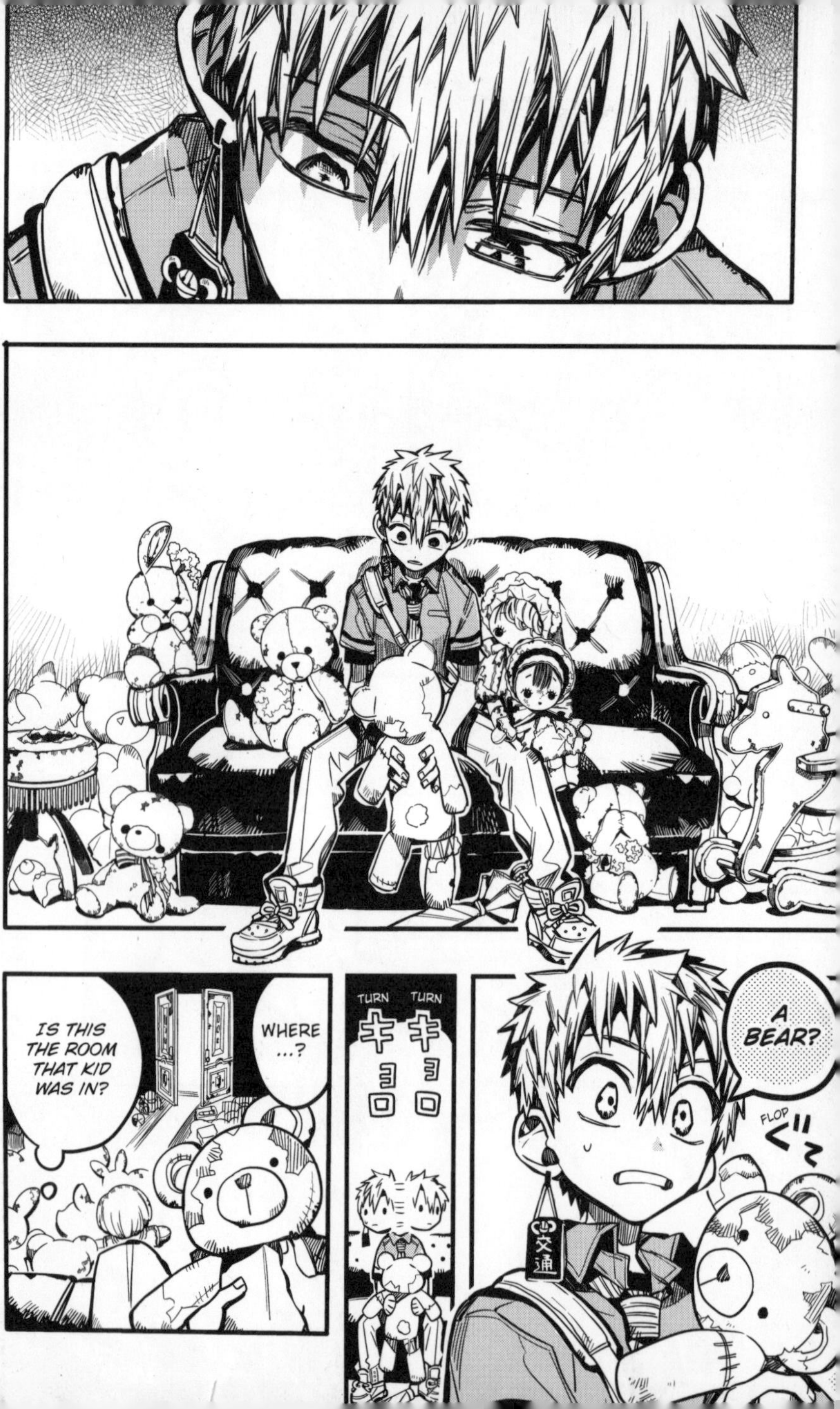
A BEAR?
FLOP
TURN TURN
キョロキョロ
WHERE ...?
IS THIS THE ROOM THAT KID WAS IN?

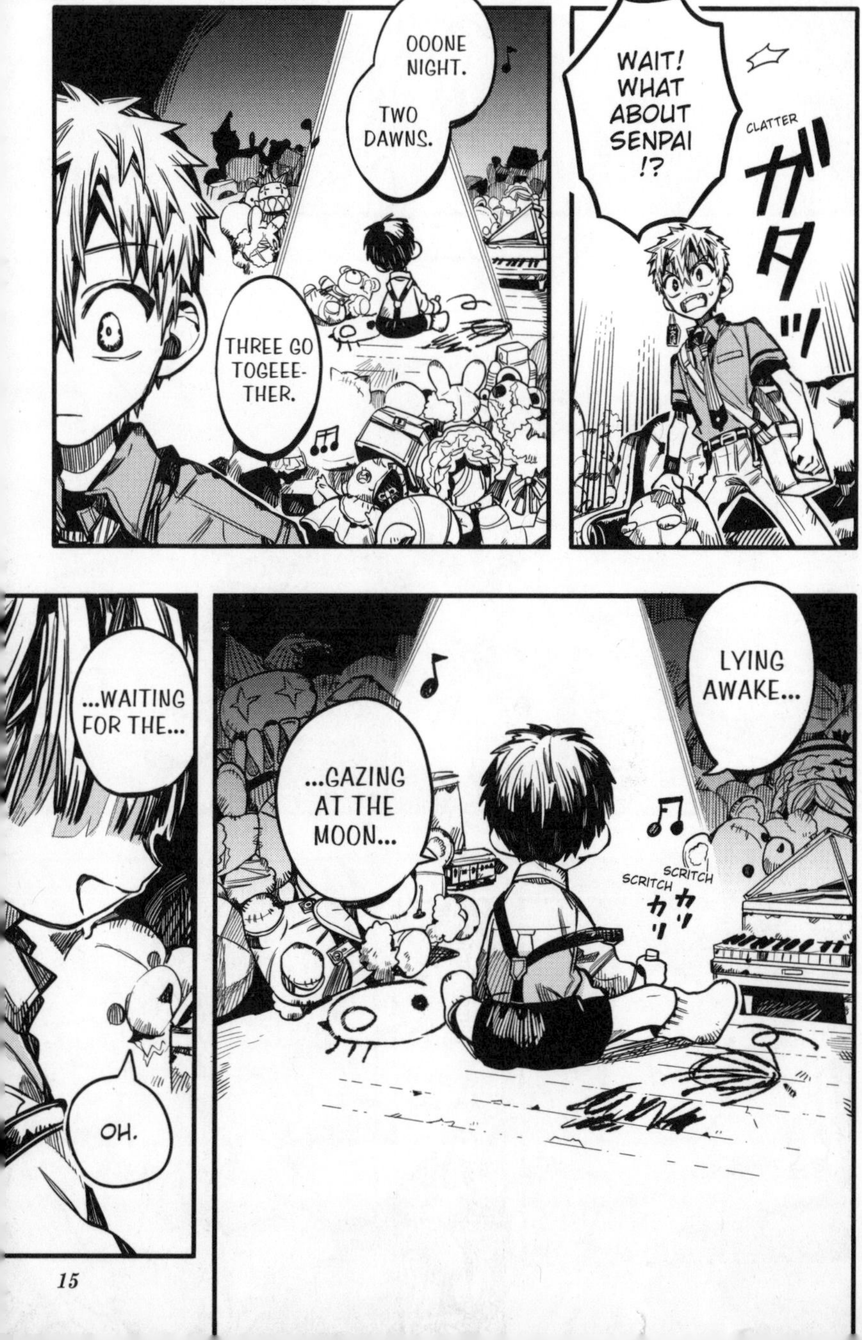
WAIT! WHAT ABOUT SENPAI !?
CLATTER
ガタッ
OOONE NIGHT.
TWO DAWNS.
THREE GO TOGEEE-THER.
LYING AWAKE...
...GAZING AT THE MOON...
SCRITCH SCRITCH
カリカリ
...WAITING FOR THE...
OH.

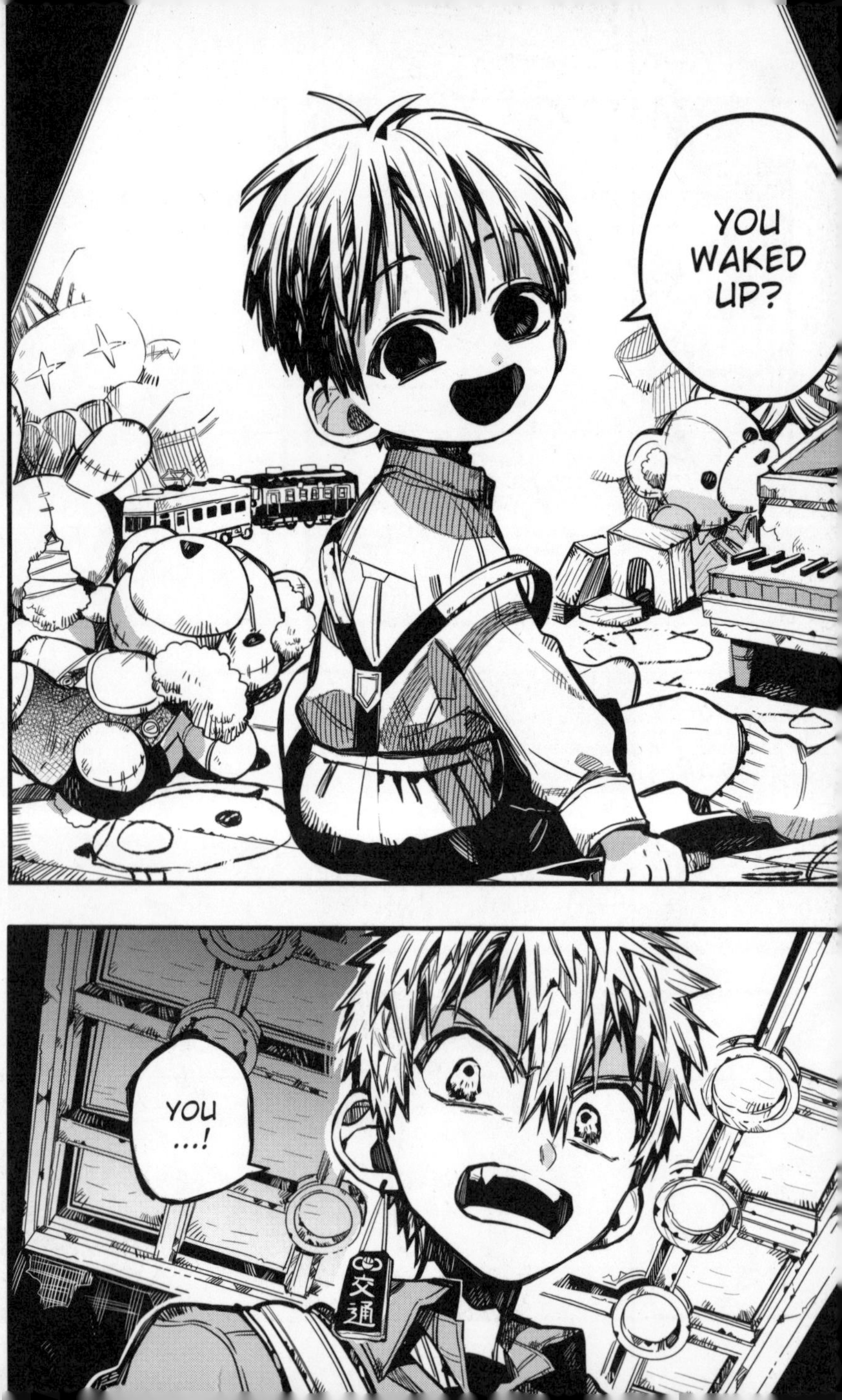
YOU WAKED UP?
YOU ...!
交通

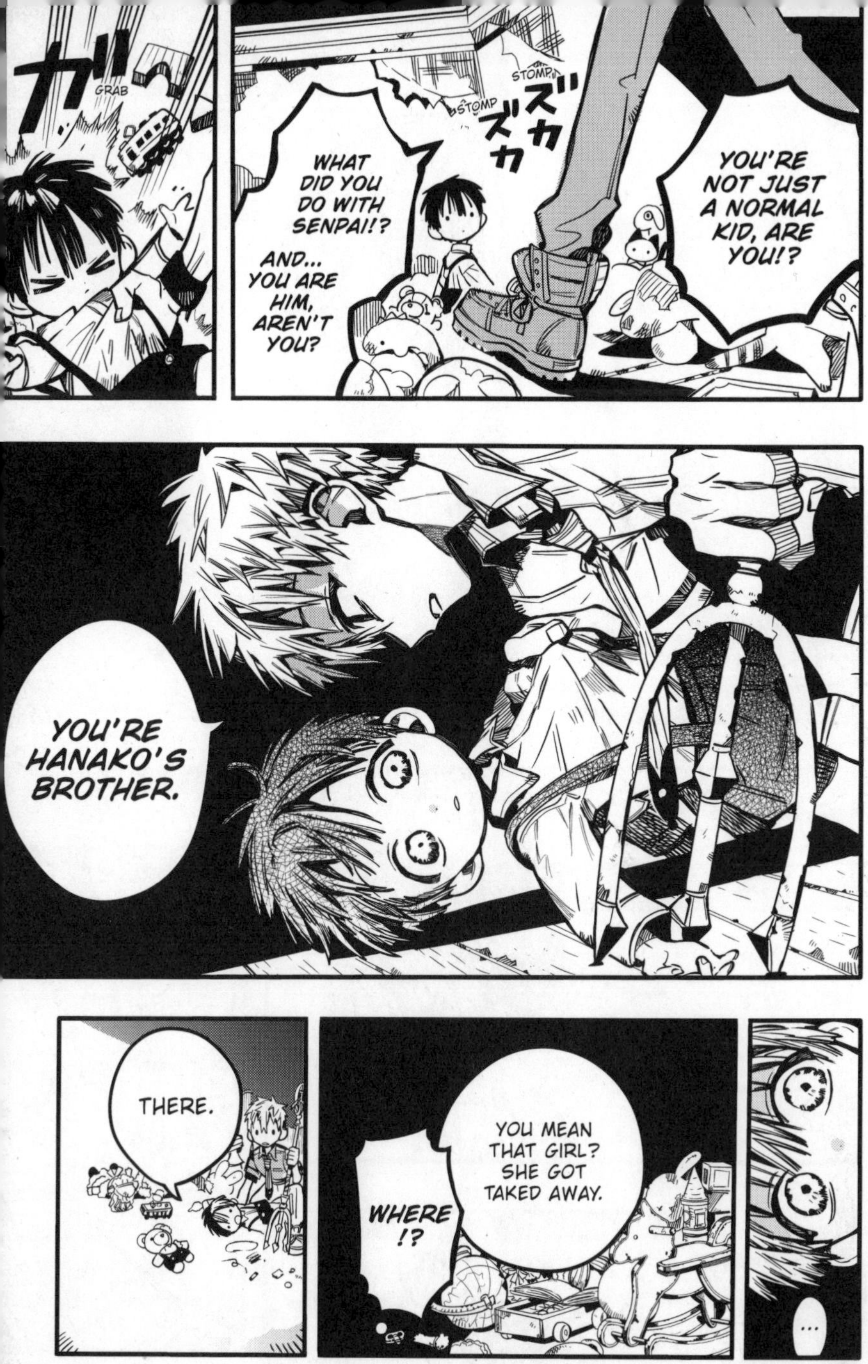

STOMP
ズカ
STOMP
ズカ
YOU'RE NOT JUST A NORMAL KID, ARE YOU!?
WHAT DID YOU DO WITH SENPAI!?
AND... YOU ARE HIM, AREN'T YOU?
ガッ
GRAB
YOU'RE HANAKO'S BROTHER.
...
YOU MEAN THAT GIRL? SHE GOT TAKED AWAY.
WHERE !?
THERE.

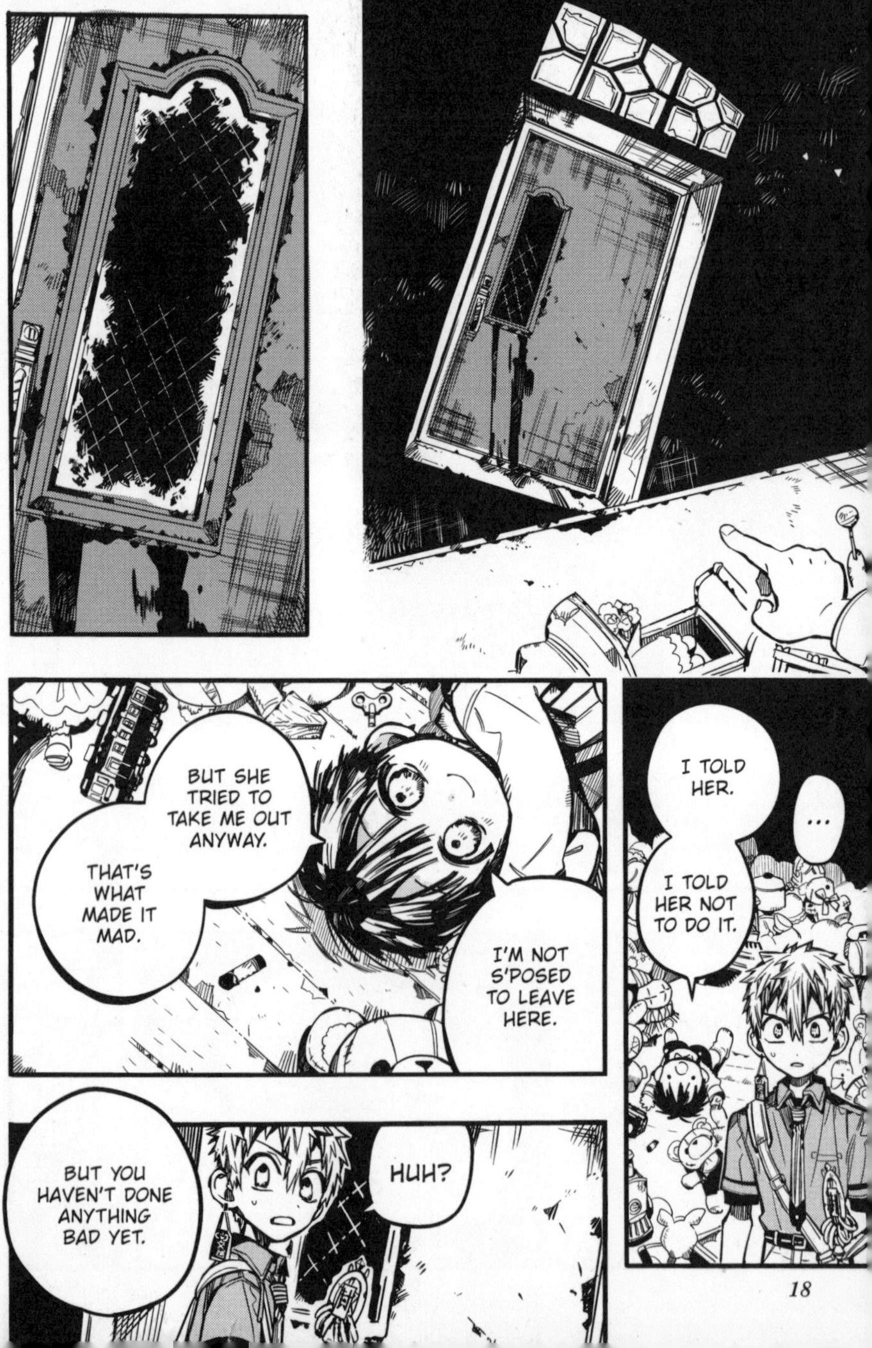
I TOLD HER.
...
I TOLD HER NOT TO DO IT.
I'M NOT S'POSED TO LEAVE HERE.
BUT SHE TRIED TO TAKE ME OUT ANYWAY.
THAT'S WHAT MADE IT MAD.
HUH?
BUT YOU HAVEN'T DONE ANYTHING BAD YET.

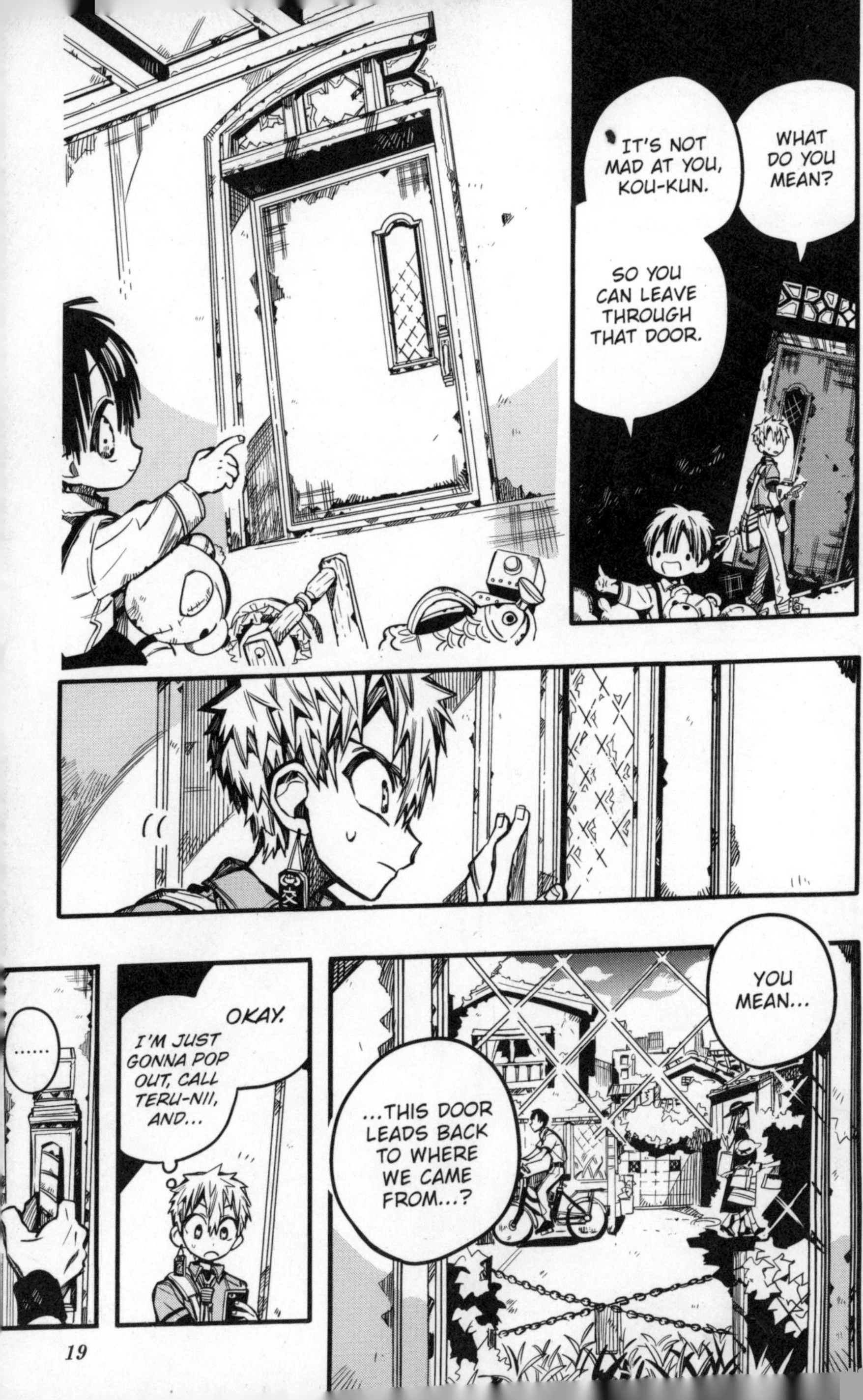
WHAT DO YOU MEAN?
IT'S NOT MAD AT YOU, KOU-KUN.
SO YOU CAN LEAVE THROUGH THAT DOOR.
YOU MEAN...
...THIS DOOR LEADS BACK TO WHERE WE CAME FROM...?
OKAY.
I'M JUST GONNA POP OUT, CALL TERU-NII, AND...
......

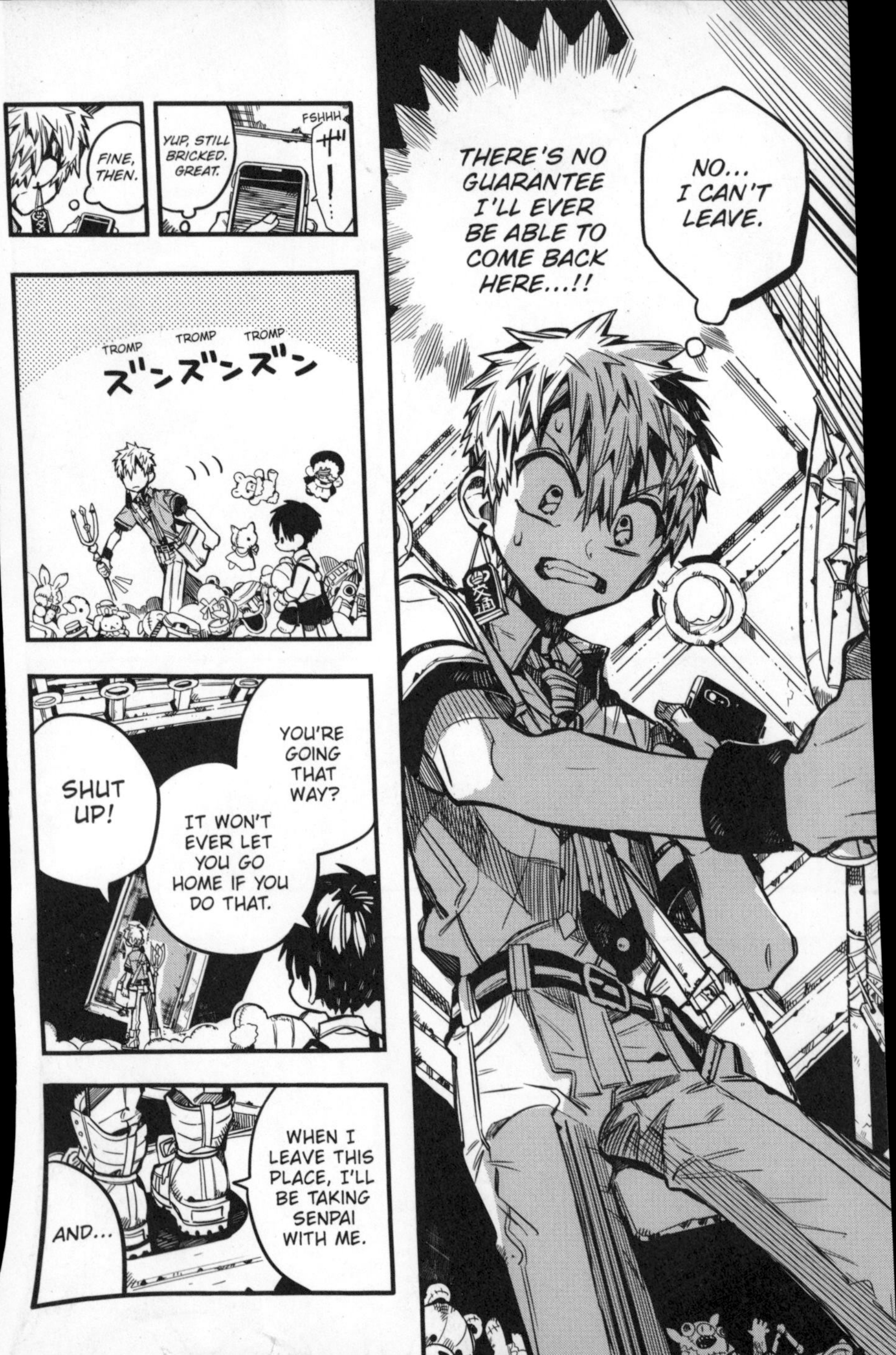
NO... I CAN'T LEAVE.
THERE'S NO GUARANTEE I'LL EVER BE ABLE TO COME BACK HERE...!!
FSHHH
YUP, STILL BRICKED. GREAT.
FINE, THEN.
TROMP TROMP TROMP
ズンズンズン
YOU'RE GOING THAT WAY?
IT WON'T EVER LET YOU GO HOME IF YOU DO THAT.
SHUT UP!
WHEN I LEAVE THIS PLACE, I'LL BE TAKING SENPAI WITH ME.
AND...

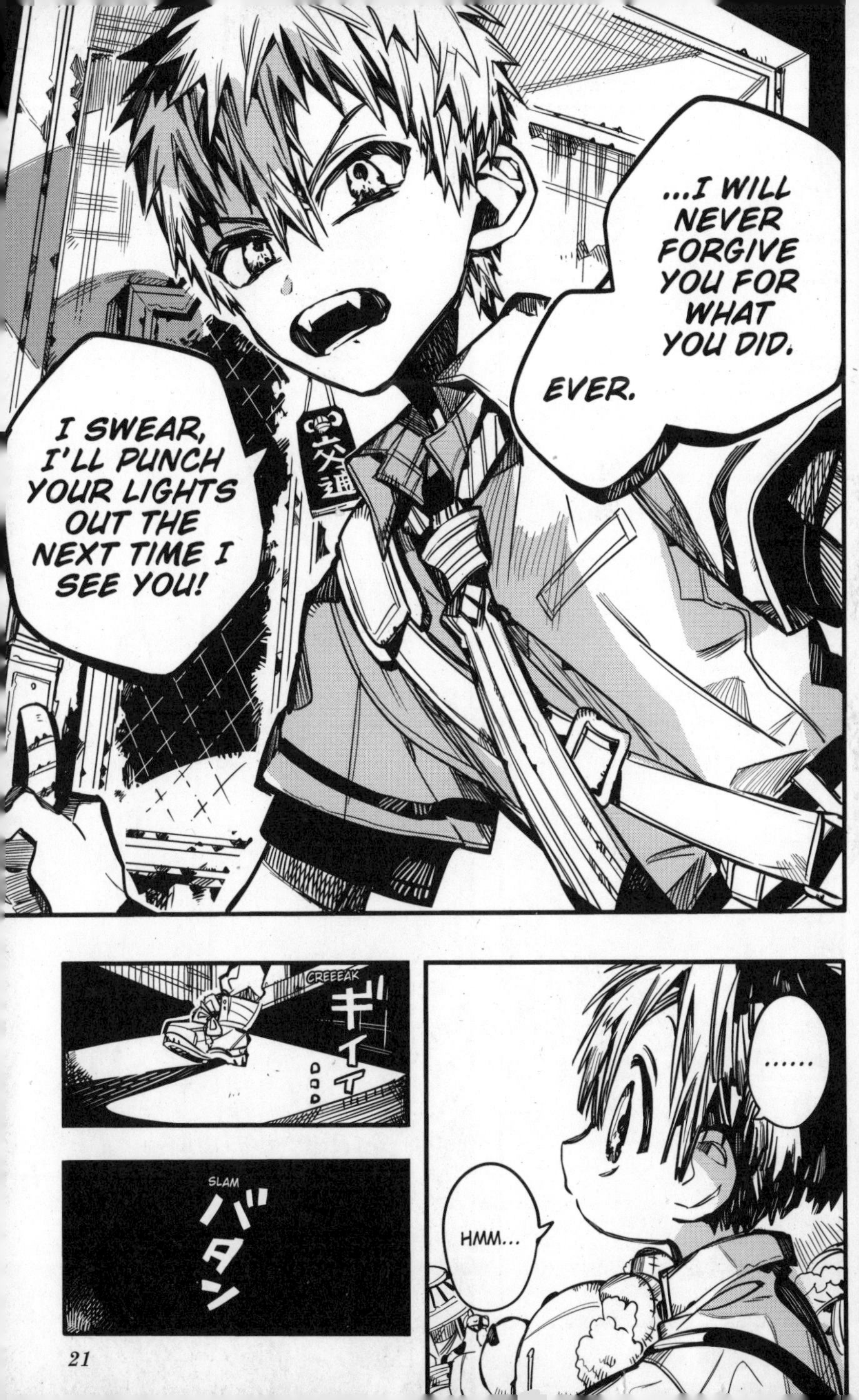
...I WILL NEVER FORGIVE YOU FOR WHAT YOU DID.
EVER.
交通
I SWEAR, I'LL PUNCH YOUR LIGHTS OUT THE NEXT TIME I SEE YOU!
......
HMM...
CREEEAK
ギイイ
SLAM
バタン

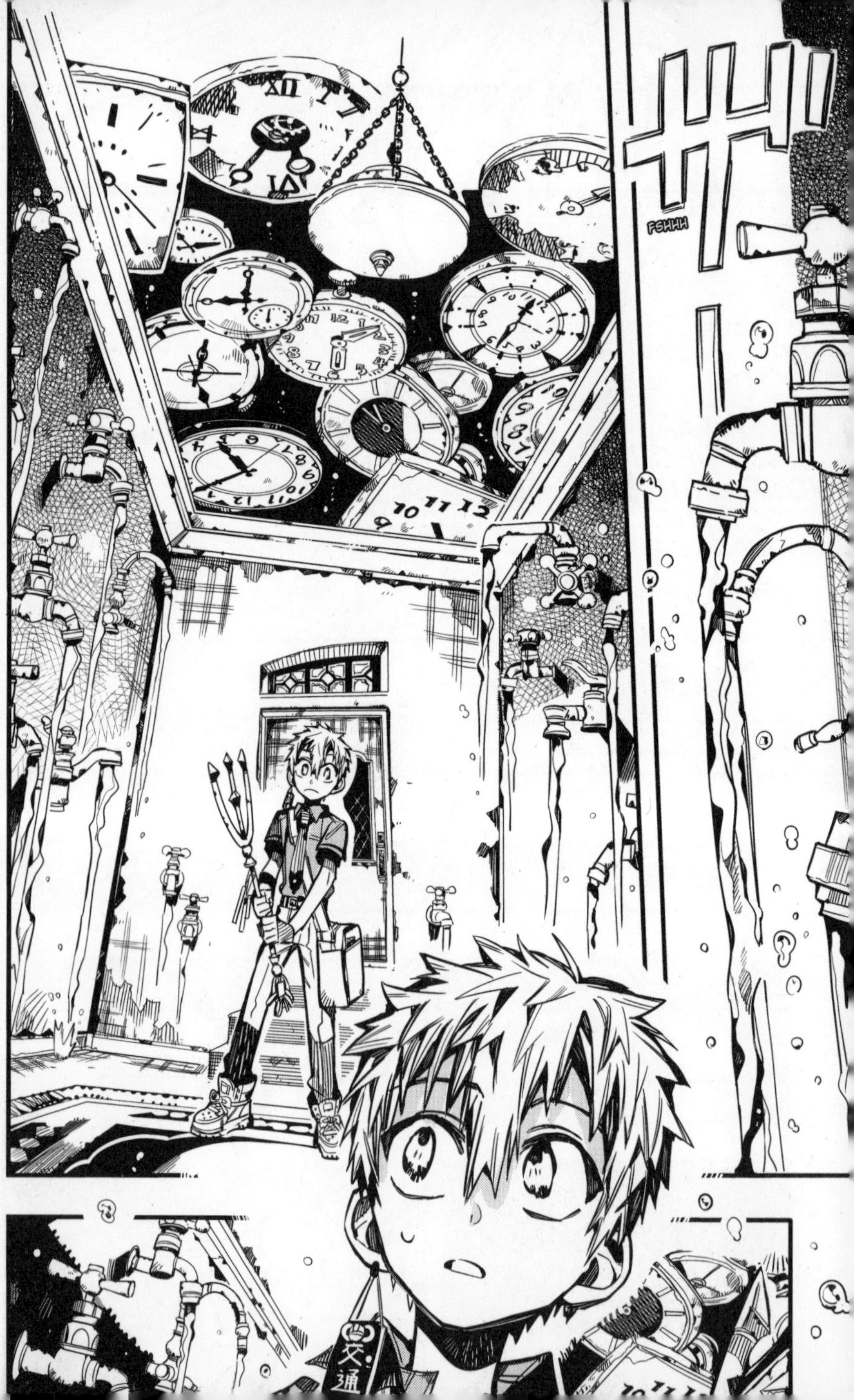
FSHHH
交通

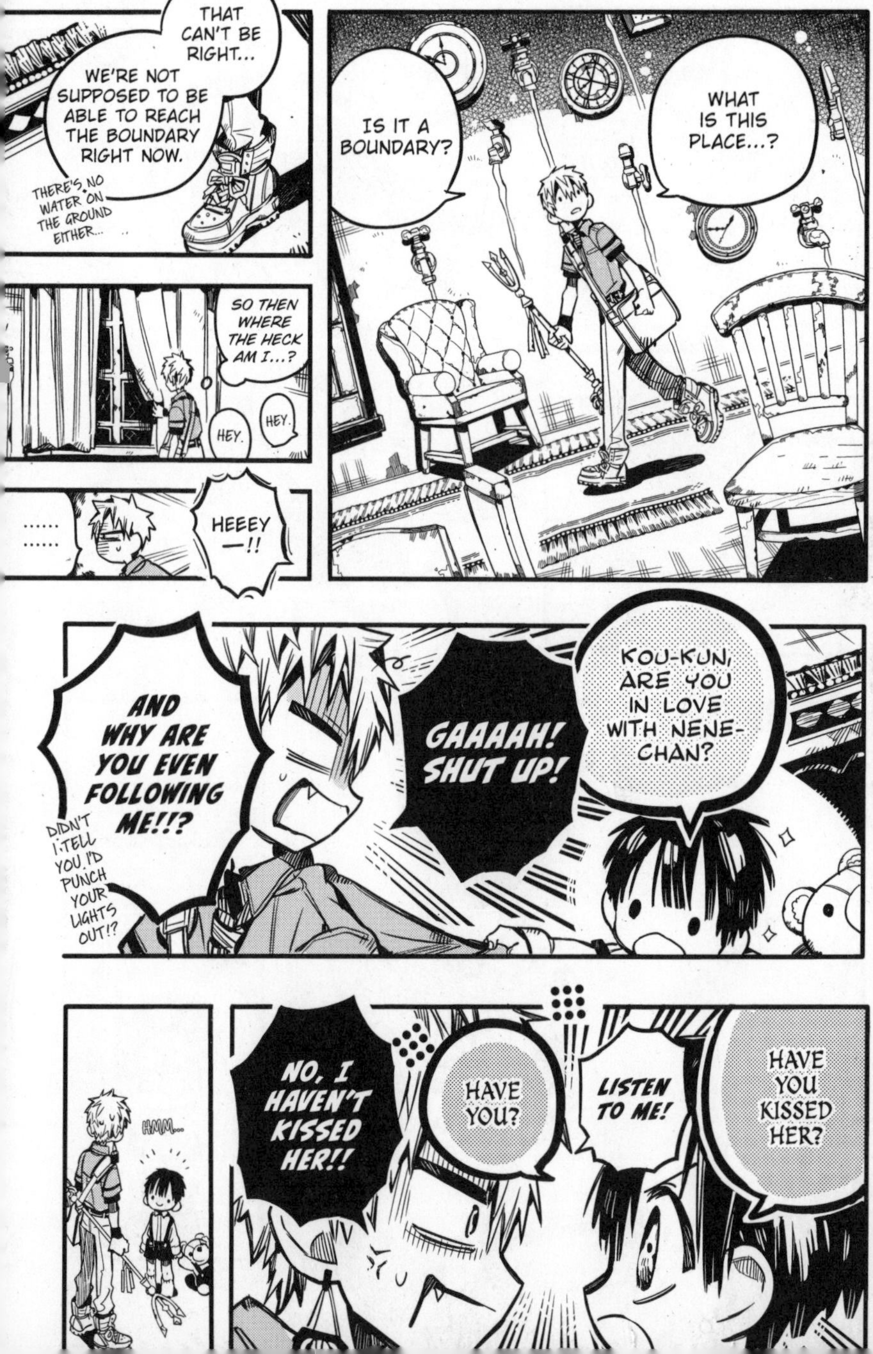
WHAT IS THIS PLACE...?
IS IT A BOUNDARY?
THAT CAN'T BE RIGHT...
WE'RE NOT SUPPOSED TO BE ABLE TO REACH THE BOUNDARY RIGHT NOW.
THERE'S NO WATER ON THE GROUND EITHER...
SO THEN WHERE THE HECK AM I...?
HEY.
HEY.
HEEEY—!!
......
......
KOU-KUN, ARE YOU IN LOVE WITH NENE-CHAN?
GAAAAH! SHUT UP!
AND WHY ARE YOU EVEN FOLLOWING ME!!?
DIDN'T I TELL YOU I'D PUNCH YOUR LIGHTS OUT!?
HAVE YOU KISSED HER?
LISTEN TO ME!
HAVE YOU?
NO, I HAVEN'T KISSED HER!!
HMM...

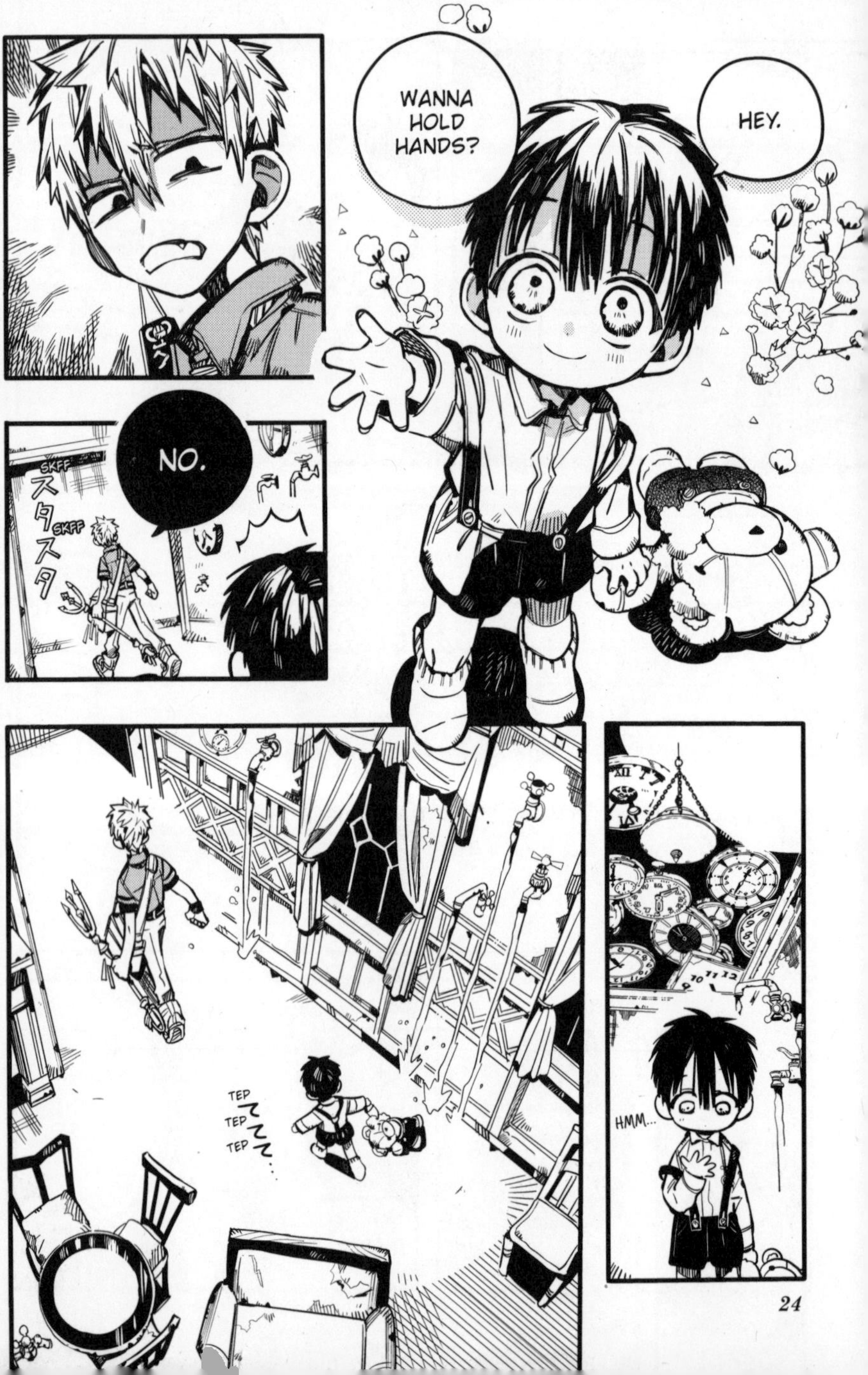
HEY.
WANNA HOLD HANDS?
NO.
SKFF
スタ
SKFF
スタ
HMM...
TEP
TEP
TEP

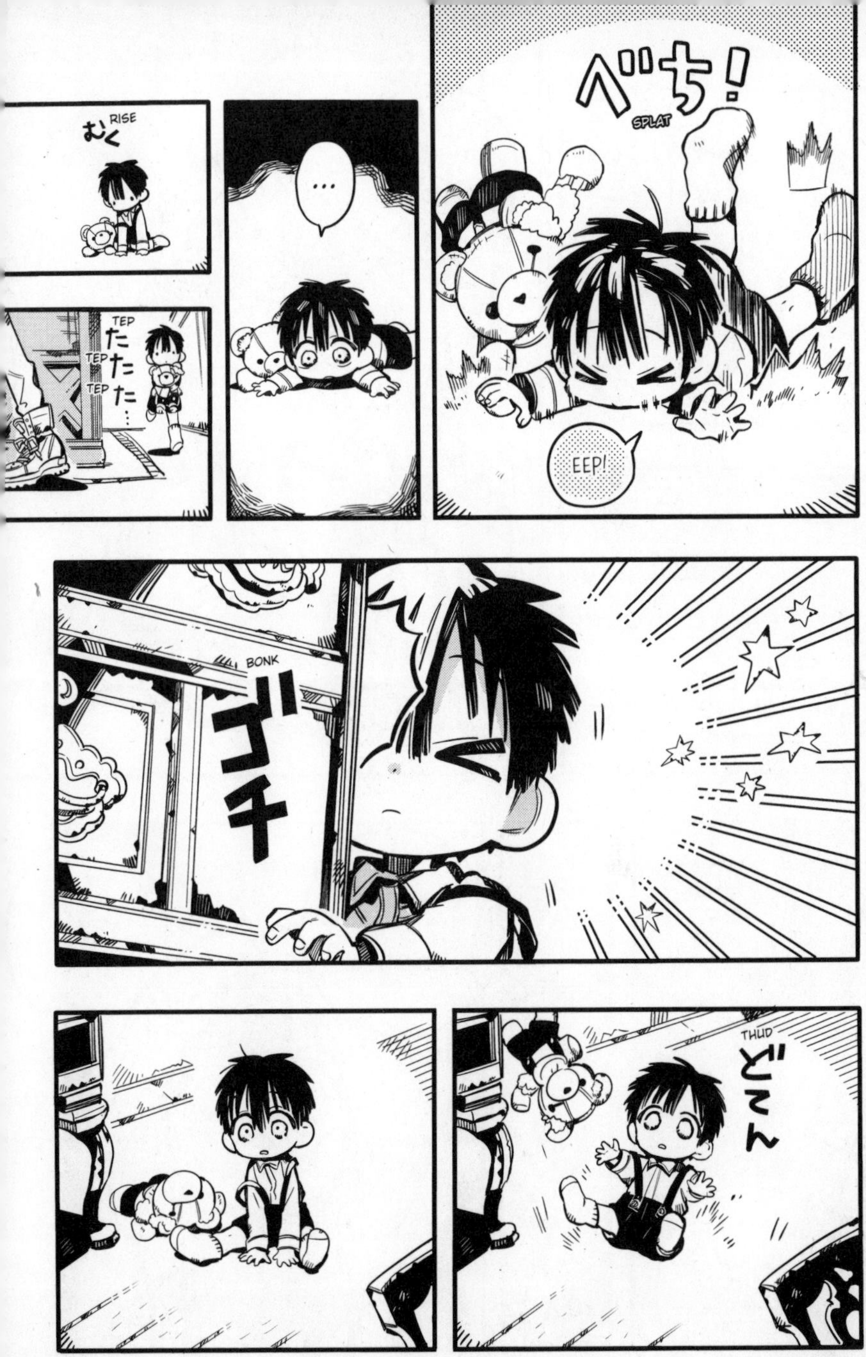
べち!
SPLAT
EEP!
...
むく
RISE
たたた...
TEP
TEP
TEP
ゴチ
BONK
どてん
THUD

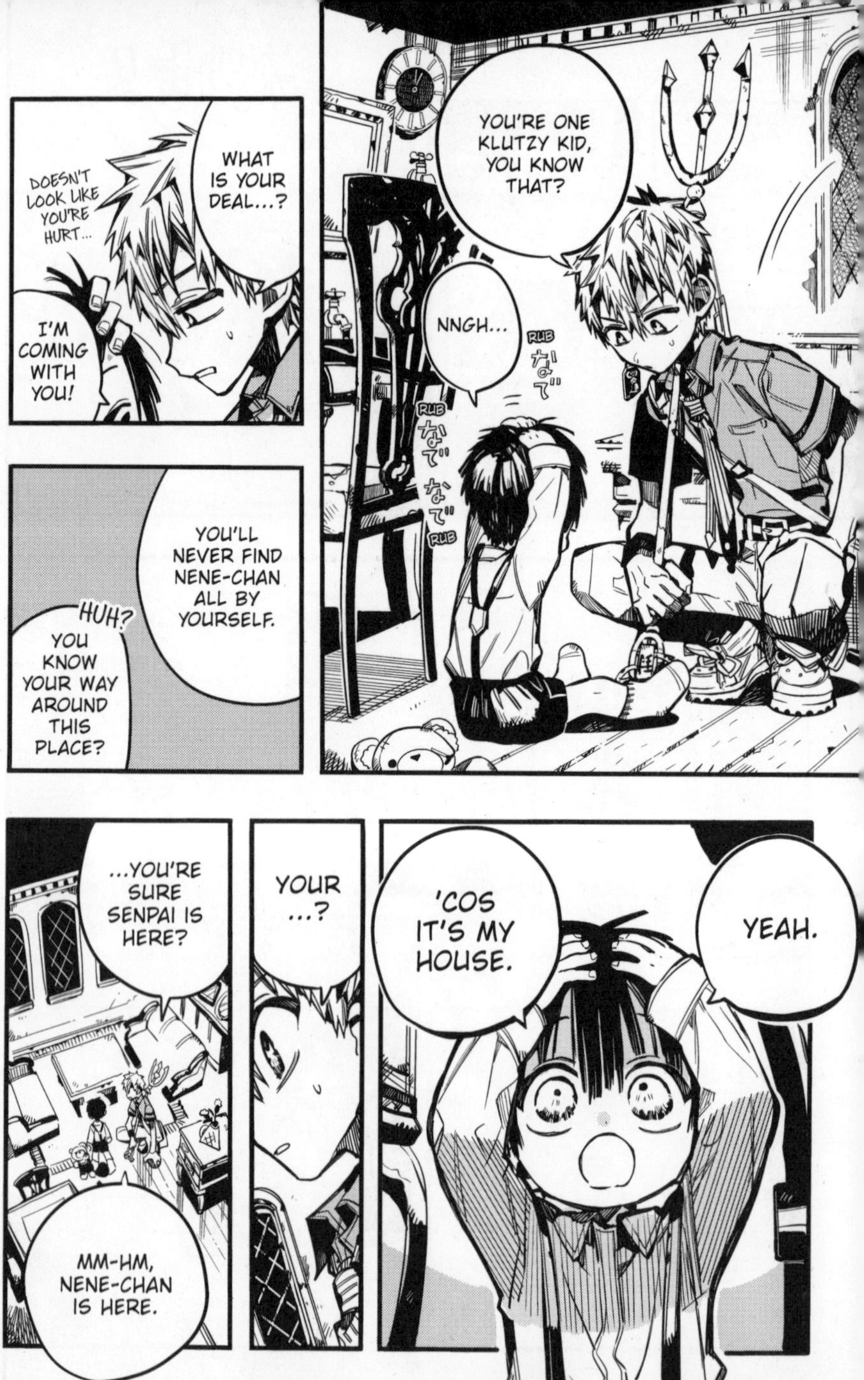
YOU'RE ONE KLUTZY KID, YOU KNOW THAT?
NNGH...
RUB なで
RUB なで
なで RUB
WHAT IS YOUR DEAL...?
DOESN'T LOOK LIKE YOU'RE HURT...
I'M COMING WITH YOU!
YOU'LL NEVER FIND NENE-CHAN ALL BY YOURSELF.
HUH?
YOU KNOW YOUR WAY AROUND THIS PLACE?
YEAH.
'COS IT'S MY HOUSE.
YOUR ...?
...YOU'RE SURE SENPAI IS HERE?
MM-HM, NENE-CHAN IS HERE.

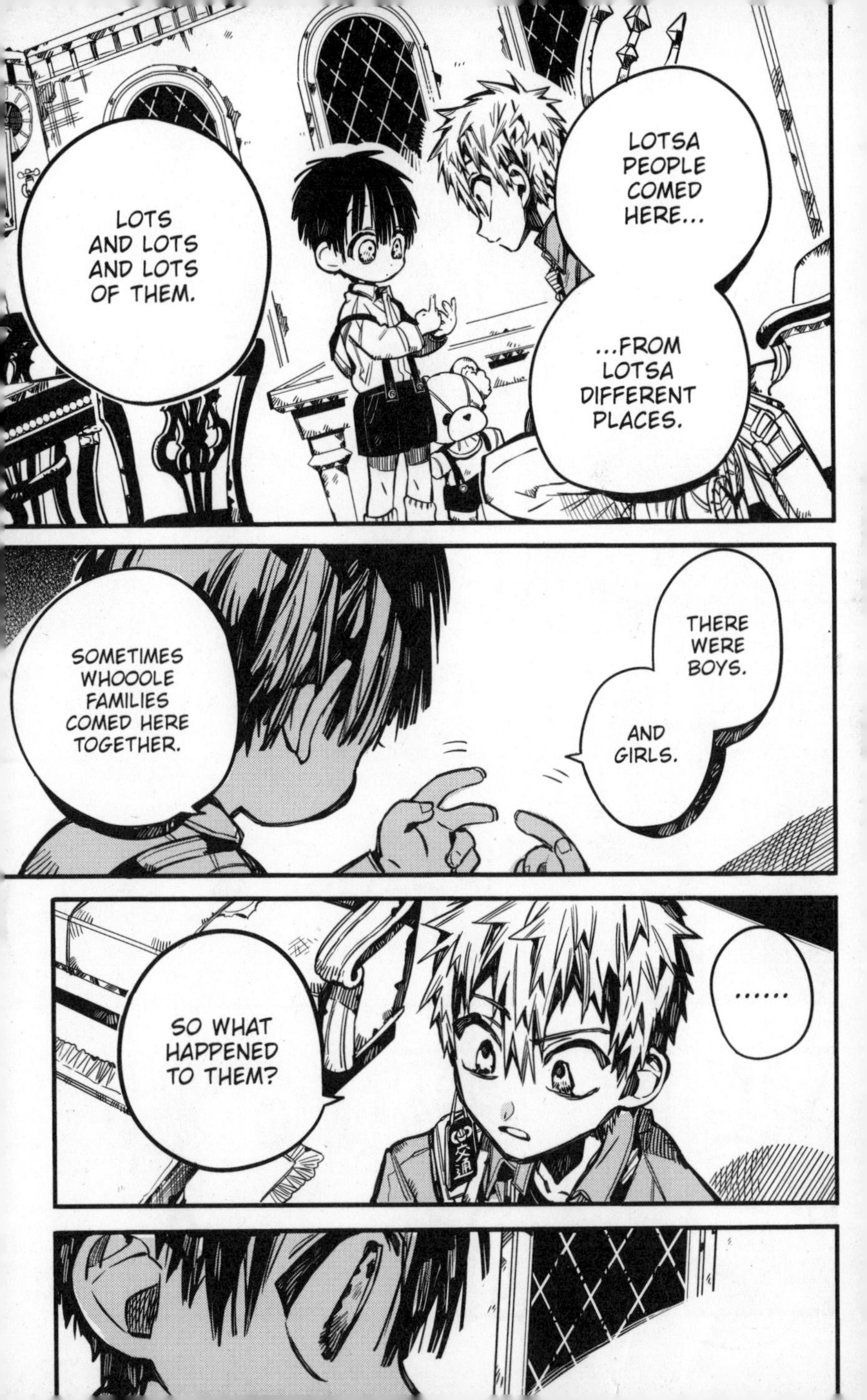
LOTSA PEOPLE COMED HERE...
...FROM LOTSA DIFFERENT PLACES.
LOTS AND LOTS AND LOTS OF THEM.
THERE WERE BOYS.
AND GIRLS.
SOMETIMES WHOOOLE FAMILIES COMED HERE TOGETHER.
......
SO WHAT HAPPENED TO THEM?

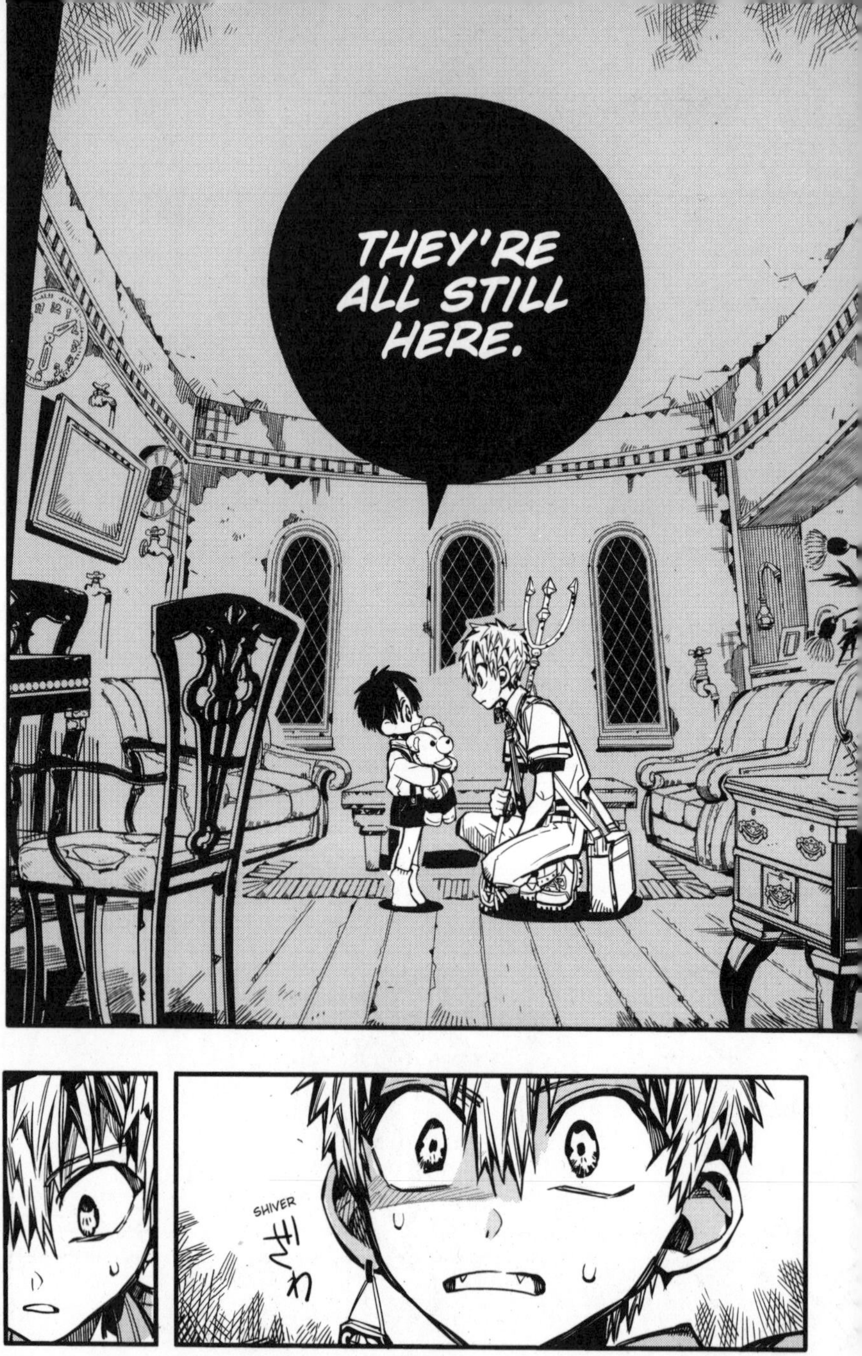
THEY'RE ALL STILL HERE.
SHIVER

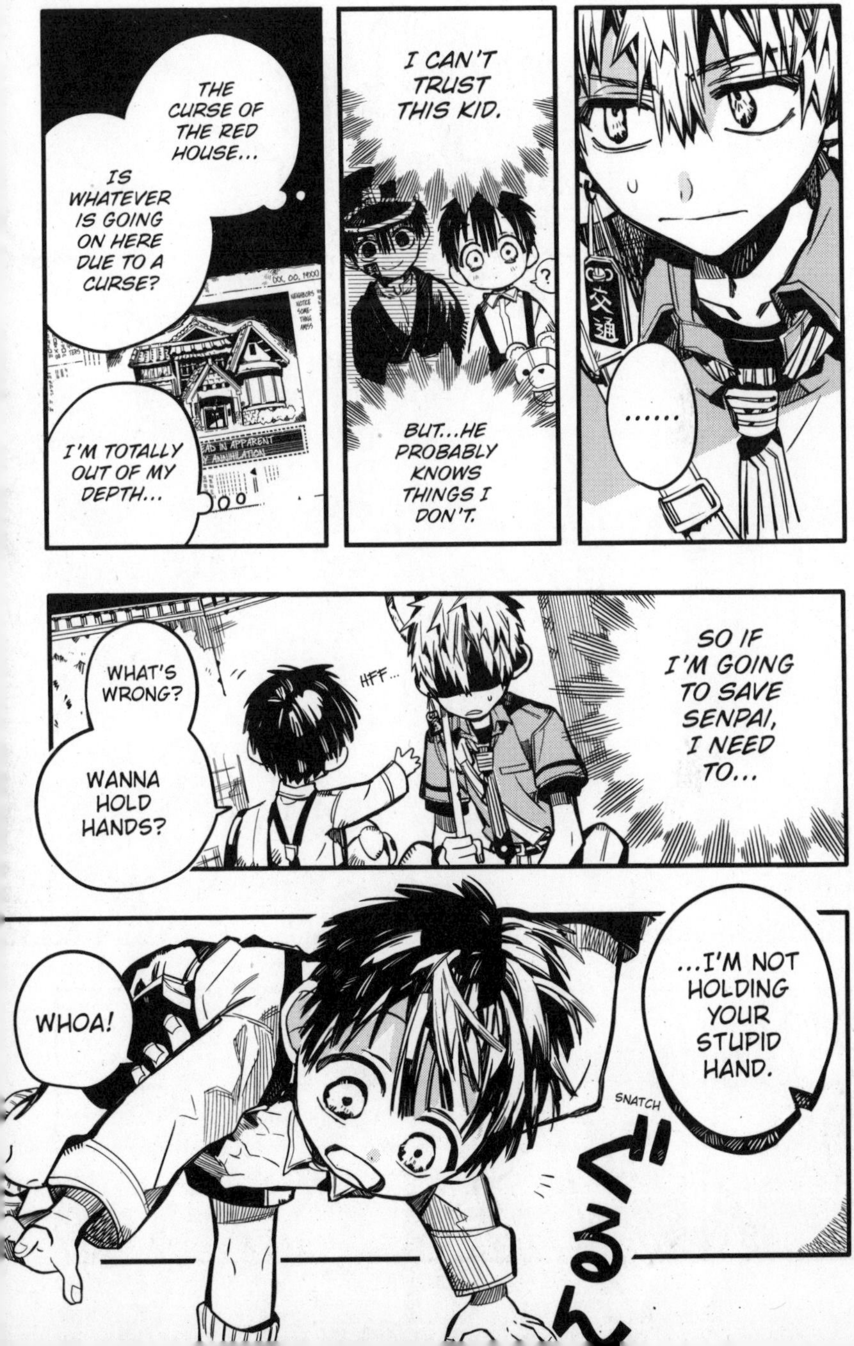
......
I CAN'T TRUST THIS KID.
BUT...HE PROBABLY KNOWS THINGS I DON'T.
THE CURSE OF THE RED HOUSE...
IS WHATEVER IS GOING ON HERE DUE TO A CURSE?
NEIGHBORS NOTICE SOME- THING AMISS
I'M TOTALLY OUT OF MY DEPTH...
SO IF I'M GOING TO SAVE SENPAI, I NEED TO...
HFF...
WHAT'S WRONG?
WANNA HOLD HANDS?
...I'M NOT HOLDING YOUR STUPID HAND.
SNATCH
WHOA!

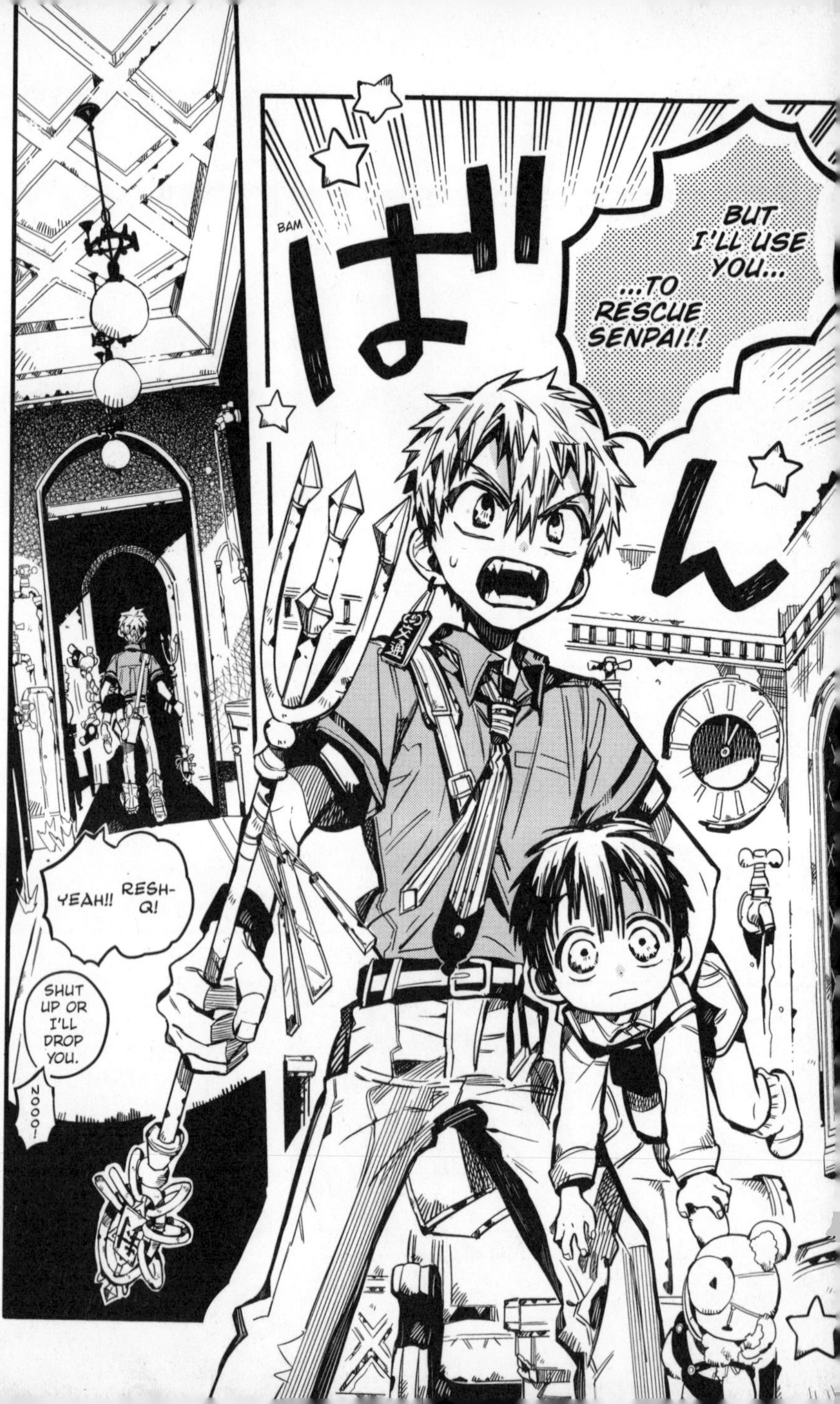
BAM
ばん
BUT I'LL USE YOU...
...TO RESCUE SENPAI!!
YEAH!! RESH-Q!
SHUT UP OR I'LL DROP YOU.
NOOOO!

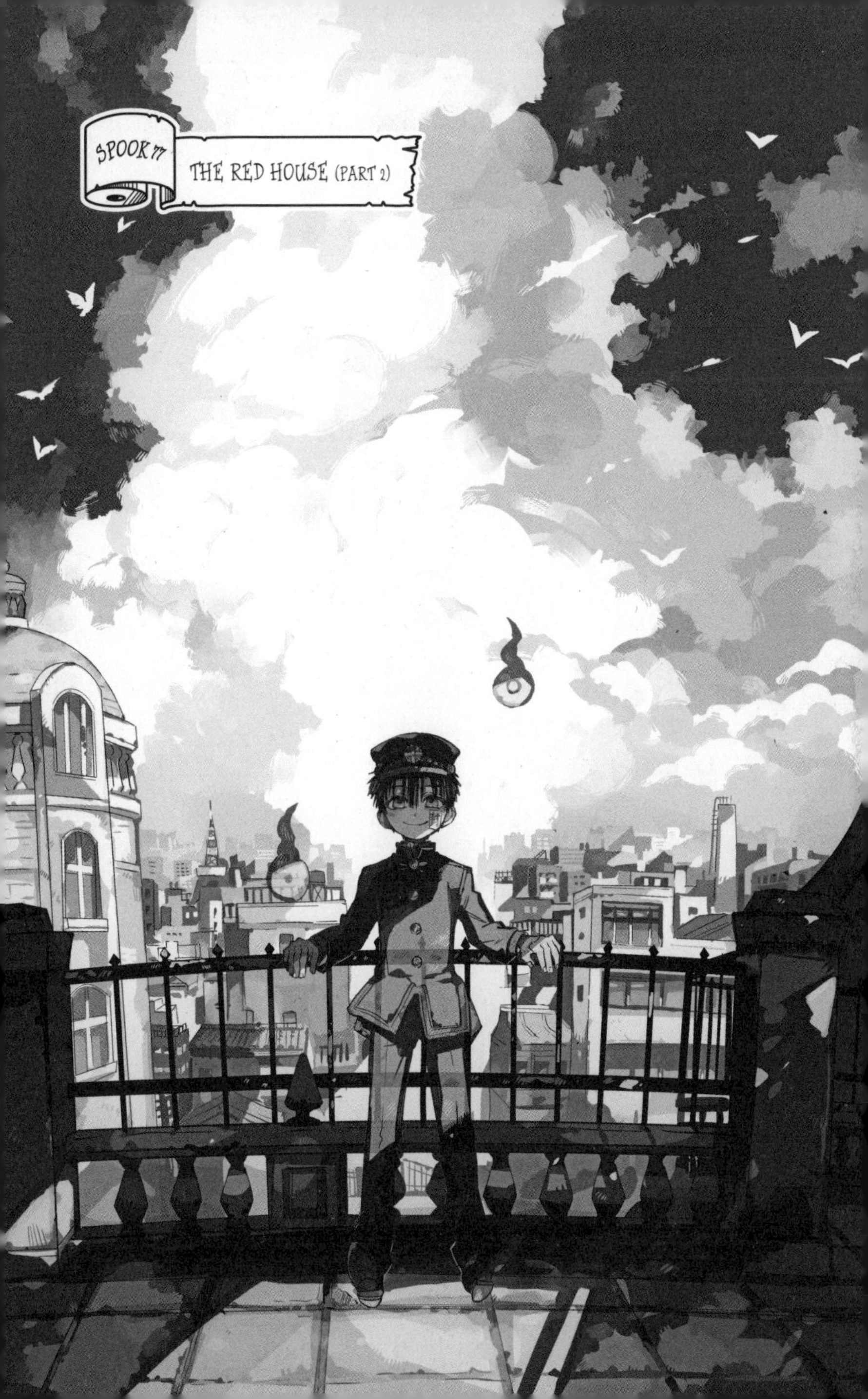
SPOOK 77
THE RED HOUSE (PART 2)

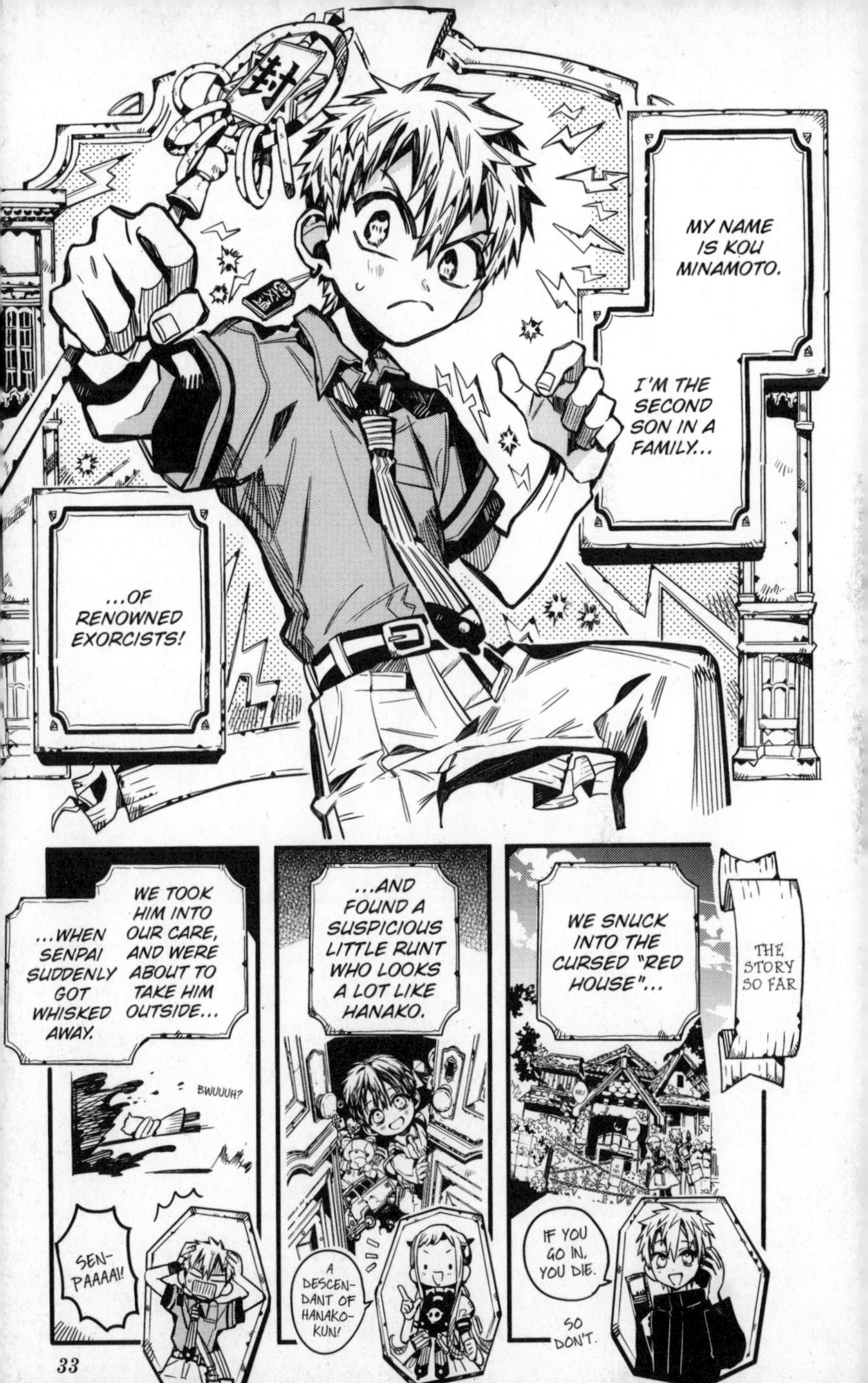
MY NAME IS KOU MINAMOTO.
I'M THE SECOND SON IN A FAMILY...
...OF RENOWNED EXORCISTS!
THE STORY SO FAR
WE SNUCK INTO THE CURSED "RED HOUSE"...
IF YOU GO IN, YOU DIE.
SO DON'T.
...AND FOUND A SUSPICIOUS LITTLE RUNT WHO LOOKS A LOT LIKE HANAKO.
A DESCEN-DANT OF HANAKO-KUN!
WE TOOK HIM INTO OUR CARE, AND WERE ABOUT TO TAKE HIM OUTSIDE...
...WHEN SENPAI SUDDENLY GOT WHISKED AWAY.
BWUUUH?
SEN-PAAAAI!

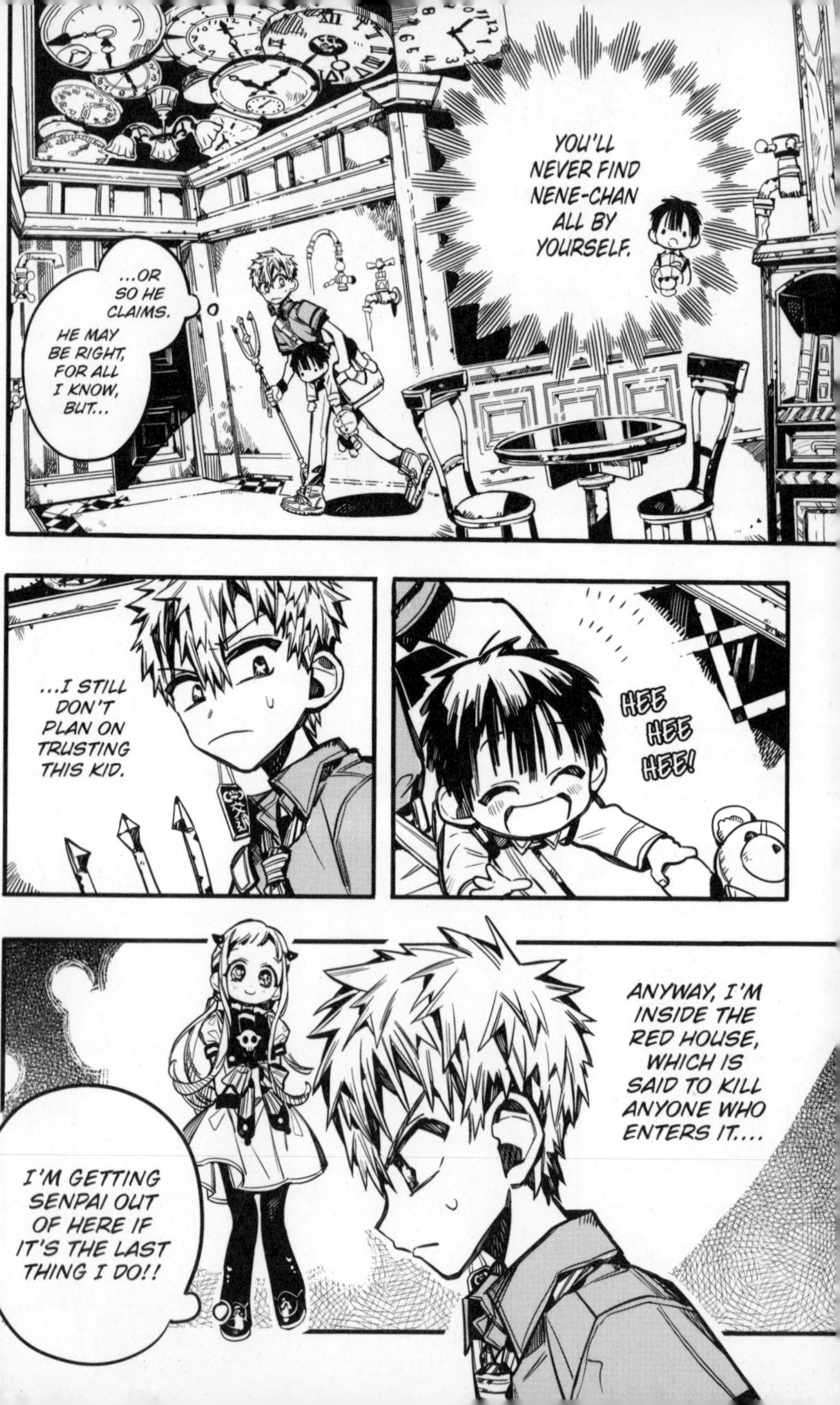
YOU'LL NEVER FIND NENE-CHAN ALL BY YOURSELF.
...OR SO HE CLAIMS.
HE MAY BE RIGHT, FOR ALL I KNOW, BUT...
HEE HEE HEE!
...I STILL DON'T PLAN ON TRUSTING THIS KID.
ANYWAY, I'M INSIDE THE RED HOUSE, WHICH IS SAID TO KILL ANYONE WHO ENTERS IT....
I'M GETTING SENPAI OUT OF HERE IF IT'S THE LAST THING I DO!!

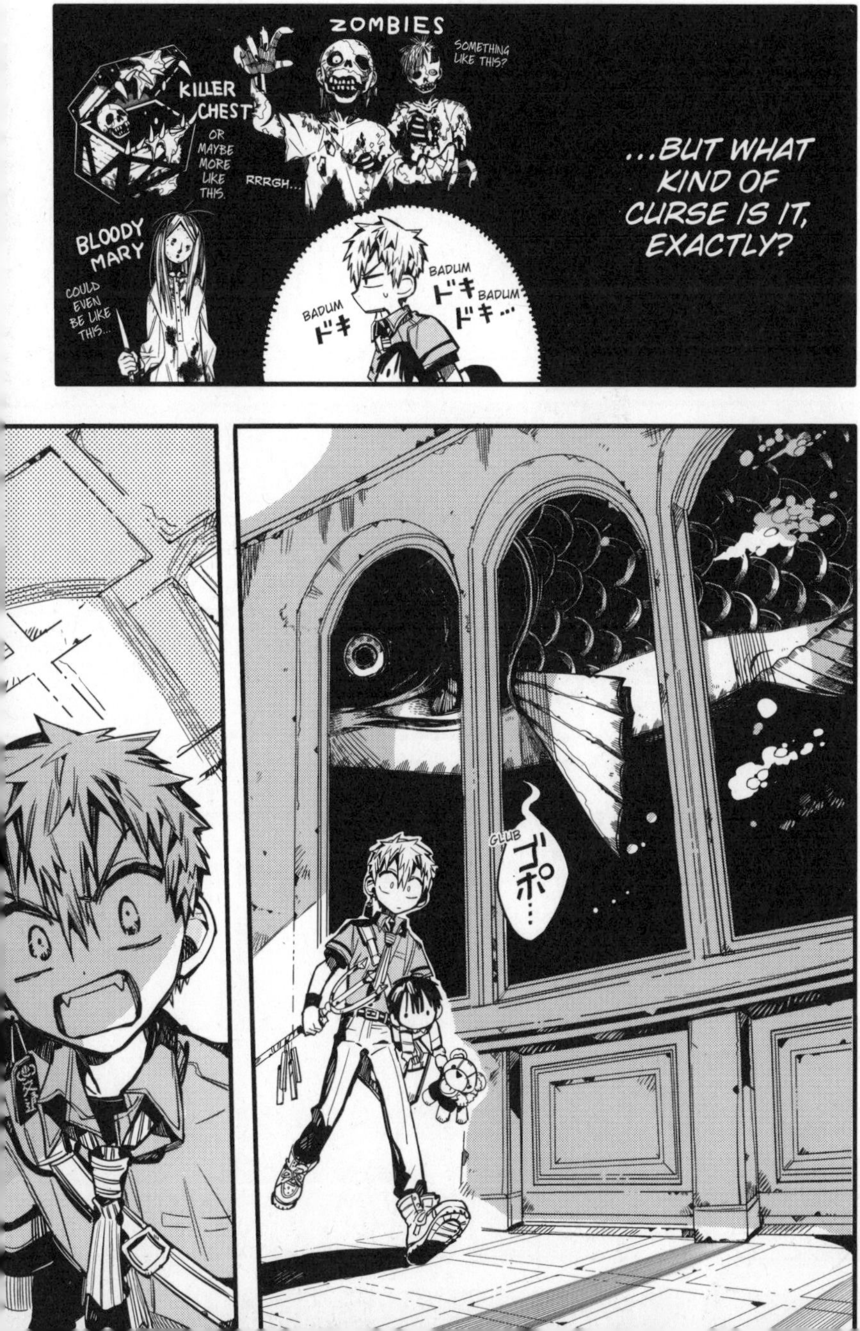
...BUT WHAT KIND OF CURSE IS IT, EXACTLY?
ZOMBIES
SOMETHING LIKE THIS?
KILLER CHEST
OR MAYBE MORE LIKE THIS.
RRRGH...
BLOODY MARY
COULD EVEN BE LIKE THIS...
BADUM ドキ
BADUM ドキ
BADUM ドキ…
GLUB ゴポ…

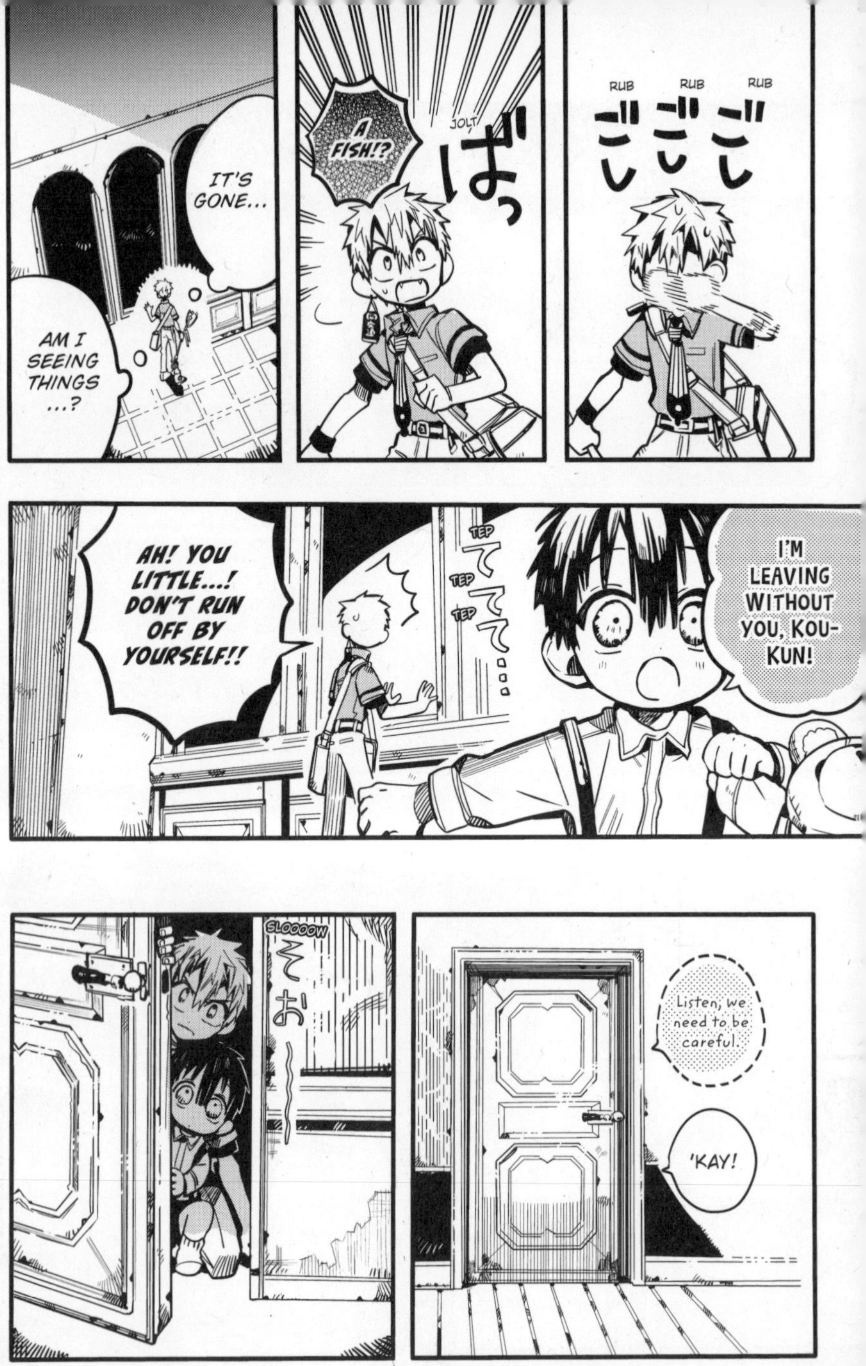
RUB RUB RUB
ごしごしごし
A FISH!?
JOLT
ぱっ
IT'S GONE...
AM I SEEING THINGS ...?
I'M LEAVING WITHOUT YOU, KOU-KUN!
TEP TEP TEP
てててて...
AH! YOU LITTLE...! DON'T RUN OFF BY YOURSELF!!
Listen, we need to be careful.
'KAY!
SLOOOOW
そぉ~~

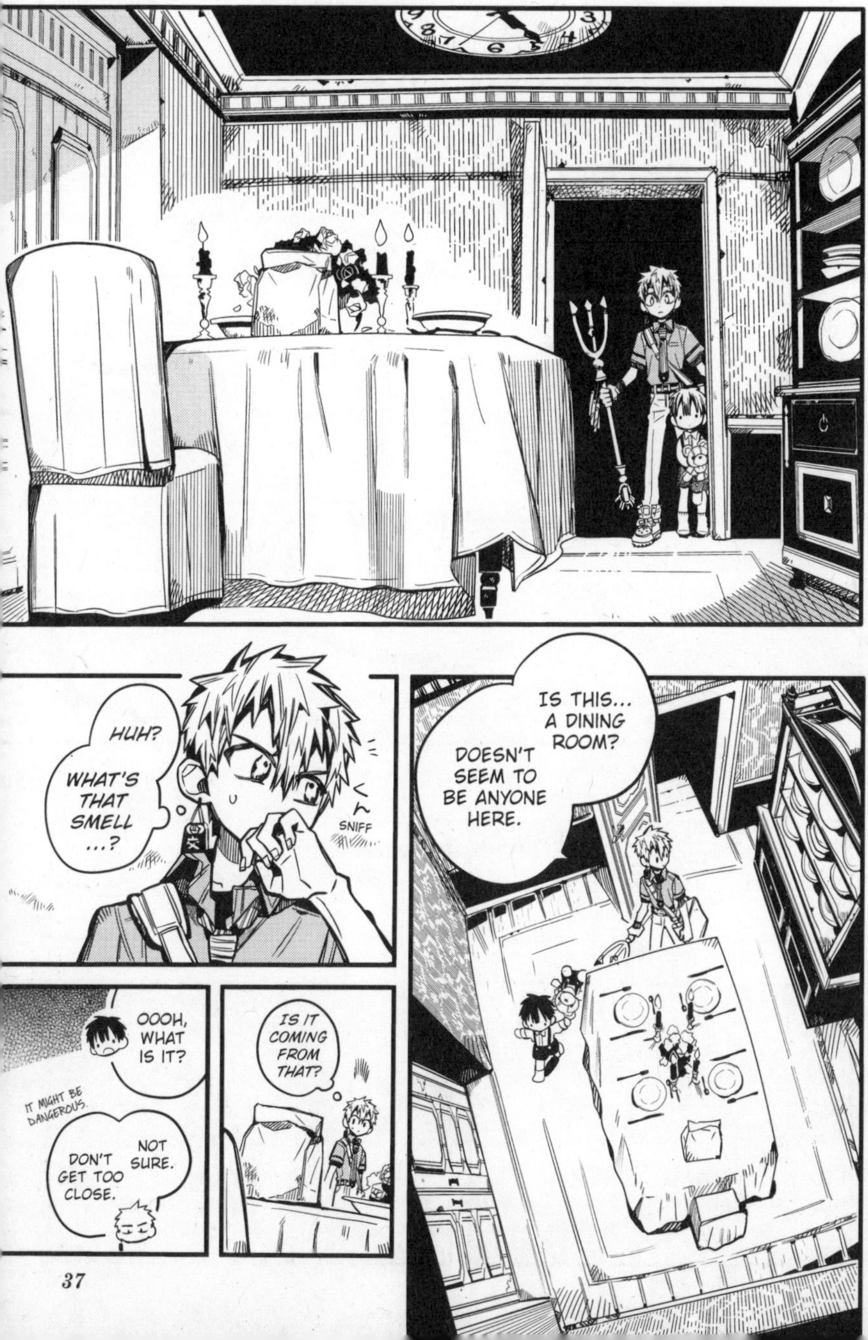
IS THIS... A DINING ROOM?
DOESN'T SEEM TO BE ANYONE HERE.
HUH?
WHAT'S THAT SMELL ...?
SNIFF
IS IT COMING FROM THAT?
OOOH, WHAT IS IT?
NOT SURE.
DON'T GET TOO CLOSE.
IT MIGHT BE DANGEROUS.

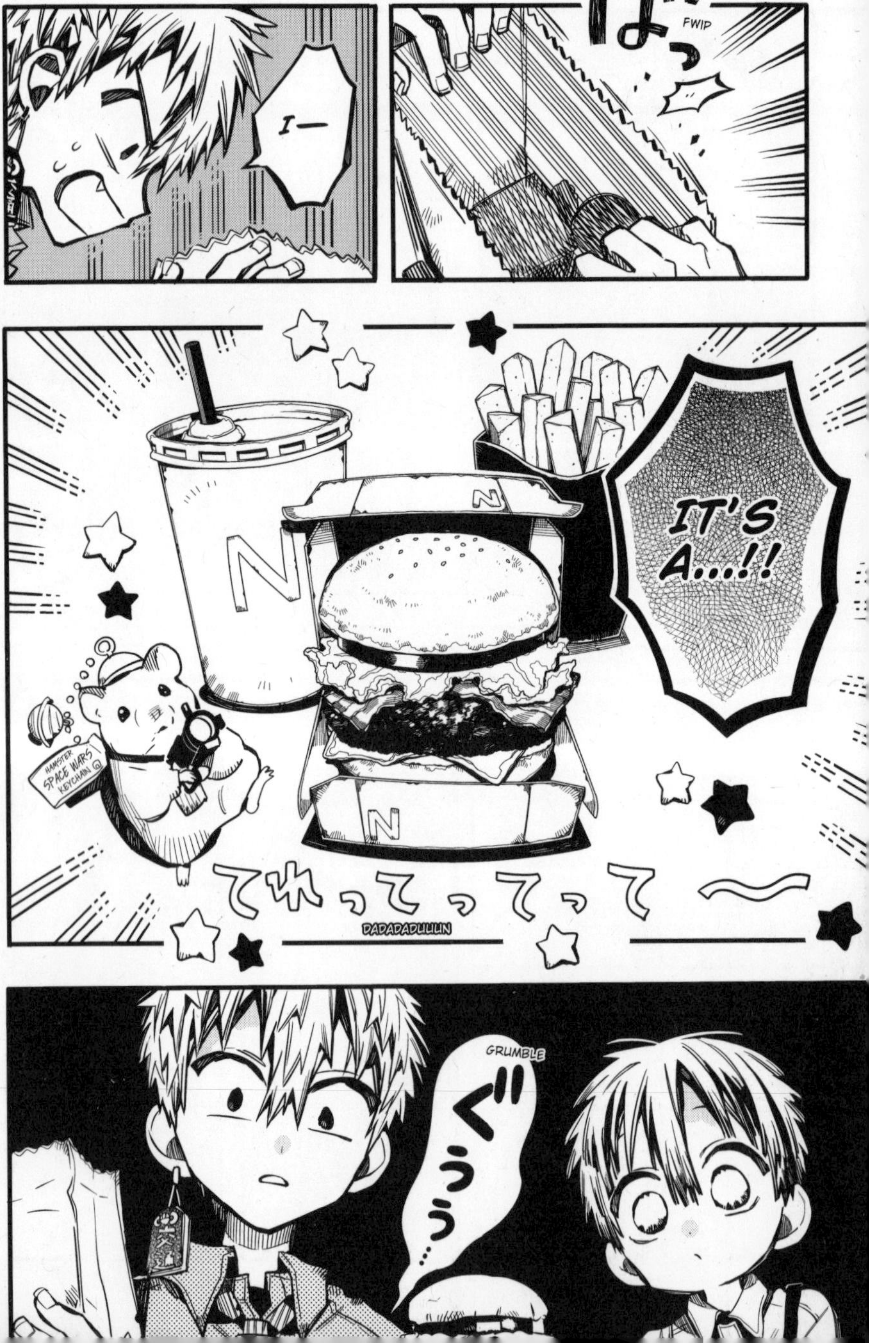
ばっ
FWIP
I—
IT'S A...!!
HAMSTER SPACE WARS KEYCHAIN
てれってってって〜
DADADADUUUN
ぐうう…
GRUMBLE

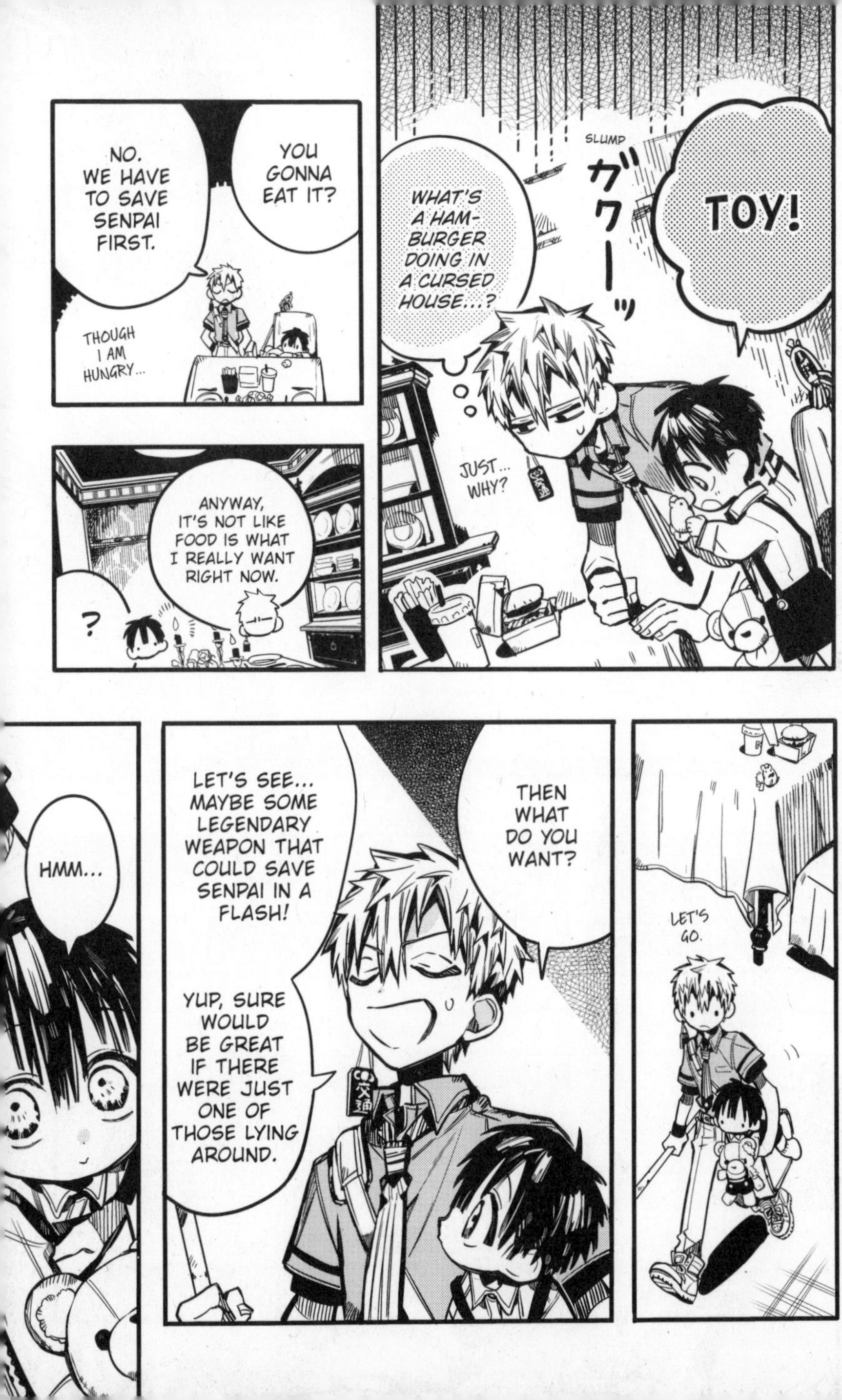
TOY!
SLUMP
ガクーッ
WHAT'S A HAMBURGER DOING IN A CURSED HOUSE...?
JUST... WHY?
YOU GONNA EAT IT?
NO. WE HAVE TO SAVE SENPAI FIRST.
THOUGH I AM HUNGRY...
ANYWAY, IT'S NOT LIKE FOOD IS WHAT I REALLY WANT RIGHT NOW.
?
LET'S GO.
THEN WHAT DO YOU WANT?
LET'S SEE... MAYBE SOME LEGENDARY WEAPON THAT COULD SAVE SENPAI IN A FLASH!
YUP, SURE WOULD BE GREAT IF THERE WERE JUST ONE OF THOSE LYING AROUND.
HMM...

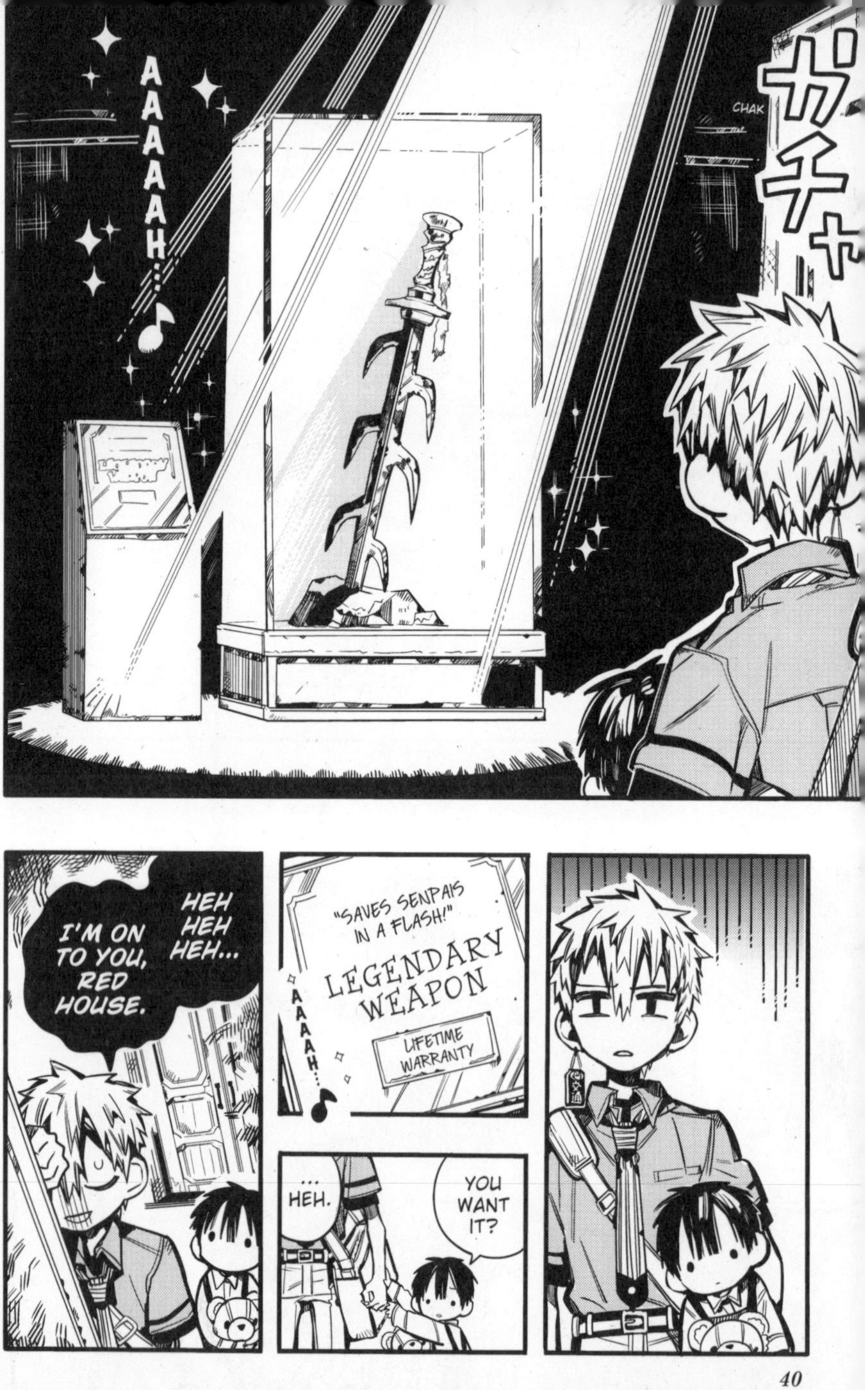
ガチャ
CHAK
AAAAAH...
"SAVES SENPAIS IN A FLASH!"
LEGENDARY WEAPON
LIFETIME WARRANTY
AAAAAH...
YOU WANT IT?
...HEH.
HEH HEH HEH...
I'M ON TO YOU, RED HOUSE.

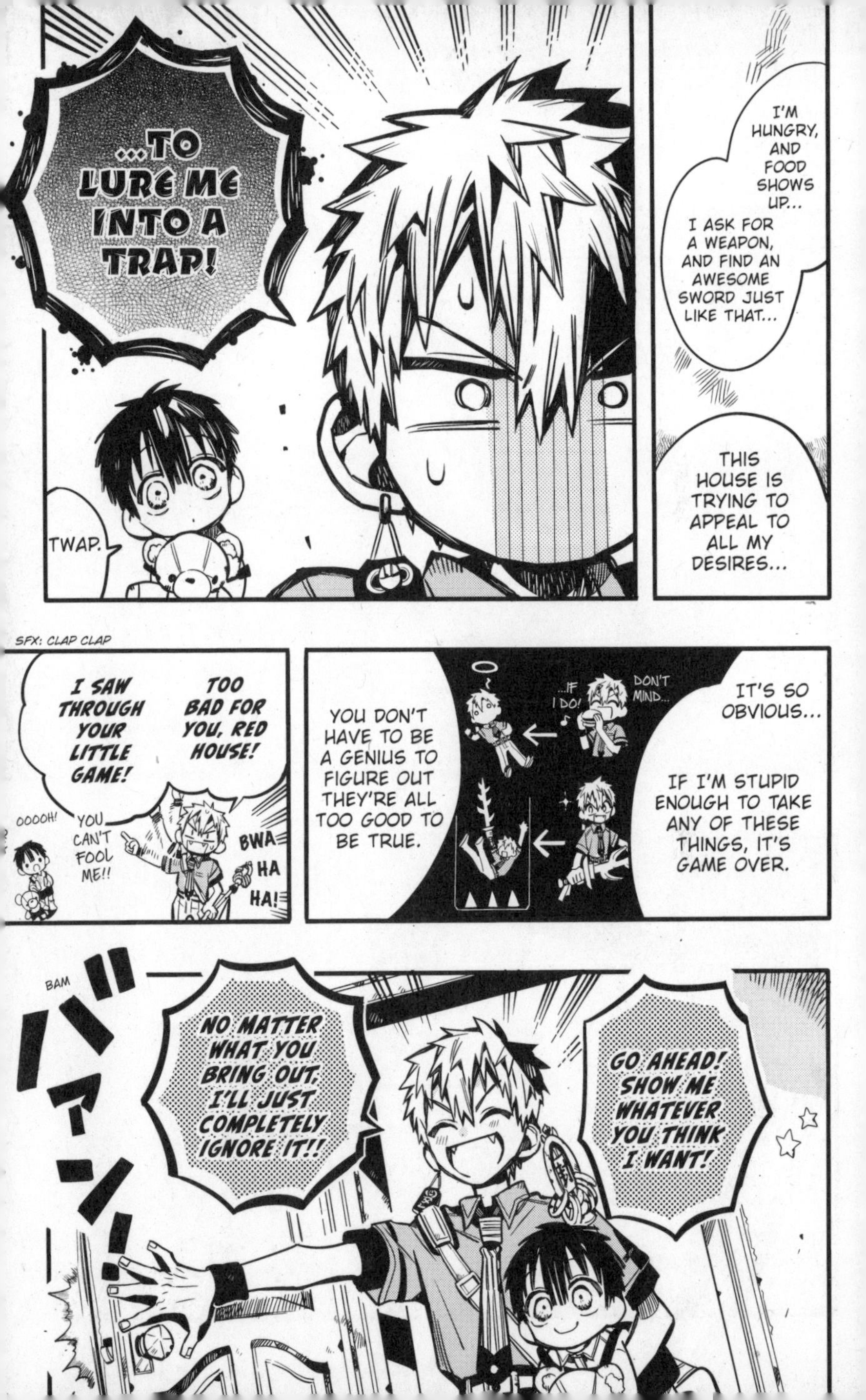
I'M HUNGRY, AND FOOD SHOWS UP...
I ASK FOR A WEAPON, AND FIND AN AWESOME SWORD JUST LIKE THAT...
THIS HOUSE IS TRYING TO APPEAL TO ALL MY DESIRES...
...TO LURE ME INTO A TRAP!
TWAP.
IT'S SO OBVIOUS...
IF I'M STUPID ENOUGH TO TAKE ANY OF THESE THINGS, IT'S GAME OVER.
DON'T MIND...
...IF I DO!
YOU DON'T HAVE TO BE A GENIUS TO FIGURE OUT THEY'RE ALL TOO GOOD TO BE TRUE.
SFX: CLAP CLAP
TOO BAD FOR YOU, RED HOUSE!
I SAW THROUGH YOUR LITTLE GAME!
BWA HA HA!
YOU CAN'T FOOL ME!!
OOOOH!
GO AHEAD! SHOW ME WHATEVER YOU THINK I WANT!
NO MATTER WHAT YOU BRING OUT, I'LL JUST COMPLETELY IGNORE IT!!
BAM

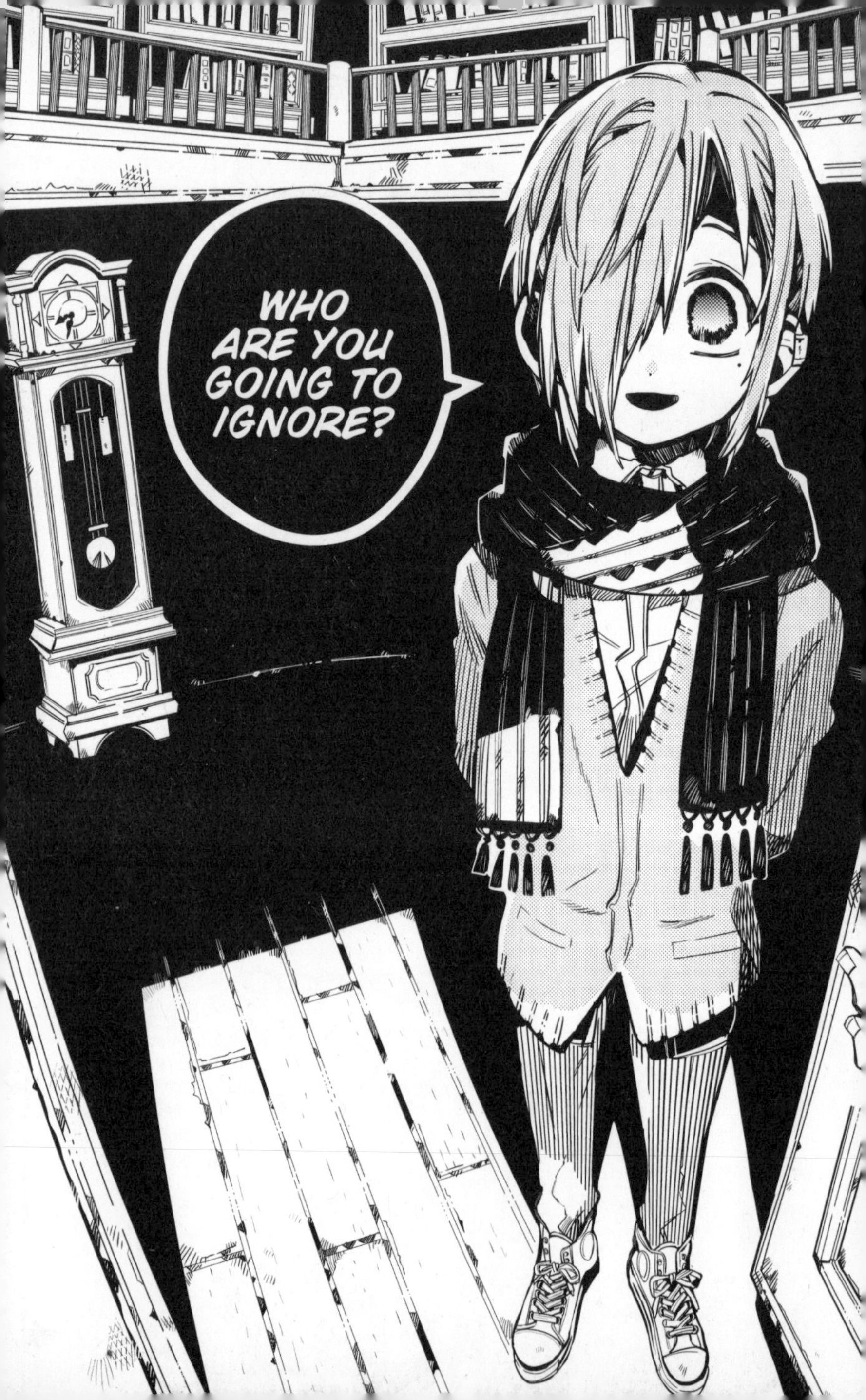
WHO ARE YOU GOING TO IGNORE?

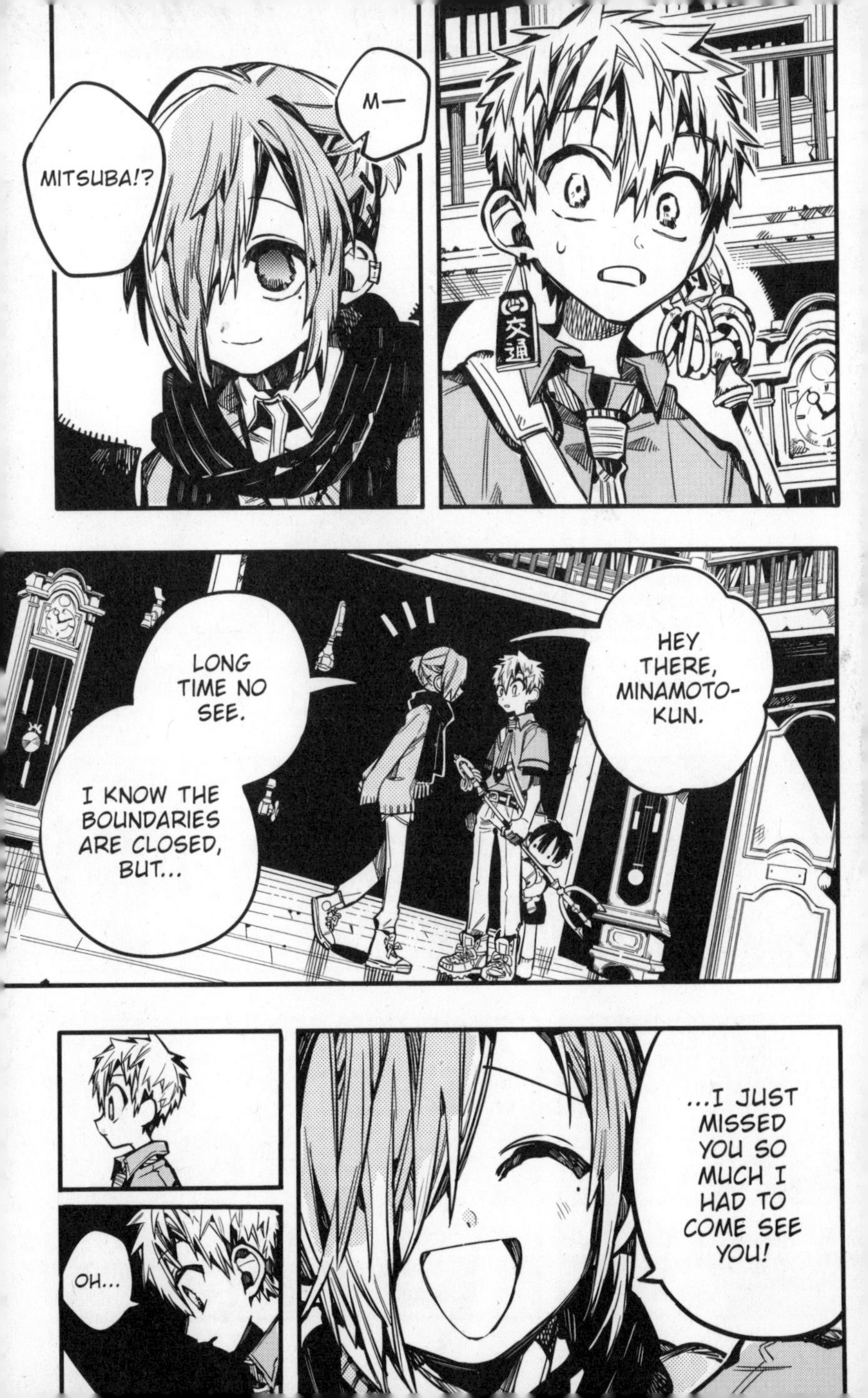
M—
MITSUBA!?
HEY THERE, MINAMOTO-KUN.
LONG TIME NO SEE.
I KNOW THE BOUNDARIES ARE CLOSED, BUT...
...I JUST MISSED YOU SO MUCH I HAD TO COME SEE YOU!
OH...

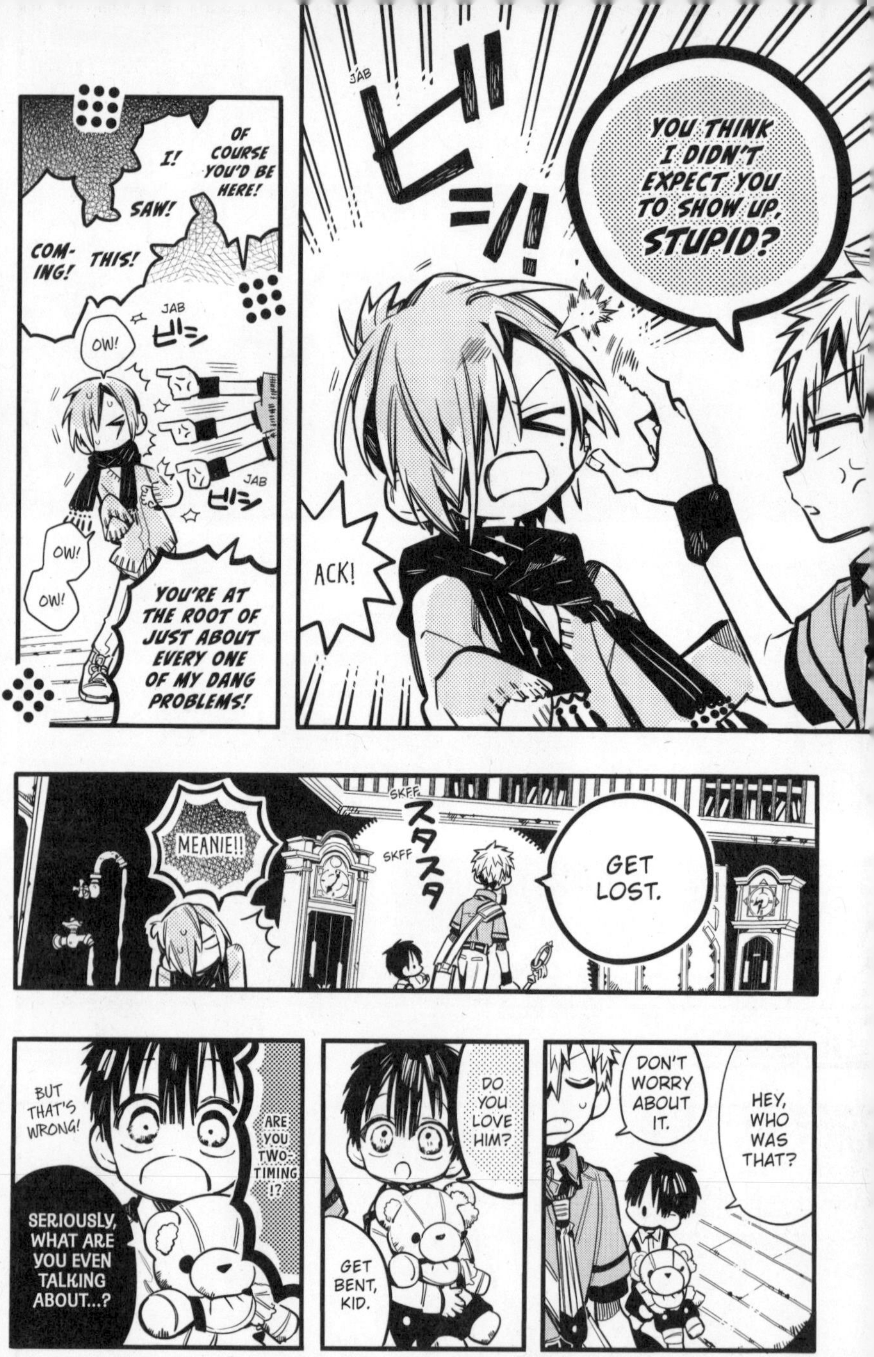
YOU THINK I DIDN'T EXPECT YOU TO SHOW UP, STUPID?
JAB
ビシッ!
ACK!
OF COURSE YOU'D BE HERE!
I!
SAW!
THIS!
COM-ING!
OW!
JAB
ビシ
JAB
ビシ
YOU'RE AT THE ROOT OF JUST ABOUT EVERY ONE OF MY DANG PROBLEMS!
OW!
OW!
GET LOST.
SKFF
SKFF
スタスタ
MEANIE!!
HEY, WHO WAS THAT?
DON'T WORRY ABOUT IT.
DO YOU LOVE HIM?
GET BENT, KID.
ARE YOU TWO-TIMING!?
BUT THAT'S WRONG!
SERIOUSLY, WHAT ARE YOU EVEN TALKING ABOUT...?

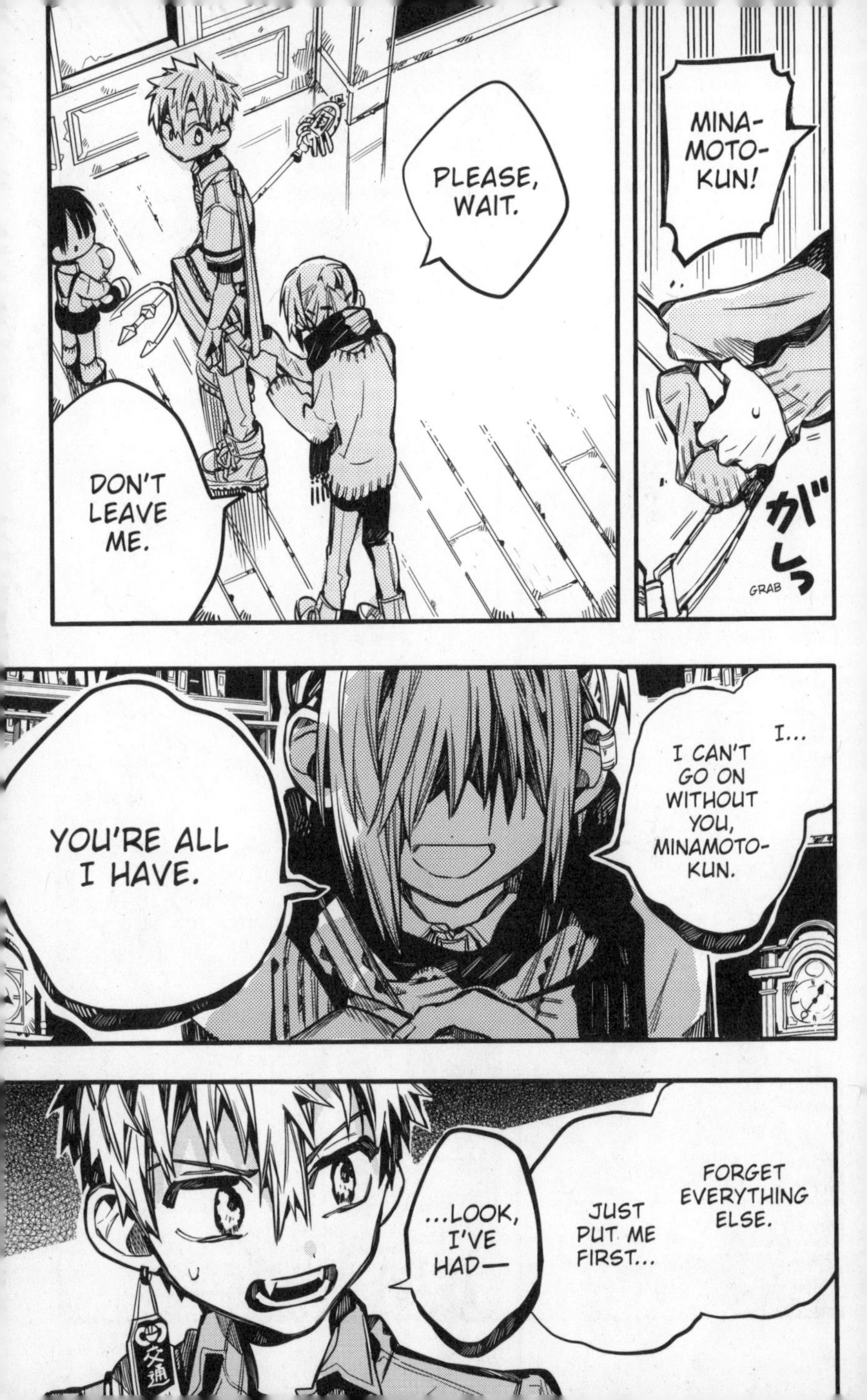
MINA-
MOTO-
KUN!
がしっ
GRAB
PLEASE, WAIT.
DON'T LEAVE ME.
I...
I CAN'T GO ON WITHOUT YOU, MINAMOTO-KUN.
YOU'RE ALL I HAVE.
FORGET EVERYTHING ELSE.
JUST PUT ME FIRST...
...LOOK, I'VE HAD—

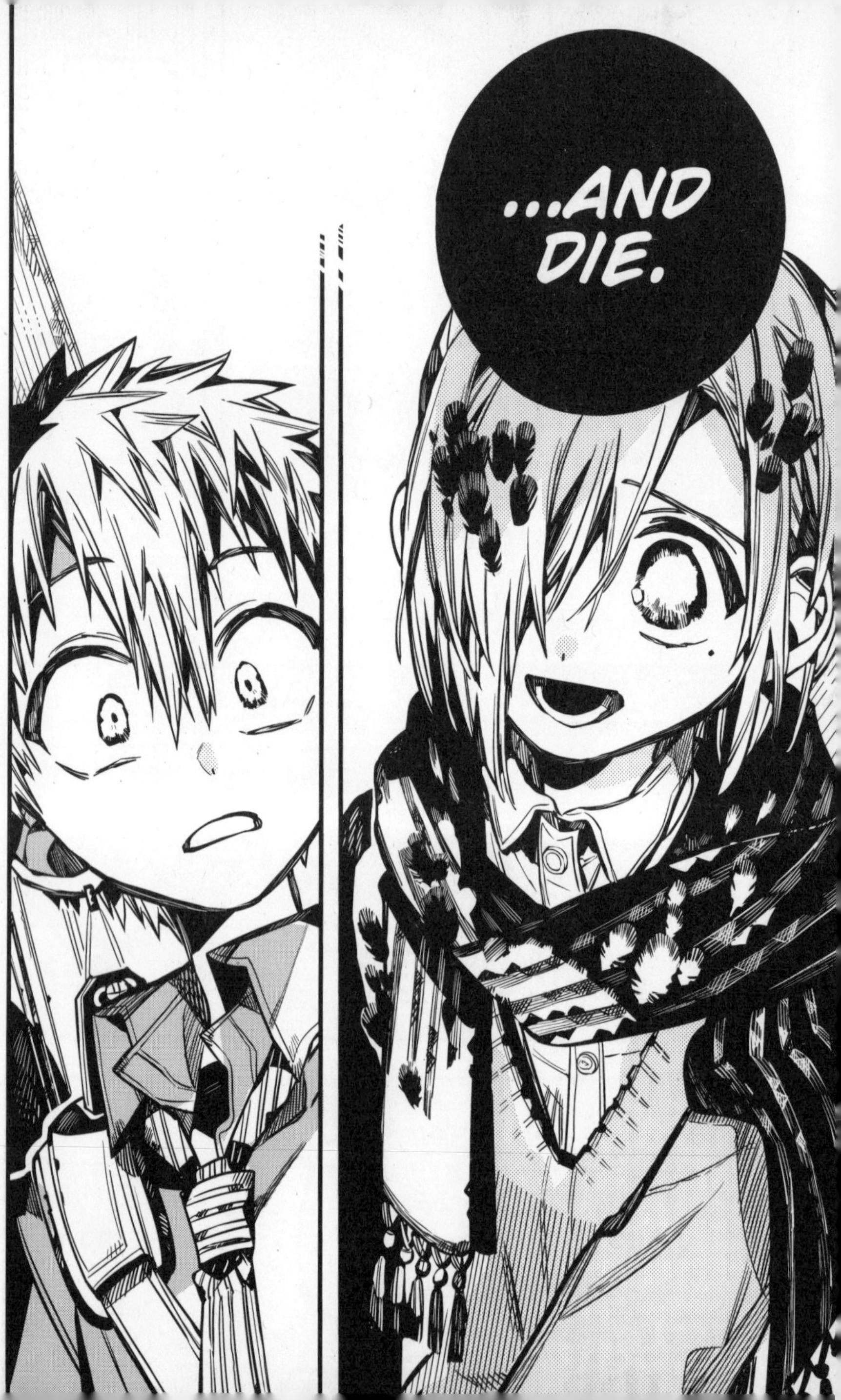
...AND DIE.

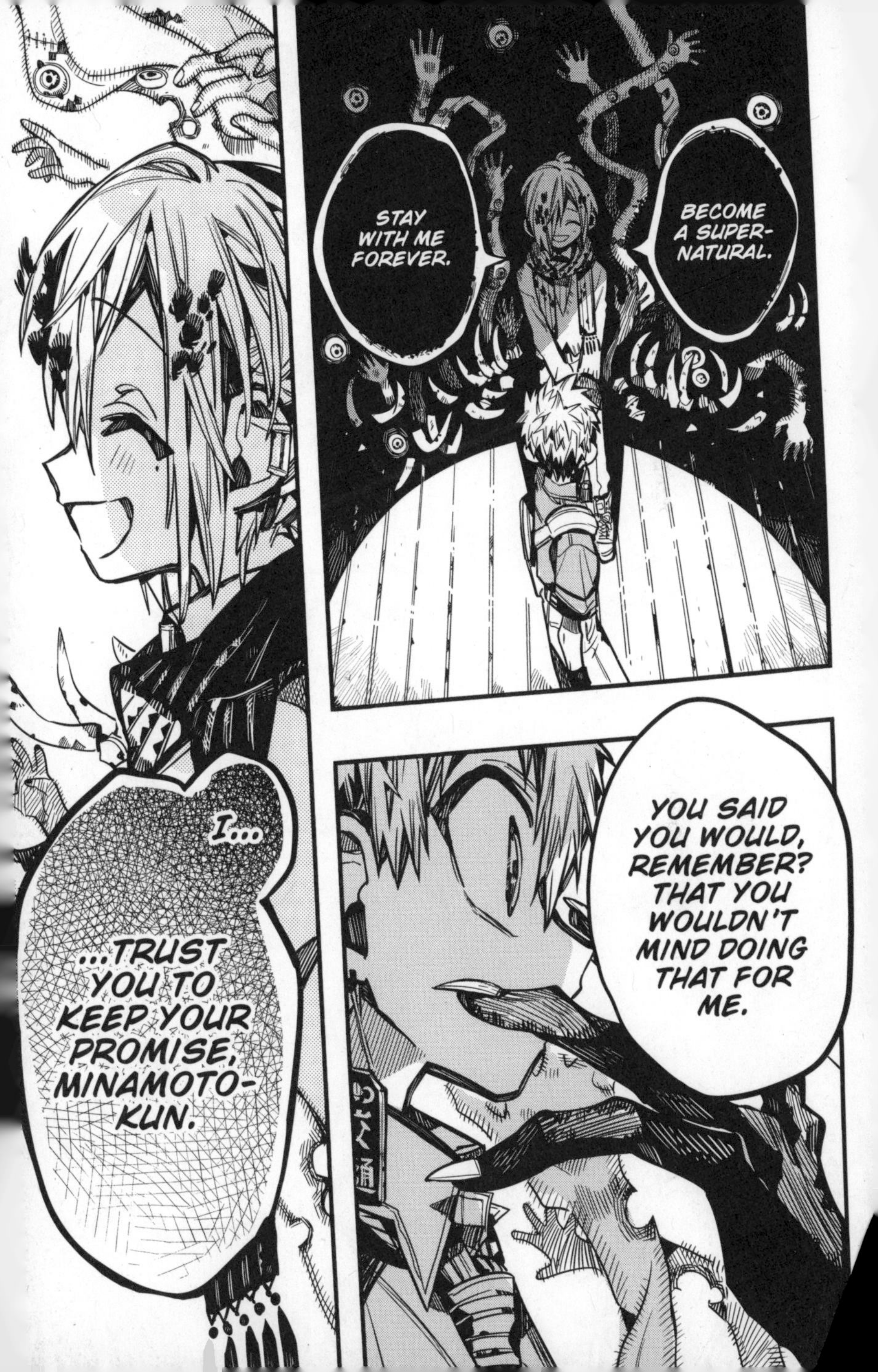
BECOME A SUPER-NATURAL.
STAY WITH ME FOREVER.
YOU SAID YOU WOULD, REMEMBER? THAT YOU WOULDN'T MIND DOING THAT FOR ME.
I...
...TRUST YOU TO KEEP YOUR PROMISE, MINAMOTO-KUN.

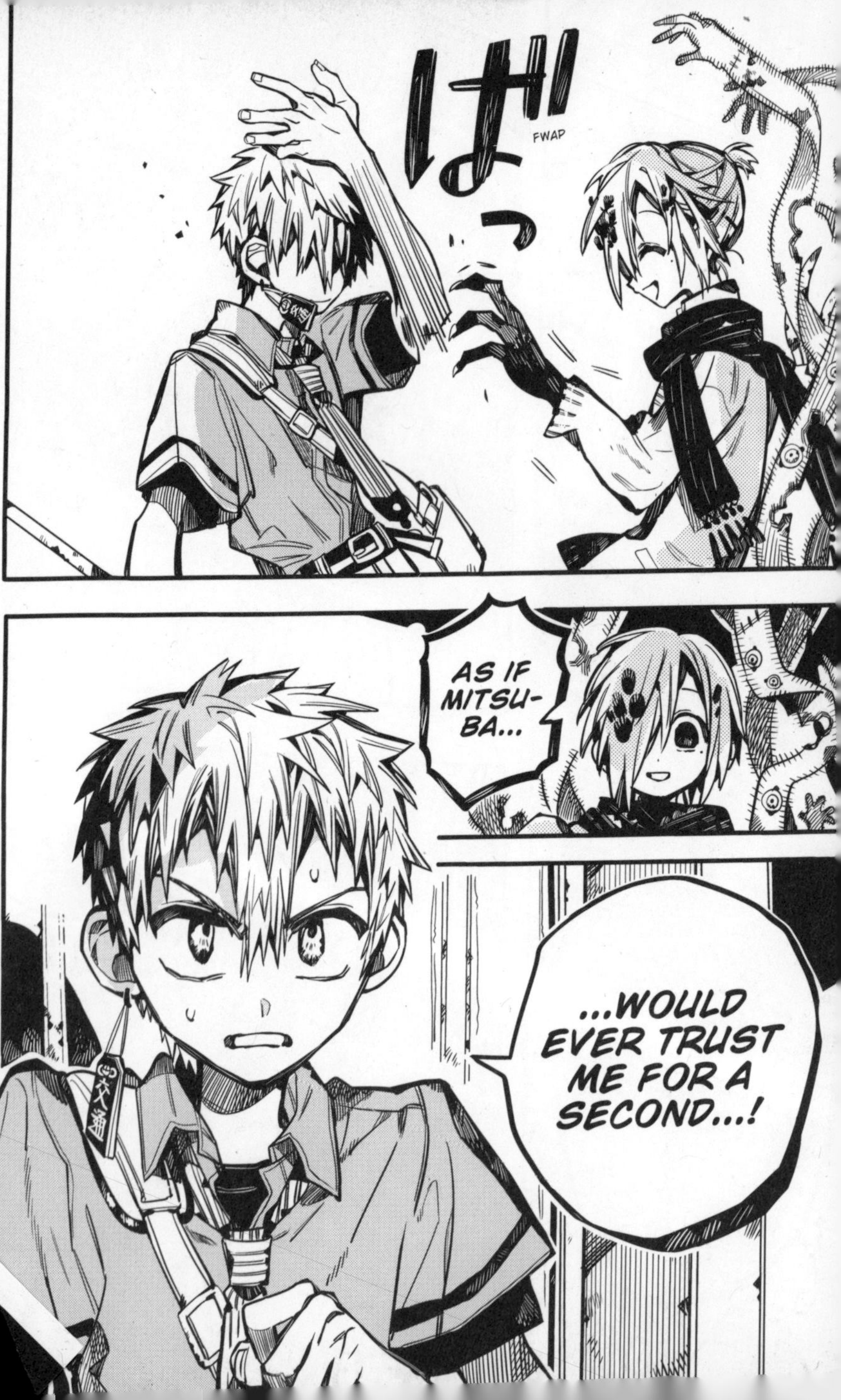
ぱっ
FWAP
AS IF MITSUBA...
...WOULD EVER TRUST ME FOR A SECOND...!

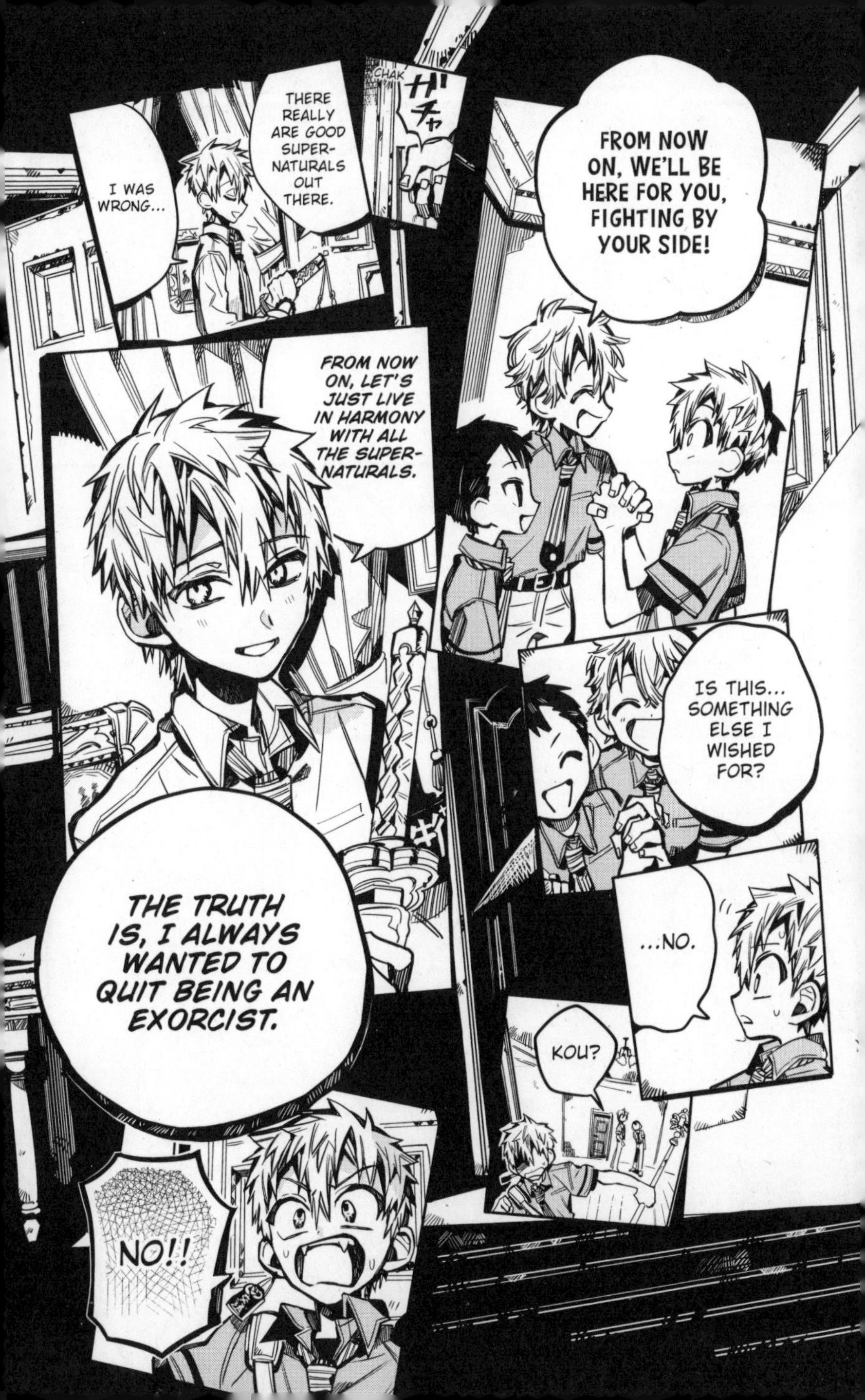
FROM NOW ON, WE'LL BE HERE FOR YOU, FIGHTING BY YOUR SIDE!
IS THIS... SOMETHING ELSE I WISHED FOR?
...NO.
KOU?
CHAK
ガチャ
THERE REALLY ARE GOOD SUPER-NATURALS OUT THERE.
I WAS WRONG...
FROM NOW ON, LET'S JUST LIVE IN HARMONY WITH ALL THE SUPER-NATURALS.
THE TRUTH IS, I ALWAYS WANTED TO QUIT BEING AN EXORCIST.
NO!!

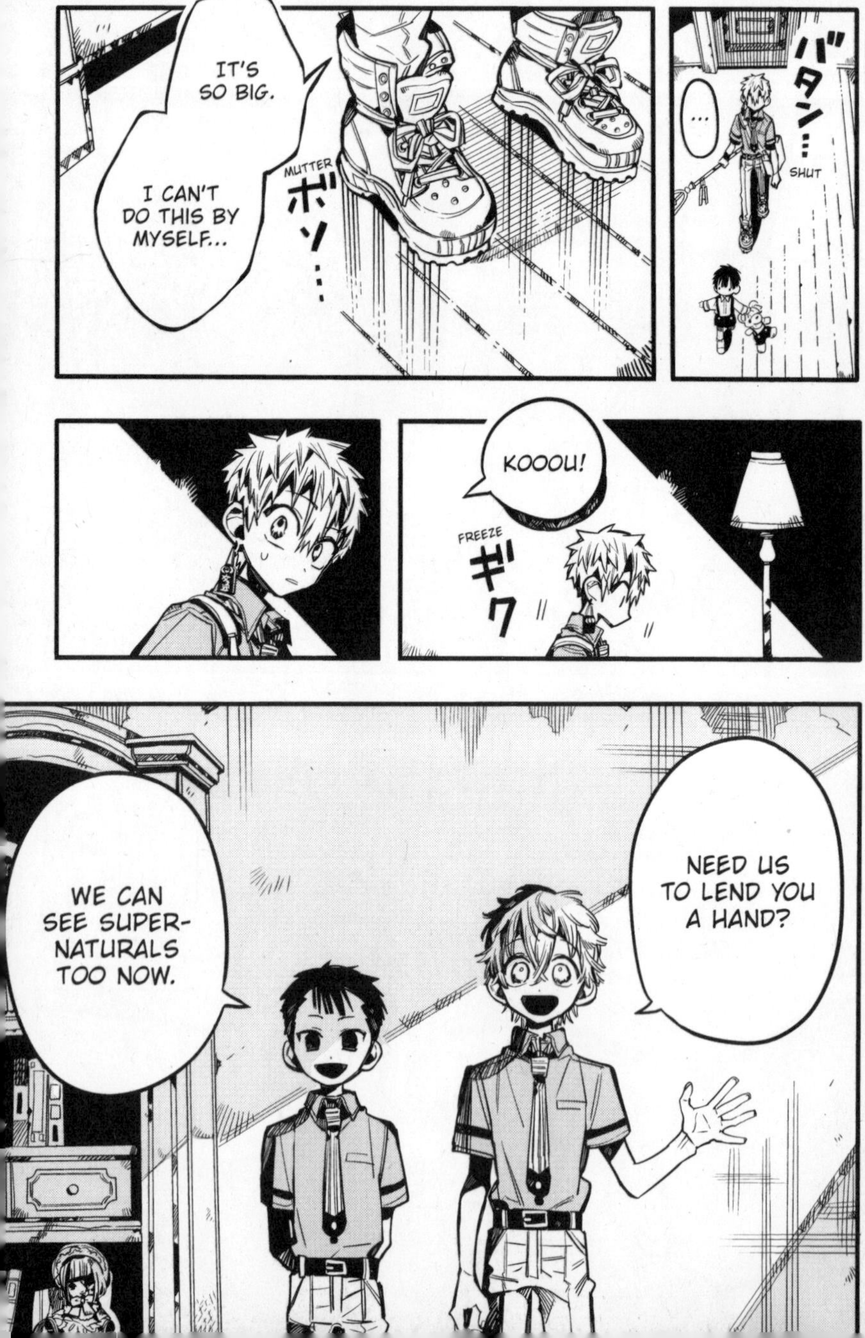

バタン…
SHUT
…
IT'S SO BIG.
I CAN'T DO THIS BY MYSELF...
ボソ…
MUTTER
KOOOU!
ギク
FREEZE
NEED US TO LEND YOU A HAND?
WE CAN SEE SUPER-NATURALS TOO NOW.

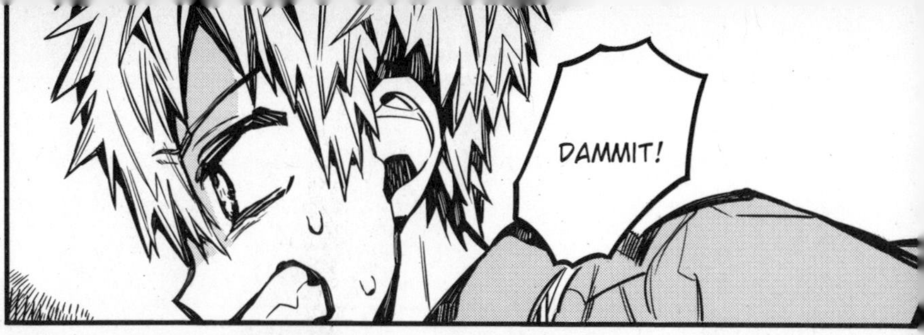
DAMMIT!
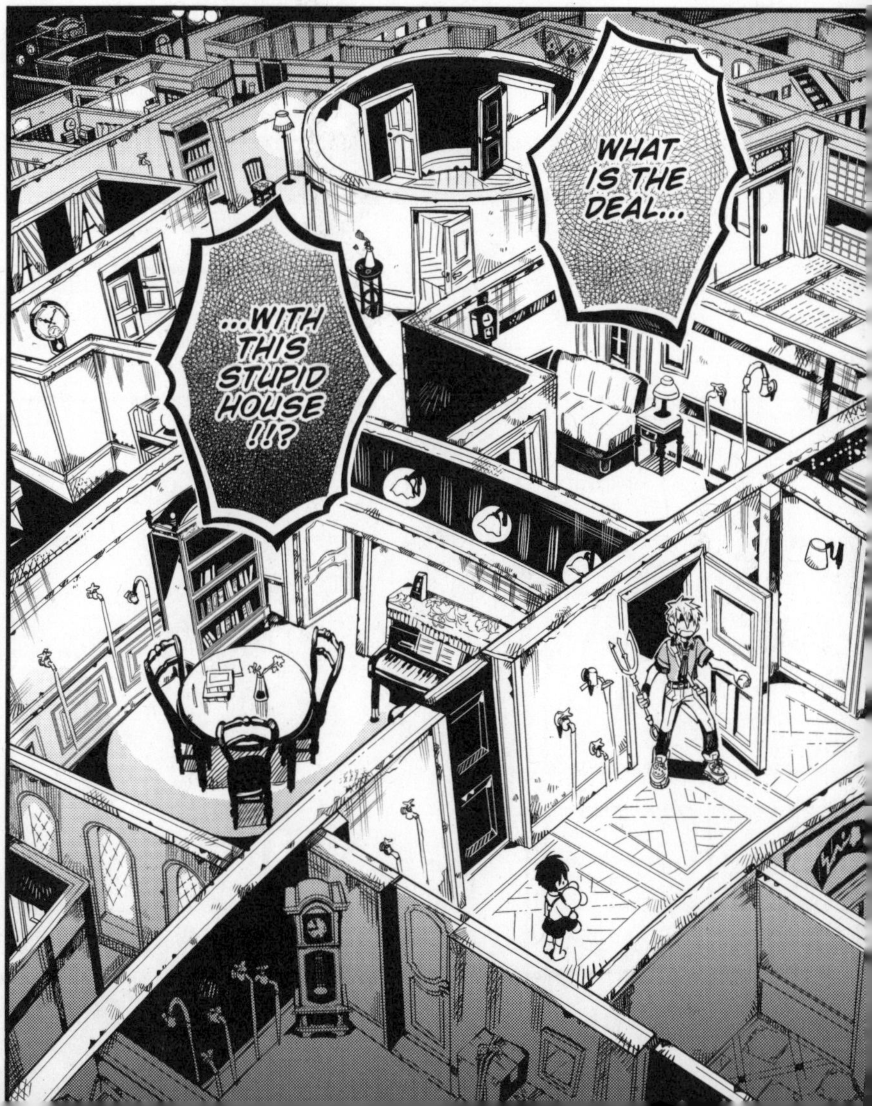
WHAT IS THE DEAL...
...WITH THIS STUPID HOUSE!!?

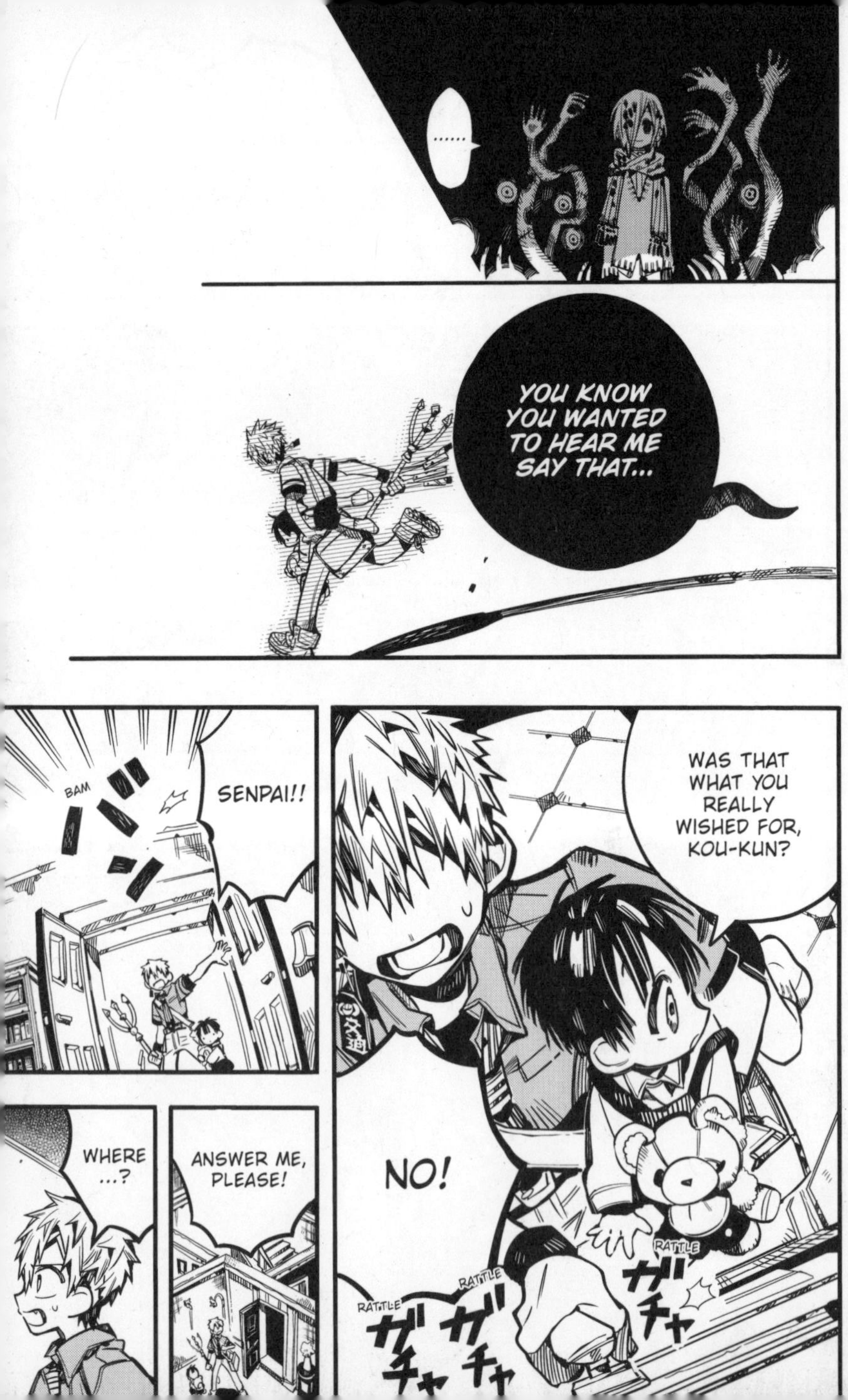
......
YOU KNOW YOU WANTED TO HEAR ME SAY THAT...
WAS THAT WHAT YOU REALLY WISHED FOR, KOU-KUN?
NO!
RATTLE
ガチャ
RATTLE
ガチャ
RATTLE
ガチャ
BAM
SENPAI!!
ANSWER ME, PLEASE!
WHERE ...?

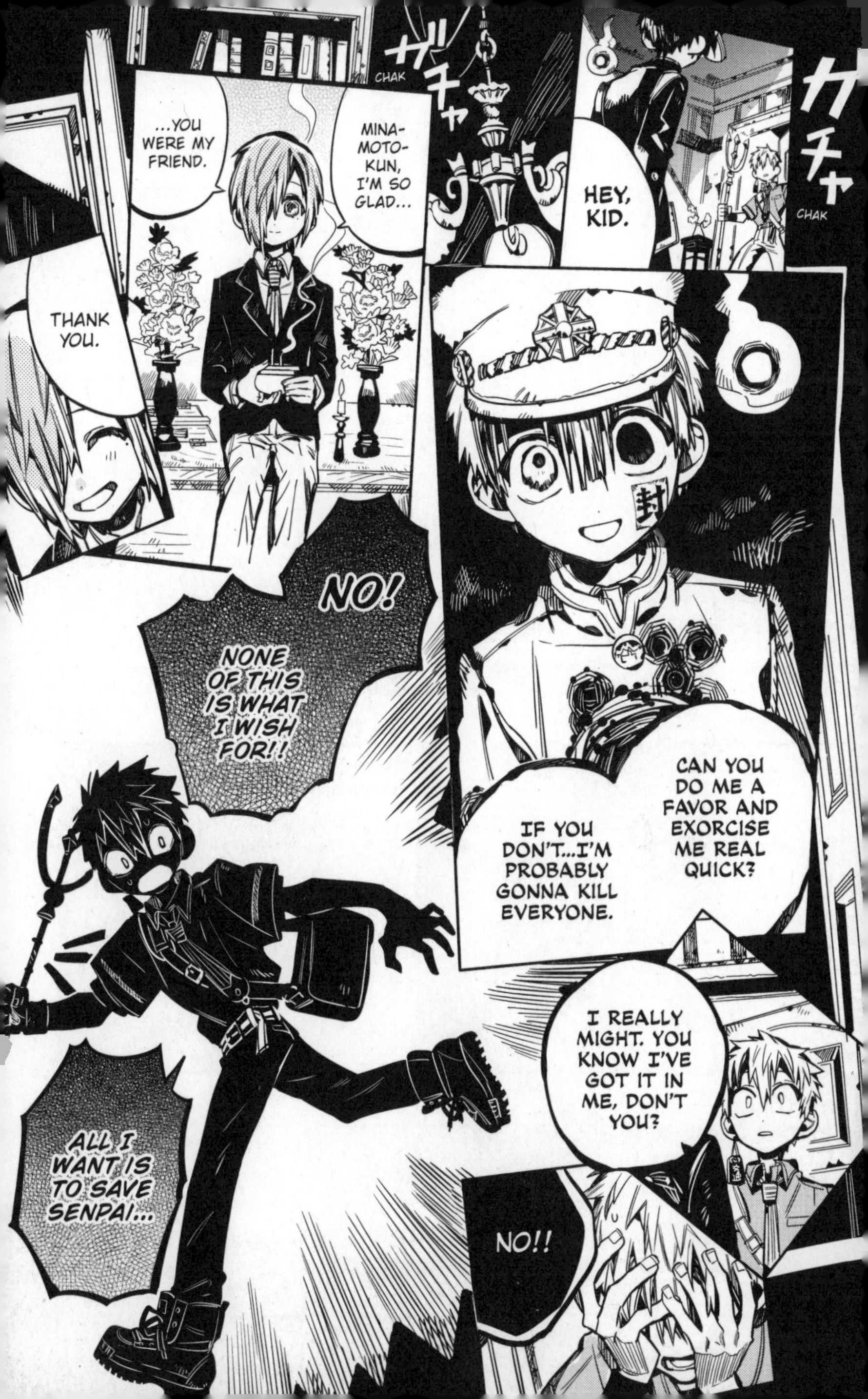
カチャ
CHAK
HEY, KID.
ガチャ
CHAK
MINA-MOTO-KUN, I'M SO GLAD...
...YOU WERE MY FRIEND.
THANK YOU.
CAN YOU DO ME A FAVOR AND EXORCISE ME REAL QUICK?
IF YOU DON'T...I'M PROBABLY GONNA KILL EVERYONE.
NO!
NONE OF THIS IS WHAT I WISH FOR!!
I REALLY MIGHT. YOU KNOW I'VE GOT IT IN ME, DON'T YOU?
NO!!
ALL I WANT IS TO SAVE SENPAI...

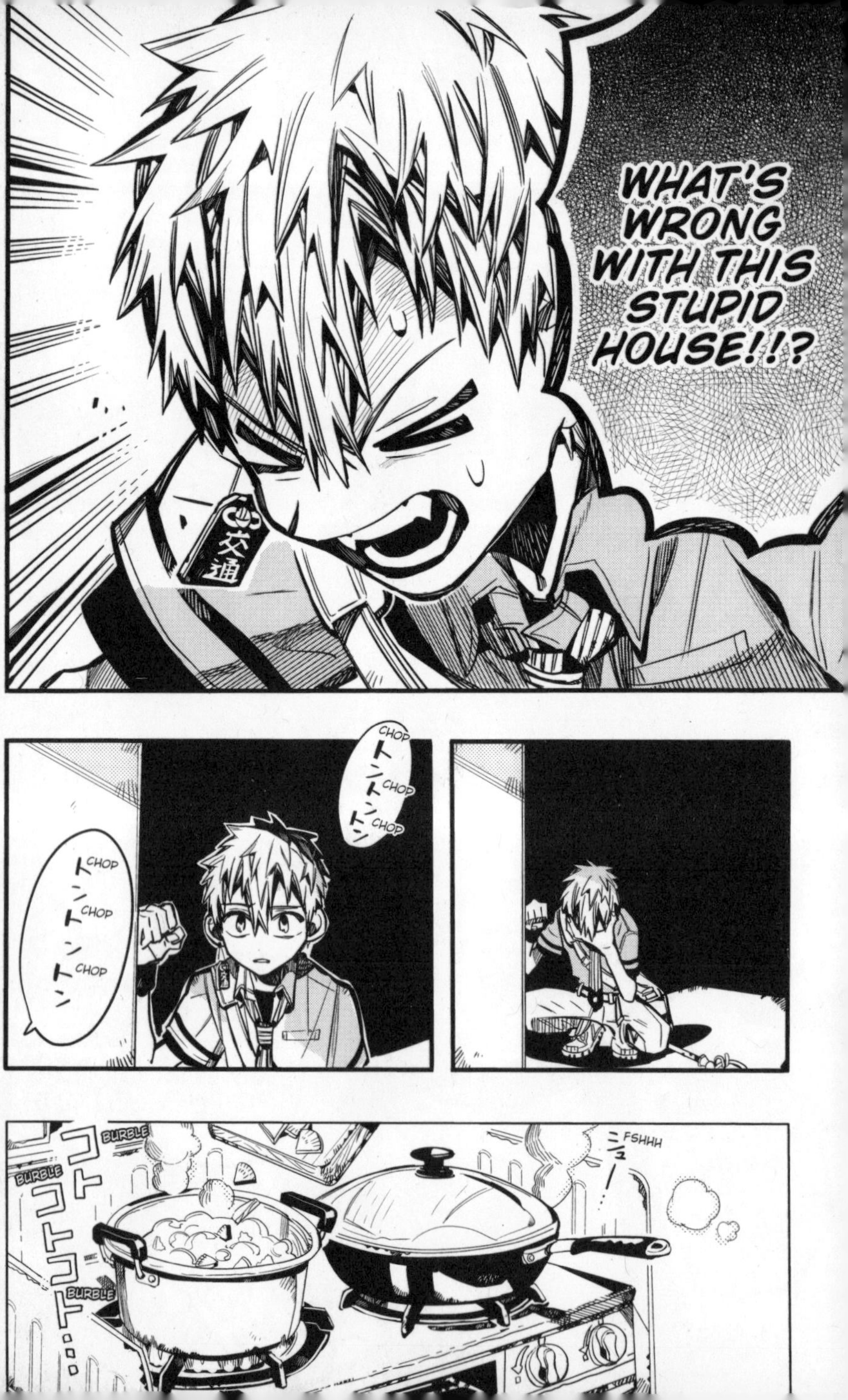
WHAT'S WRONG WITH THIS STUPID HOUSE!!?
トントントン
CHOP CHOP CHOP
トントントン
CHOP CHOP CHOP
ジュ
FSHHH
コトコトコト...
BURBLE BURBLE BURBLE

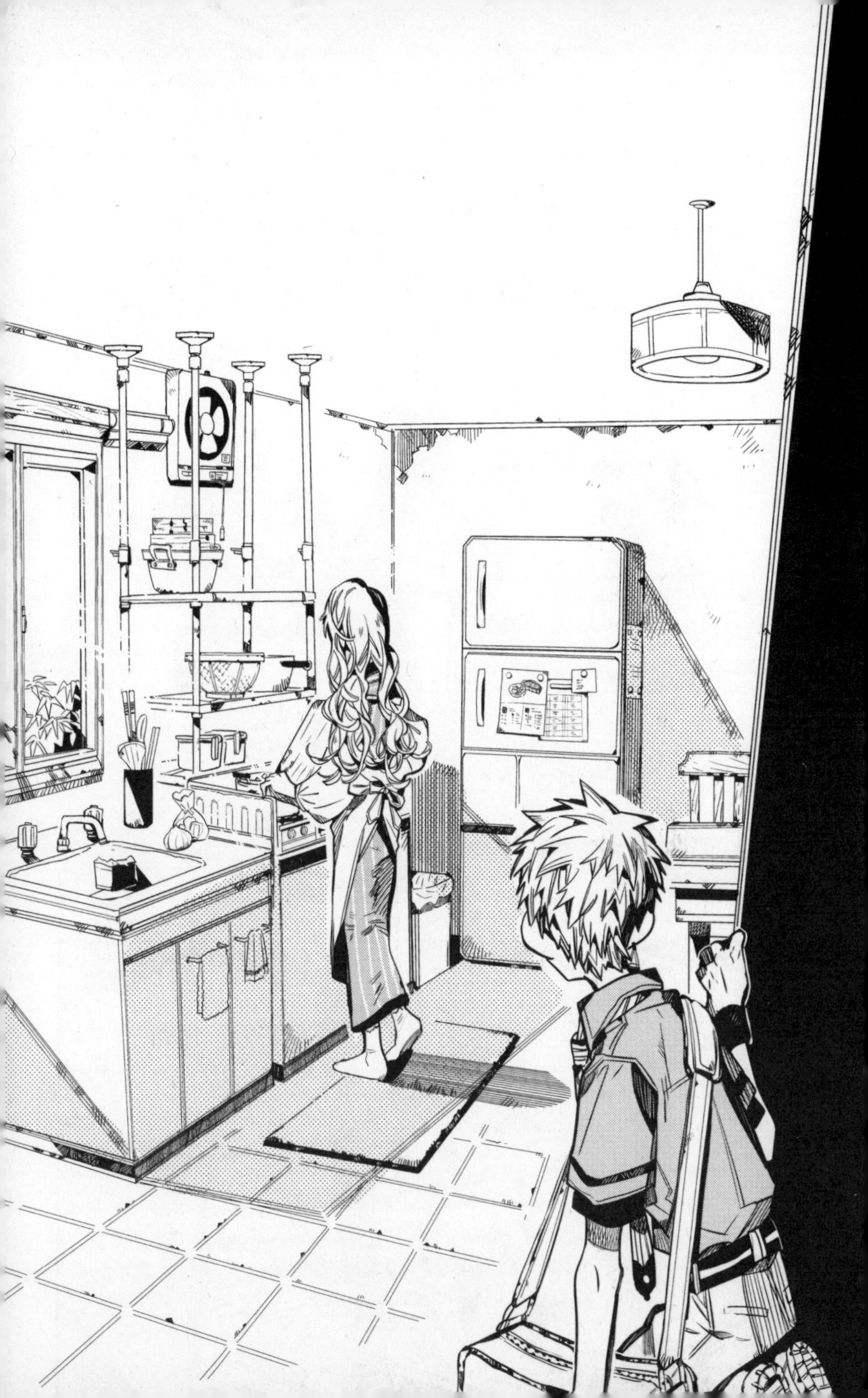

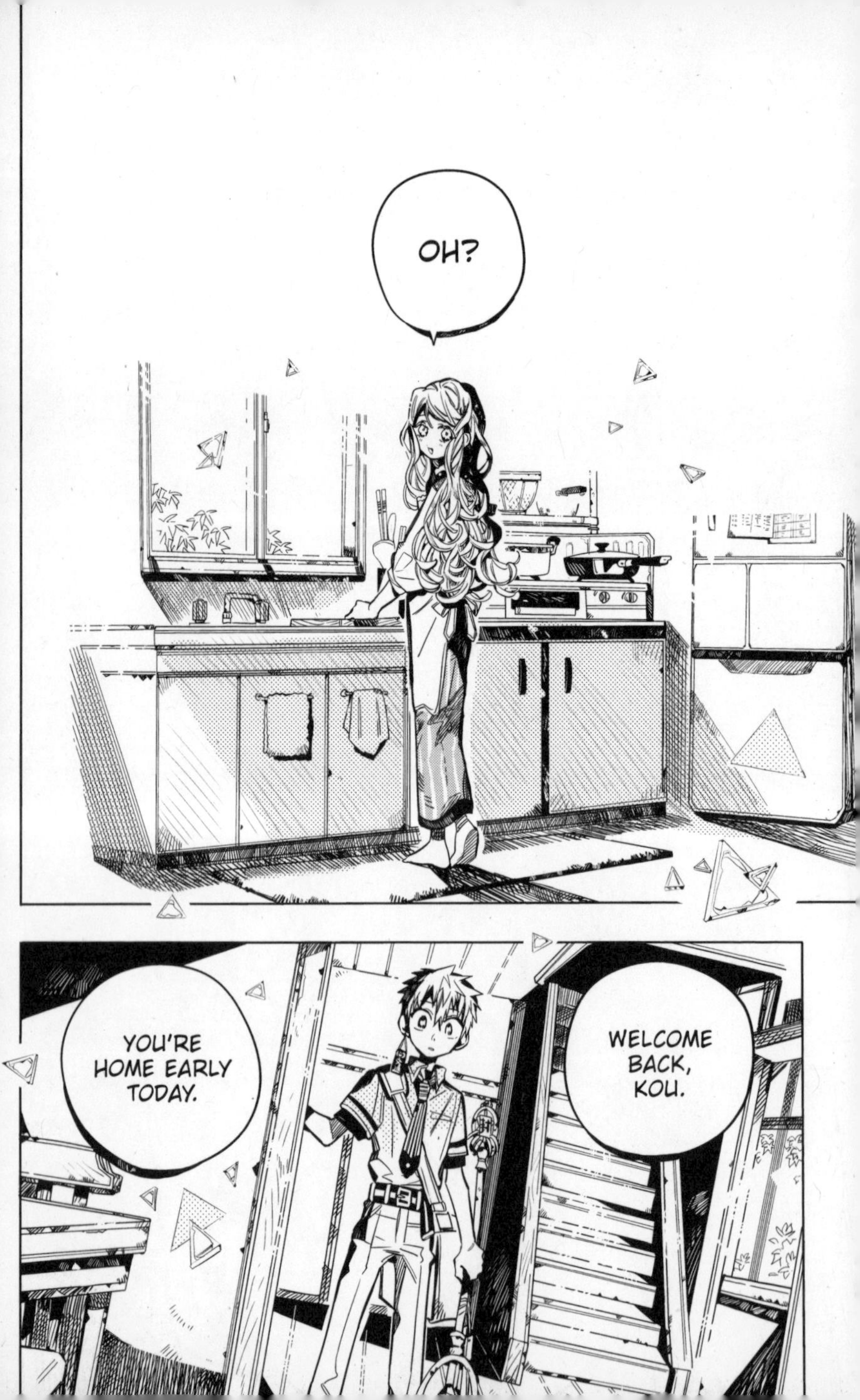
OH?
WELCOME BACK, KOU.
YOU'RE HOME EARLY TODAY.

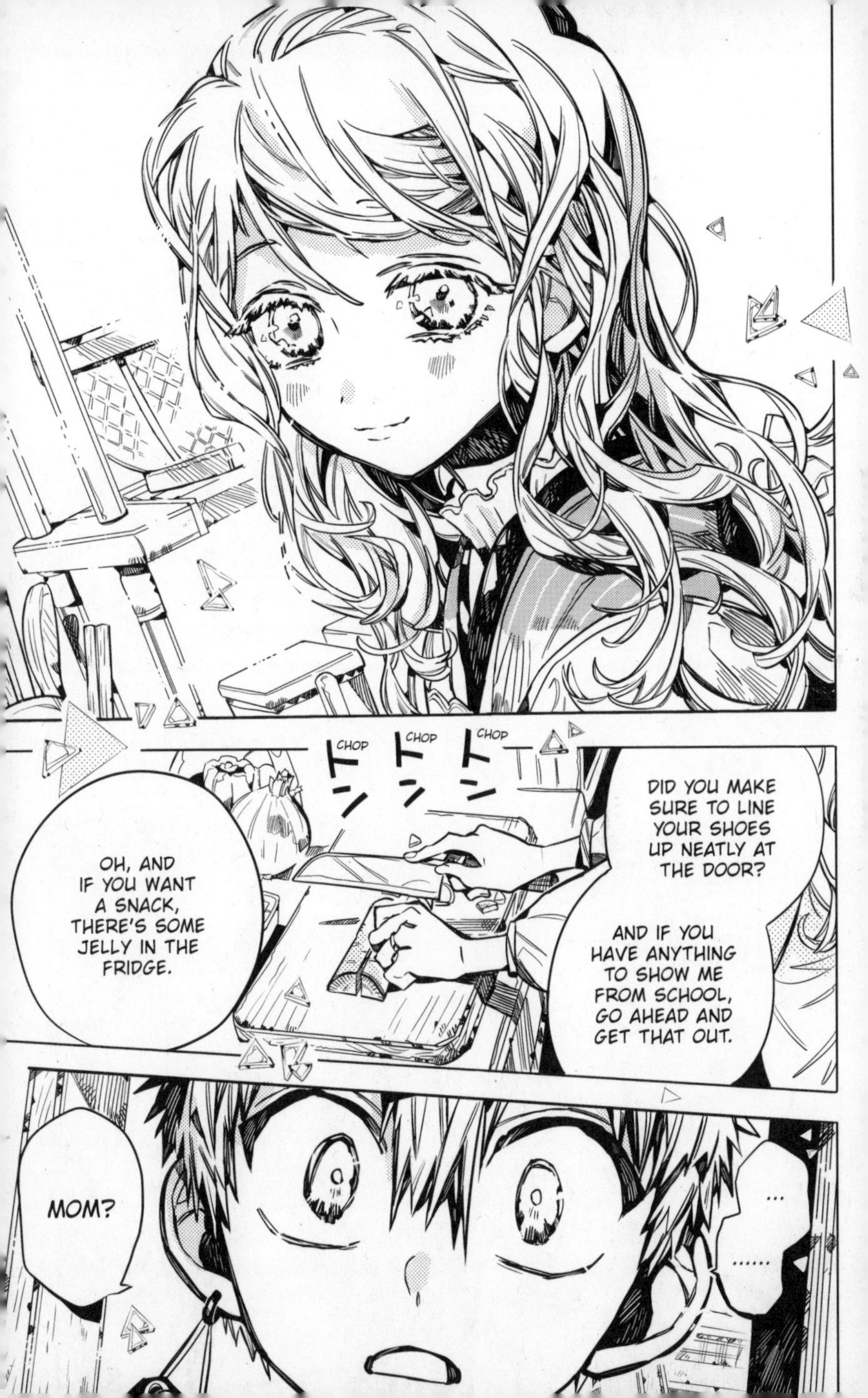
CHOP
CHOP
CHOP
DID YOU MAKE SURE TO LINE YOUR SHOES UP NEATLY AT THE DOOR?
AND IF YOU HAVE ANYTHING TO SHOW ME FROM SCHOOL, GO AHEAD AND GET THAT OUT.
OH, AND IF YOU WANT A SNACK, THERE'S SOME JELLY IN THE FRIDGE.
...
......
MOM?

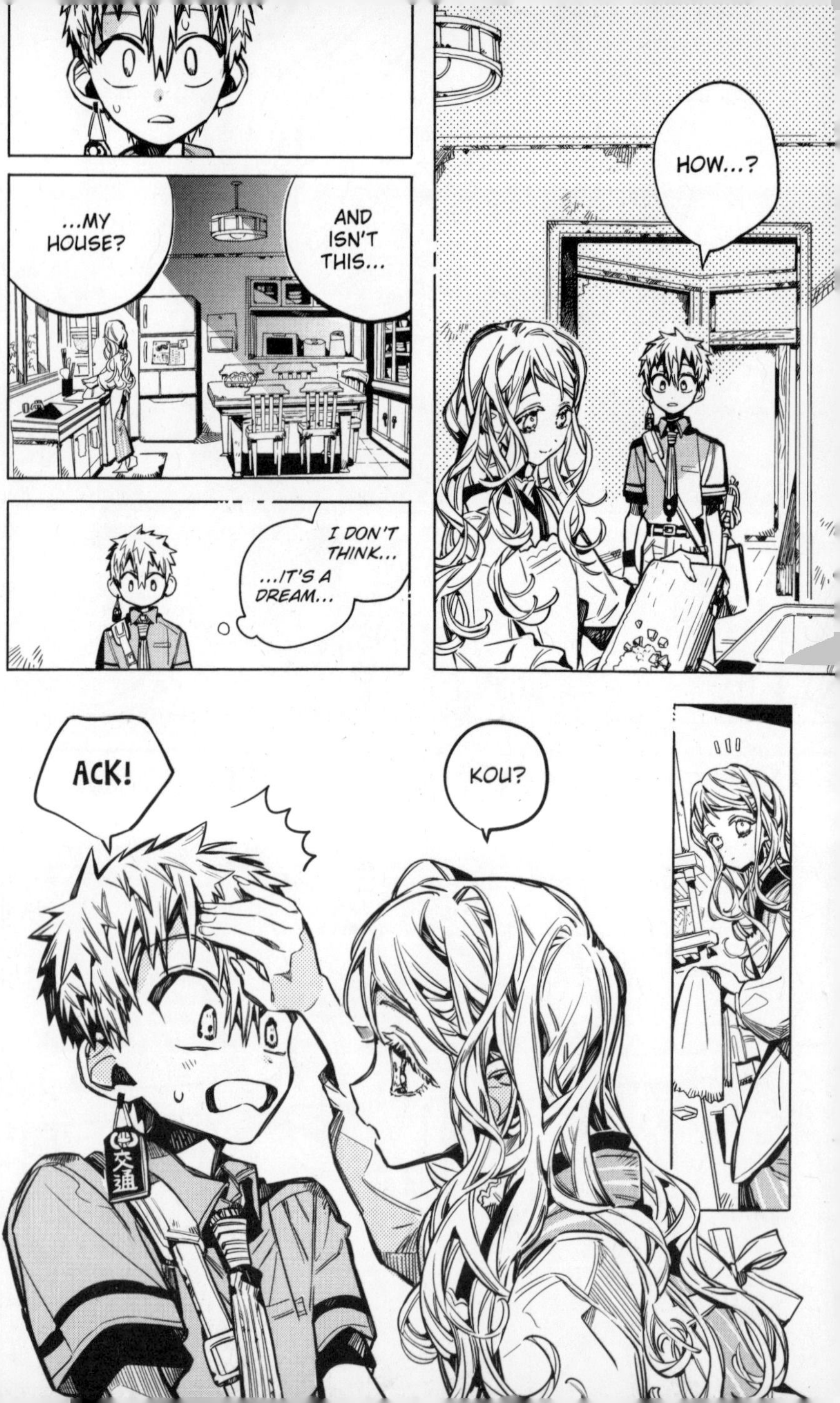
HOW...?
AND ISN'T THIS...
...MY HOUSE?
I DON'T THINK...
...IT'S A DREAM...
KOU?
ACK!

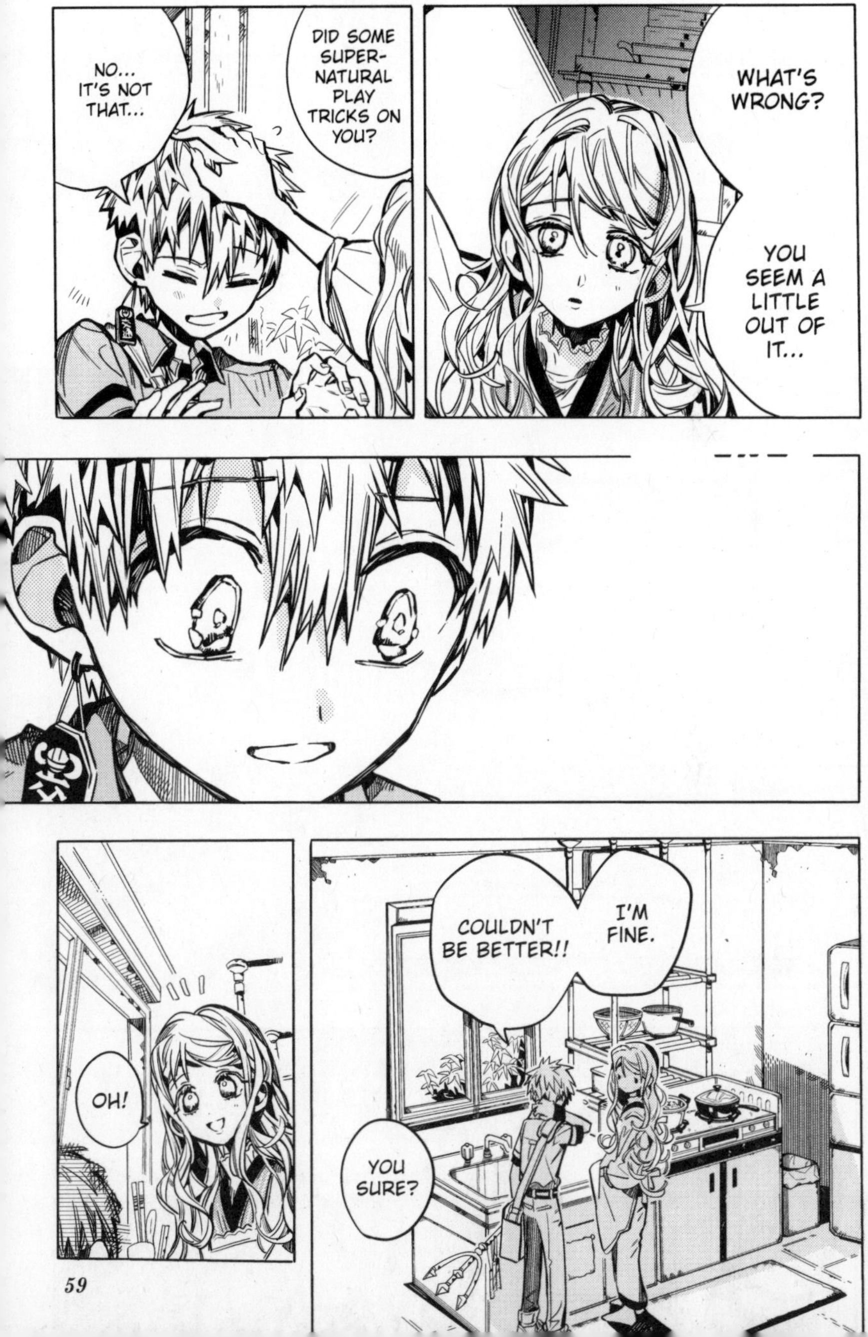
WHAT'S WRONG?
YOU SEEM A LITTLE OUT OF IT...
DID SOME SUPER-NATURAL PLAY TRICKS ON YOU?
NO... IT'S NOT THAT...
I'M FINE.
COULDN'T BE BETTER!!
YOU SURE?
OH!

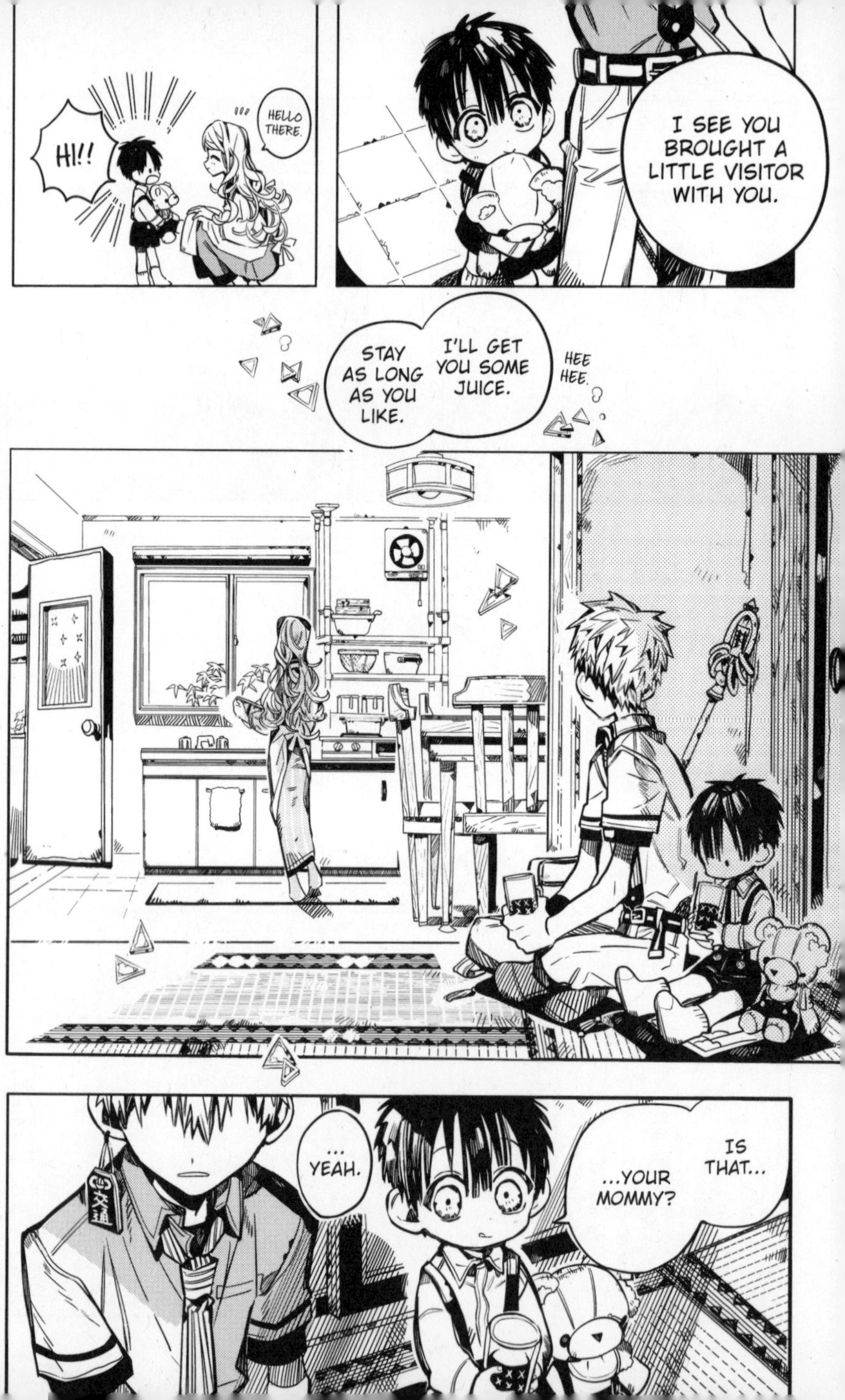
I SEE YOU BROUGHT A LITTLE VISITOR WITH YOU.
HELLO THERE.
HI!!
HEE HEE.
I'LL GET YOU SOME JUICE.
STAY AS LONG AS YOU LIKE.
IS THAT...
...YOUR MOMMY?
... YEAH.

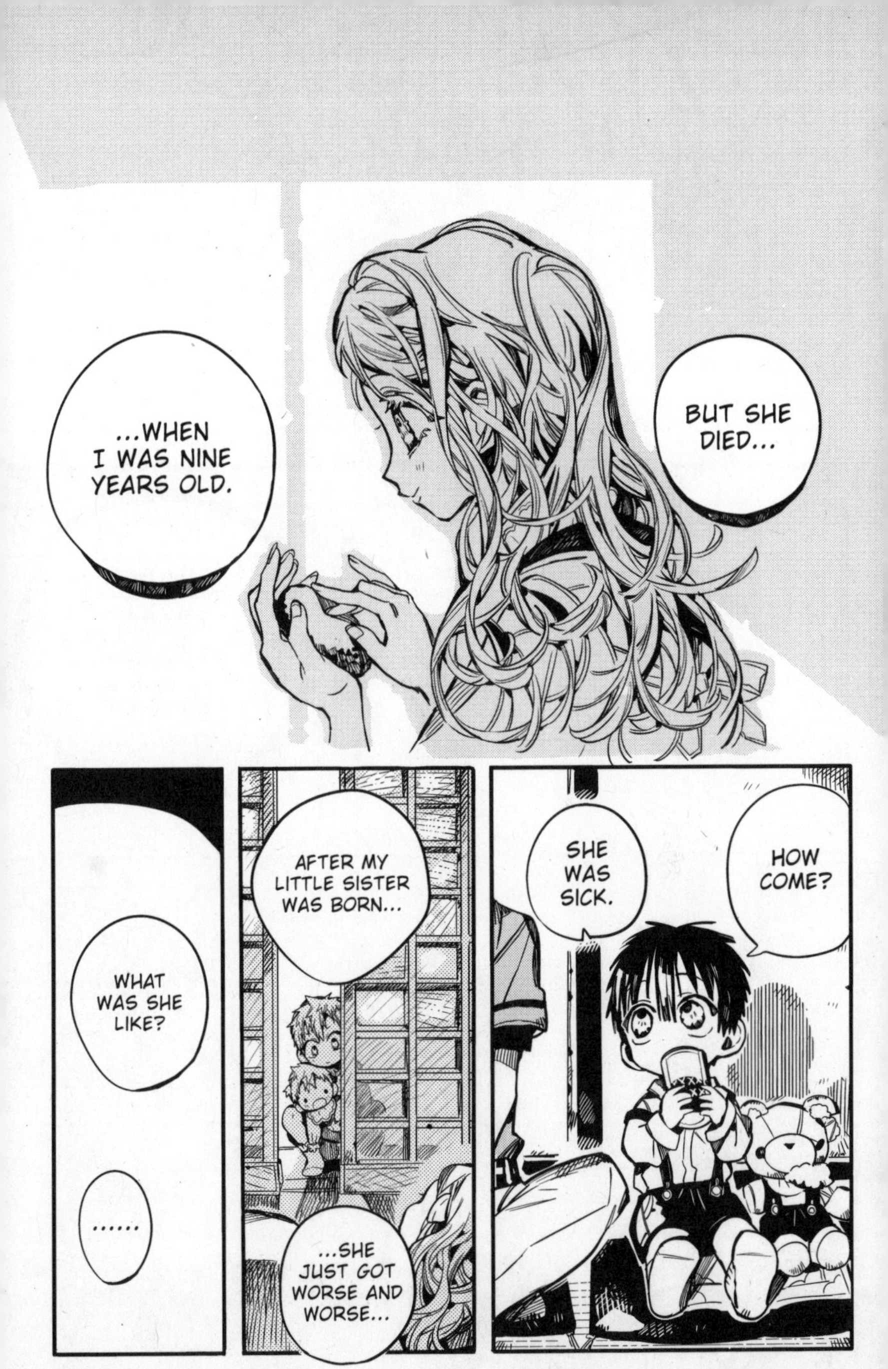
BUT SHE DIED...
...WHEN I WAS NINE YEARS OLD.
HOW COME?
SHE WAS SICK.
AFTER MY LITTLE SISTER WAS BORN...
...SHE JUST GOT WORSE AND WORSE...
WHAT WAS SHE LIKE?
......

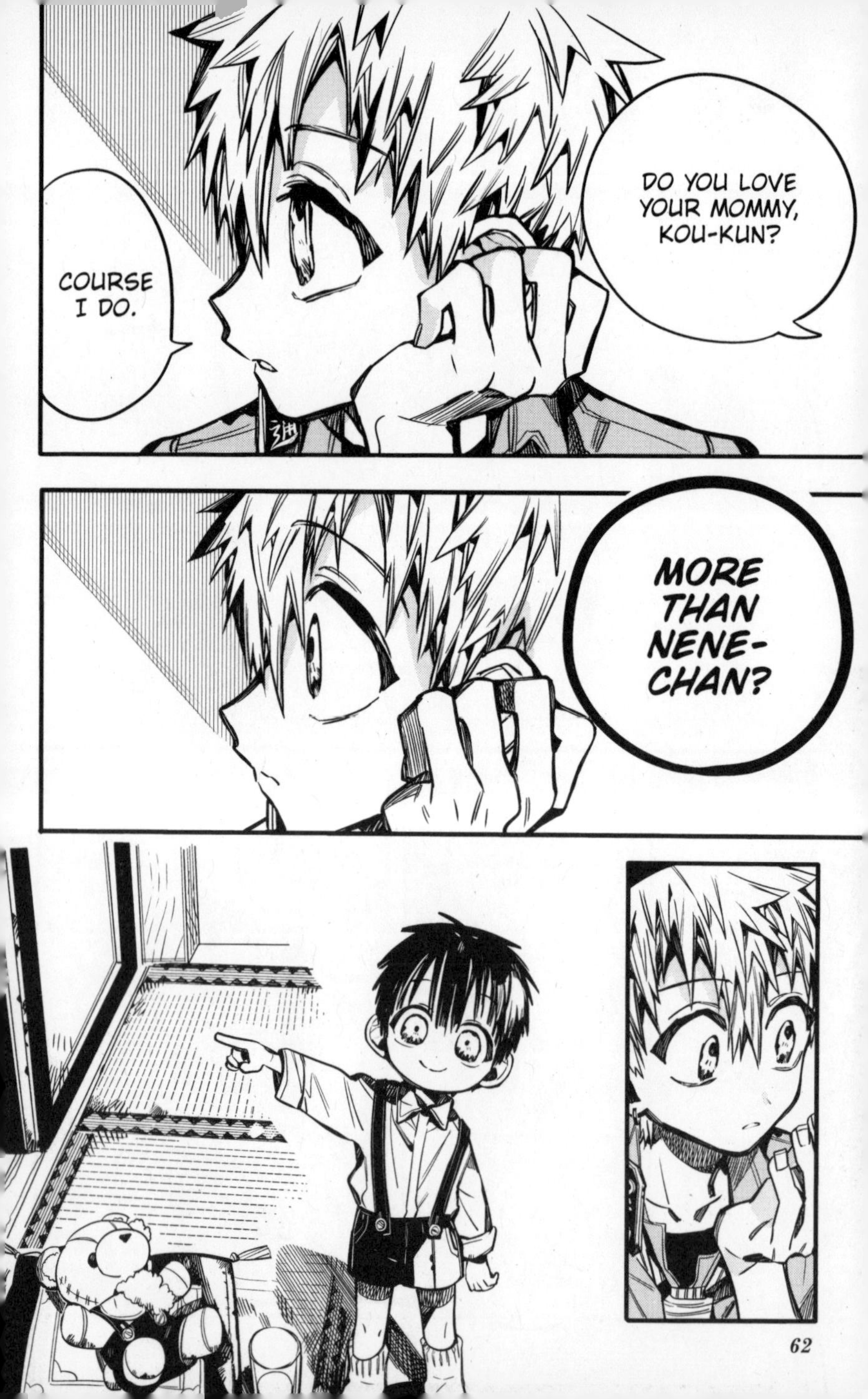
DO YOU LOVE YOUR MOMMY, KOU-KUN?
COURSE I DO.
MORE THAN NENE-CHAN?

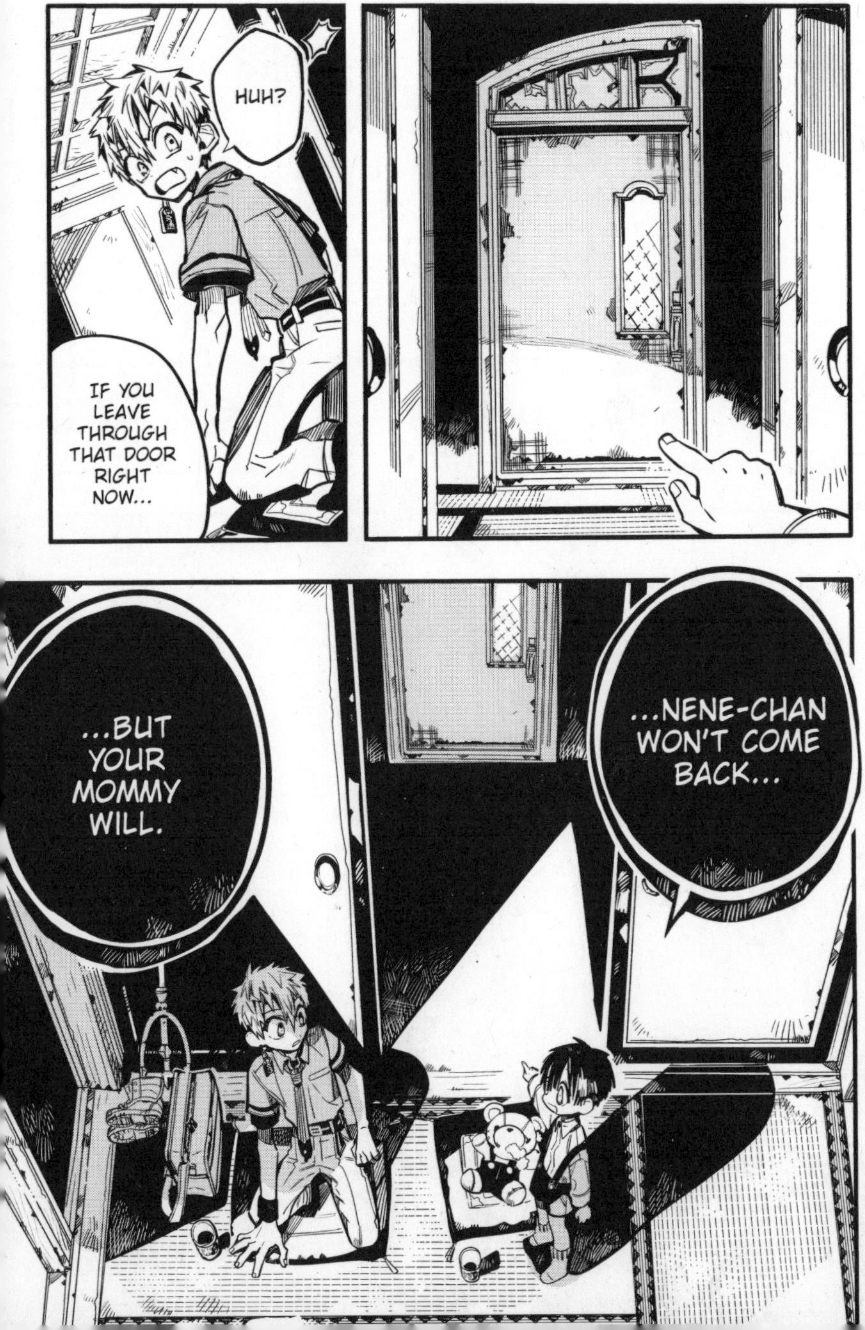
HUH?
IF YOU LEAVE THROUGH THAT DOOR RIGHT NOW...
...NENE-CHAN WON'T COME BACK...
...BUT YOUR MOMMY WILL.

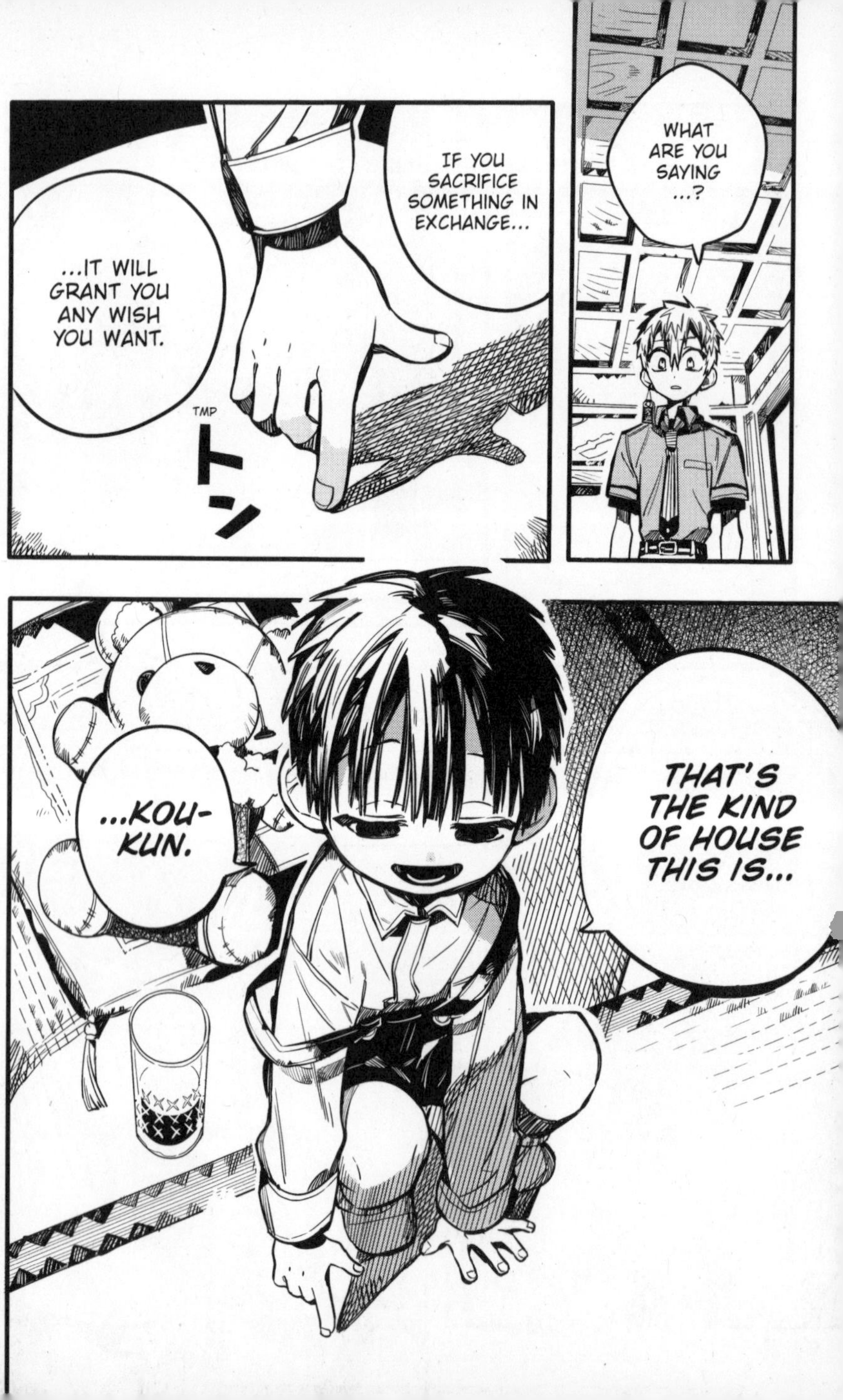
WHAT ARE YOU SAYING ...?
IF YOU SACRIFICE SOMETHING IN EXCHANGE...
...IT WILL GRANT YOU ANY WISH YOU WANT.
TMP
トッ
THAT'S THE KIND OF HOUSE THIS IS...
...KOU-KUN.

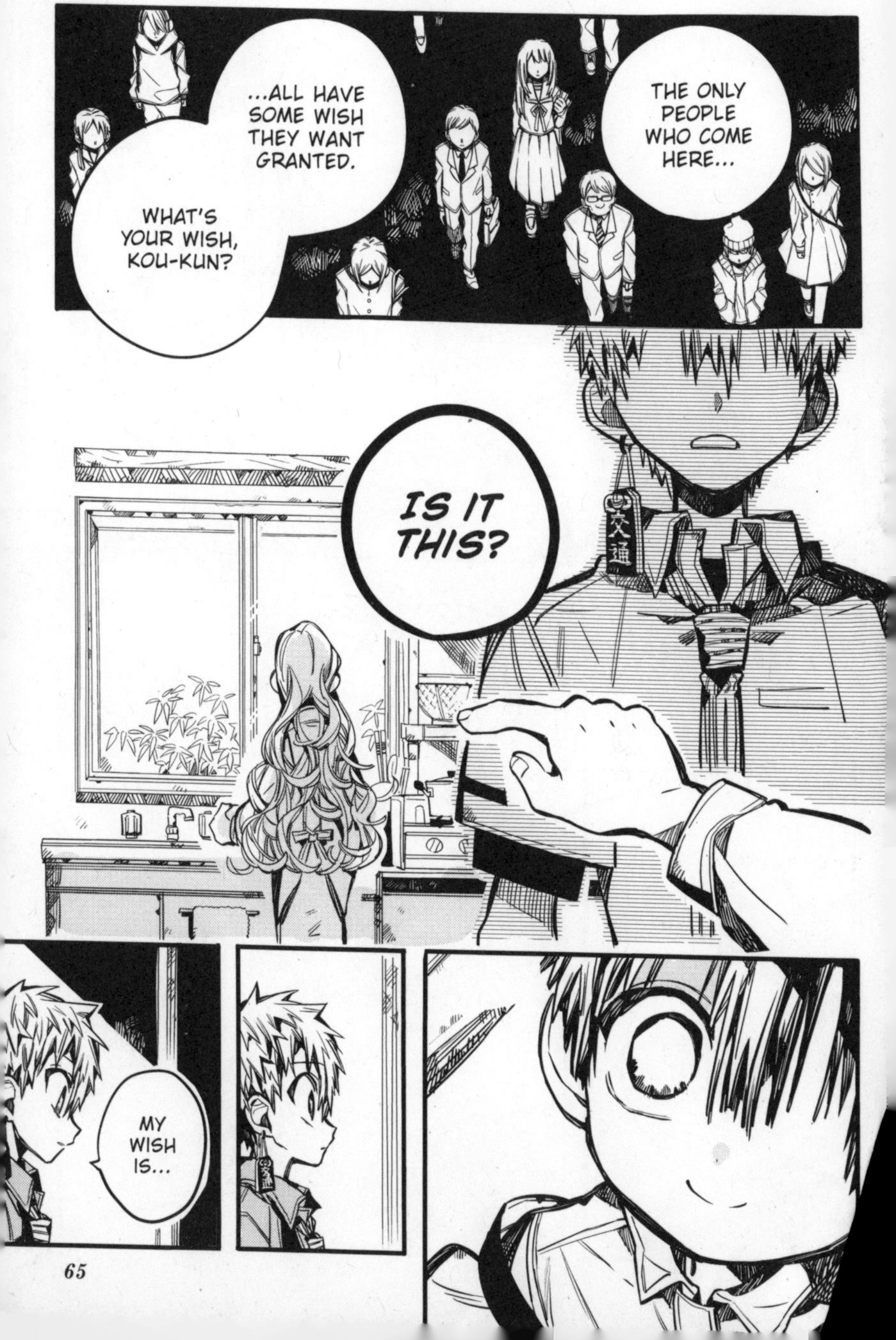
THE ONLY PEOPLE WHO COME HERE...
...ALL HAVE SOME WISH THEY WANT GRANTED.
WHAT'S YOUR WISH, KOU-KUN?
IS IT THIS?
MY WISH IS...

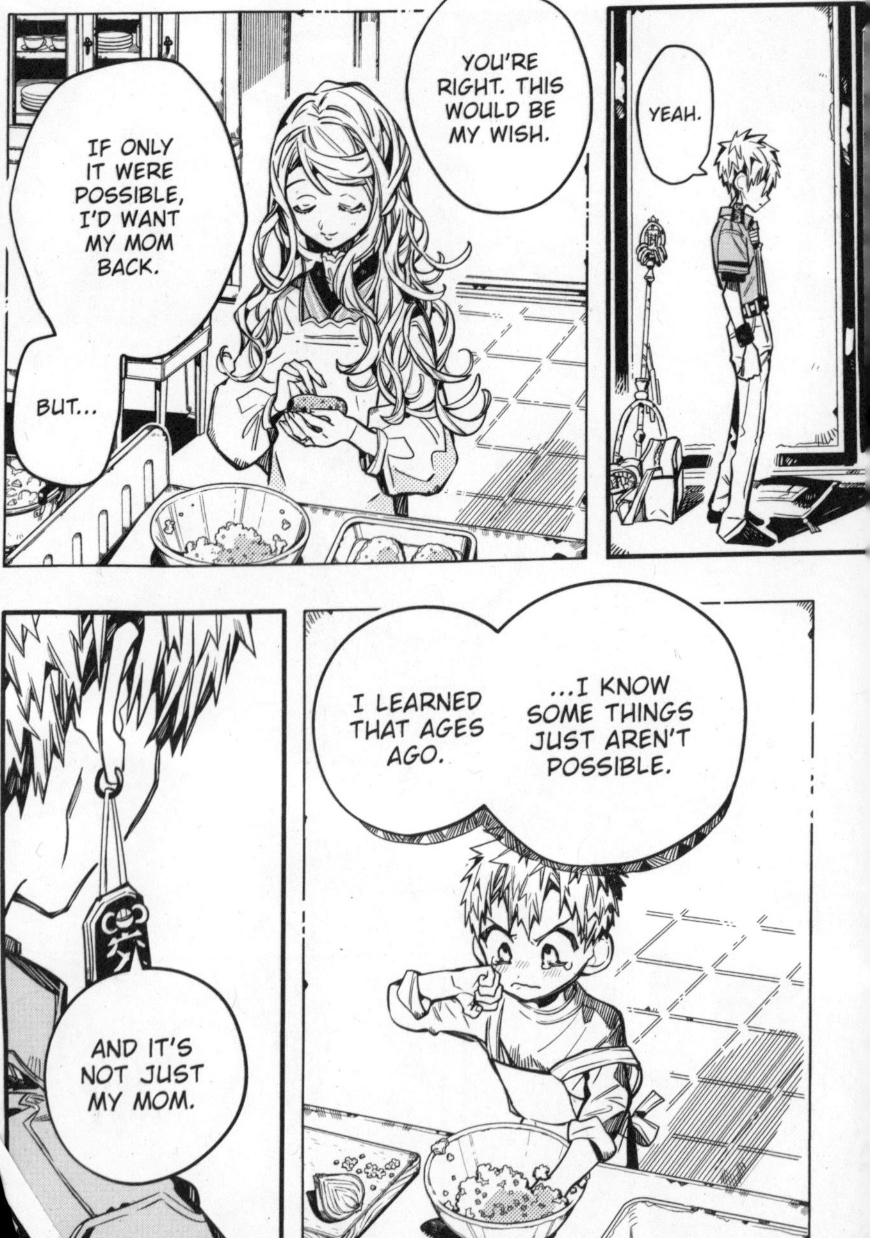
YEAH.
YOU'RE RIGHT. THIS WOULD BE MY WISH.
IF ONLY IT WERE POSSIBLE, I'D WANT MY MOM BACK.
BUT...
...I KNOW SOME THINGS JUST AREN'T POSSIBLE.
I LEARNED THAT AGES AGO.
AND IT'S NOT JUST MY MOM.

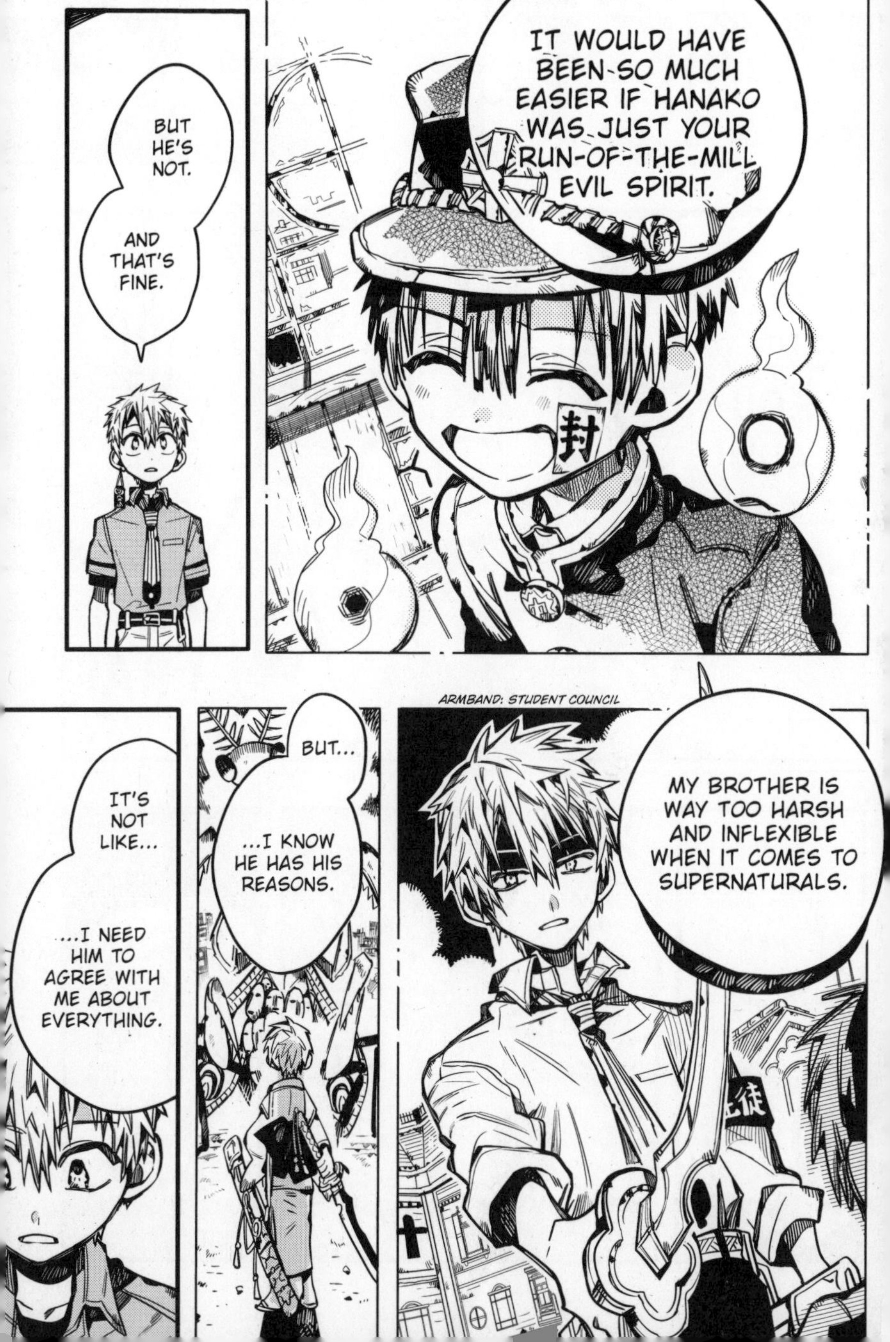
IT WOULD HAVE BEEN SO MUCH EASIER IF HANAKO WAS JUST YOUR RUN-OF-THE-MILL EVIL SPIRIT.
BUT HE'S NOT.
AND THAT'S FINE.
ARMBAND: STUDENT COUNCIL
MY BROTHER IS WAY TOO HARSH AND INFLEXIBLE WHEN IT COMES TO SUPERNATURALS.
BUT...
...I KNOW HE HAS HIS REASONS.
IT'S NOT LIKE...
...I NEED HIM TO AGREE WITH ME ABOUT EVERYTHING.

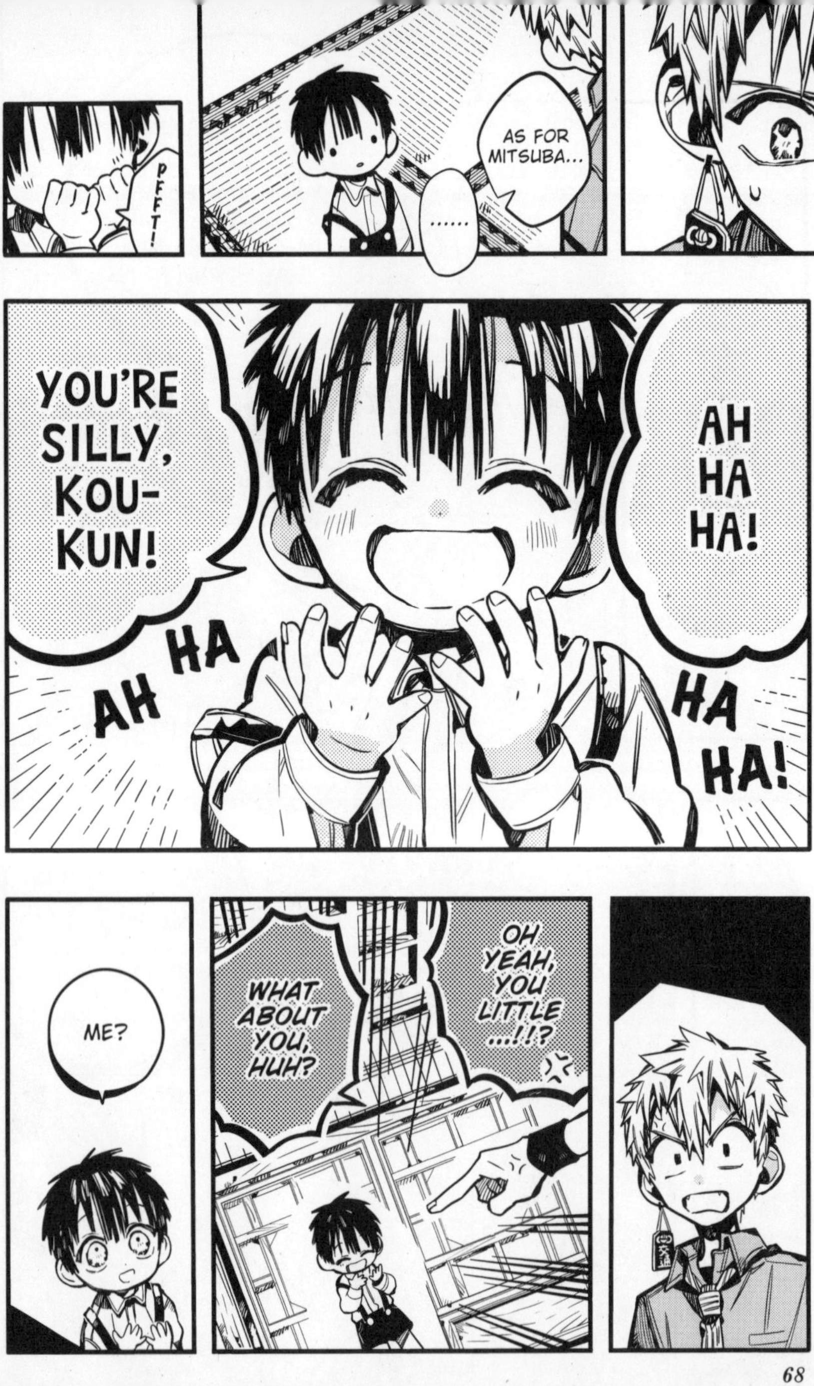
AS FOR MITSUBA...
......
PFFT!
AH HA HA!
YOU'RE SILLY, KOU-KUN!
HA HA!
AH HA
OH YEAH, YOU LITTLE ...!!?
WHAT ABOUT YOU, HUH?
ME?

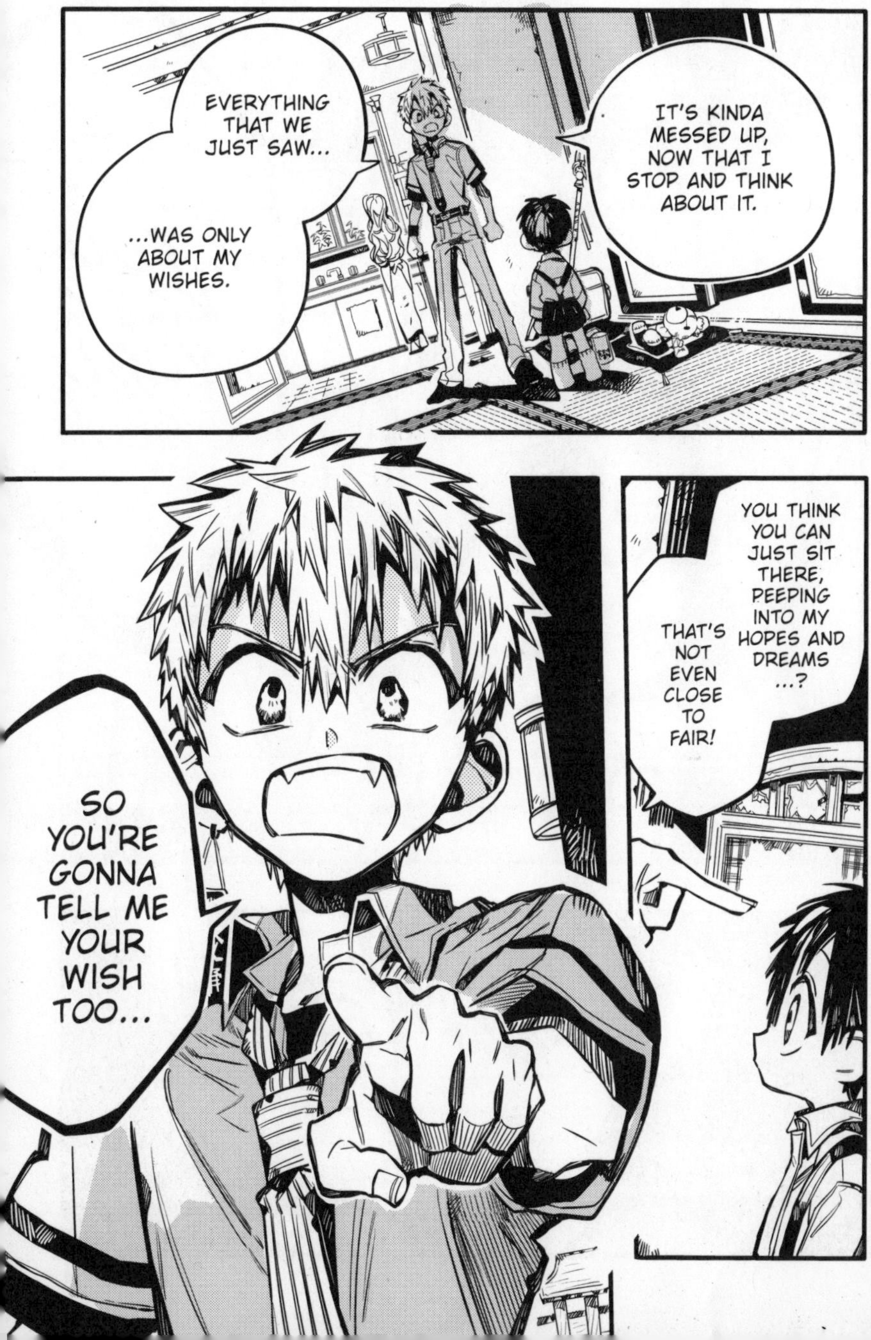
IT'S KINDA MESSED UP, NOW THAT I STOP AND THINK ABOUT IT.
EVERYTHING THAT WE JUST SAW...
...WAS ONLY ABOUT MY WISHES.
YOU THINK YOU CAN JUST SIT THERE, PEEPING INTO MY HOPES AND DREAMS ...?
THAT'S NOT EVEN CLOSE TO FAIR!
SO YOU'RE GONNA TELL ME YOUR WISH TOO...

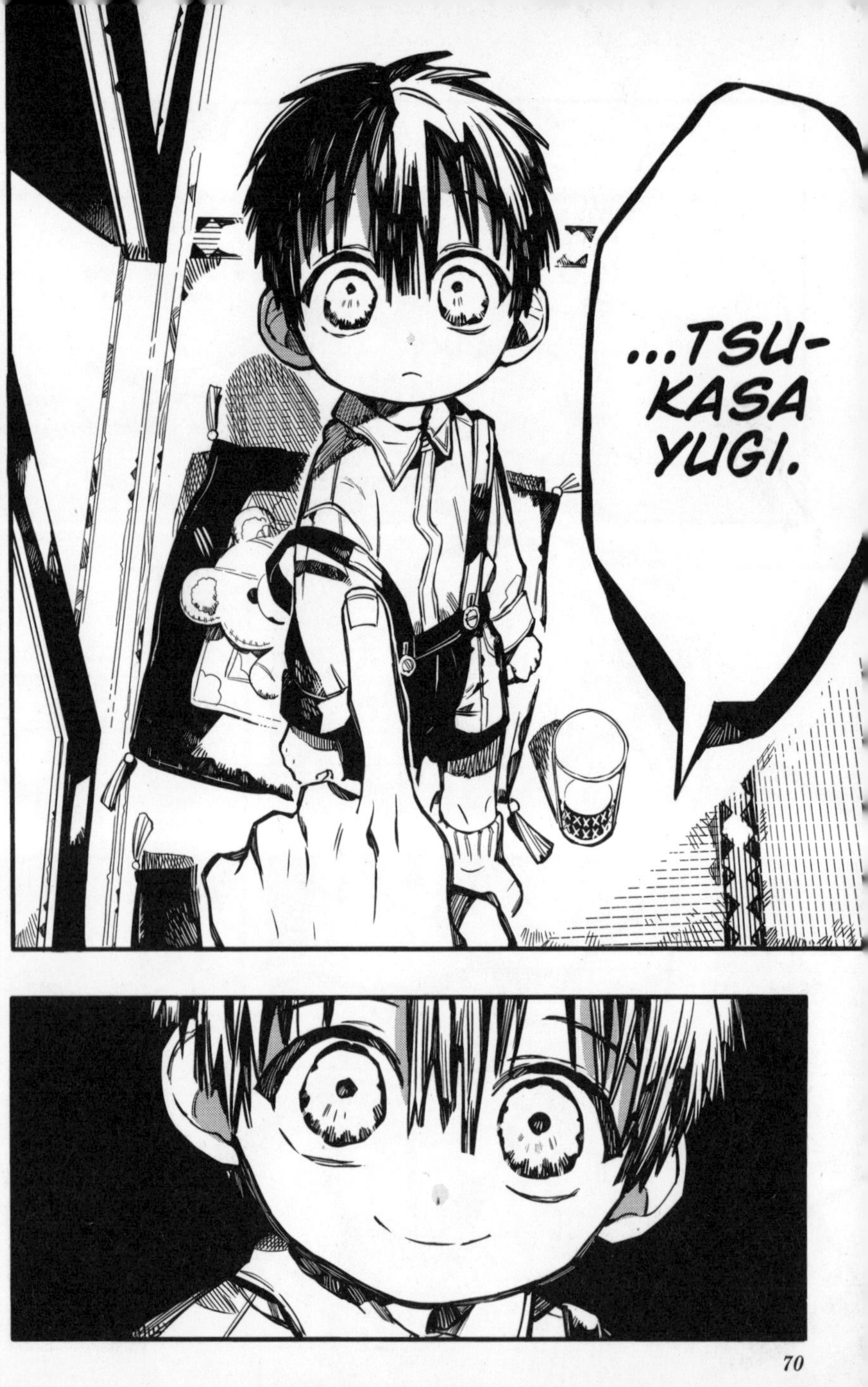
...TSU-
KASA
YUGI.

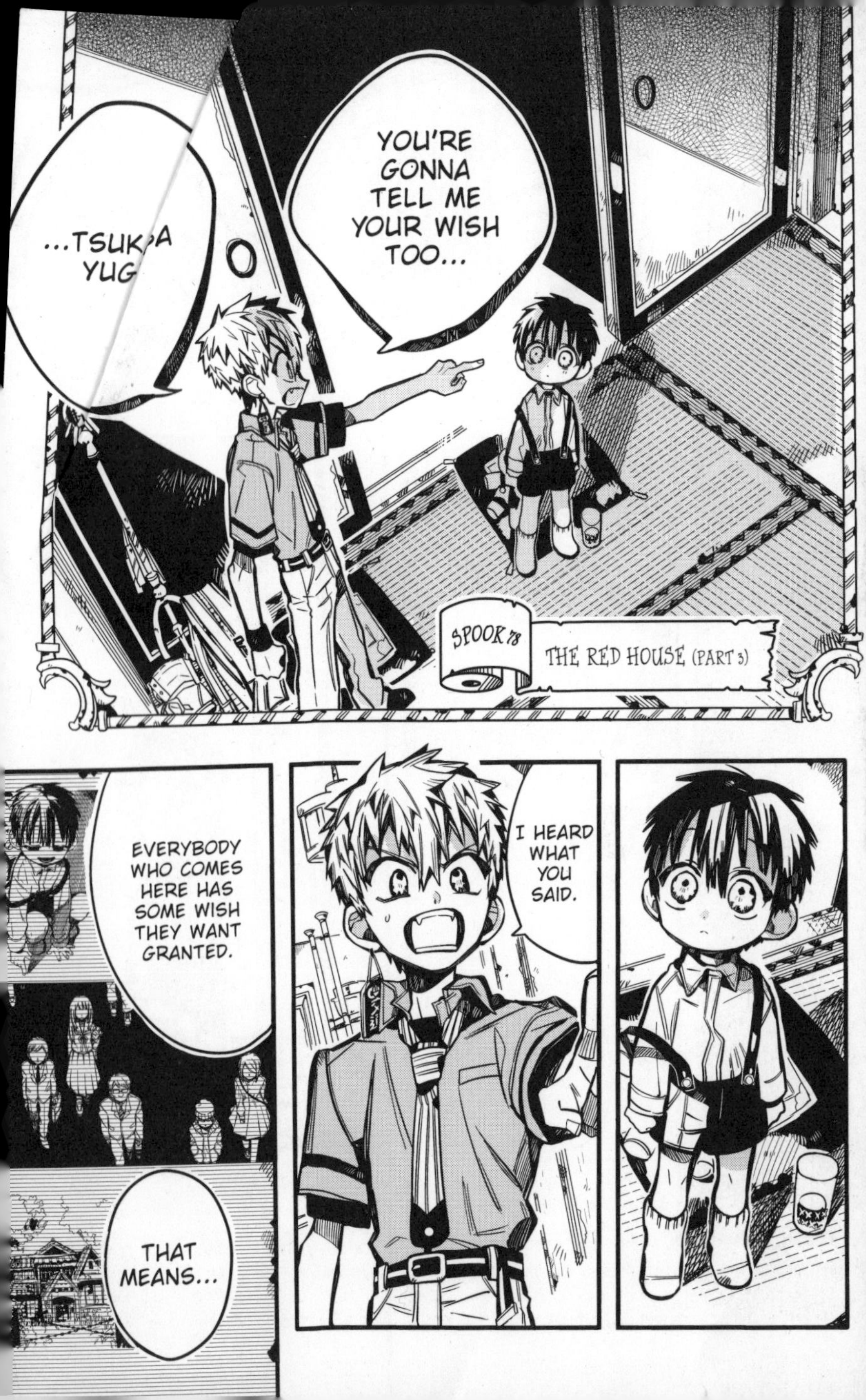

YOU'RE GONNA TELL ME YOUR WISH TOO...
...TSUK A YUG
SPOOK 78
THE RED HOUSE (PART 3)
I HEARD WHAT YOU SAID.
EVERYBODY WHO COMES HERE HAS SOME WISH THEY WANT GRANTED.
THAT MEANS...

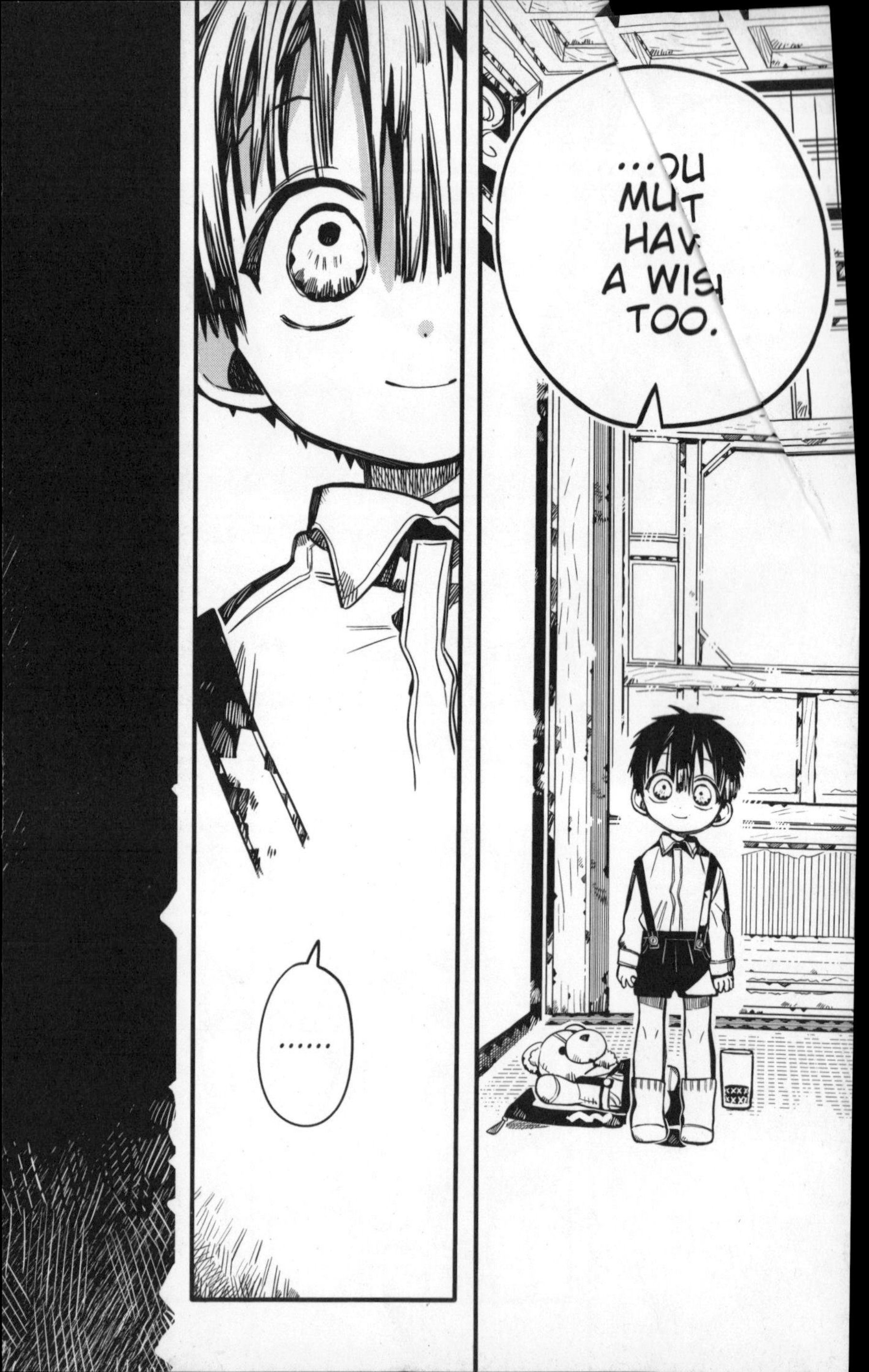
...OU MUT HAV A WIS TOO.
......

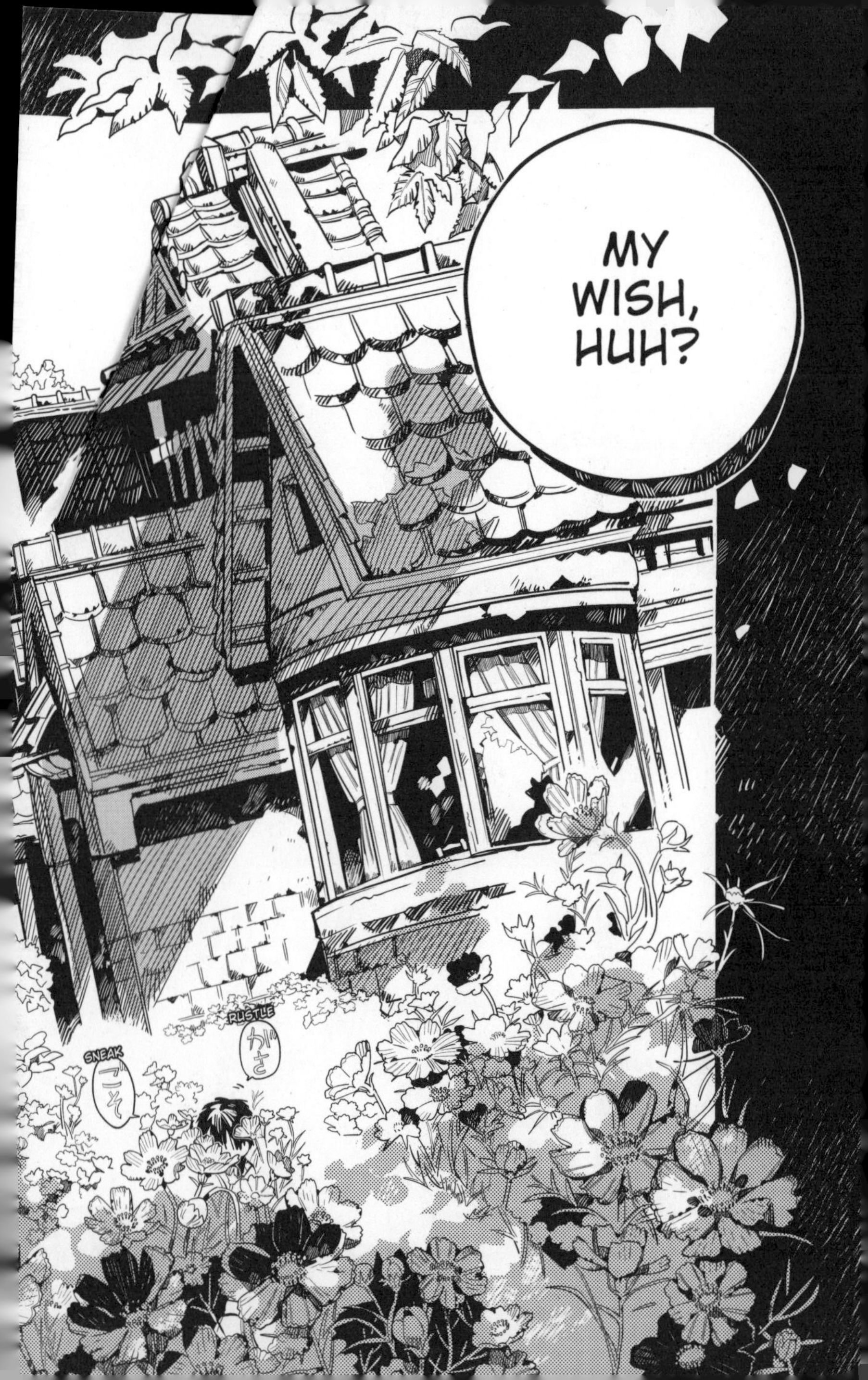
MY WISH, HUH?
RUSTLE
がさ
SNEAK
こそ

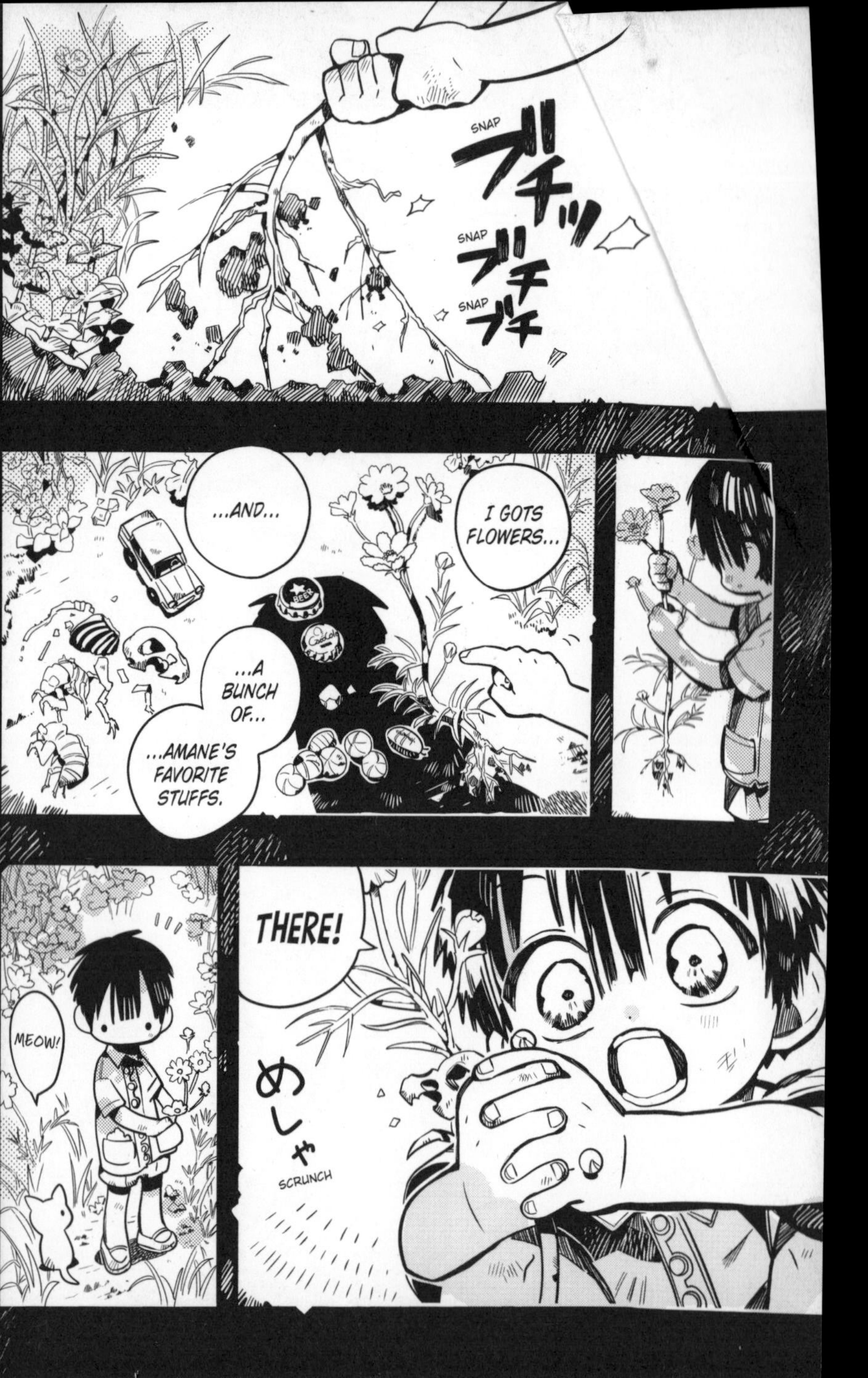
ブチッ
SNAP
ブチ
SNAP
ブチ
SNAP
I GOTS FLOWERS...
...AND...
...A BUNCH OF...
...AMANE'S FAVORITE STUFFS.
THERE!
めしゃ
SCRUNCH
MEOW!

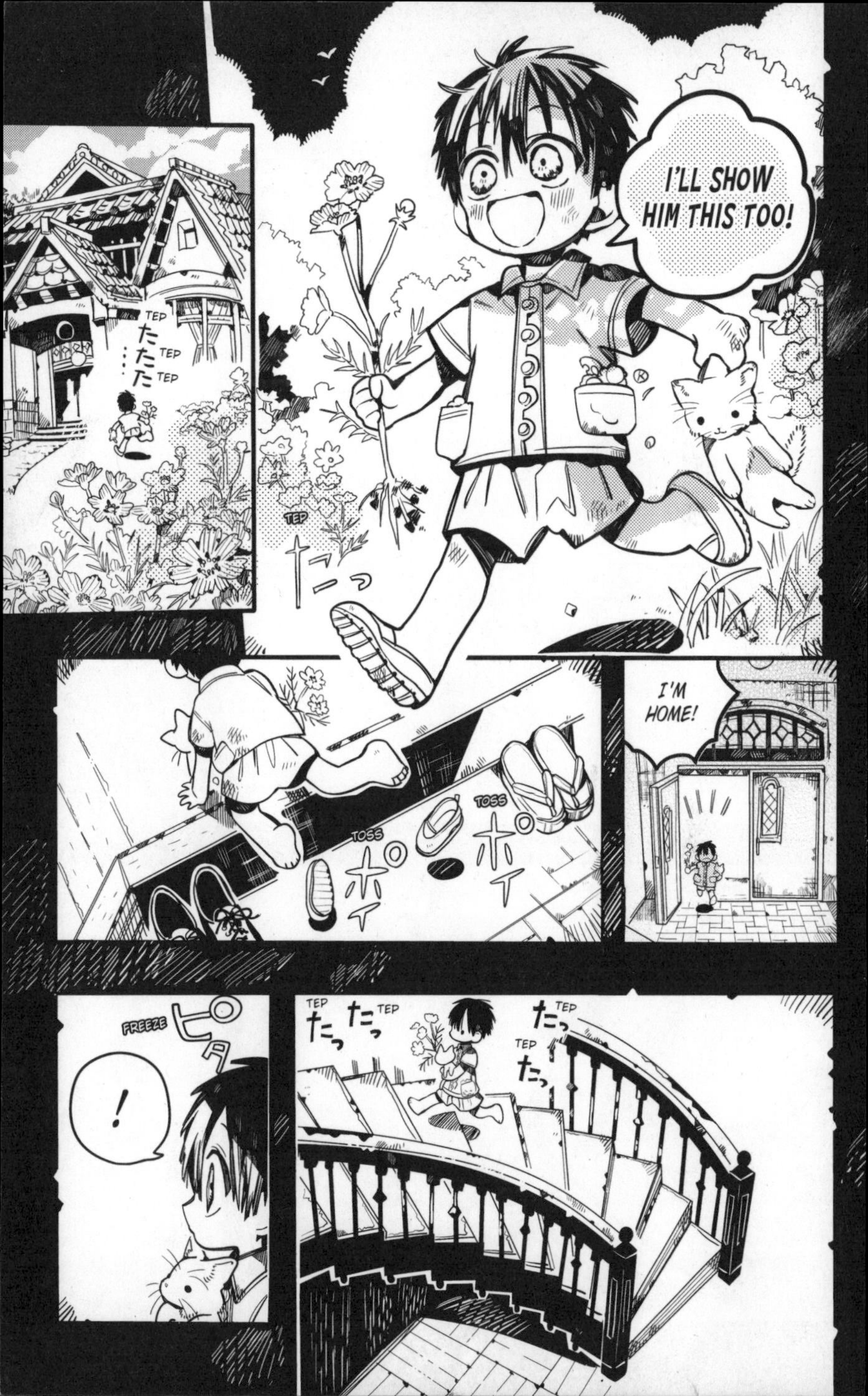
I'LL SHOW HIM THIS TOO!
TEP
たーっ
TEP
たたた
TEP
TEP
I'M HOME!
TOSS
ポイ
TOSS
ポイ
TEP
たっ
TEP
たっ
TEP
たっ
TEP
たっ
FREEZE
ピタ
!

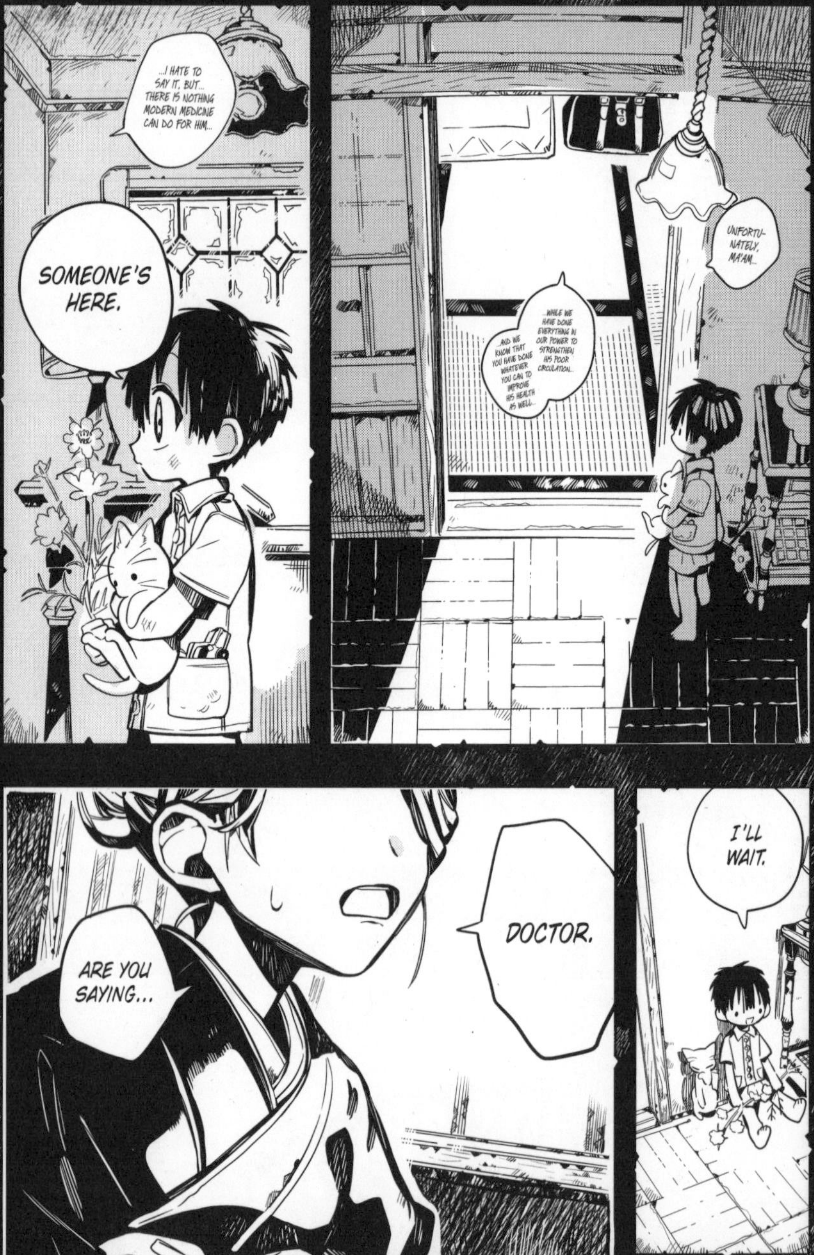
UNFORTUNATELY, MA'AM...
...WHILE WE HAVE DONE EVERYTHING IN OUR POWER TO STRENGTHEN HIS POOR CIRCULATION...
...AND WE KNOW THAT YOU HAVE DONE WHATEVER YOU CAN TO IMPROVE HIS HEALTH AS WELL...
...I HATE TO SAY IT, BUT... THERE IS NOTHING MODERN MEDICINE CAN DO FOR HIM...
SOMEONE'S HERE.
I'LL WAIT.
DOCTOR.
ARE YOU SAYING...

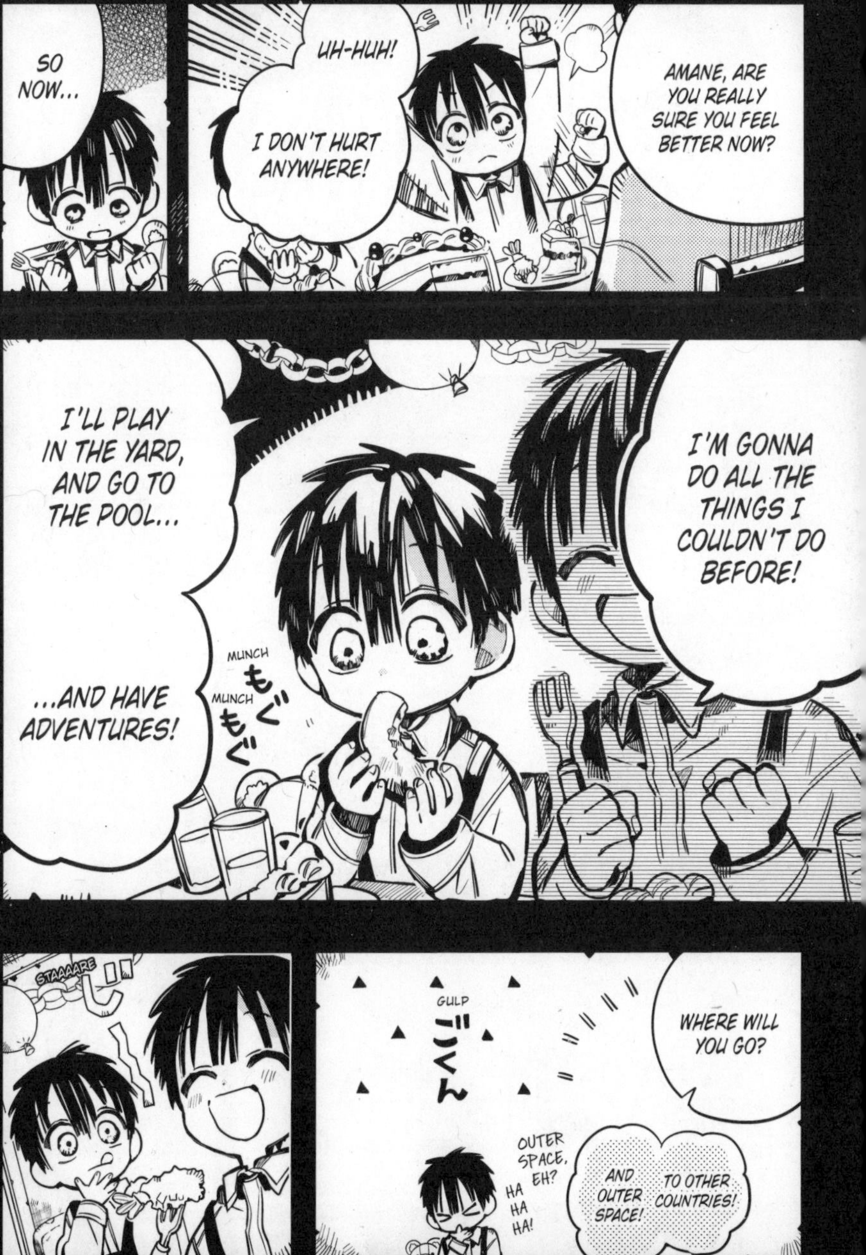
AMANE, ARE YOU REALLY SURE YOU FEEL BETTER NOW?
UH-HUH!
I DON'T HURT ANYWHERE!
SO NOW...
I'M GONNA DO ALL THE THINGS I COULDN'T DO BEFORE!
I'LL PLAY IN THE YARD, AND GO TO THE POOL...
MUNCH もぐ
MUNCH もぐ
...AND HAVE ADVENTURES!
WHERE WILL YOU GO?
GULP
TO OTHER COUNTRIES!
AND OUTER SPACE!
OUTER SPACE, EH?
HA HA HA!
STAAAARE

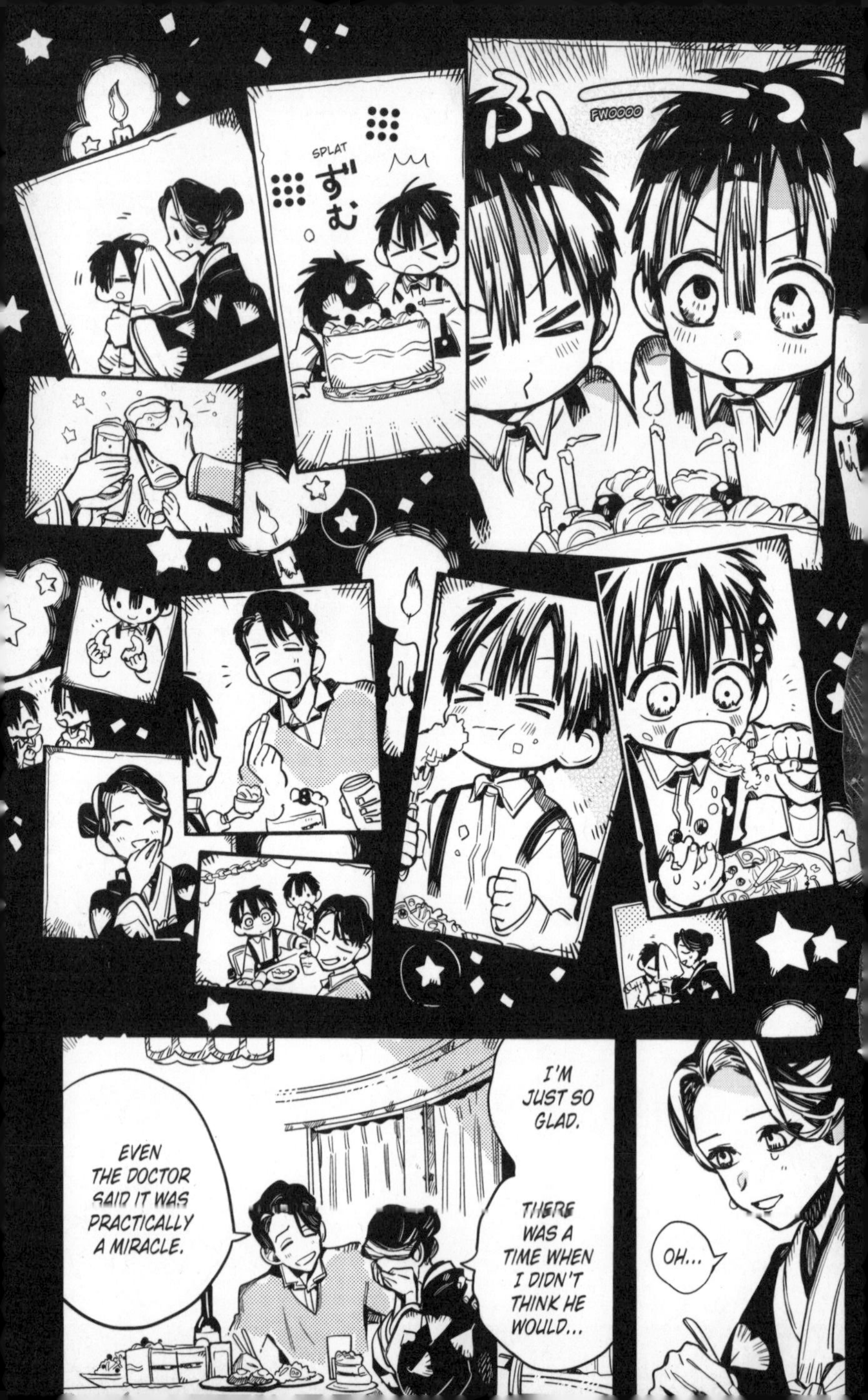

ふーっ
FWOOOO
SPLAT
ずむ
OH...
I'M JUST SO GLAD.
THERE WAS A TIME WHEN I DIDN'T THINK HE WOULD...
EVEN THE DOCTOR SAID IT WAS PRACTICALLY A MIRACLE.

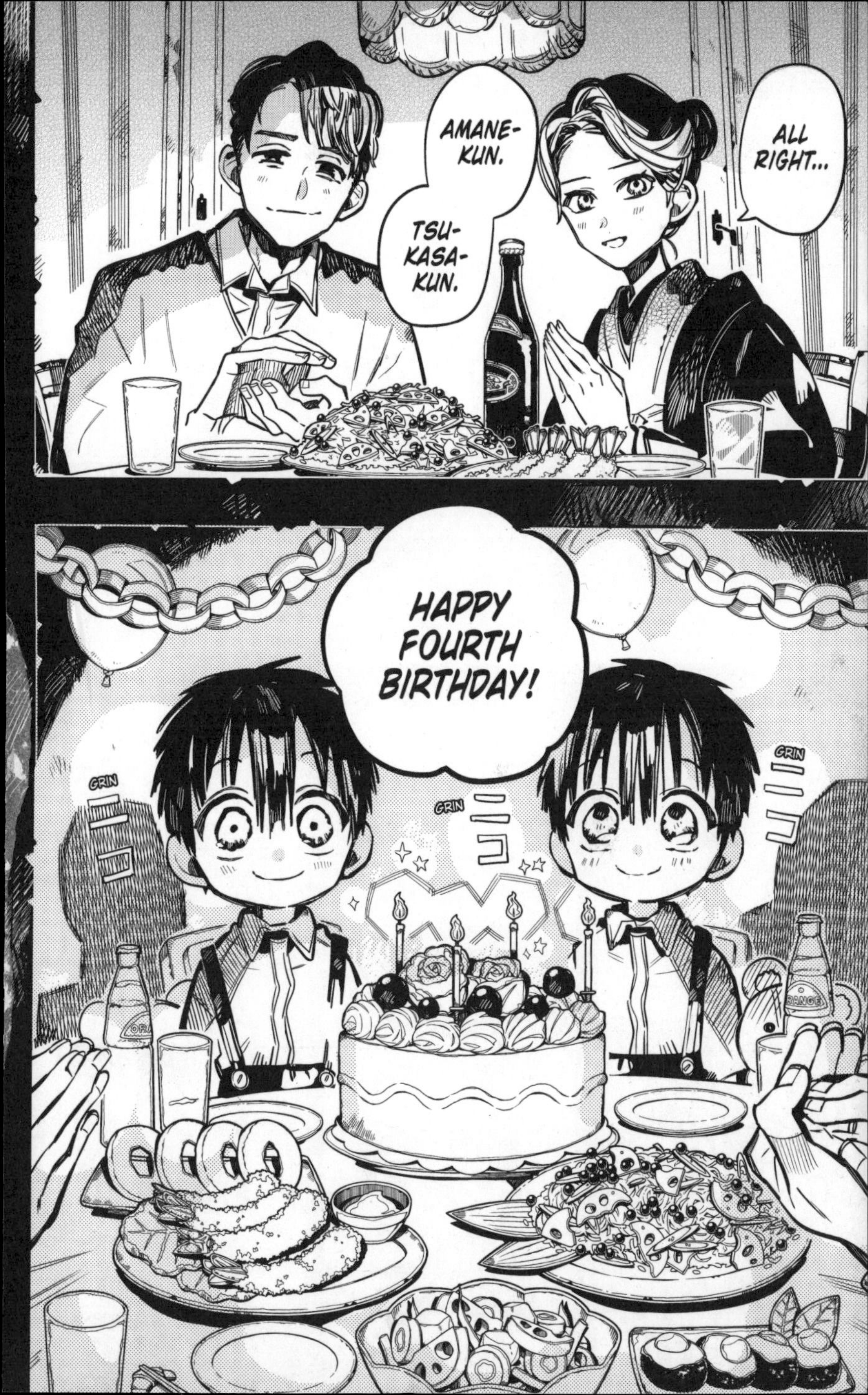
ALL RIGHT...
AMANE-KUN.
TSU-KASA-KUN.
HAPPY FOURTH BIRTHDAY!
GRIN
GRIN
GRIN
ORANGE

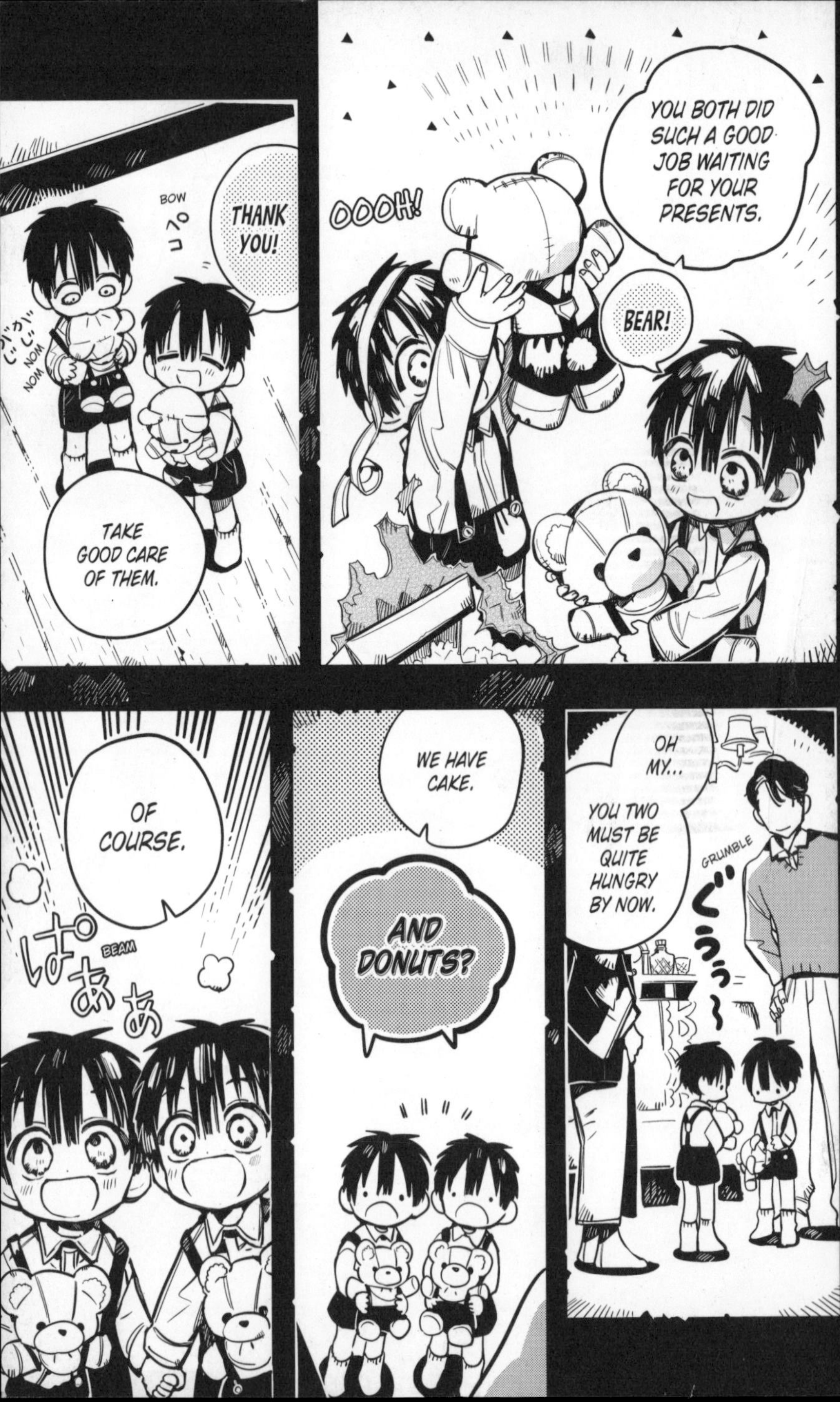
YOU BOTH DID SUCH A GOOD JOB WAITING FOR YOUR PRESENTS.
OOOH!
BEAR!
BOW
THANK YOU!
NOM NOM
TAKE GOOD CARE OF THEM.
OH MY...
YOU TWO MUST BE QUITE HUNGRY BY NOW.
GRUMBLE
ぐぅぅ~
WE HAVE CAKE.
AND DONUTS?
OF COURSE.
ぱあぁ
BEAM

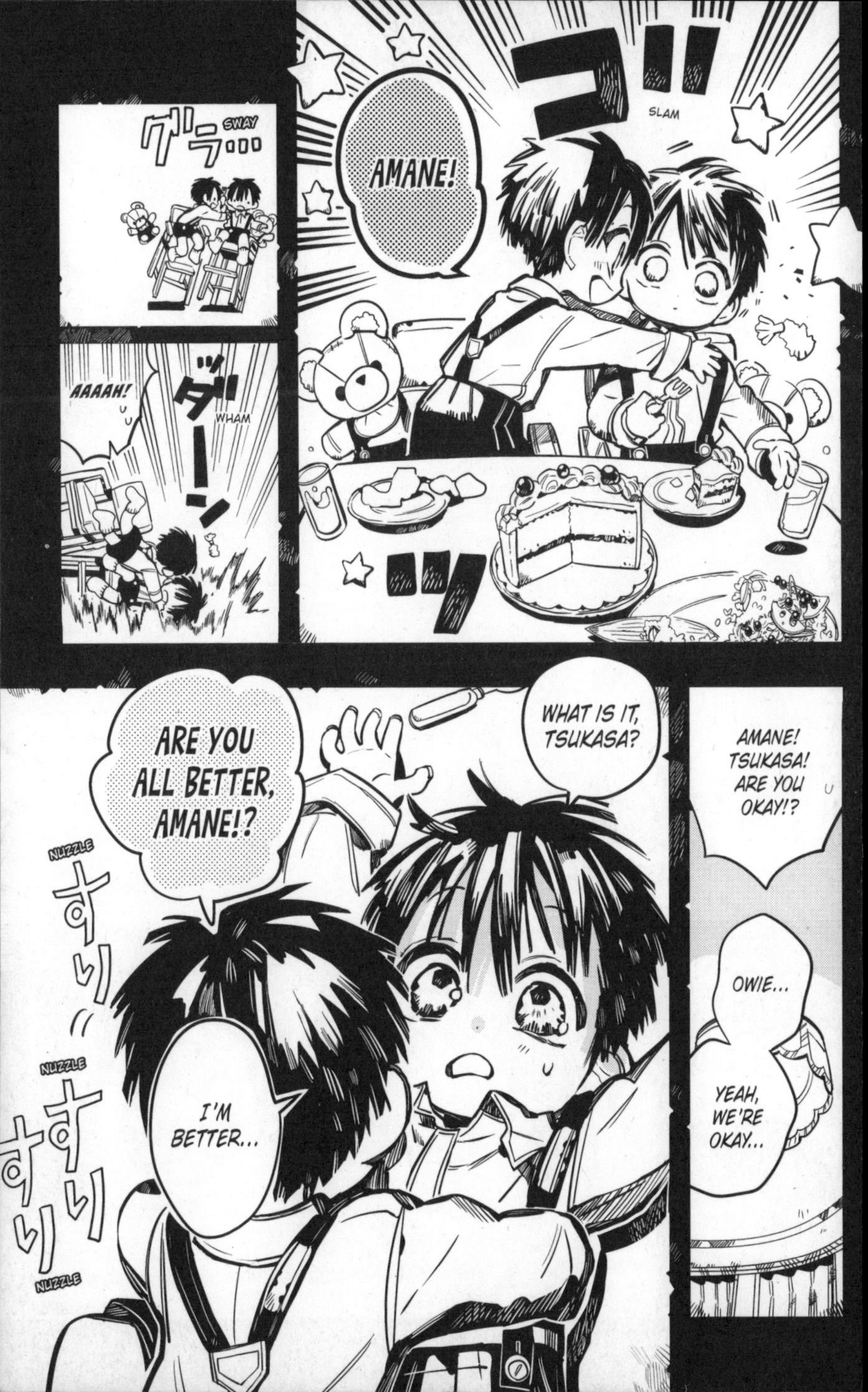

SLAM
AMANE!
SWAY
AAAAH!
WHAM
AMANE! TSUKASA! ARE YOU OKAY!?
OWIE...
YEAH, WE'RE OKAY...
WHAT IS IT, TSUKASA?
ARE YOU ALL BETTER, AMANE!?
NUZZLE
NUZZLE
NUZZLE
I'M BETTER...

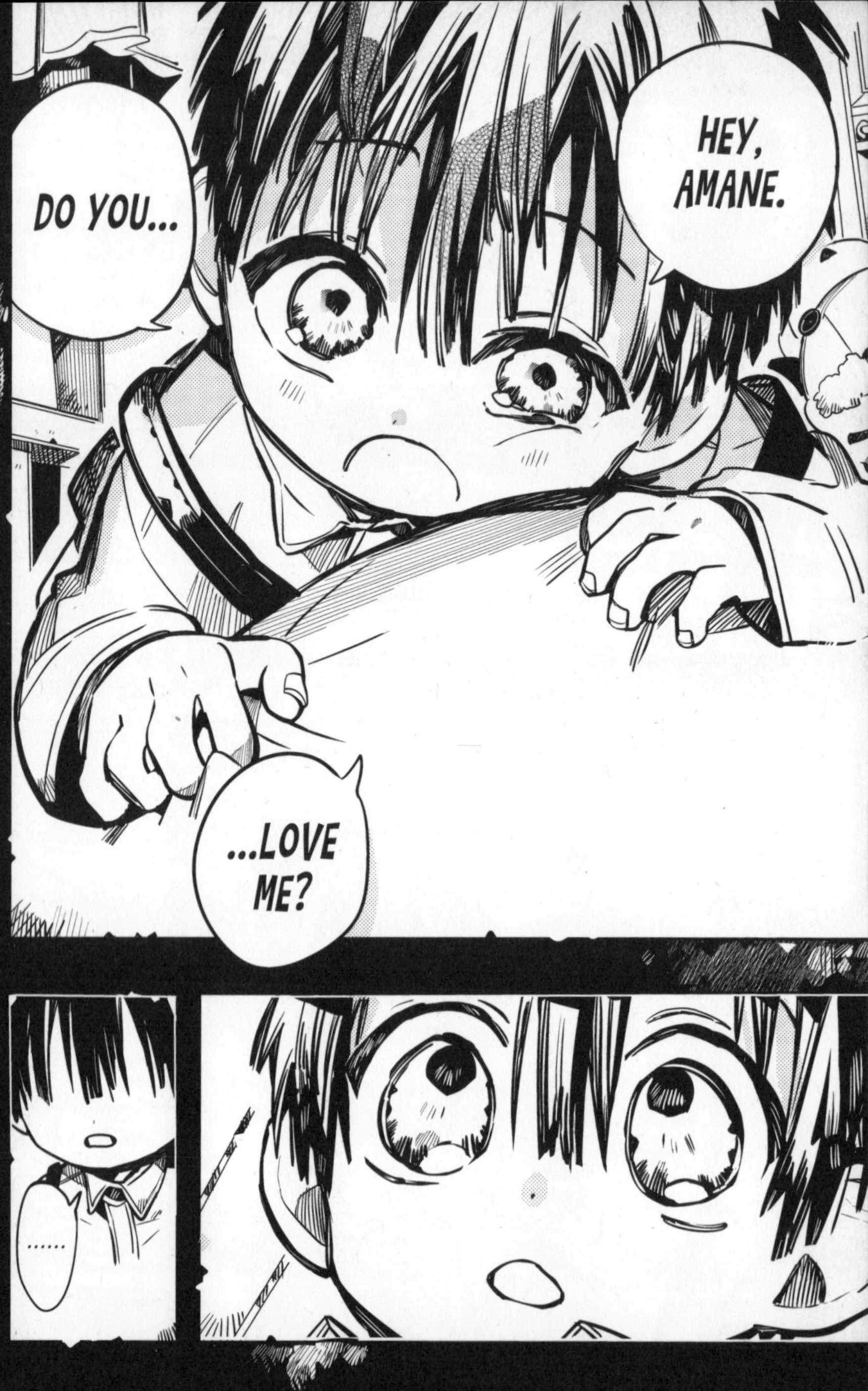
HEY, AMANE.
DO YOU...
...LOVE ME?
......

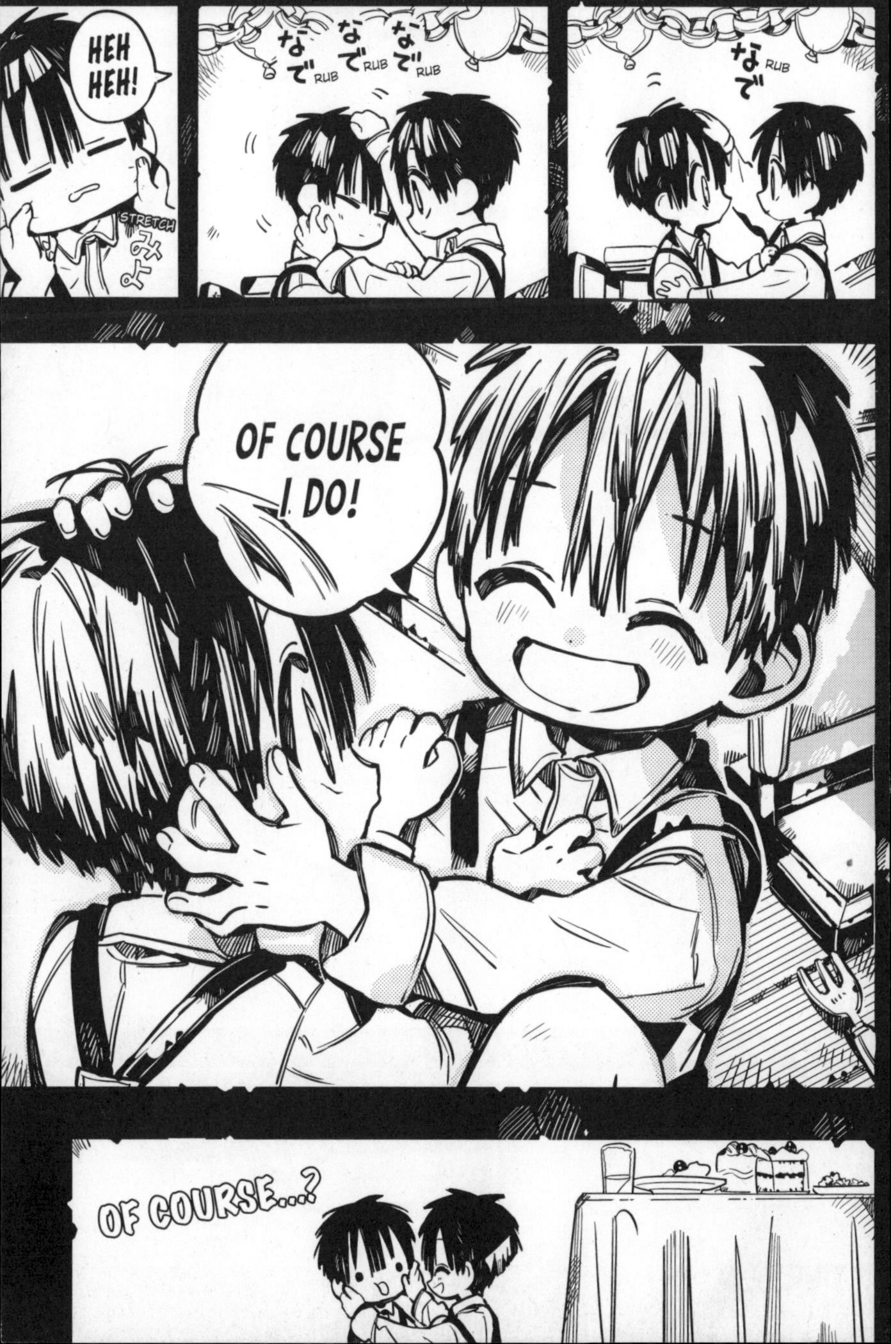
なで RUB
なで RUB
なで RUB
なで RUB
HEH HEH!
STRETCH
みょ
OF COURSE I DO!
OF COURSE...?

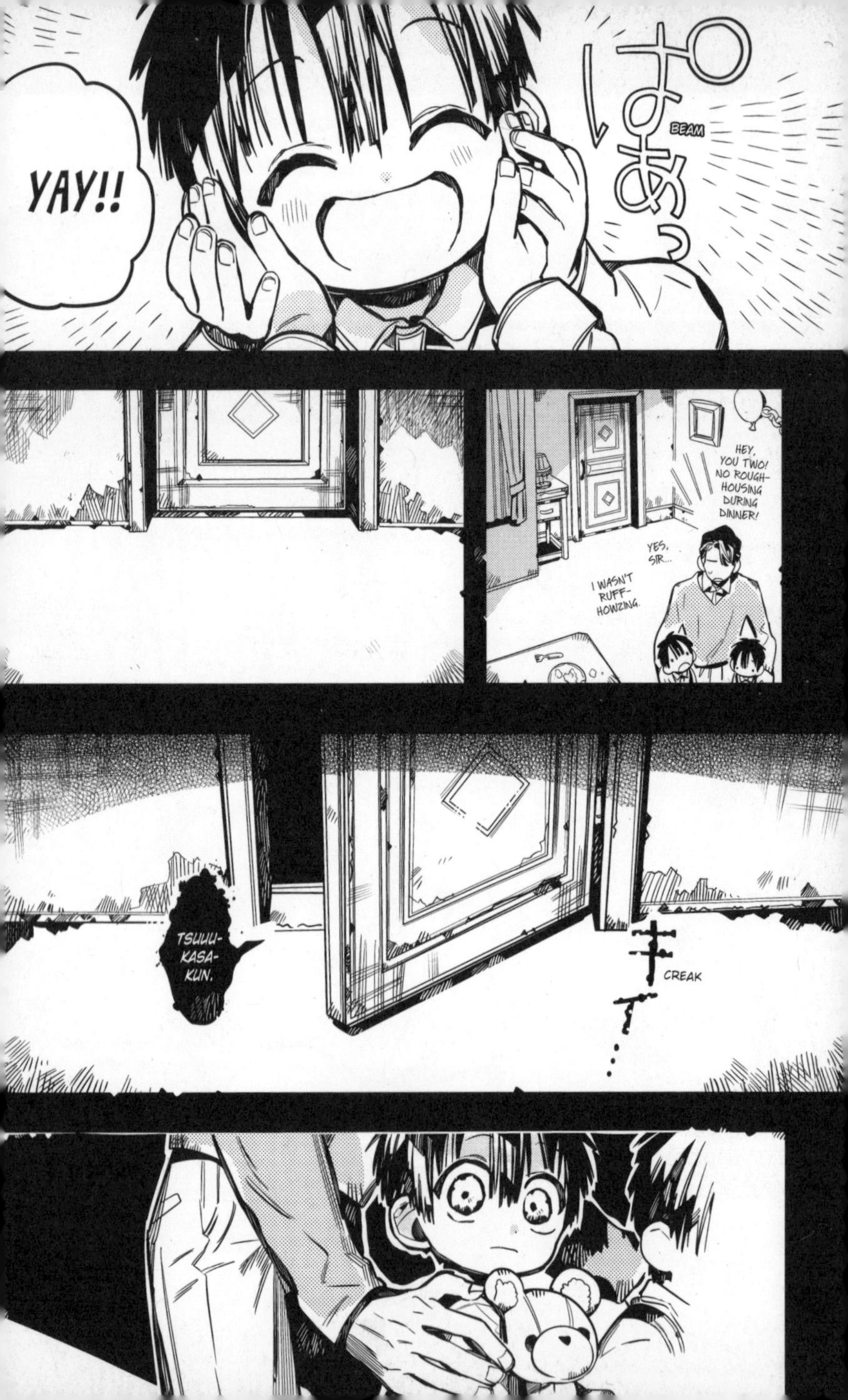
ぱあっ
BEAM
YAY!!
HEY, YOU TWO! NO ROUGH-HOUSING DURING DINNER!
YES, SIR...
I WASN'T RUFF-HOWZING.
CREAK
TSUUU-KASA-KUN.

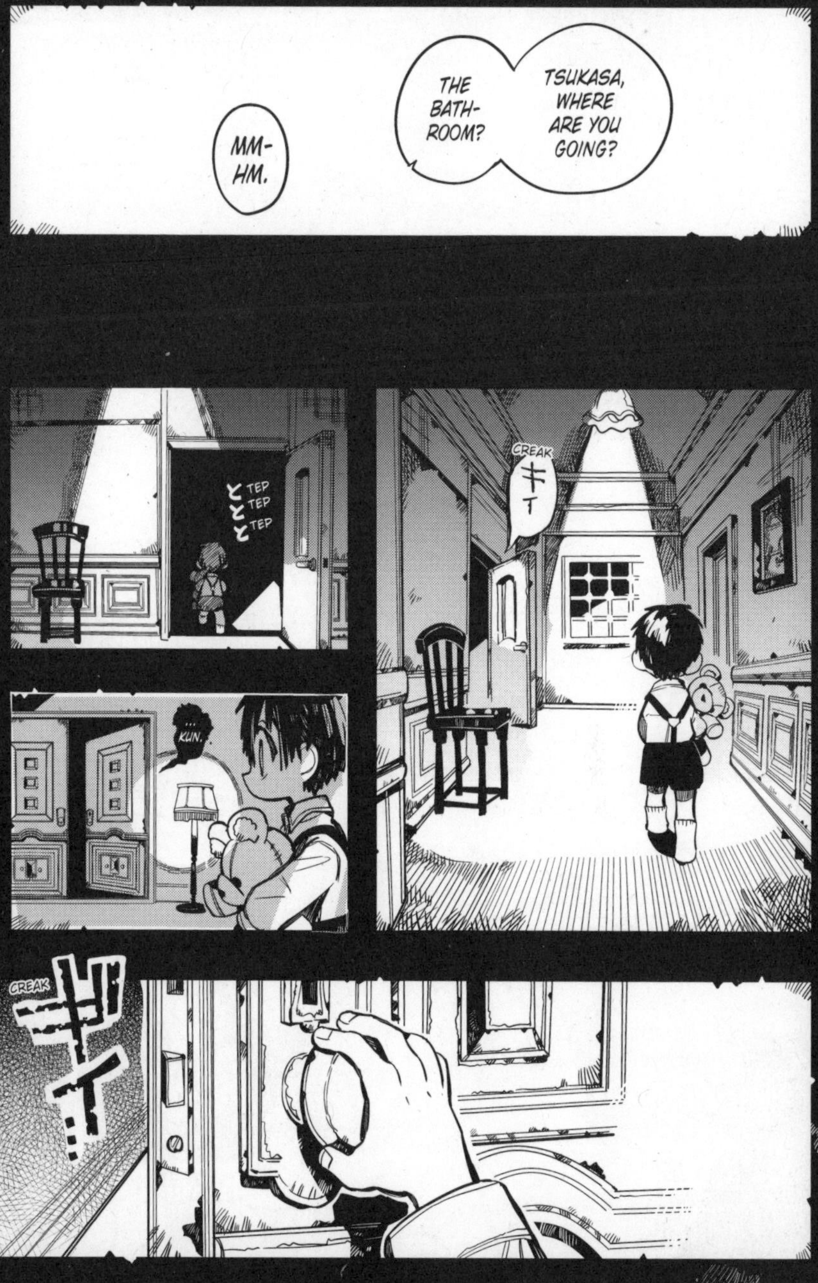
TSUKASA, WHERE ARE YOU GOING?
THE BATH-ROOM?
MM-HM.
CREAK
TEP TEP TEP
...KUN.
CREAK

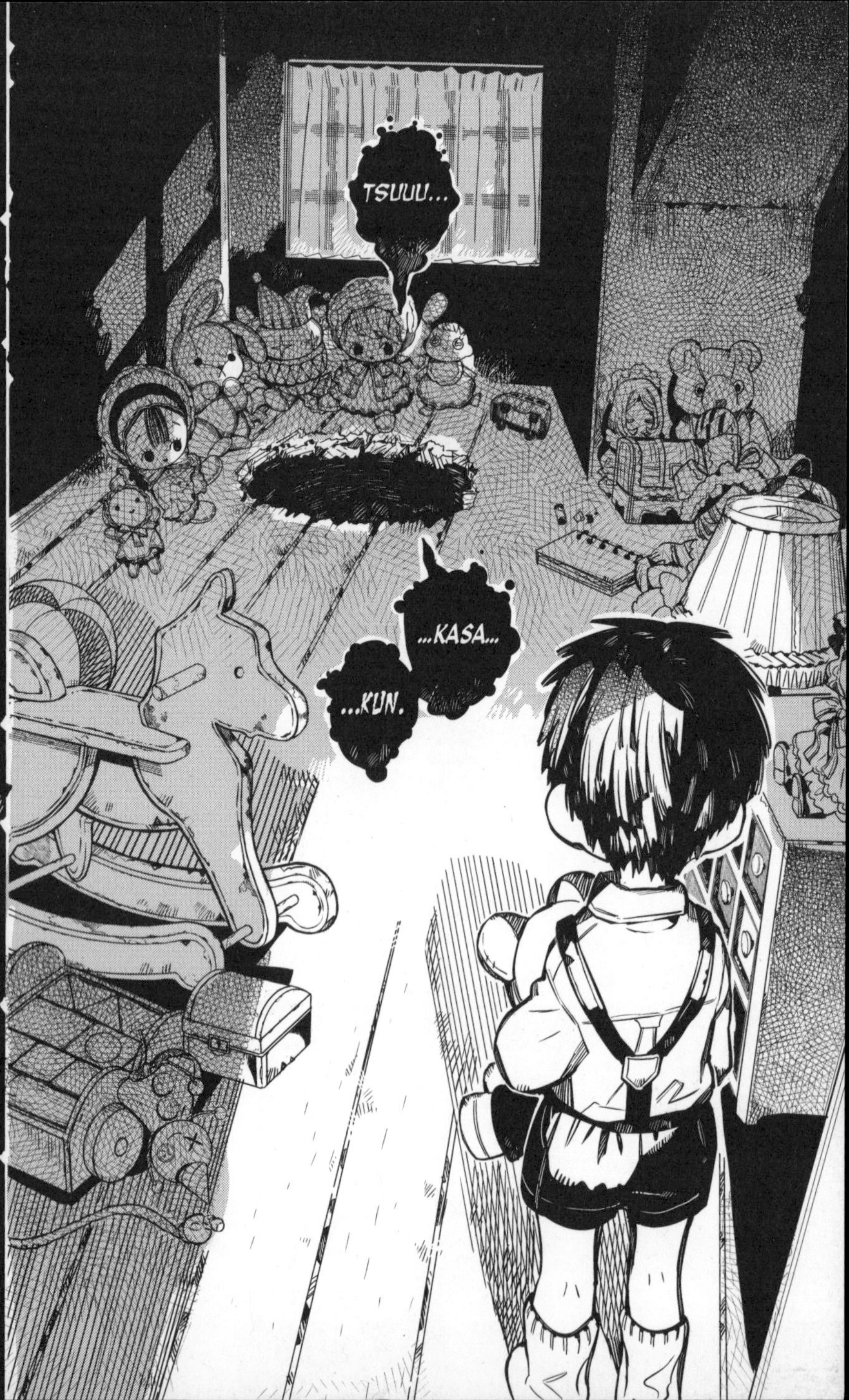
TSUUU...
...KASA...
...KUN.

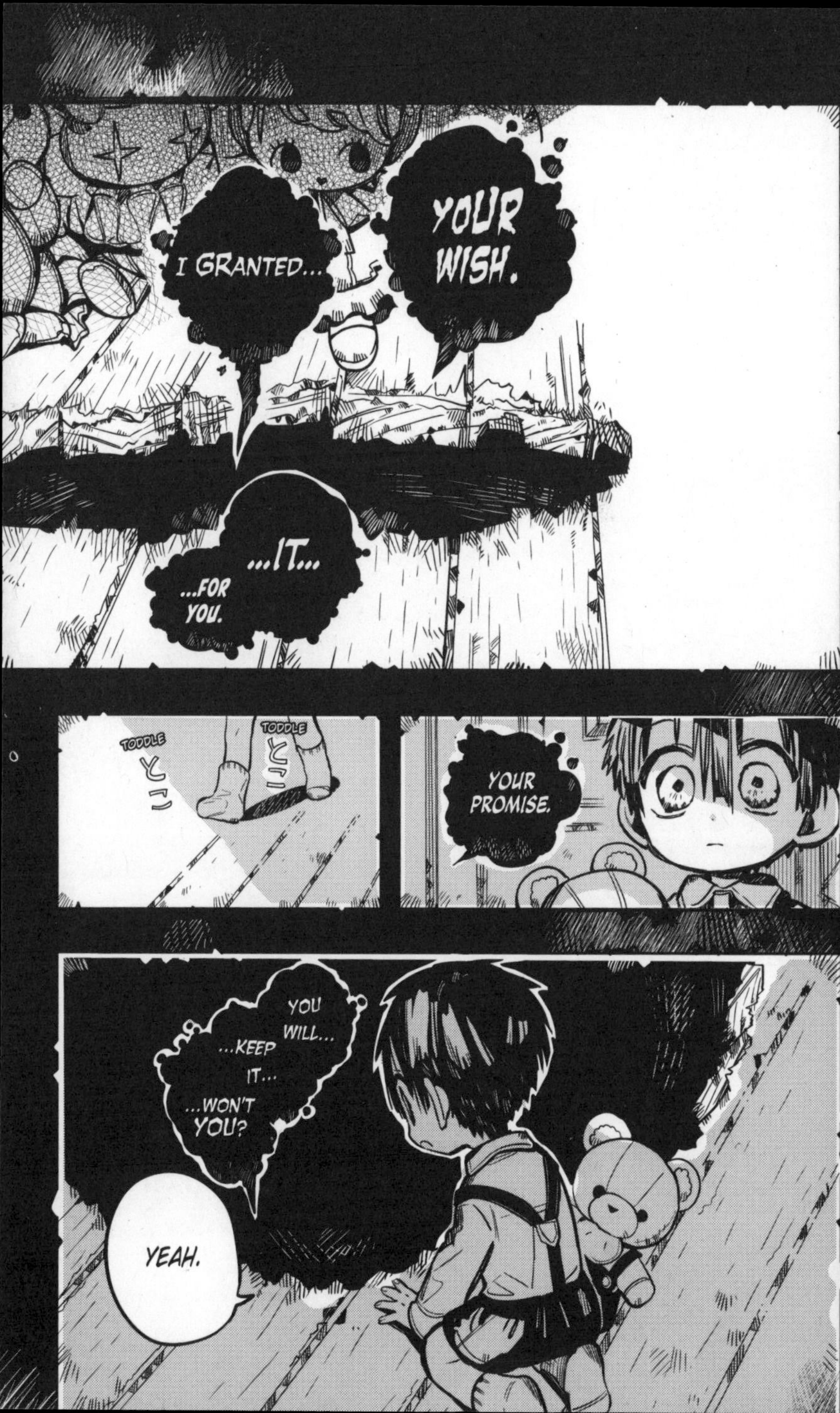
YOUR WISH.
I GRANTED...
...IT...
...FOR YOU.
YOUR PROMISE.
TODDLE とこ
TODDLE とこ
YOU WILL... ...KEEP IT... ...WON'T YOU?
YEAH.

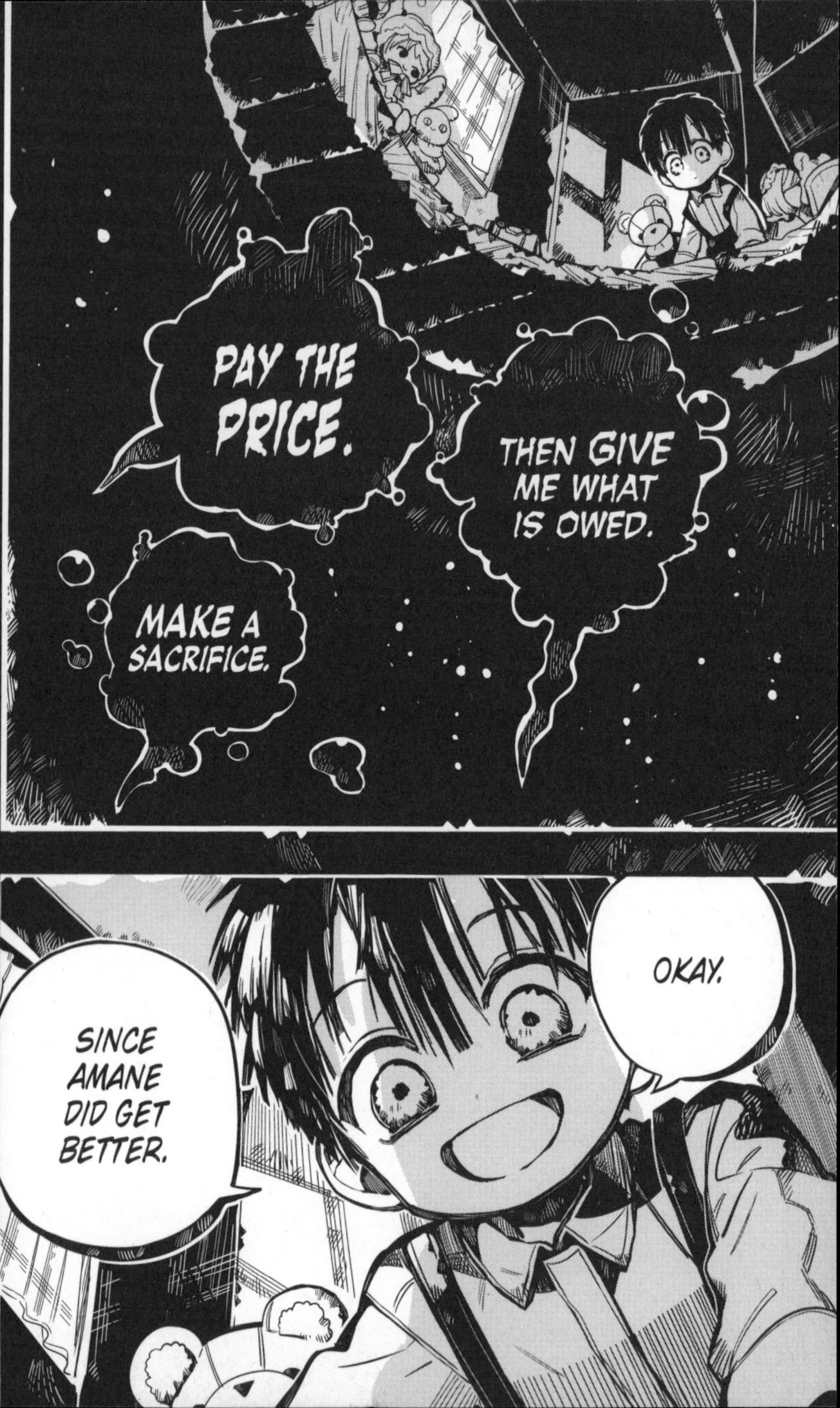
THEN GIVE ME WHAT IS OWED.
PAY THE PRICE.
MAKE A SACRIFICE.
OKAY.
SINCE AMANE DID GET BETTER.

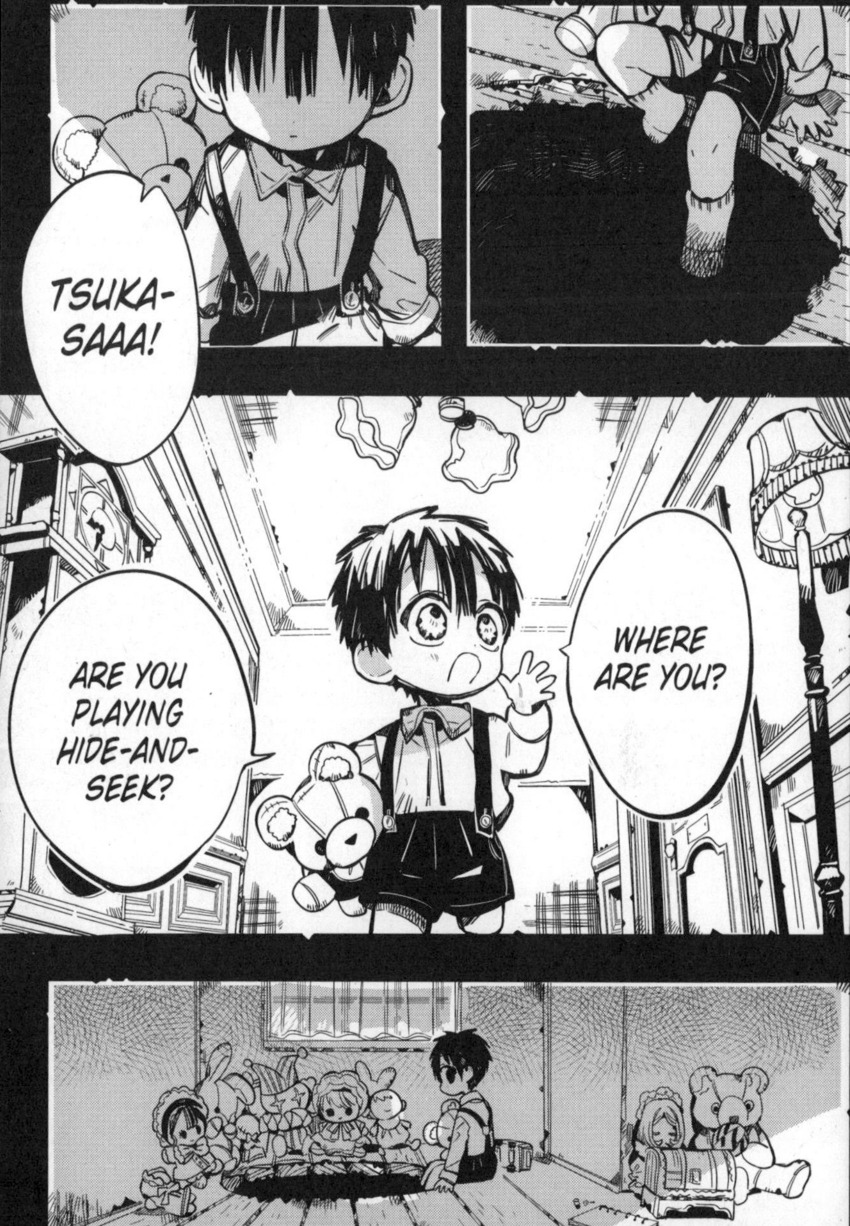
TSUKA-SAAA!
WHERE ARE YOU?
ARE YOU PLAYING HIDE-AND-SEEK?

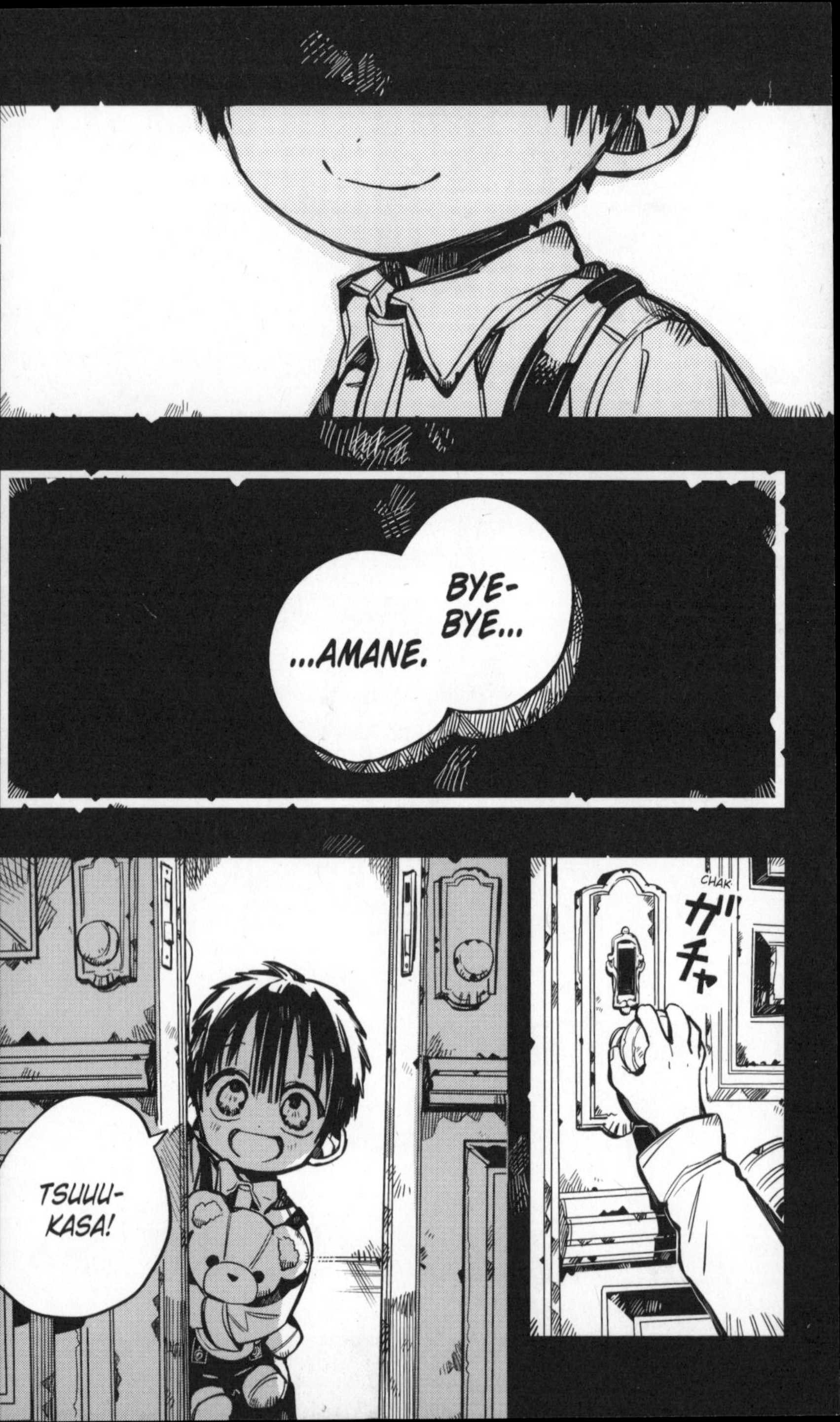
BYE-BYE... ...AMANE.
CHAK
ガチャ
TSUUU-KASA!

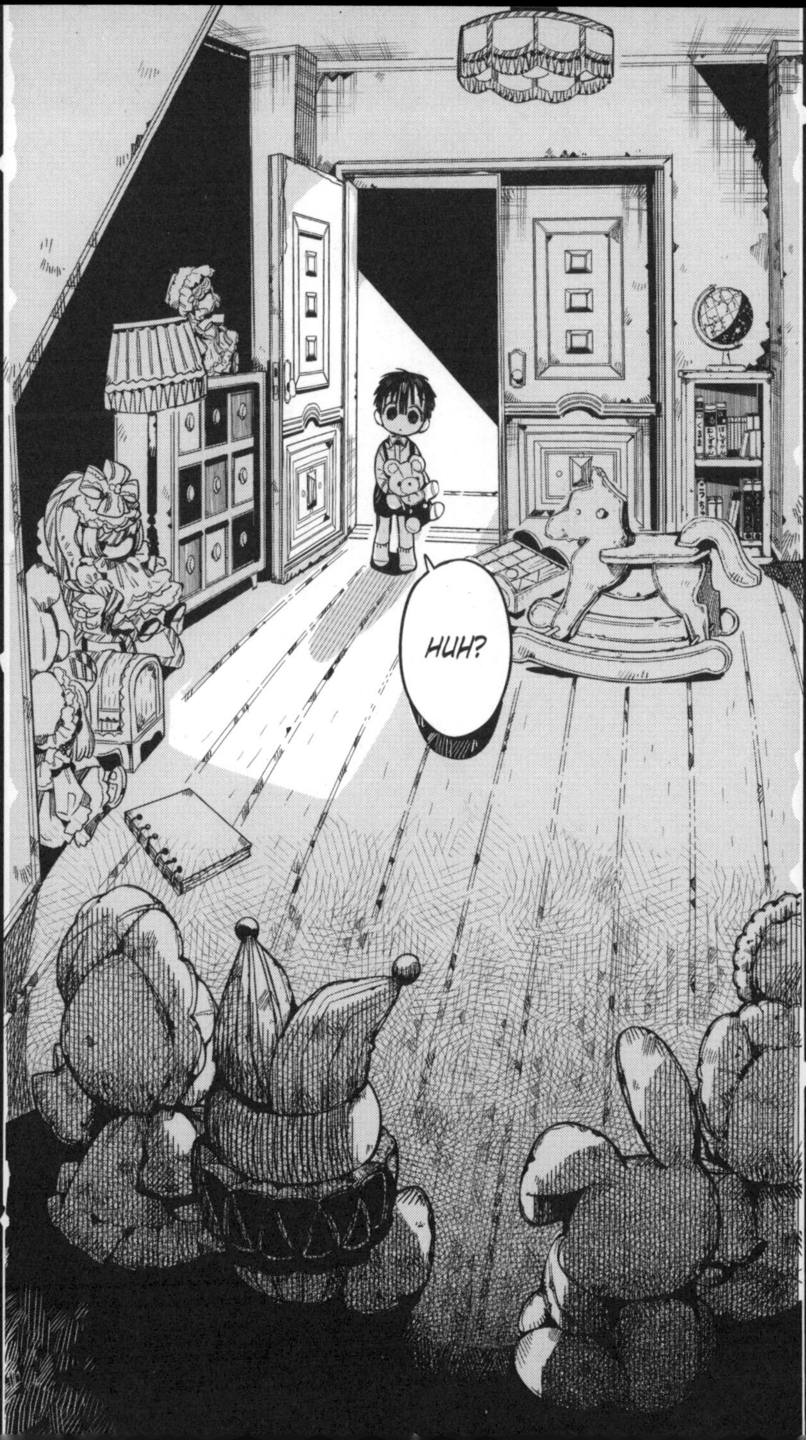
HUH?

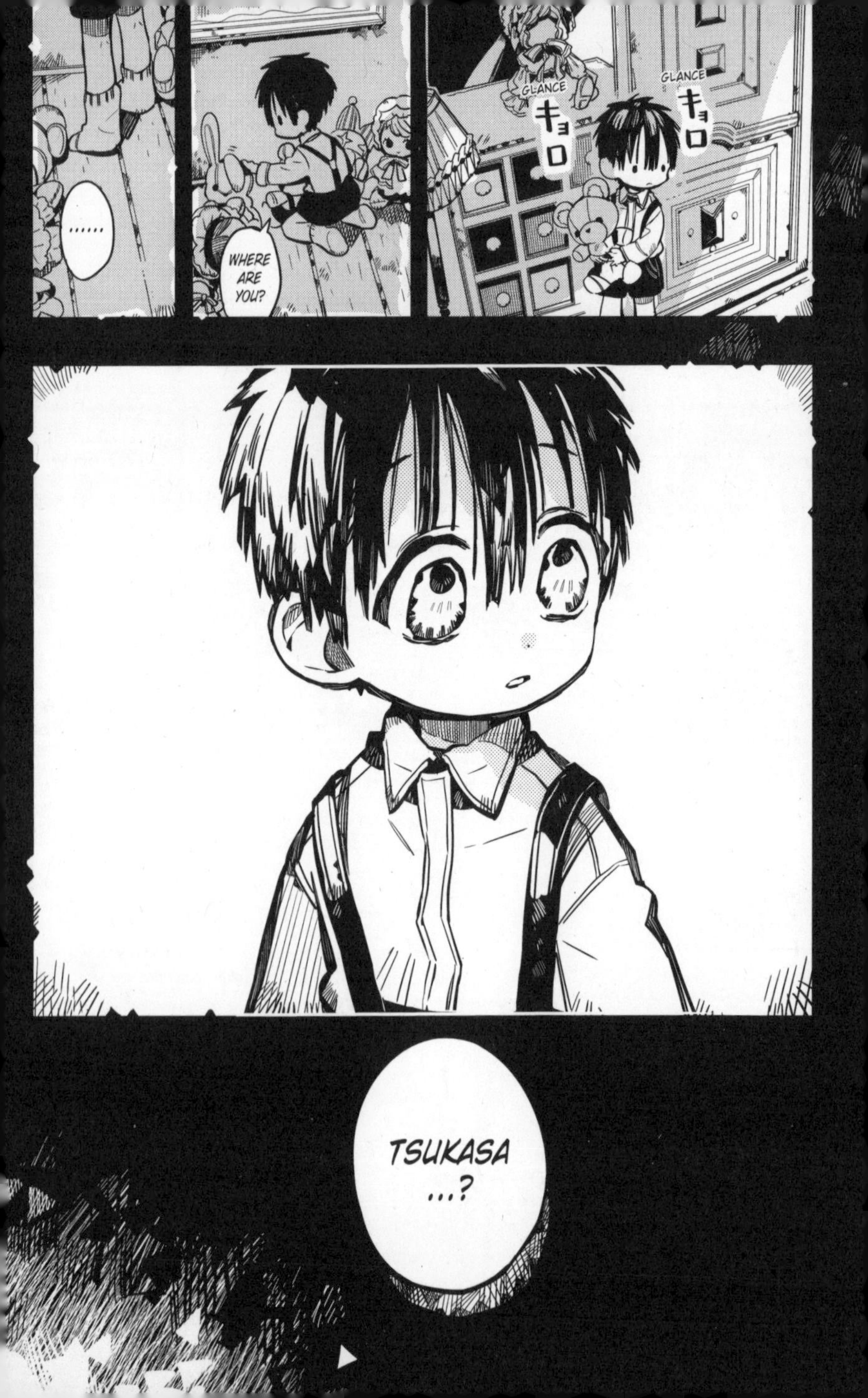
GLANCE
キョロ
GLANCE
キョロ
WHERE ARE YOU?
......
TSUKASA ...?

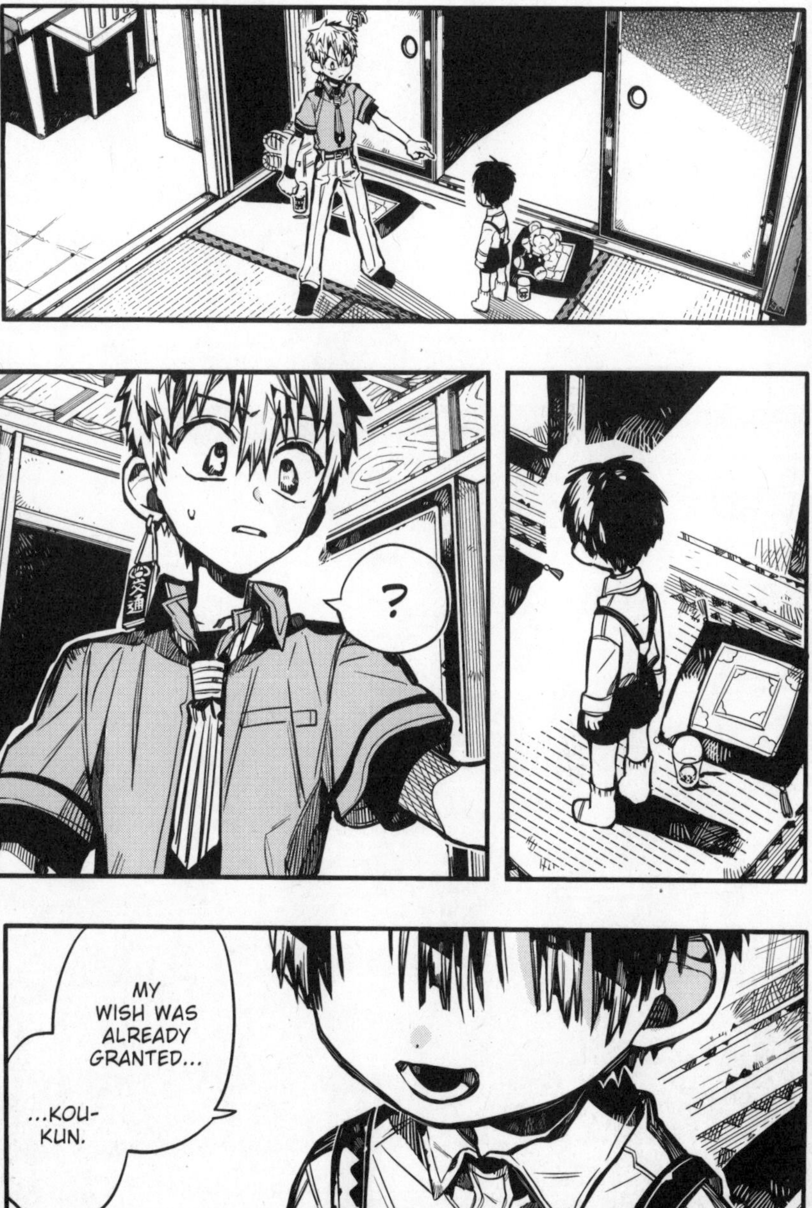
?
MY WISH WAS ALREADY GRANTED...
...KOU-KUN.

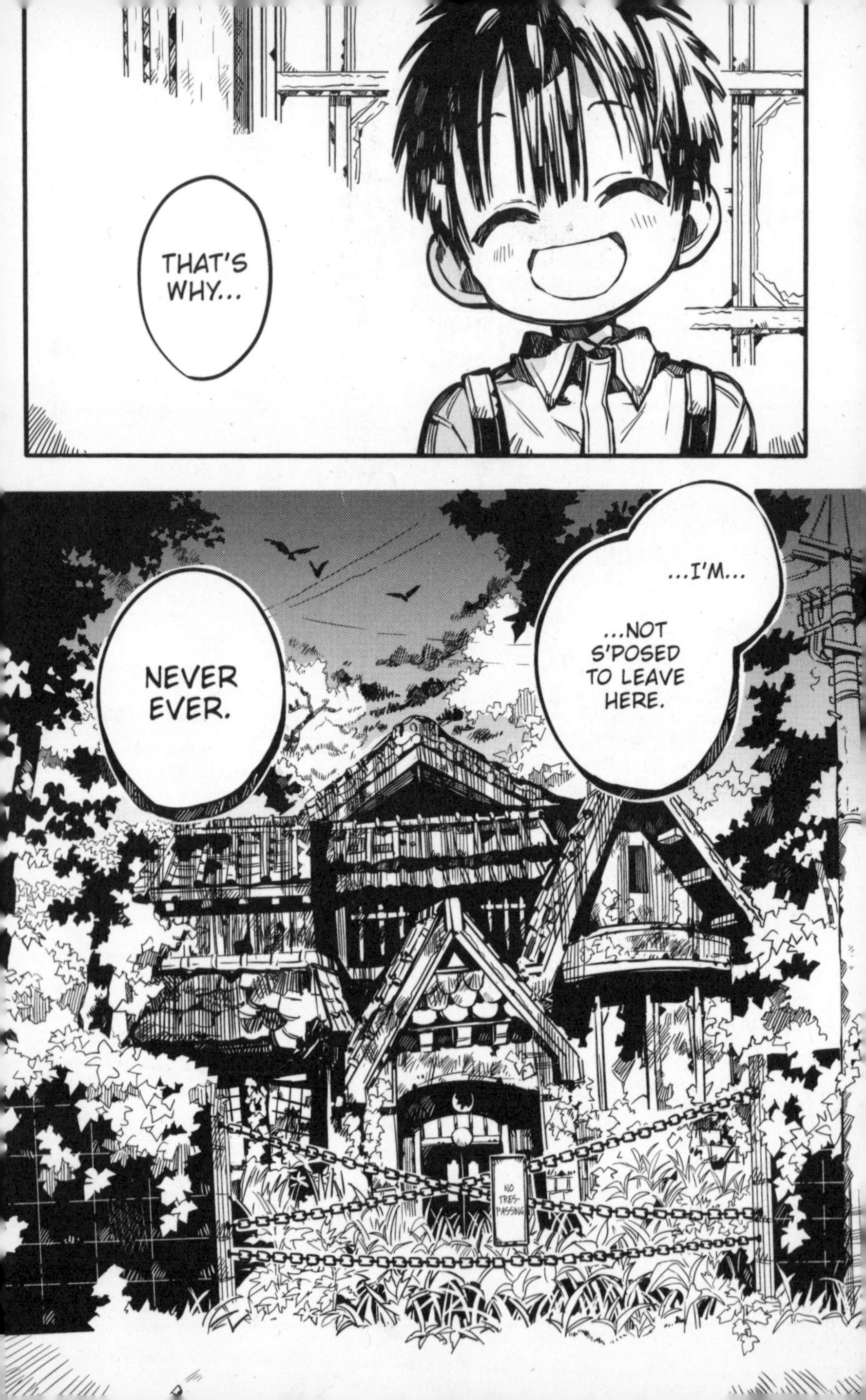
THAT'S WHY...
...I'M...
...NOT S'POSED TO LEAVE HERE.
NEVER EVER.
NO TRES-PASSING

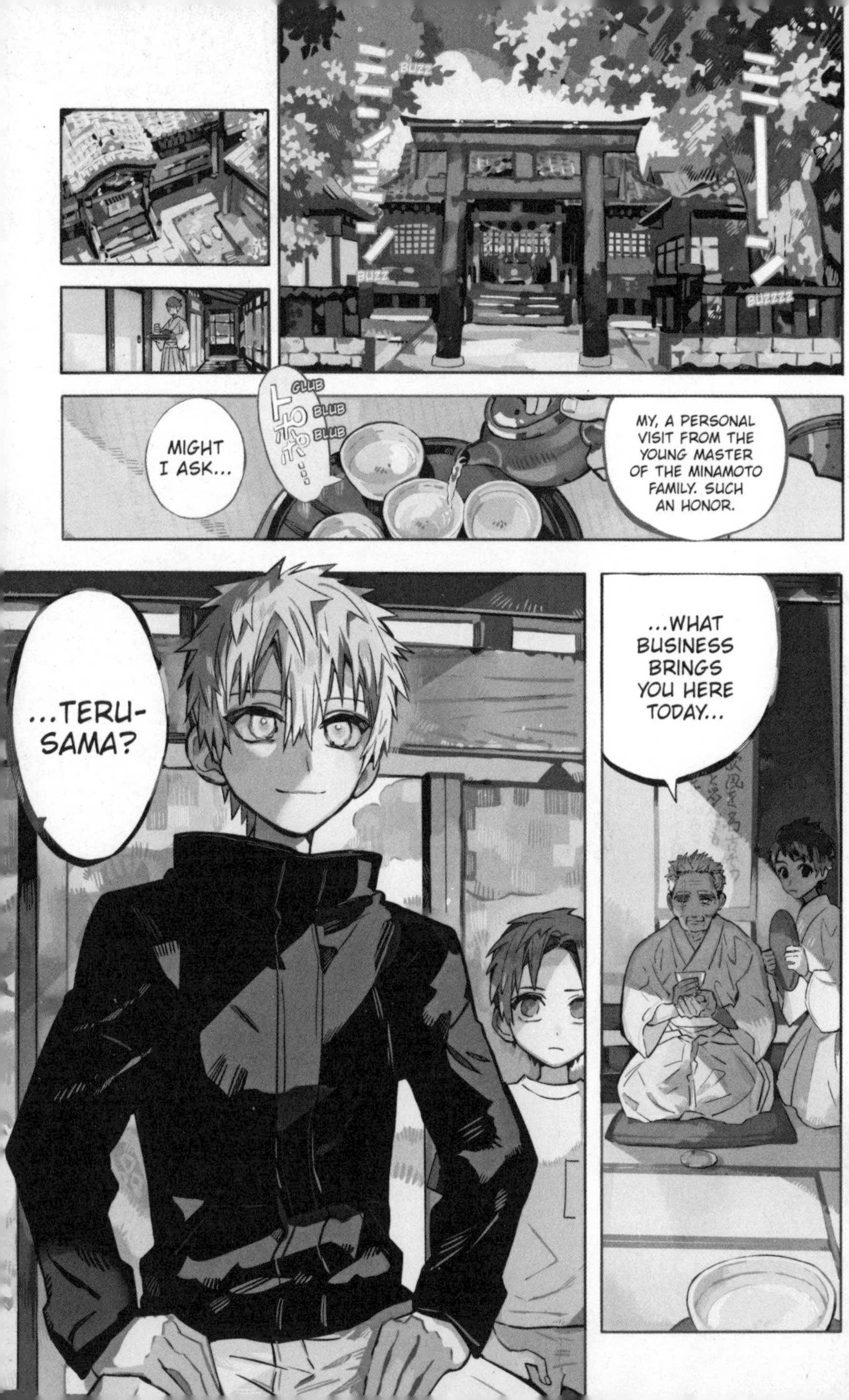
BUZZ
BUZZ
BUZZZZ
MY, A PERSONAL VISIT FROM THE YOUNG MASTER OF THE MINAMOTO FAMILY. SUCH AN HONOR.
GLUB BLUB BLUB
MIGHT I ASK...
...WHAT BUSINESS BRINGS YOU HERE TODAY...
...TERU-SAMA?

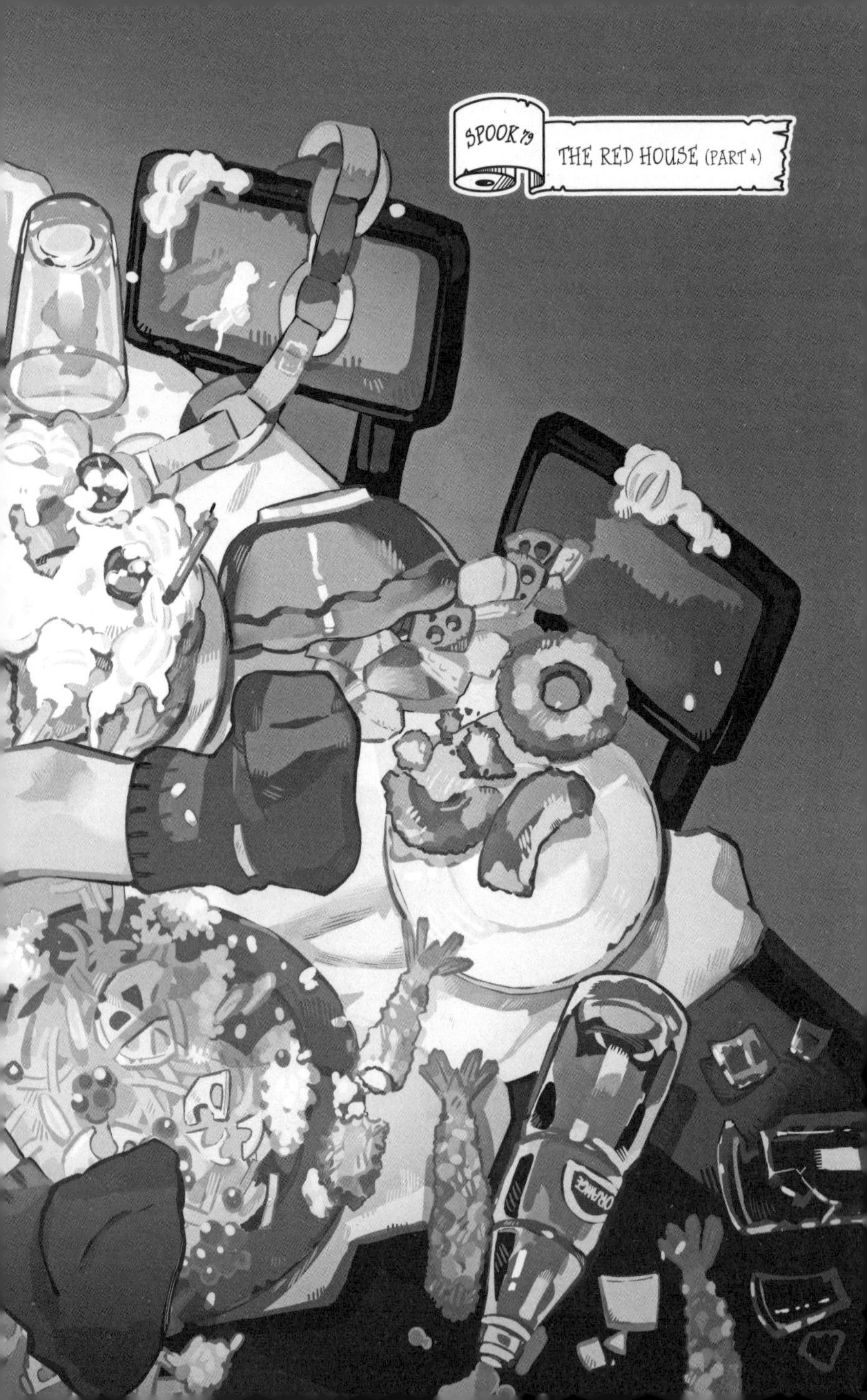
SPOOK 79
THE RED HOUSE (PART 4)
ORANGE

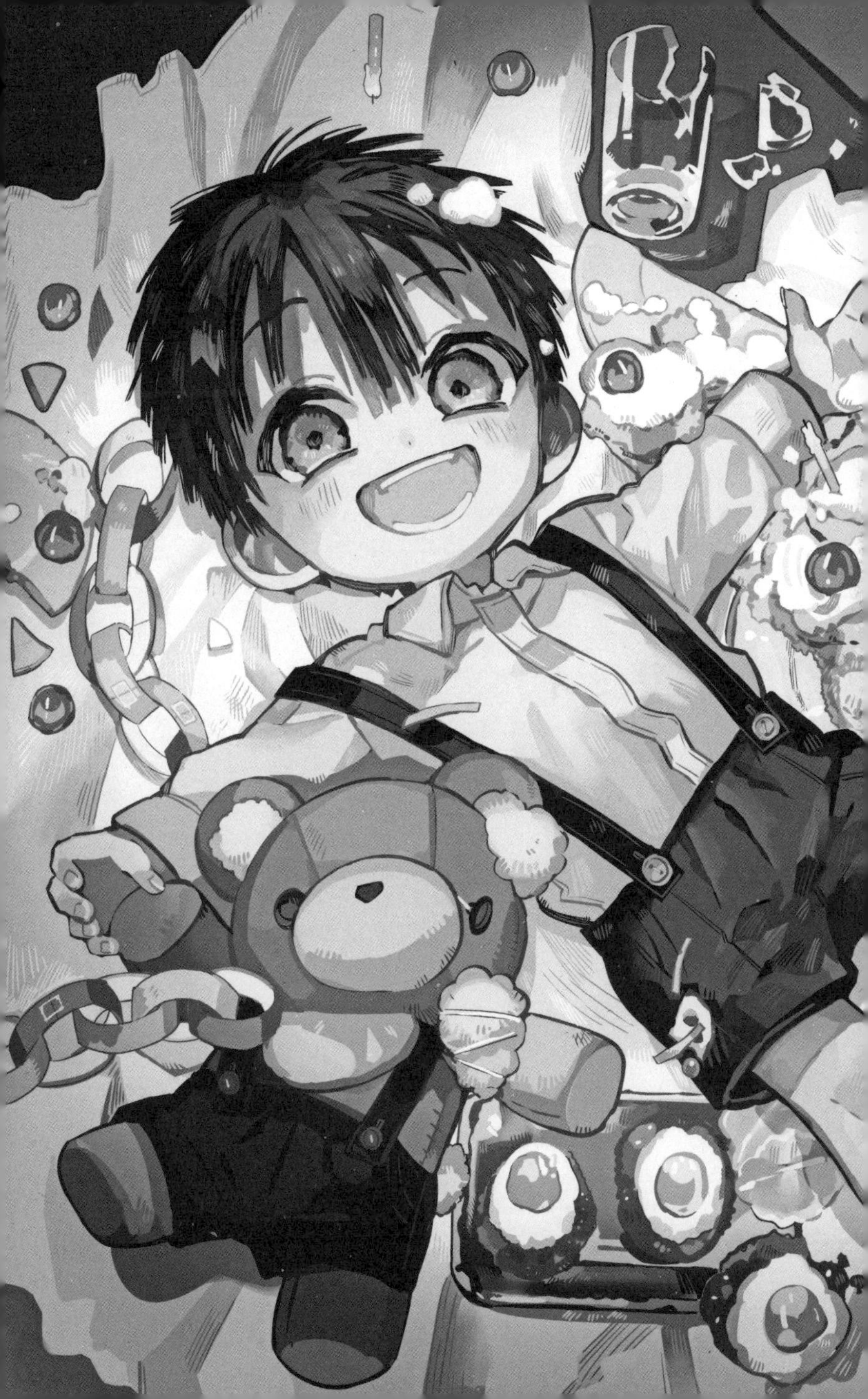

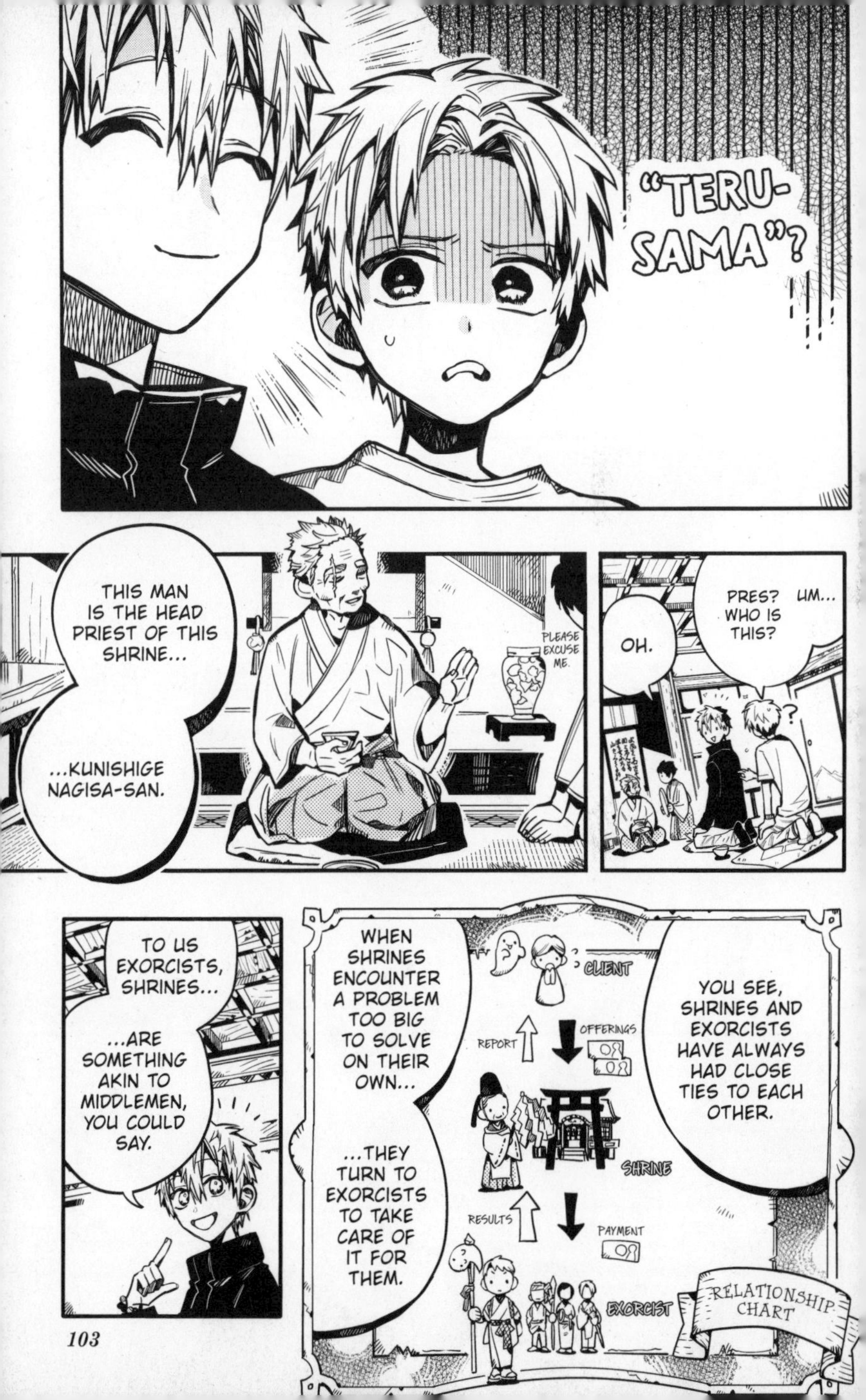
"TERU-SAMA"?
PRES? UM... WHO IS THIS?
OH.
PLEASE EXCUSE ME.
THIS MAN IS THE HEAD PRIEST OF THIS SHRINE...
...KUNISHIGE NAGISA-SAN.
YOU SEE, SHRINES AND EXORCISTS HAVE ALWAYS HAD CLOSE TIES TO EACH OTHER.
WHEN SHRINES ENCOUNTER A PROBLEM TOO BIG TO SOLVE ON THEIR OWN...
...THEY TURN TO EXORCISTS TO TAKE CARE OF IT FOR THEM.
CLIENT
REPORT
OFFERINGS
SHRINE
RESULTS
PAYMENT
EXORCIST
RELATIONSHIP CHART
TO US EXORCISTS, SHRINES...
...ARE SOMETHING AKIN TO MIDDLEMEN, YOU COULD SAY.

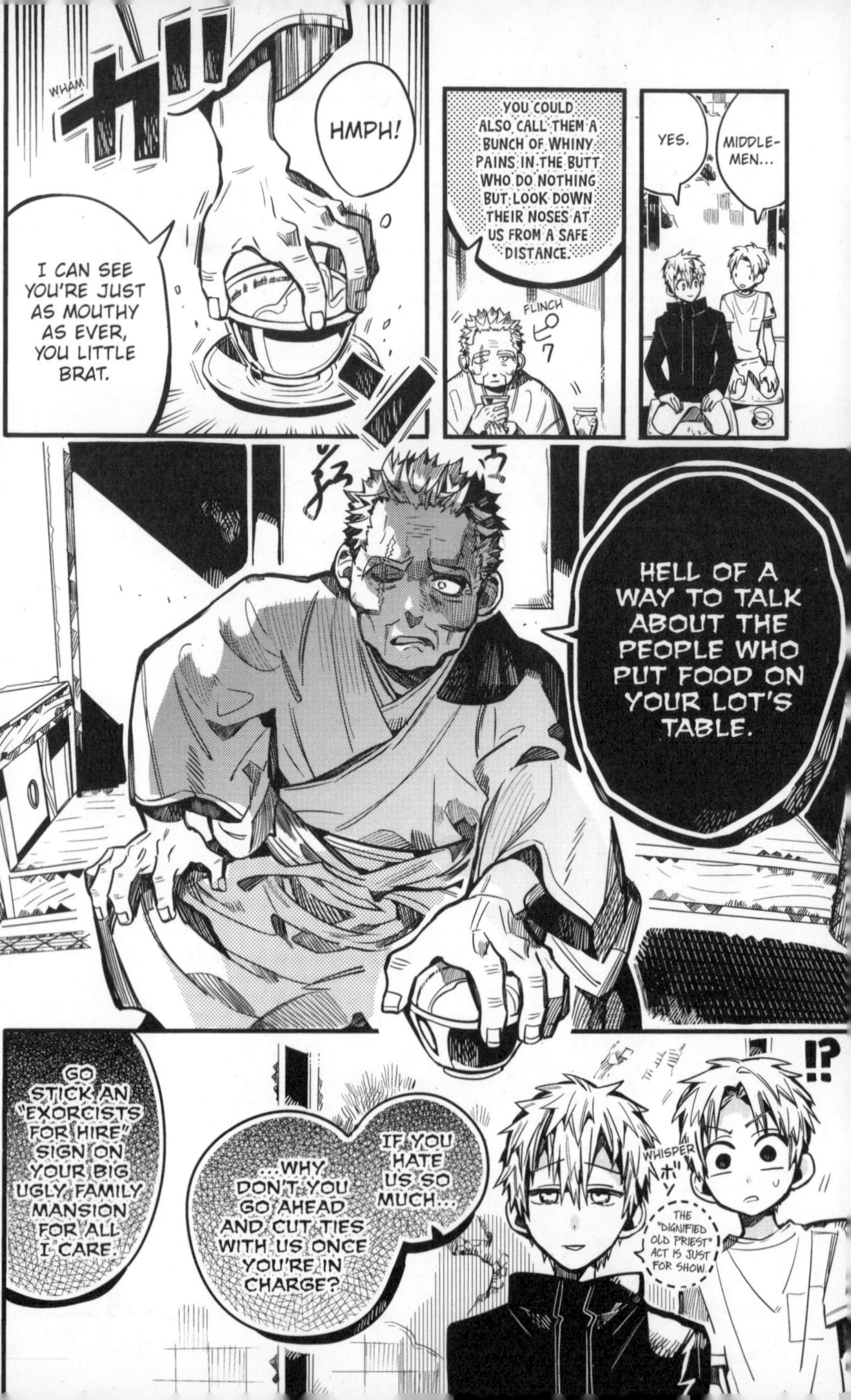
MIDDLE-MEN...
YES.
YOU COULD ALSO CALL THEM A BUNCH OF WHINY PAINS IN THE BUTT WHO DO NOTHING BUT LOOK DOWN THEIR NOSES AT US FROM A SAFE DISTANCE.
FLINCH
ピク
HMPH!
WHAM
I CAN SEE YOU'RE JUST AS MOUTHY AS EVER, YOU LITTLE BRAT.
HELL OF A WAY TO TALK ABOUT THE PEOPLE WHO PUT FOOD ON YOUR LOT'S TABLE.
!?
WHISPER
ボソ
THE "DIGNIFIED OLD PRIEST" ACT IS JUST FOR SHOW.
IF YOU HATE US SO MUCH...
...WHY DON'T YOU GO AHEAD AND CUT TIES WITH US ONCE YOU'RE IN CHARGE?
GO STICK AN "EXORCISTS FOR HIRE" SIGN ON YOUR BIG UGLY FAMILY MANSION FOR ALL I CARE.

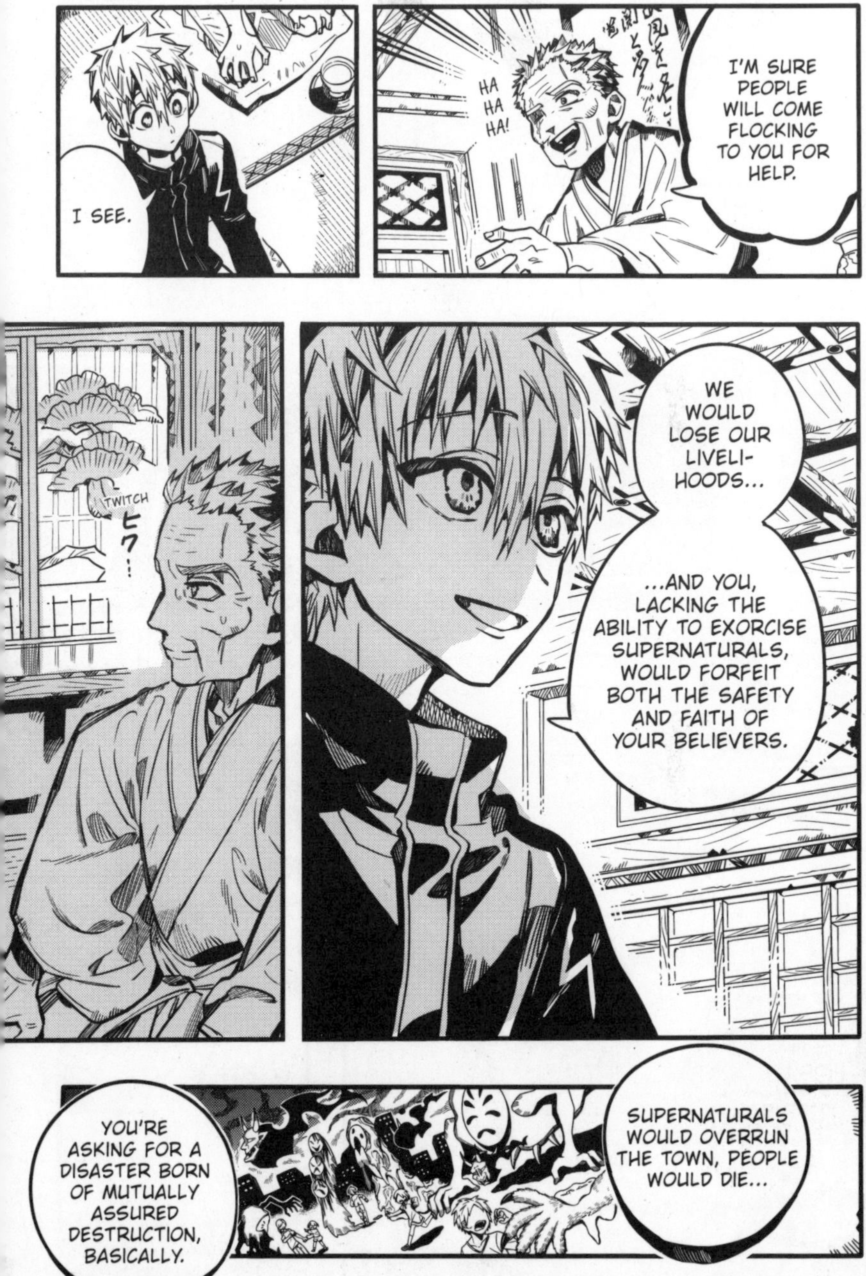
I'M SURE PEOPLE WILL COME FLOCKING TO YOU FOR HELP.
HA HA HA!
I SEE.
WE WOULD LOSE OUR LIVELI-HOODS...
...AND YOU, LACKING THE ABILITY TO EXORCISE SUPERNATURALS, WOULD FORFEIT BOTH THE SAFETY AND FAITH OF YOUR BELIEVERS.
TWITCH
ヒク
SUPERNATURALS WOULD OVERRUN THE TOWN, PEOPLE WOULD DIE...
YOU'RE ASKING FOR A DISASTER BORN OF MUTUALLY ASSURED DESTRUCTION, BASICALLY.

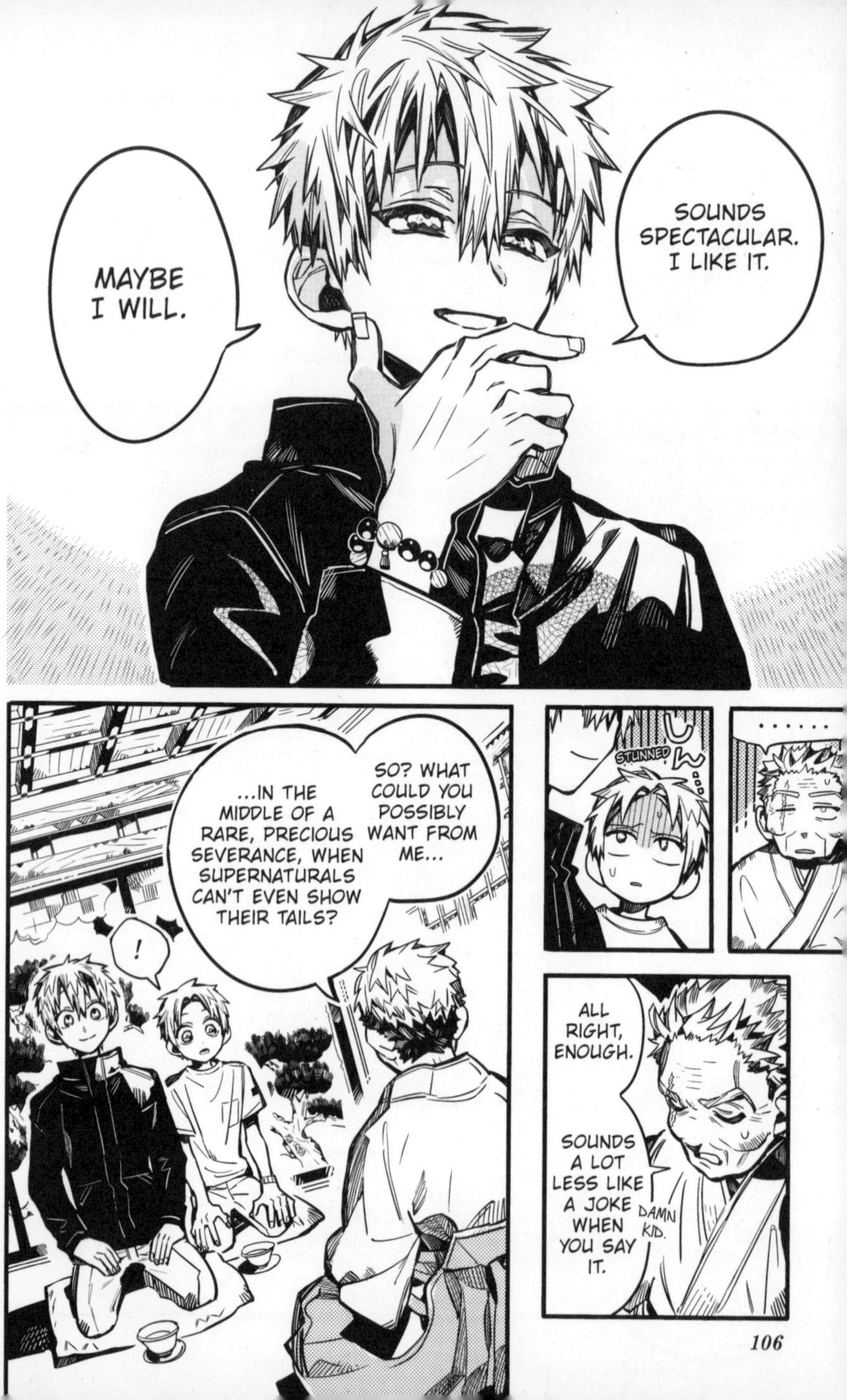
SOUNDS SPECTACULAR. I LIKE IT.
MAYBE I WILL.
......
STUNNED
ALL RIGHT, ENOUGH.
SOUNDS A LOT LESS LIKE A JOKE WHEN YOU SAY IT.
DAMN KID.
SO? WHAT COULD YOU POSSIBLY WANT FROM ME...
...IN THE MIDDLE OF A RARE, PRECIOUS SEVERANCE, WHEN SUPERNATURALS CAN'T EVEN SHOW THEIR TAILS?
!

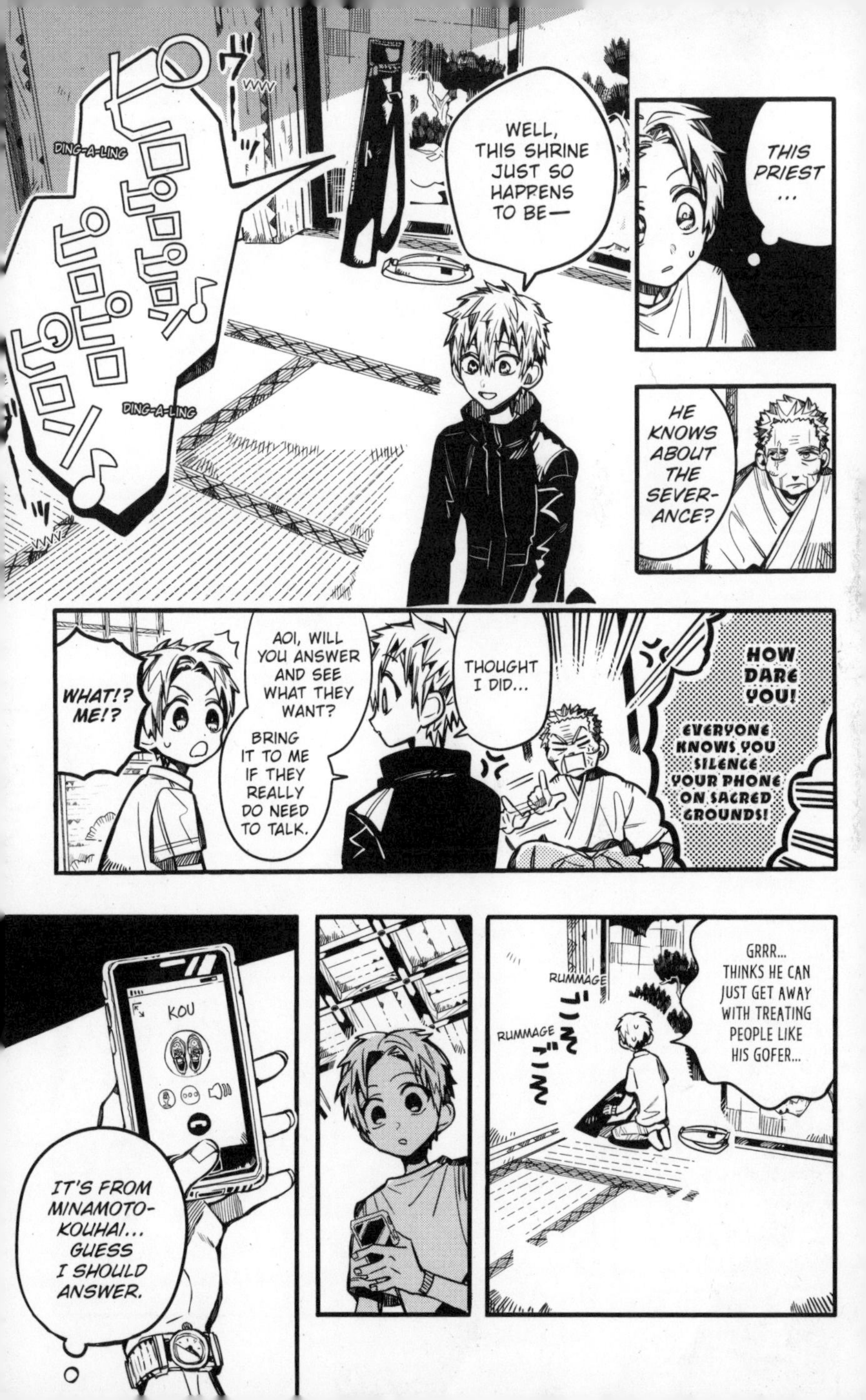

THIS PRIEST...
HE KNOWS ABOUT THE SEVER-ANCE?
WELL, THIS SHRINE JUST SO HAPPENS TO BE—
DING-A-LING
DING-A-LING
HOW DARE YOU!
EVERYONE KNOWS YOU SILENCE YOUR PHONE ON SACRED GROUNDS!
THOUGHT I DID...
AOI, WILL YOU ANSWER AND SEE WHAT THEY WANT?
BRING IT TO ME IF THEY REALLY DO NEED TO TALK.
WHAT!? ME!?
GRRR... THINKS HE CAN JUST GET AWAY WITH TREATING PEOPLE LIKE HIS GOFER...
RUMMAGE
RUMMAGE
KOU
IT'S FROM MINAMOTO-KOUHAI... GUESS I SHOULD ANSWER.

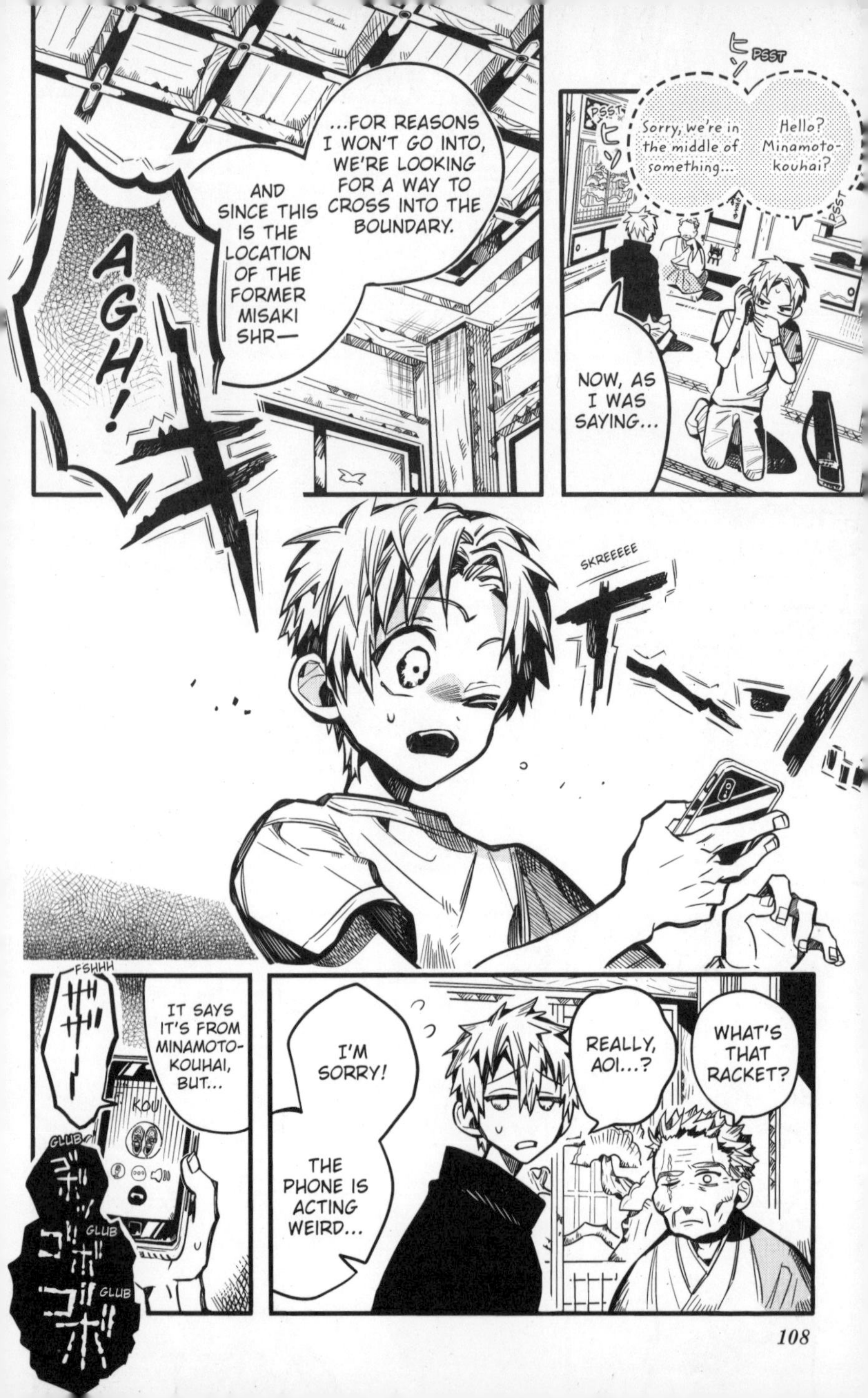
PSST
Hello? Minamoto-kouhai?
Sorry, we're in the middle of something...
PSST
PSST
NOW, AS I WAS SAYING...
...FOR REASONS I WON'T GO INTO, WE'RE LOOKING FOR A WAY TO CROSS INTO THE BOUNDARY.
AND SINCE THIS IS THE LOCATION OF THE FORMER MISAKI SHR—
AGH!
SKREEEEE
WHAT'S THAT RACKET?
REALLY, AOI...?
I'M SORRY!
THE PHONE IS ACTING WEIRD...
FSHHH
IT SAYS IT'S FROM MINAMOTO-KOUHAI, BUT...
KOU
GLUB
GLUB
GLUB

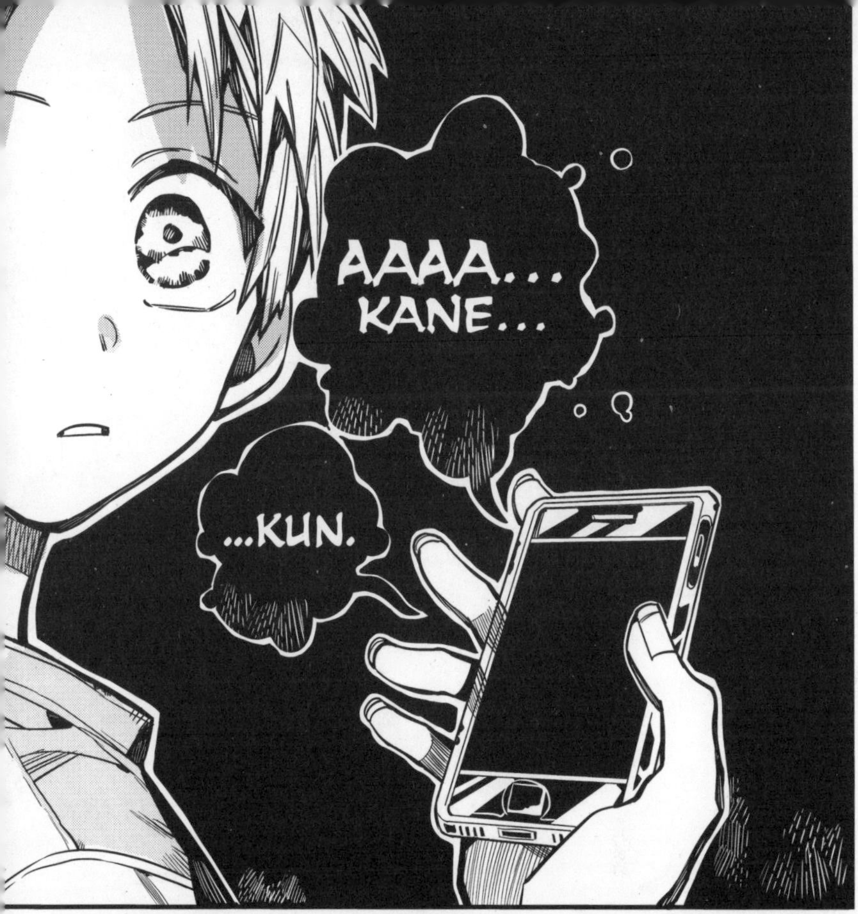
AAAA... KANE...
...KUN.
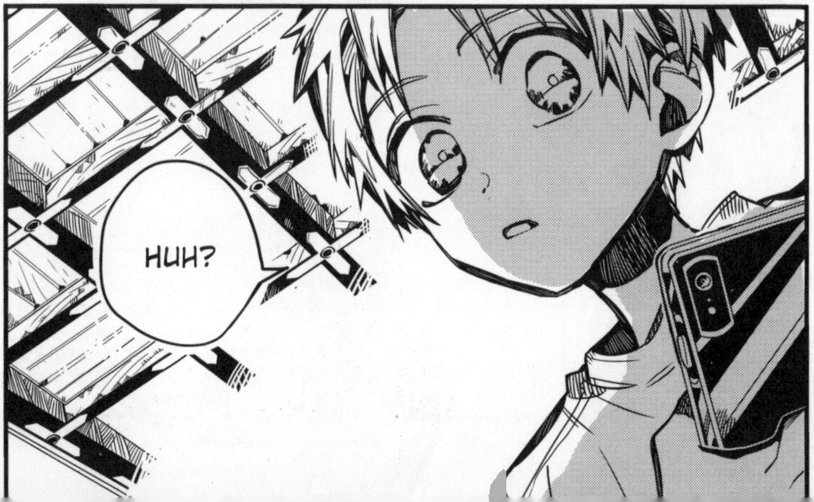
HUH?

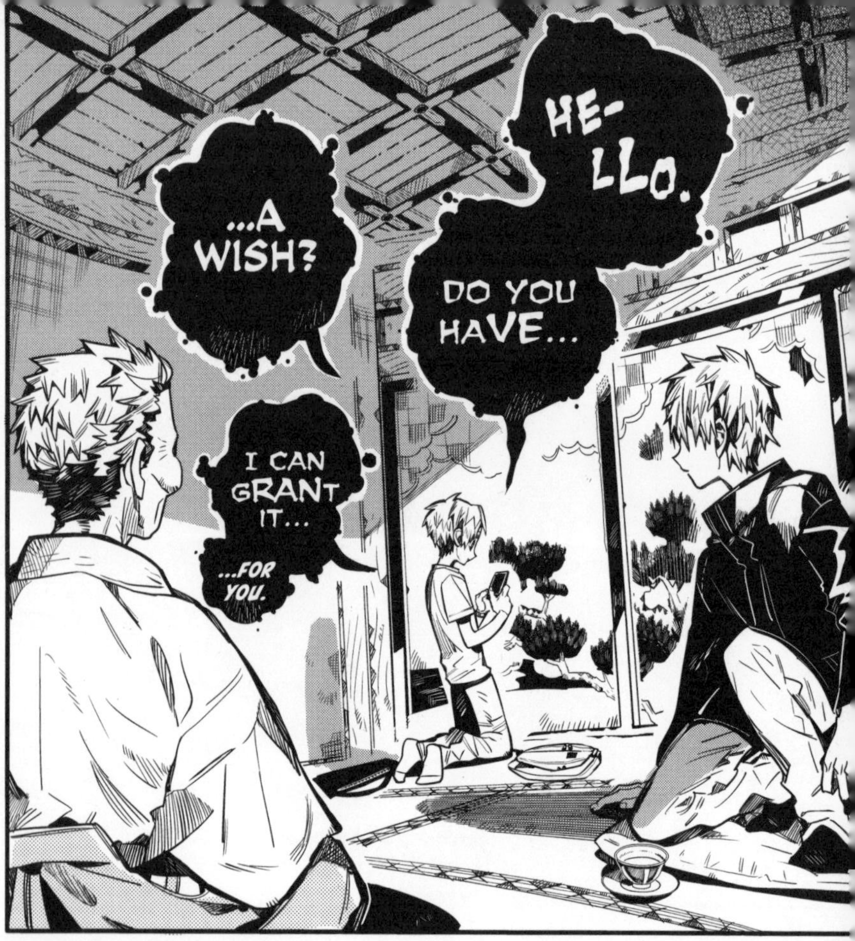
HE-
LLO.
DO YOU HAVE...
...A WISH?
I CAN GRANT IT...
...FOR YOU.

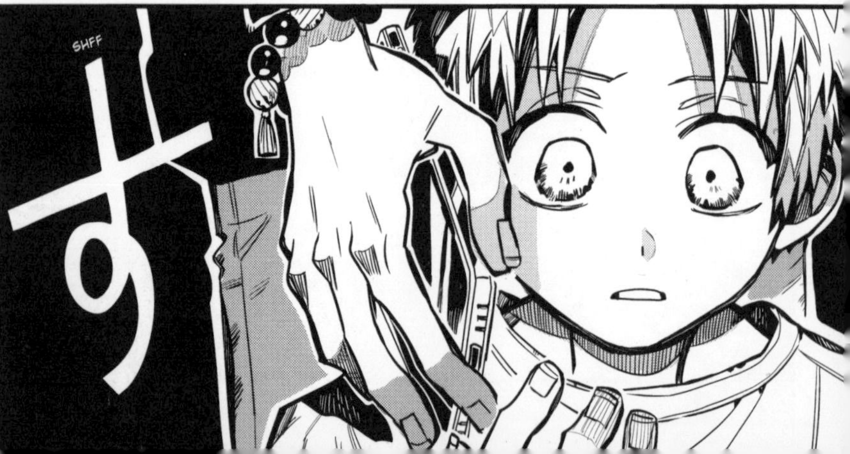
SHFF
す

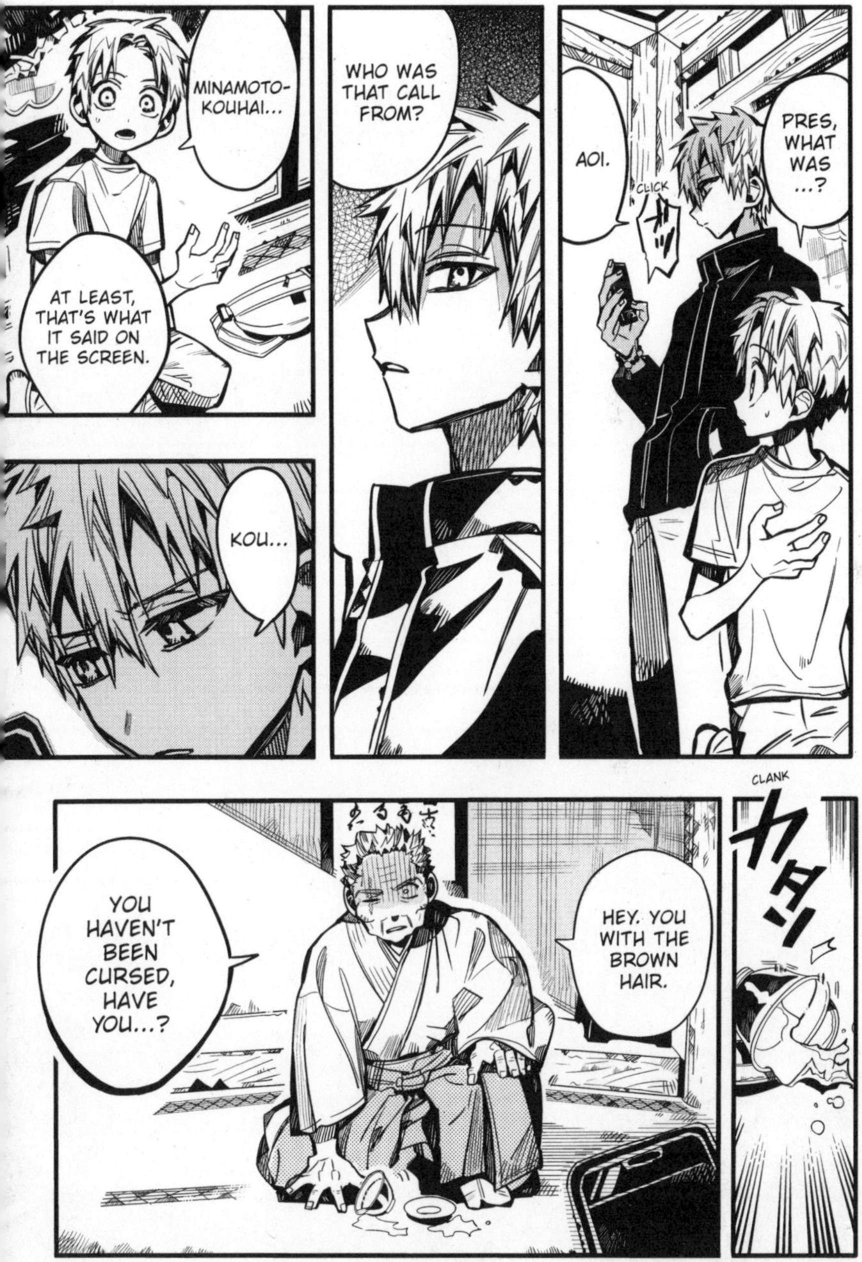
PRES, WHAT WAS ...?
CLICK
AOI.
WHO WAS THAT CALL FROM?
MINAMOTO-KOUHAI...
AT LEAST, THAT'S WHAT IT SAID ON THE SCREEN.
KOU...
CLANK
HEY. YOU WITH THE BROWN HAIR.
YOU HAVEN'T BEEN CURSED, HAVE YOU...?

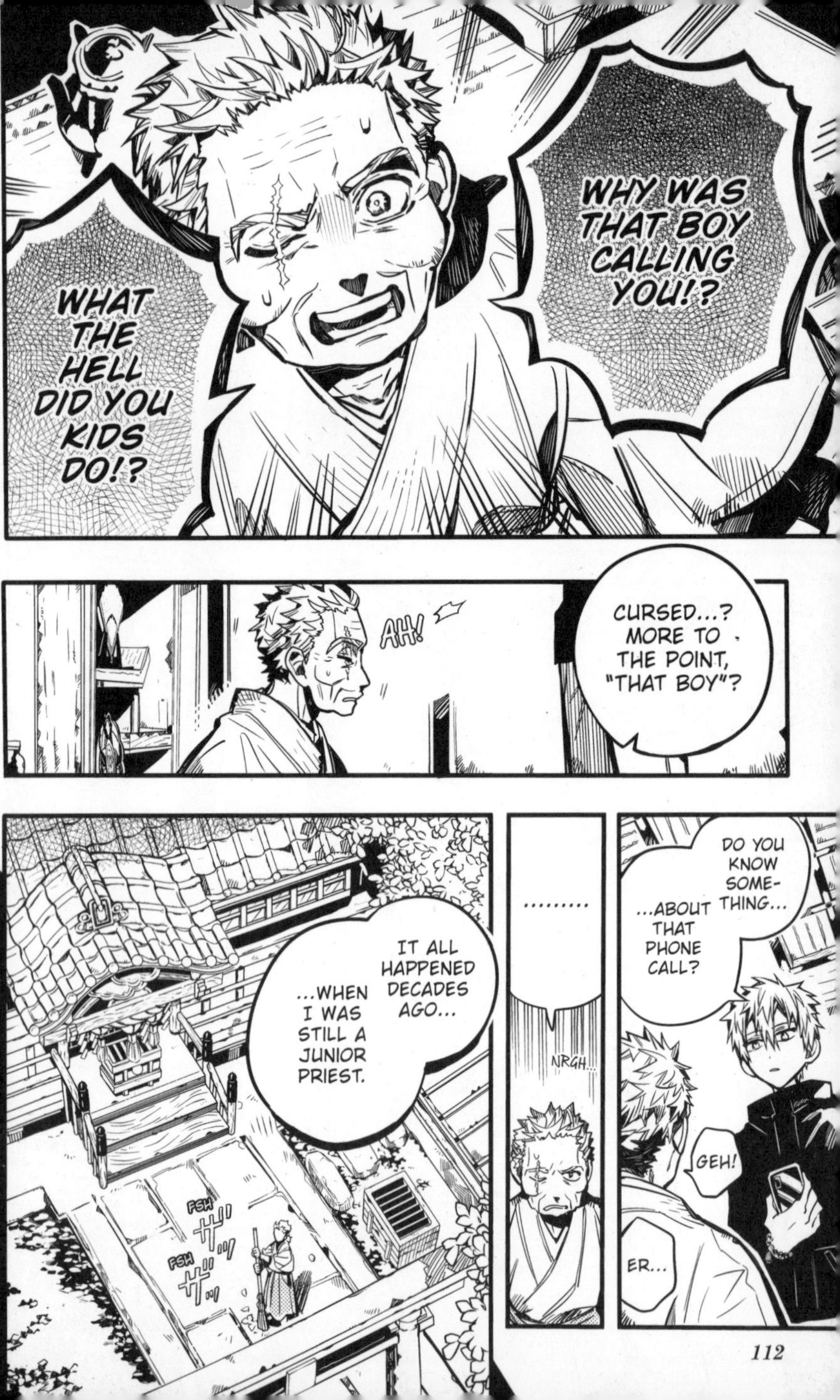
WHY WAS THAT BOY CALLING YOU!?
WHAT THE HELL DID YOU KIDS DO!?
CURSED...? MORE TO THE POINT, "THAT BOY"?
AH!
DO YOU KNOW SOME-THING...
...ABOUT THAT PHONE CALL?
GEH!
ER...
....
NRGH...
IT ALL HAPPENED DECADES AGO...
...WHEN I WAS STILL A JUNIOR PRIEST.
FSH
FSH

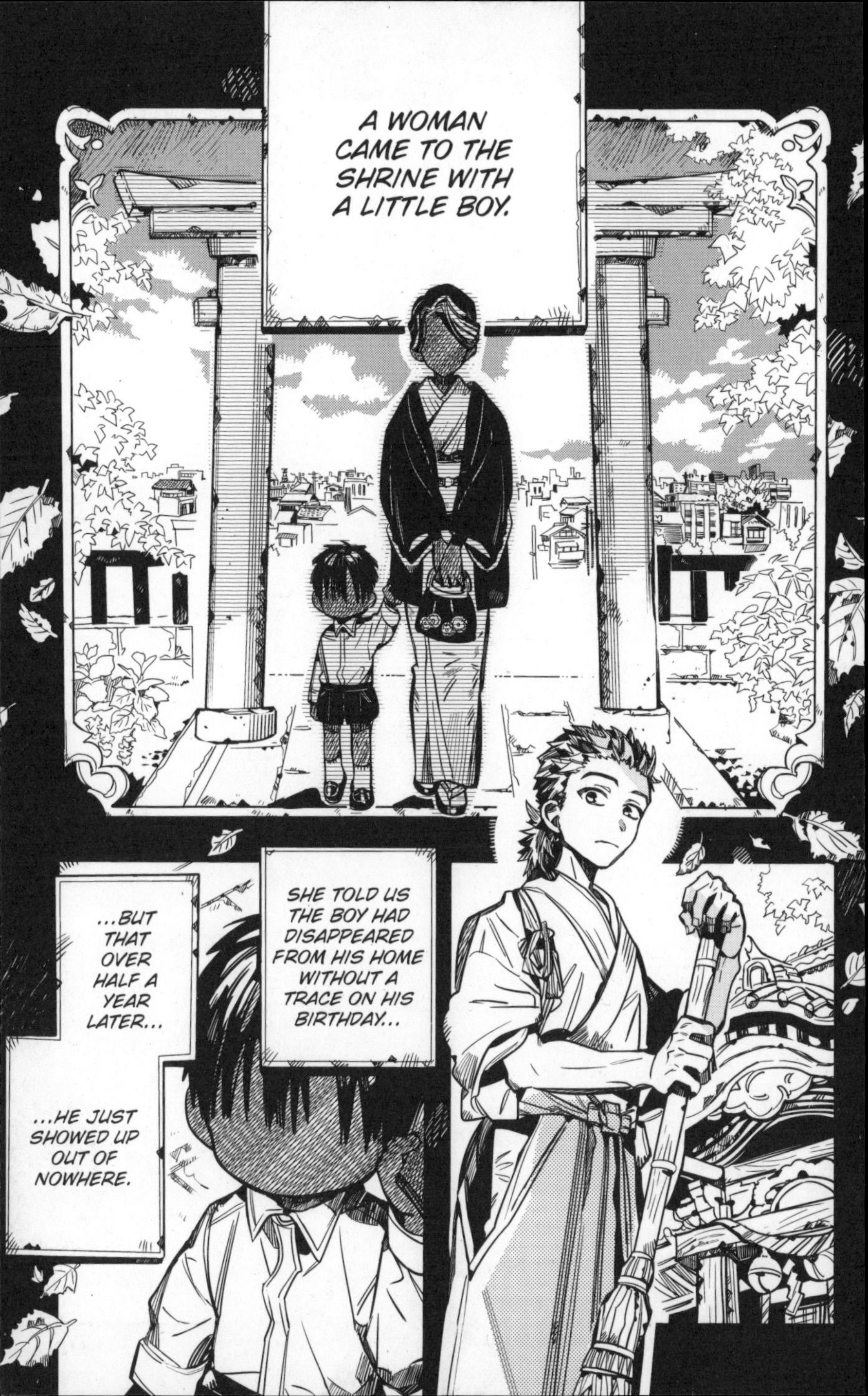

A WOMAN CAME TO THE SHRINE WITH A LITTLE BOY.
SHE TOLD US THE BOY HAD DISAPPEARED FROM HIS HOME WITHOUT A TRACE ON HIS BIRTHDAY...
...BUT THAT OVER HALF A YEAR LATER...
...HE JUST SHOWED UP OUT OF NOWHERE.

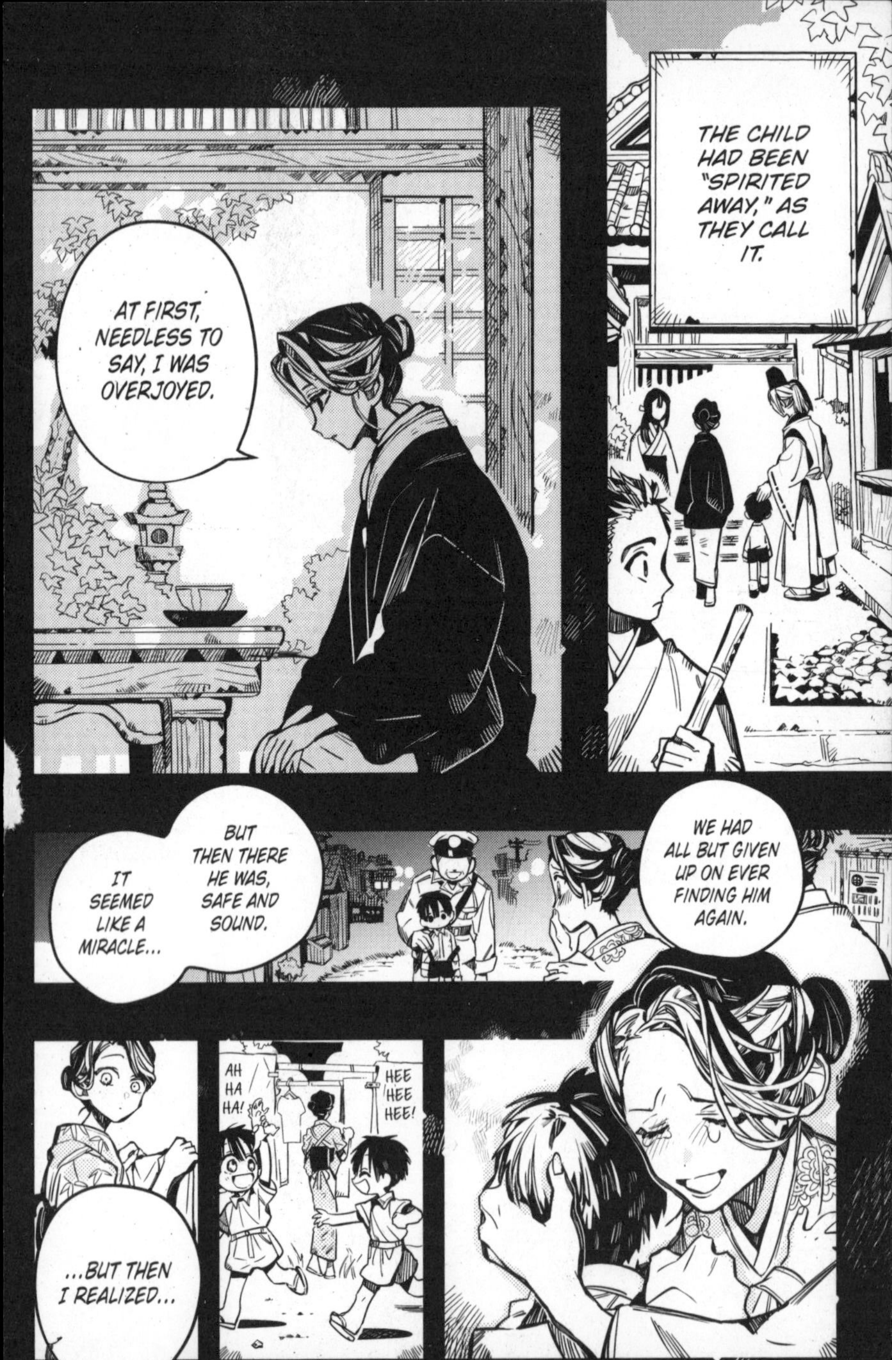
THE CHILD HAD BEEN "SPIRITED AWAY," AS THEY CALL IT.
AT FIRST, NEEDLESS TO SAY, I WAS OVERJOYED.
WE HAD ALL BUT GIVEN UP ON EVER FINDING HIM AGAIN.
BUT THEN THERE HE WAS, SAFE AND SOUND.
IT SEEMED LIKE A MIRACLE...
HEE HEE HEE!
AH HA HA!
...BUT THEN I REALIZED...

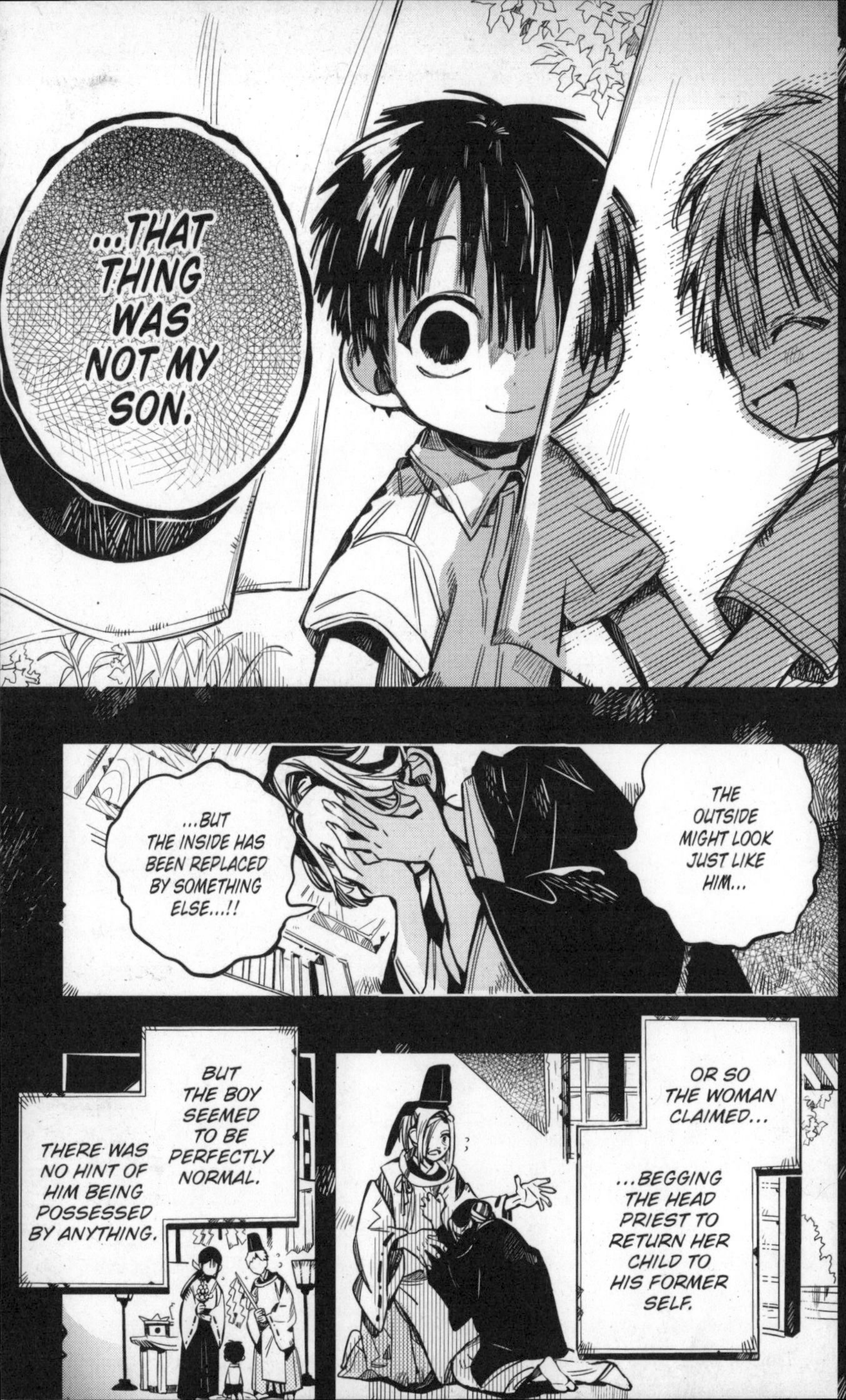
...THAT THING WAS NOT MY SON.
THE OUTSIDE MIGHT LOOK JUST LIKE HIM...
...BUT THE INSIDE HAS BEEN REPLACED BY SOMETHING ELSE...!!
OR SO THE WOMAN CLAIMED...
...BEGGING THE HEAD PRIEST TO RETURN HER CHILD TO HIS FORMER SELF.
BUT THE BOY SEEMED TO BE PERFECTLY NORMAL.
THERE WAS NO HINT OF HIM BEING POSSESSED BY ANYTHING.

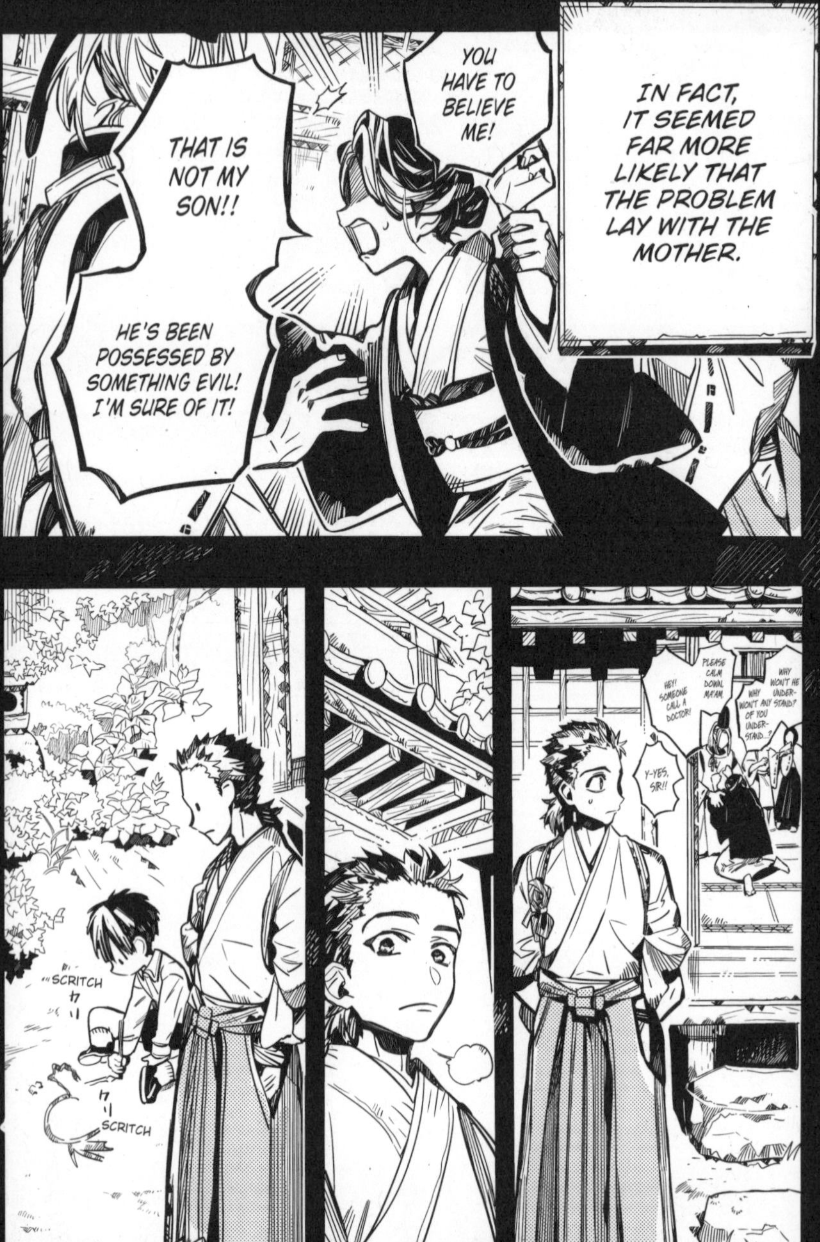
IN FACT, IT SEEMED FAR MORE LIKELY THAT THE PROBLEM LAY WITH THE MOTHER.
YOU HAVE TO BELIEVE ME!
THAT IS NOT MY SON!!
HE'S BEEN POSSESSED BY SOMETHING EVIL! I'M SURE OF IT!
WHY WON'T HE UNDER-STAND?
WHY WON'T ANY OF YOU UNDER-STAND...?
PLEASE CALM DOWN, MA'AM.
HEY! SOMEONE CALL A DOCTOR!
Y-YES, SIR!!
SCRITCH
カリ
カリ
SCRITCH

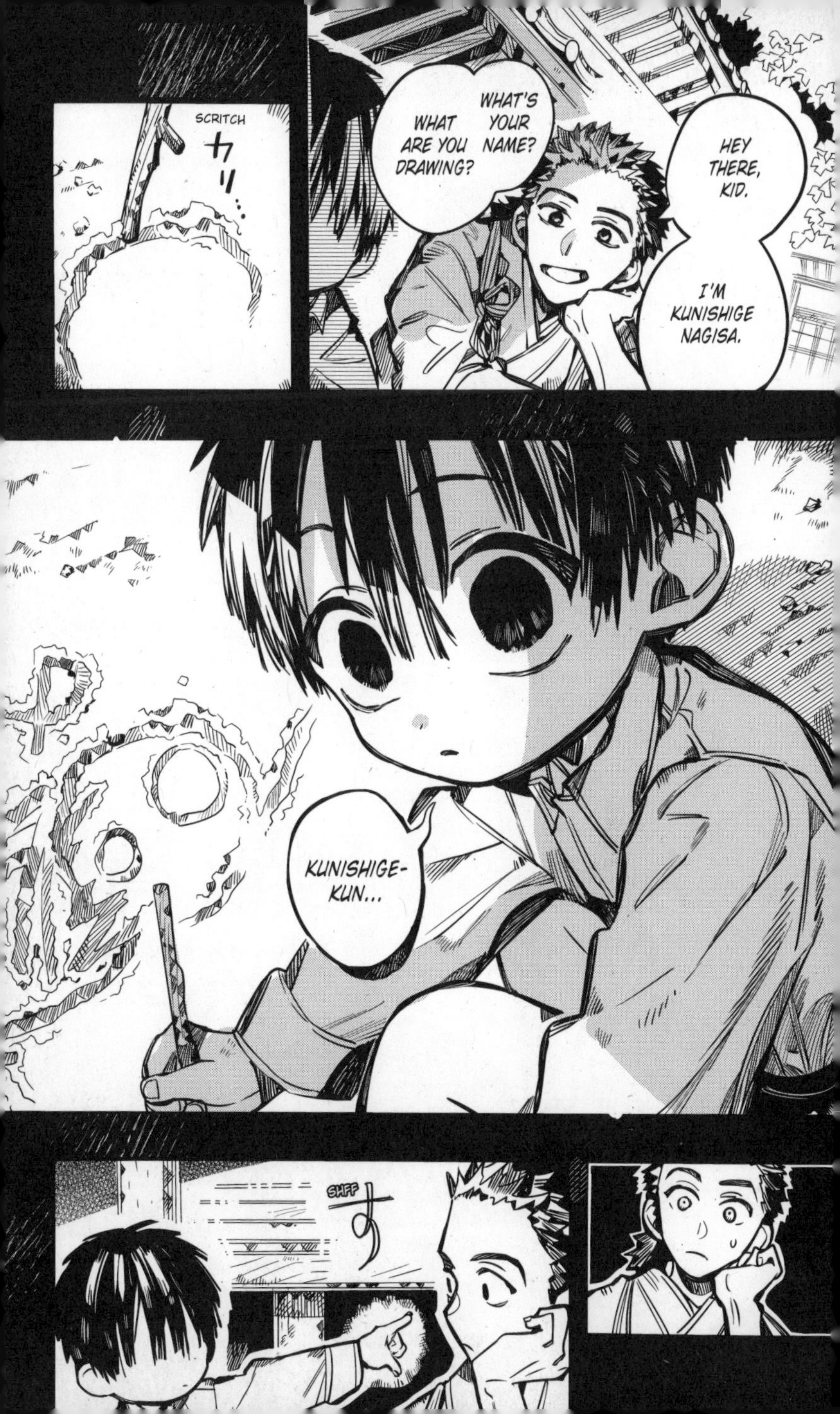
HEY THERE, KID.
I'M KUNISHIGE NAGISA.
WHAT'S YOUR NAME?
WHAT ARE YOU DRAWING?
SCRITCH
カリ…
KUNISHIGE-KUN...
SHFF
す

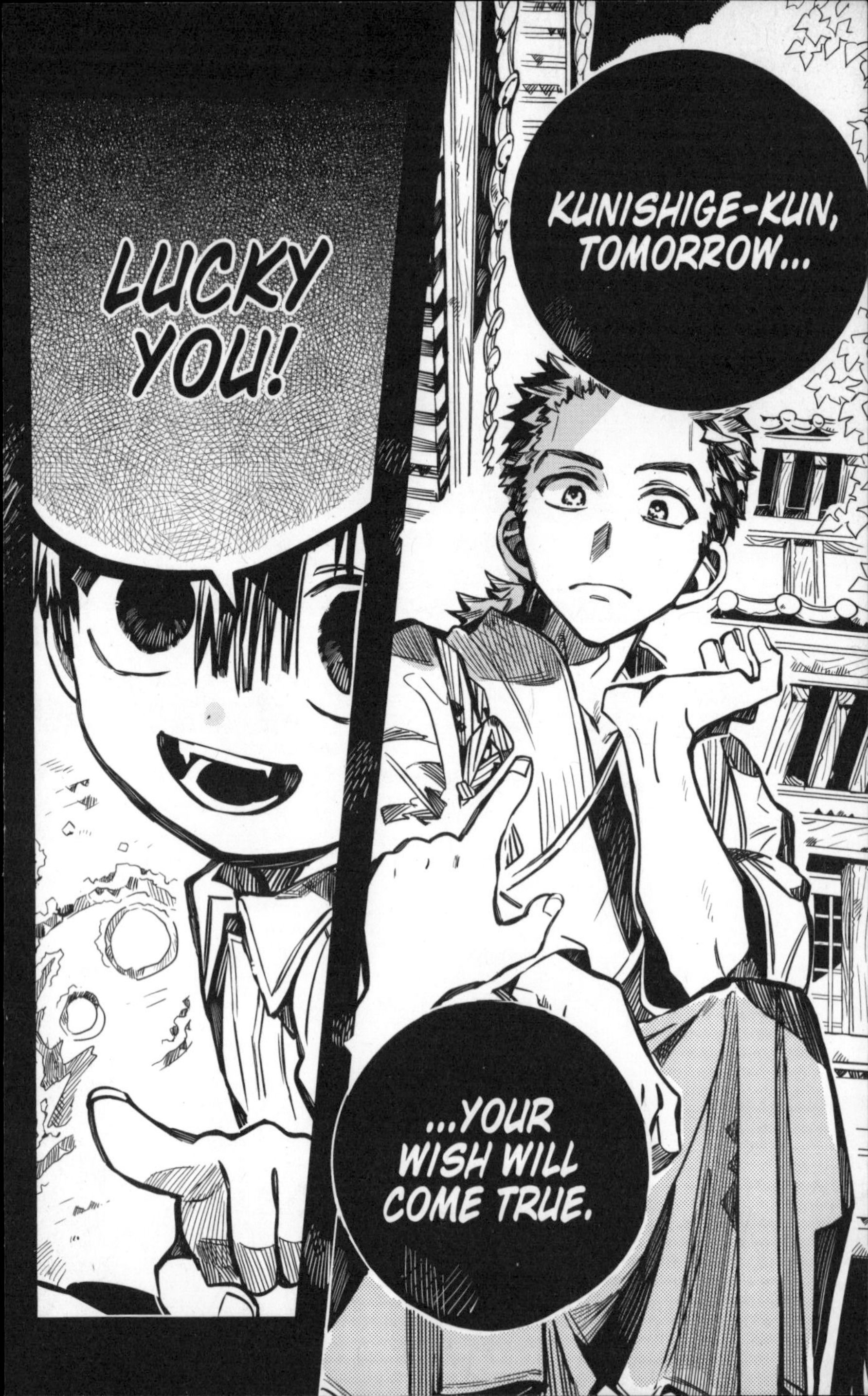
KUNISHIGE-KUN, TOMORROW...
...YOUR WISH WILL COME TRUE.
LUCKY YOU!

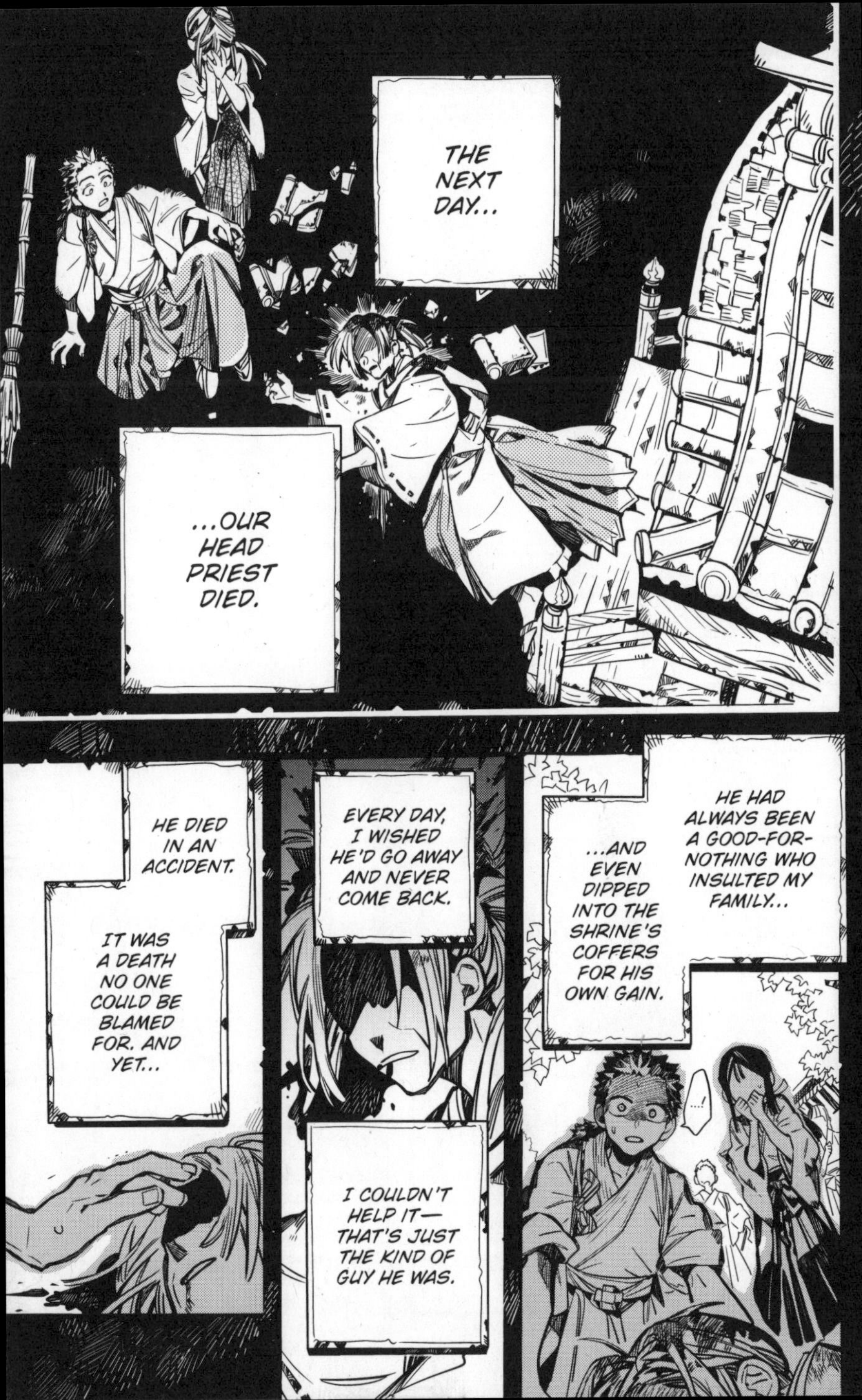
THE NEXT DAY...
...OUR HEAD PRIEST DIED.
HE HAD ALWAYS BEEN A GOOD-FOR-NOTHING WHO INSULTED MY FAMILY...
...AND EVEN DIPPED INTO THE SHRINE'S COFFERS FOR HIS OWN GAIN.
...!
EVERY DAY, I WISHED HE'D GO AWAY AND NEVER COME BACK.
I COULDN'T HELP IT—THAT'S JUST THE KIND OF GUY HE WAS.
HE DIED IN AN ACCIDENT.
IT WAS A DEATH NO ONE COULD BE BLAMED FOR. AND YET...

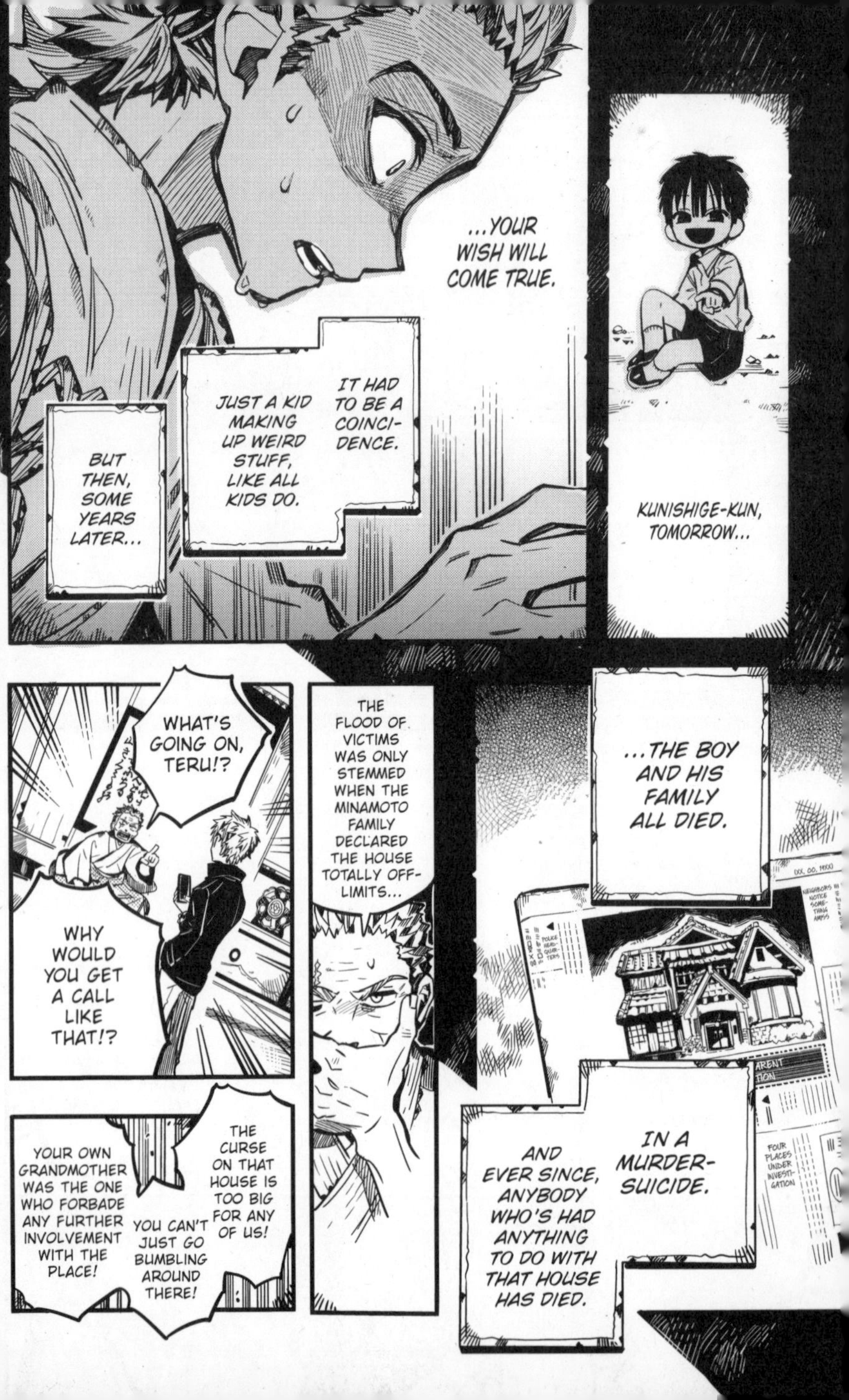
KUNISHIGE-KUN, TOMORROW...
...YOUR WISH WILL COME TRUE.
IT HAD TO BE A COINCIDENCE.
JUST A KID MAKING UP WEIRD STUFF, LIKE ALL KIDS DO.
BUT THEN, SOME YEARS LATER...
...THE BOY AND HIS FAMILY ALL DIED.
POLICE HEADQUARTERS
IN A MURDER-SUICIDE.
AND EVER SINCE, ANYBODY WHO'S HAD ANYTHING TO DO WITH THAT HOUSE HAS DIED.
FOUR PLACES UNDER INVESTIGATION
THE FLOOD OF VICTIMS WAS ONLY STEMMED WHEN THE MINAMOTO FAMILY DECLARED THE HOUSE TOTALLY OFF-LIMITS...
WHAT'S GOING ON, TERU!?
WHY WOULD YOU GET A CALL LIKE THAT!?
THE CURSE ON THAT HOUSE IS TOO BIG FOR ANY OF US!
YOU CAN'T JUST GO BUMBLING AROUND THERE!
YOUR OWN GRANDMOTHER WAS THE ONE WHO FORBADE ANY FURTHER INVOLVEMENT WITH THE PLACE!

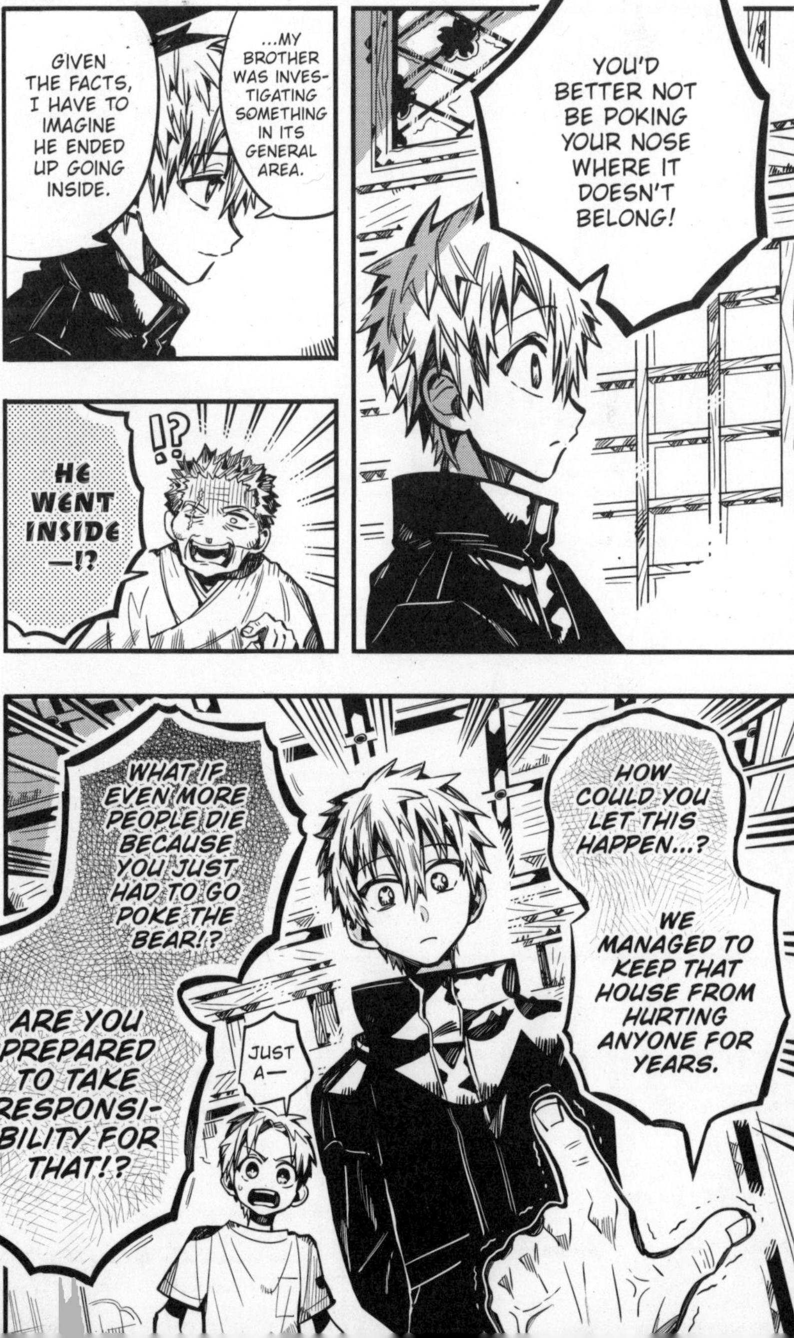
YOU'D BETTER NOT BE POKING YOUR NOSE WHERE IT DOESN'T BELONG!
...MY BROTHER WAS INVES-TIGATING SOMETHING IN ITS GENERAL AREA.
GIVEN THE FACTS, I HAVE TO IMAGINE HE ENDED UP GOING INSIDE.
!?
HE WENT INSIDE—!?
HOW COULD YOU LET THIS HAPPEN...?
WE MANAGED TO KEEP THAT HOUSE FROM HURTING ANYONE FOR YEARS.
WHAT IF EVEN MORE PEOPLE DIE BECAUSE YOU JUST HAD TO GO POKE THE BEAR!?
JUST A—
ARE YOU PREPARED TO TAKE RESPONSI-BILITY FOR THAT!?

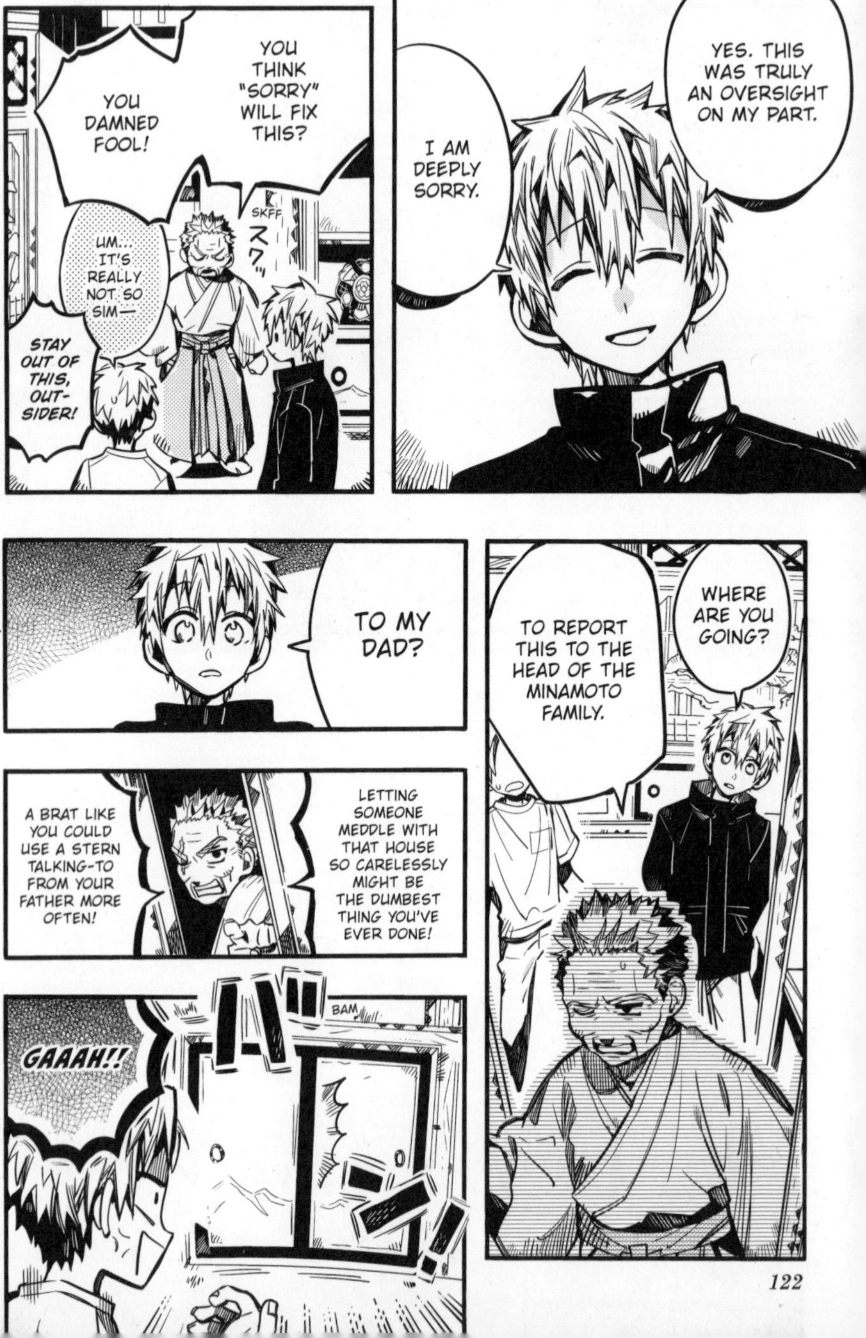
YES. THIS WAS TRULY AN OVERSIGHT ON MY PART.
I AM DEEPLY SORRY.
YOU THINK "SORRY" WILL FIX THIS?
YOU DAMNED FOOL!
SKFF
UM... IT'S REALLY NOT SO SIM—
STAY OUT OF THIS, OUT-SIDER!
WHERE ARE YOU GOING?
TO REPORT THIS TO THE HEAD OF THE MINAMOTO FAMILY.
TO MY DAD?
LETTING SOMEONE MEDDLE WITH THAT HOUSE SO CARELESSLY MIGHT BE THE DUMBEST THING YOU'VE EVER DONE!
A BRAT LIKE YOU COULD USE A STERN TALKING-TO FROM YOUR FATHER MORE OFTEN!
BAM
GAAAH!!

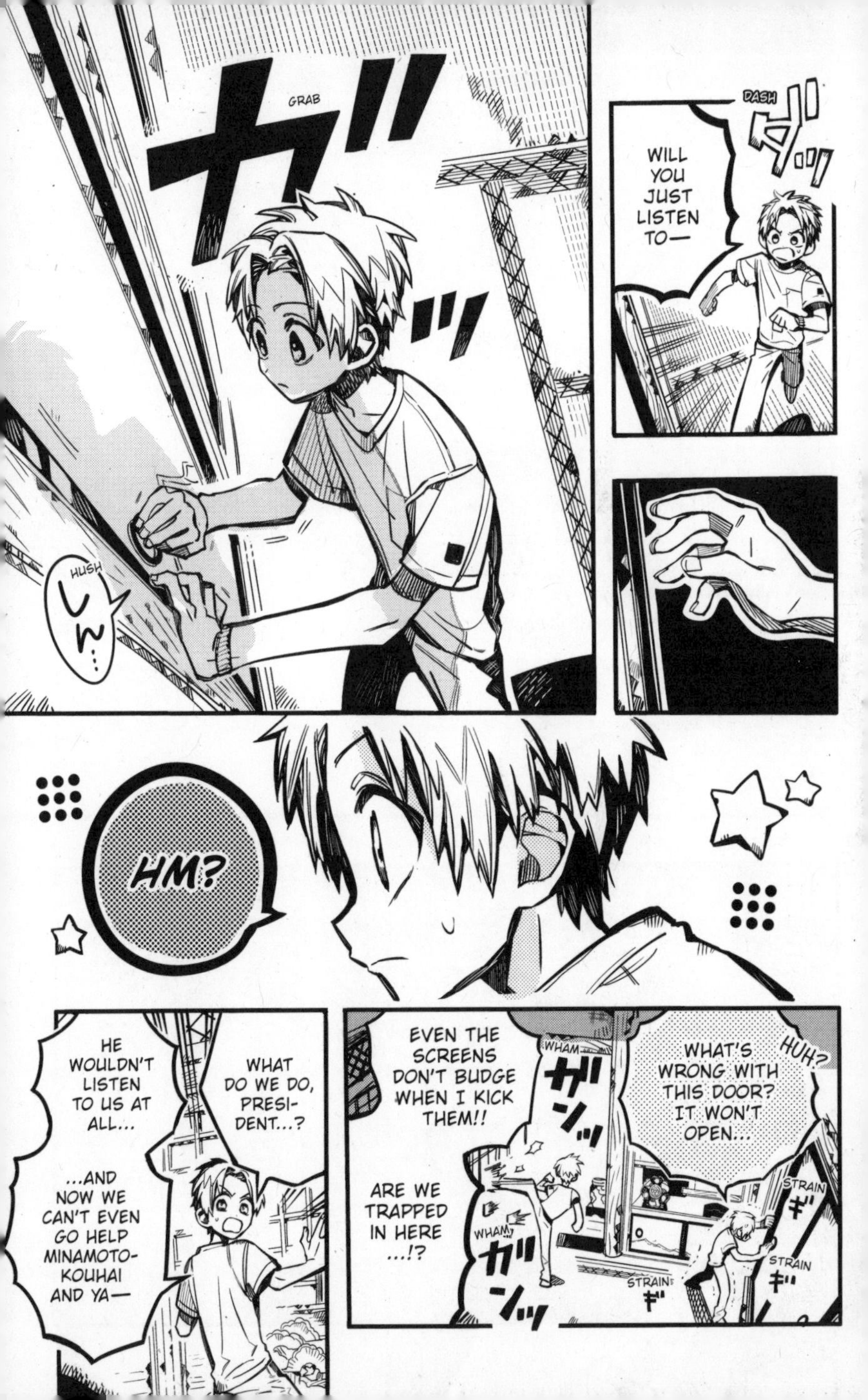
DASH
ダッ
WILL YOU JUST LISTEN TO—
GRAB
ガッ
HUSH
しん…
HM?
HUH?
WHAT'S WRONG WITH THIS DOOR? IT WON'T OPEN...
STRAIN
ギ
STRAIN
ギ
STRAIN
ギ
WHAM
ガンッ
EVEN THE SCREENS DON'T BUDGE WHEN I KICK THEM!!
WHAM
ガンッ
ARE WE TRAPPED IN HERE ...!?
WHAT DO WE DO, PRESI-DENT...?
HE WOULDN'T LISTEN TO US AT ALL...
...AND NOW WE CAN'T EVEN GO HELP MINAMOTO-KOUHAI AND YA—

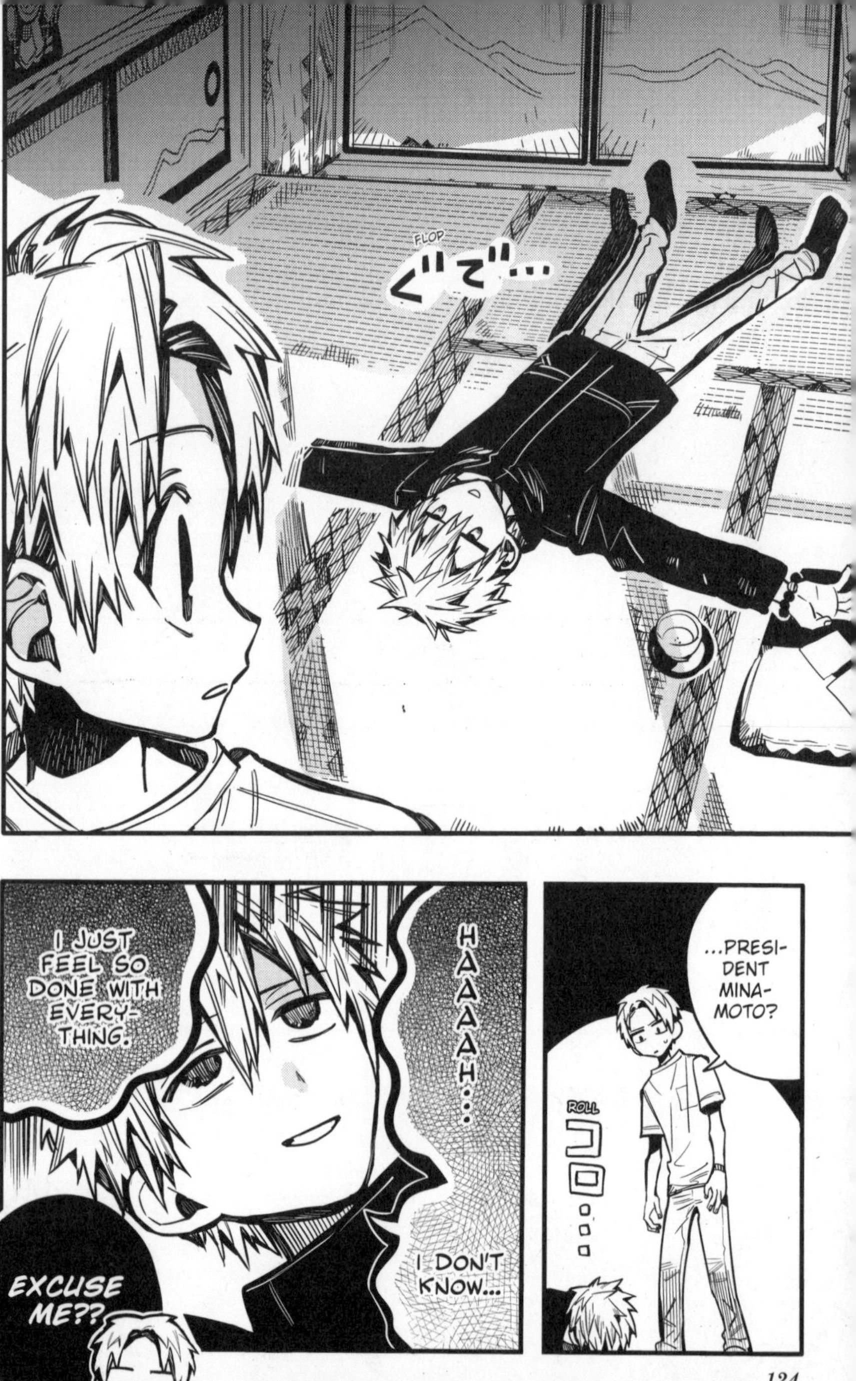
FLOP
ぐで…
...PRESI-DENT MINA-MOTO?
ROLL
コロ…
HAAAAH...
I JUST FEEL SO DONE WITH EVERY-THING.
I DON'T KNOW...
EXCUSE ME??

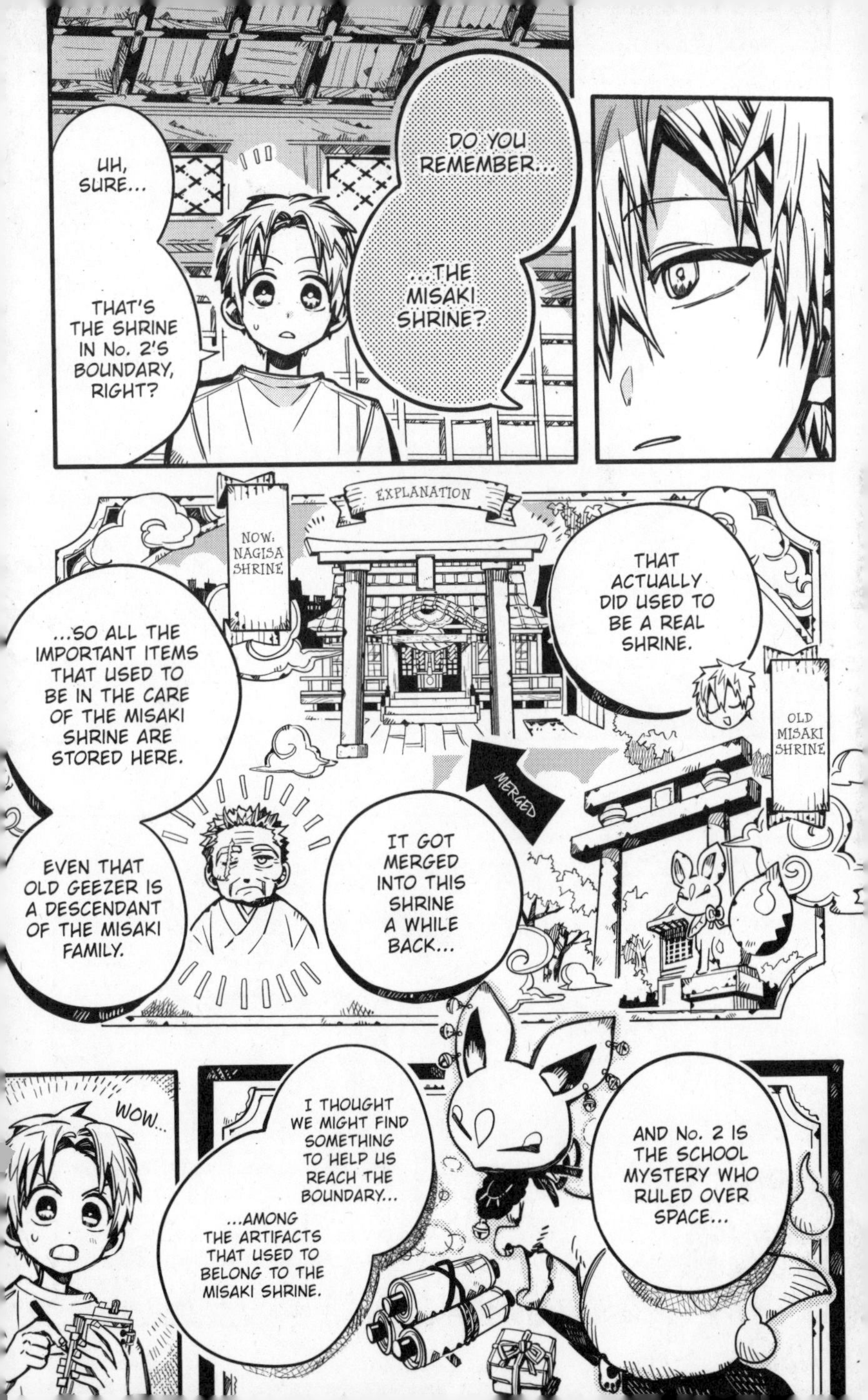
DO YOU REMEMBER...
...THE MISAKI SHRINE?
UH, SURE...
THAT'S THE SHRINE IN No. 2'S BOUNDARY, RIGHT?
EXPLANATION
OLD MISAKI SHRINE
THAT ACTUALLY DID USED TO BE A REAL SHRINE.
MERGED
IT GOT MERGED INTO THIS SHRINE A WHILE BACK...
NOW: NAGISA SHRINE
...SO ALL THE IMPORTANT ITEMS THAT USED TO BE IN THE CARE OF THE MISAKI SHRINE ARE STORED HERE.
EVEN THAT OLD GEEZER IS A DESCENDANT OF THE MISAKI FAMILY.
AND No. 2 IS THE SCHOOL MYSTERY WHO RULED OVER SPACE...
I THOUGHT WE MIGHT FIND SOMETHING TO HELP US REACH THE BOUNDARY...
...AMONG THE ARTIFACTS THAT USED TO BELONG TO THE MISAKI SHRINE.
WOW...

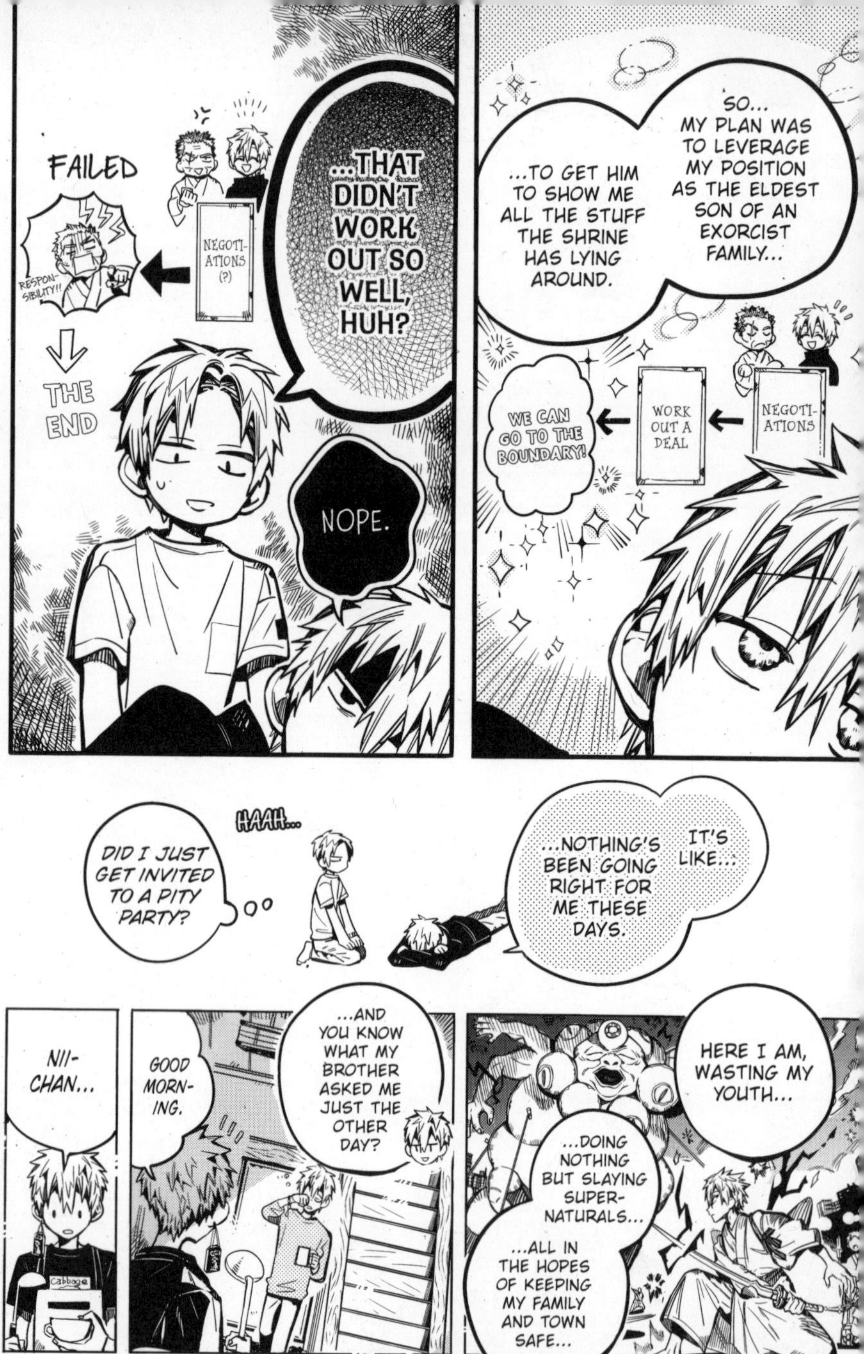
SO... MY PLAN WAS TO LEVERAGE MY POSITION AS THE ELDEST SON OF AN EXORCIST FAMILY...
...TO GET HIM TO SHOW ME ALL THE STUFF THE SHRINE HAS LYING AROUND.
NEGOTI-ATIONS
WORK OUT A DEAL
WE CAN GO TO THE BOUNDARY!
...THAT DIDN'T WORK OUT SO WELL, HUH?
NOPE.
NEGOTI-ATIONS (?)
RESPON-SIBILITY!!
FAILED
THE END
IT'S LIKE...
...NOTHING'S BEEN GOING RIGHT FOR ME THESE DAYS.
HAAH...
DID I JUST GET INVITED TO A PITY PARTY?
HERE I AM, WASTING MY YOUTH...
...DOING NOTHING BUT SLAYING SUPER-NATURALS...
...ALL IN THE HOPES OF KEEPING MY FAMILY AND TOWN SAFE...
...AND YOU KNOW WHAT MY BROTHER ASKED ME JUST THE OTHER DAY?
GOOD MORN-ING.
NII-CHAN...
Cabbage

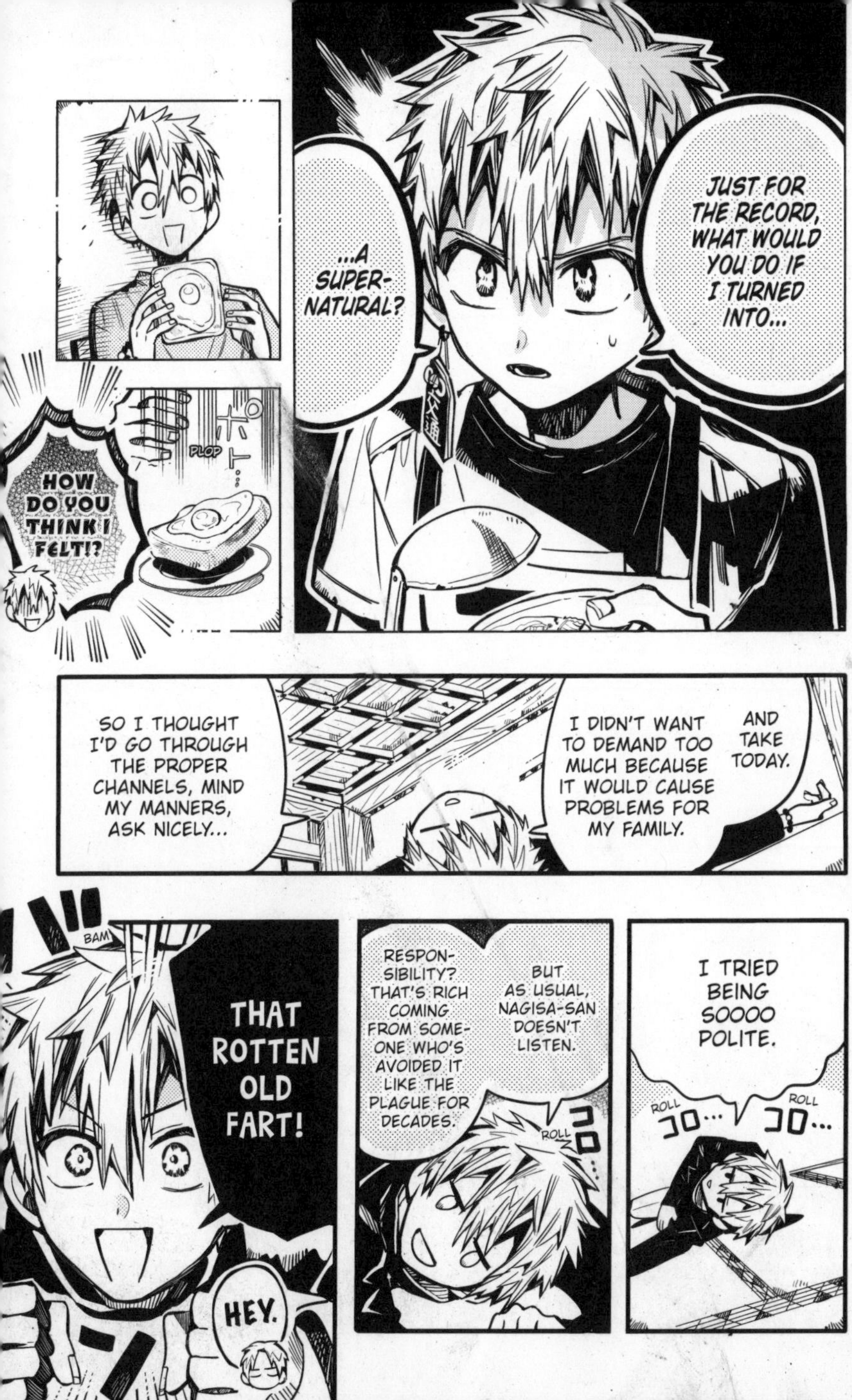
JUST FOR THE RECORD, WHAT WOULD YOU DO IF I TURNED INTO...
...A SUPER-NATURAL?
ポト
PLOP
HOW DO YOU THINK I FELT!?
AND TAKE TODAY.
I DIDN'T WANT TO DEMAND TOO MUCH BECAUSE IT WOULD CAUSE PROBLEMS FOR MY FAMILY.
SO I THOUGHT I'D GO THROUGH THE PROPER CHANNELS, MIND MY MANNERS, ASK NICELY...
I TRIED BEING SOOOO POLITE.
コロ...
ROLL
コロ...
ROLL
BUT AS USUAL, NAGISA-SAN DOESN'T LISTEN.
RESPON-SIBILITY? THAT'S RICH COMING FROM SOME-ONE WHO'S AVOIDED IT LIKE THE PLAGUE FOR DECADES.
コロ...
ROLL
BAM
THAT ROTTEN OLD FART!
HEY.

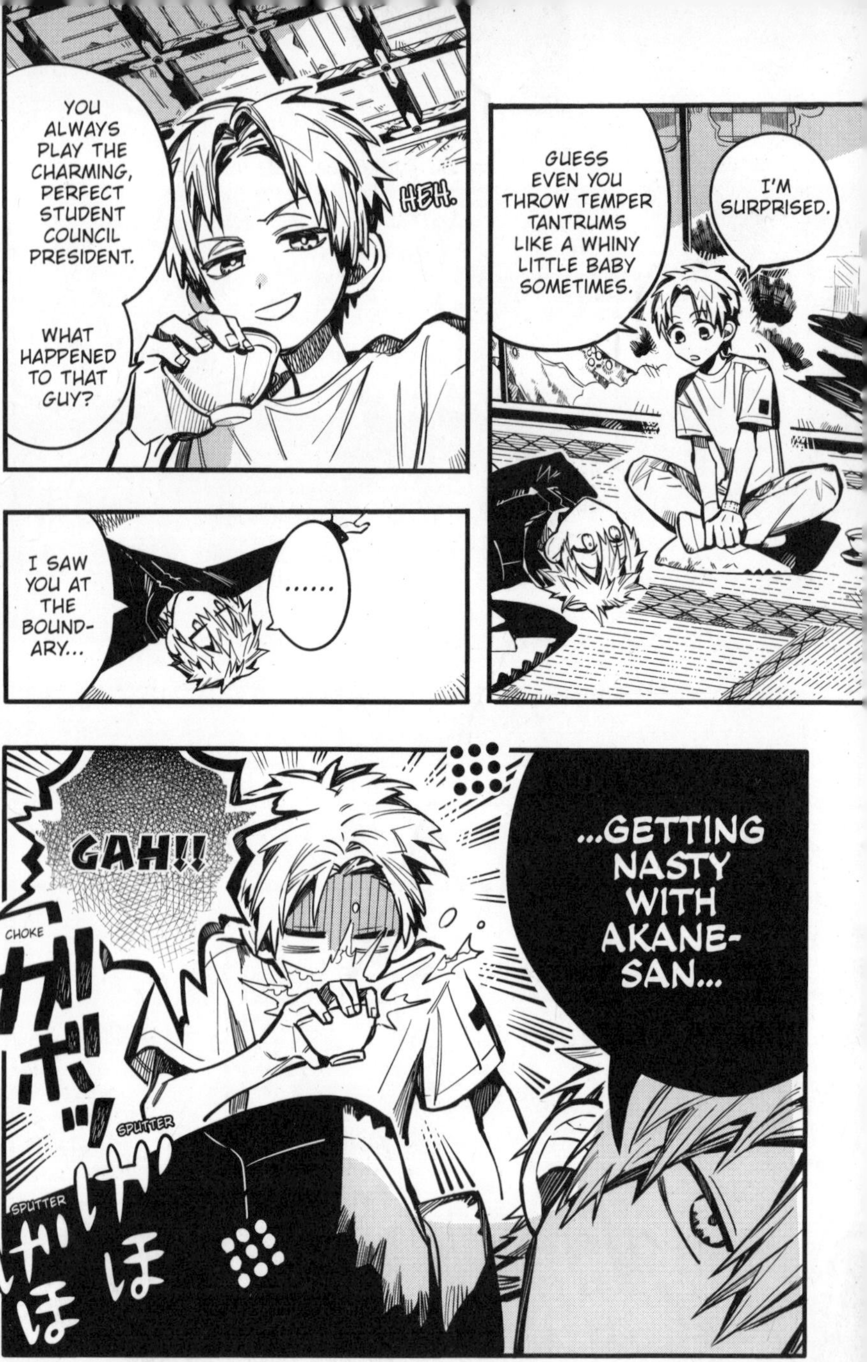
I'M SURPRISED.
GUESS EVEN YOU THROW TEMPER TANTRUMS LIKE A WHINY LITTLE BABY SOMETIMES.
YOU ALWAYS PLAY THE CHARMING, PERFECT STUDENT COUNCIL PRESIDENT.
HEH.
WHAT HAPPENED TO THAT GUY?
......
I SAW YOU AT THE BOUNDARY...
...GETTING NASTY WITH AKANE-SAN...
GAH!!
CHOKE
ガボッ
SPUTTER
SPUTTER
げほげほ

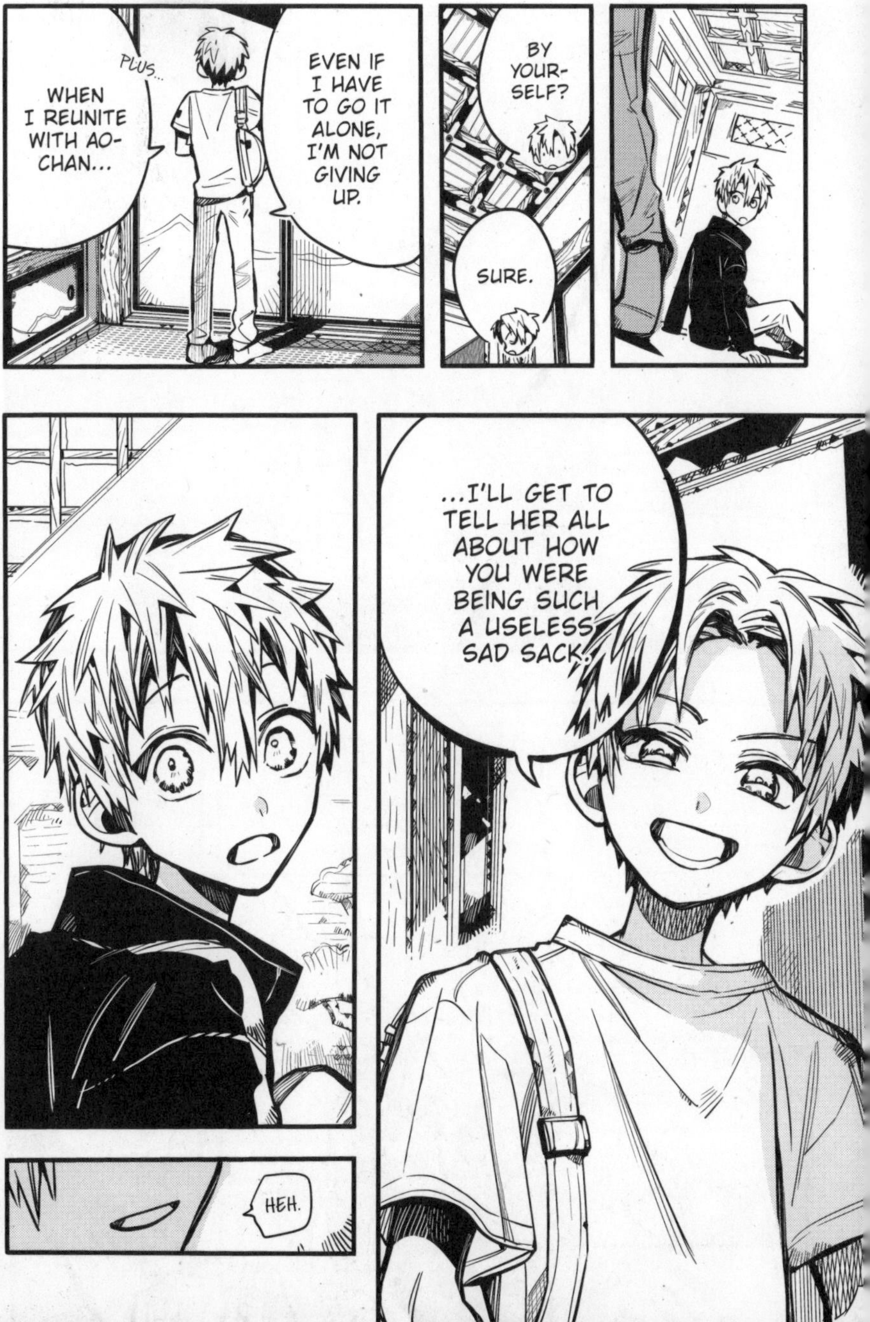
BY YOUR-SELF?
SURE.
EVEN IF I HAVE TO GO IT ALONE, I'M NOT GIVING UP.
PLUS...
WHEN I REUNITE WITH AO-CHAN...
...I'LL GET TO TELL HER ALL ABOUT HOW YOU WERE BEING SUCH A USELESS SAD SACK.
HEH.

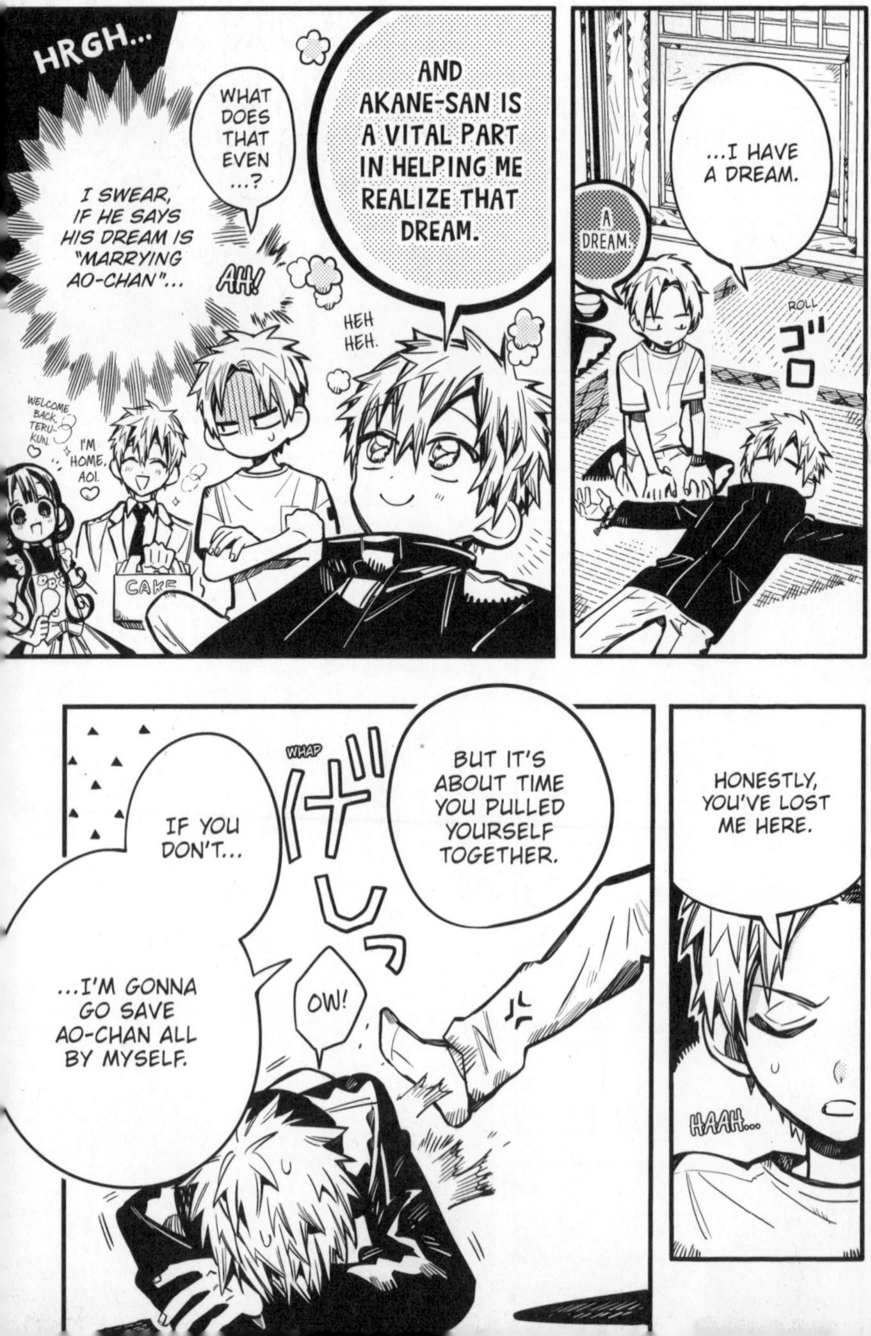
...I HAVE A DREAM.
A DREAM.
ROLL
ゴロ
AND AKANE-SAN IS A VITAL PART IN HELPING ME REALIZE THAT DREAM.
HEH HEH.
WHAT DOES THAT EVEN ...?
AH!
HRGH...
I SWEAR, IF HE SAYS HIS DREAM IS "MARRYING AO-CHAN"...
I'M HOME, AOI.
WELCOME BACK, TERU-KUN.
CAKE
HONESTLY, YOU'VE LOST ME HERE.
HAAH...
BUT IT'S ABOUT TIME YOU PULLED YOURSELF TOGETHER.
WHAP
げしっ
IF YOU DON'T...
OW!
...I'M GONNA GO SAVE AO-CHAN ALL BY MYSELF.

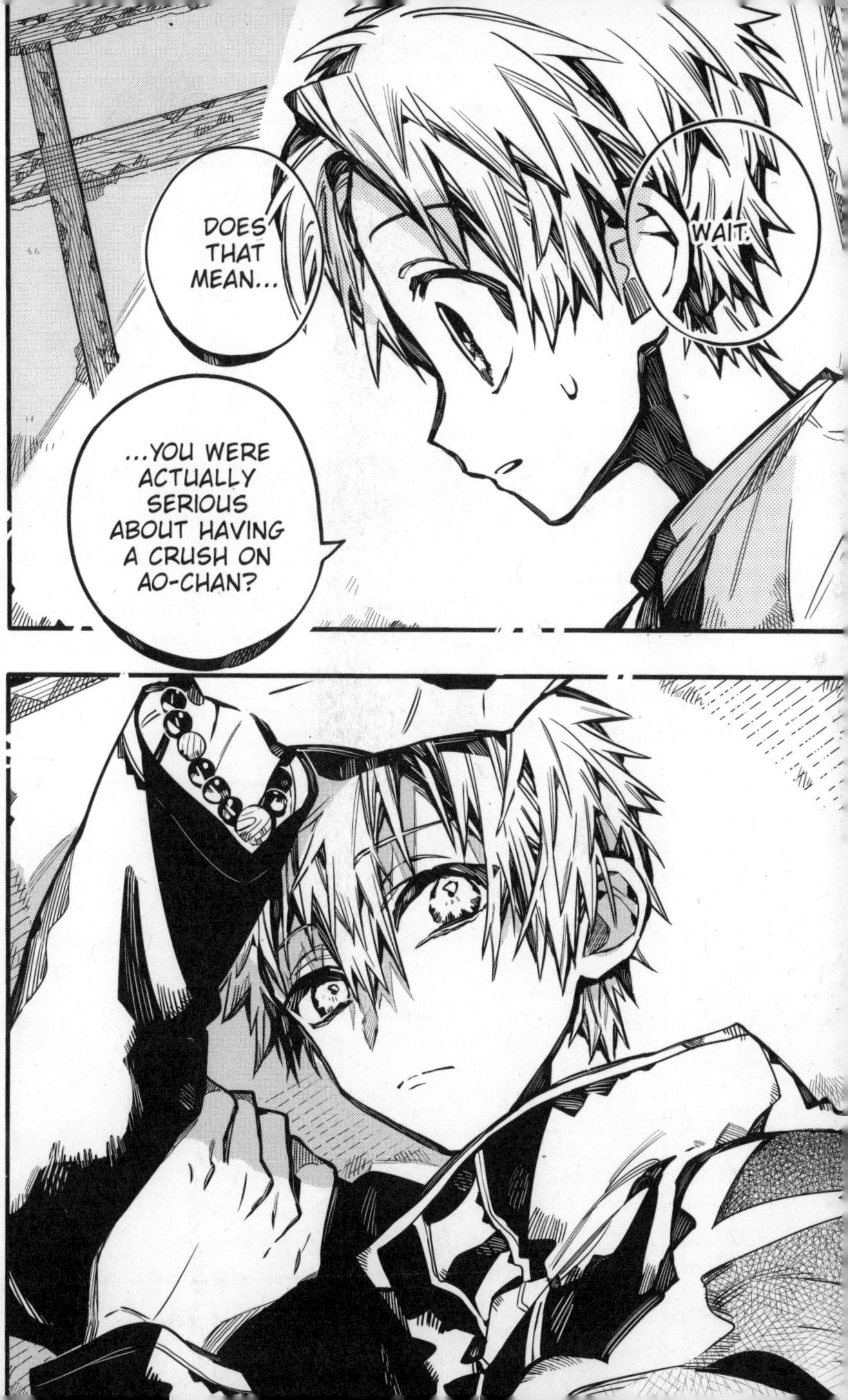
WAIT.
DOES THAT MEAN...
...YOU WERE ACTUALLY SERIOUS ABOUT HAVING A CRUSH ON AO-CHAN?

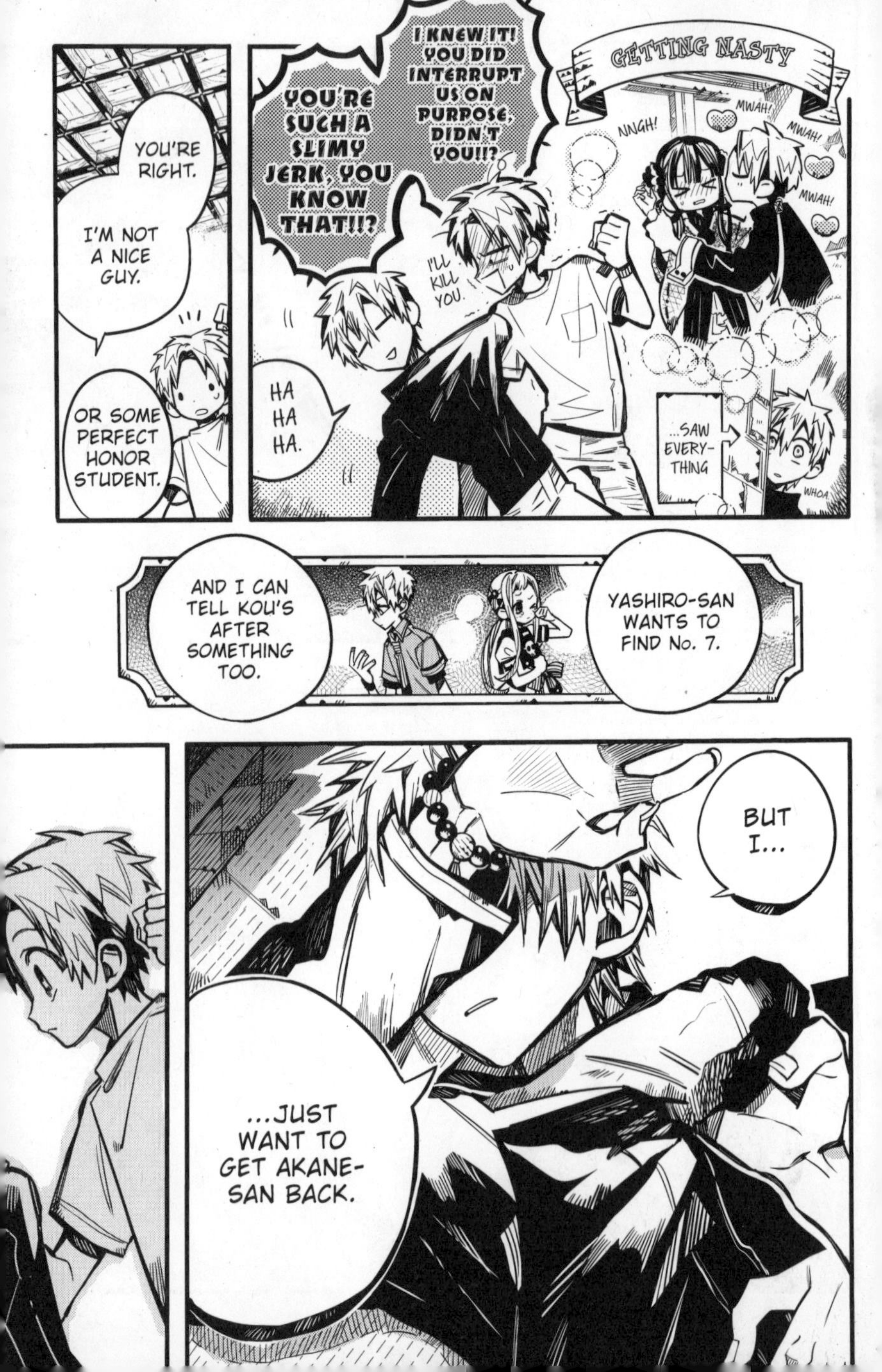
GETTING NASTY
MWAH!
MWAH!
MWAH!
NNGH!
I KNEW IT! YOU DID INTERRUPT US ON PURPOSE, DIDN'T YOU!!?
YOU'RE SUCH A SLIMY JERK, YOU KNOW THAT!!?
I'LL KILL YOU.
...SAW EVERYTHING
WHOA
HA HA HA.
YOU'RE RIGHT.
I'M NOT A NICE GUY.
OR SOME PERFECT HONOR STUDENT.
YASHIRO-SAN WANTS TO FIND No. 7.
AND I CAN TELL KOU'S AFTER SOMETHING TOO.
BUT I...
...JUST WANT TO GET AKANE-SAN BACK.

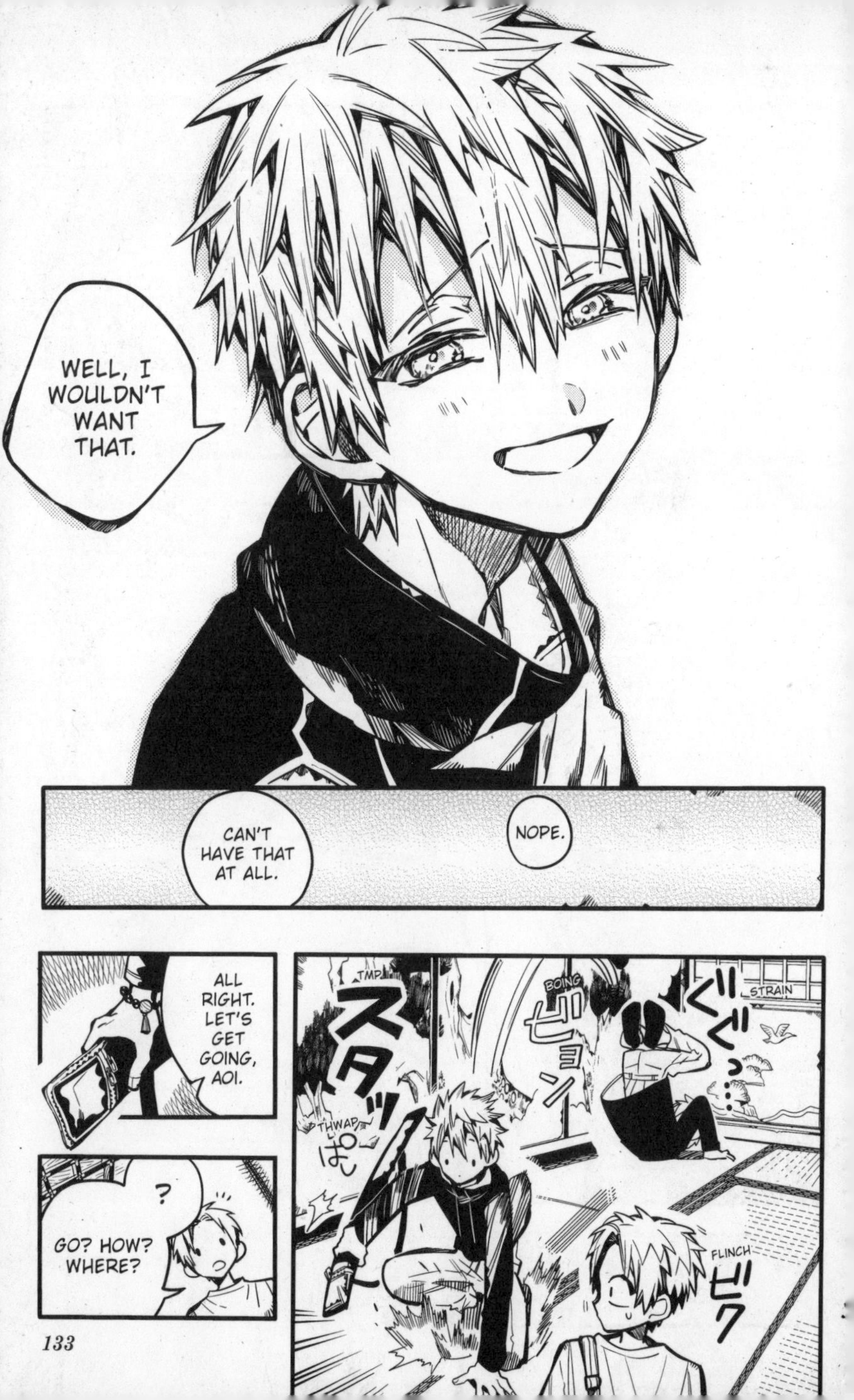
WELL, I WOULDN'T WANT THAT.
NOPE.
CAN'T HAVE THAT AT ALL.
STRAIN
ぐぐっ…
BOING
ピョン
TMP
スタッ
THWAP
ぱし
FLINCH
ビク
ALL RIGHT. LET'S GET GOING, AOI.
?
GO? HOW? WHERE?

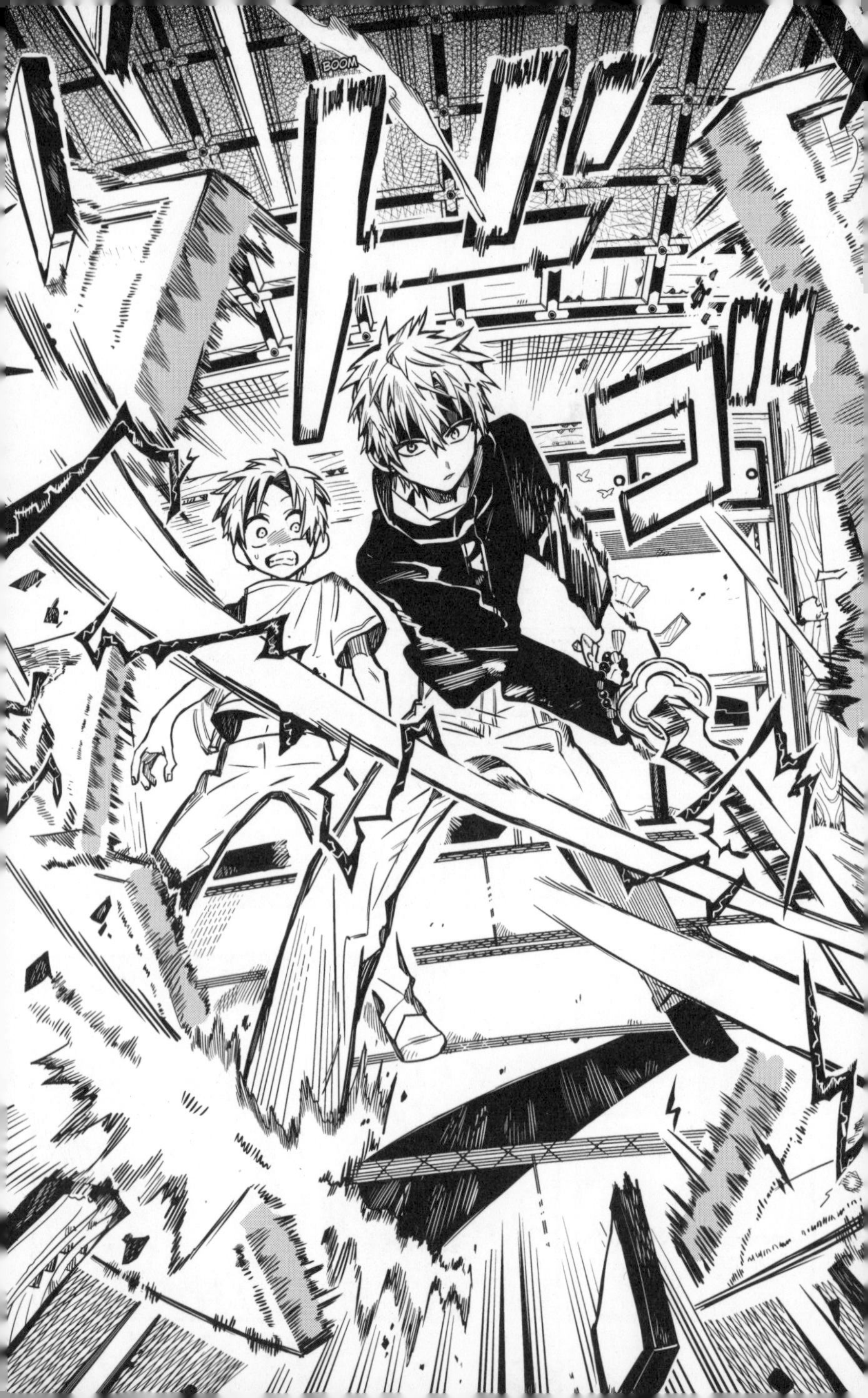
BOOM

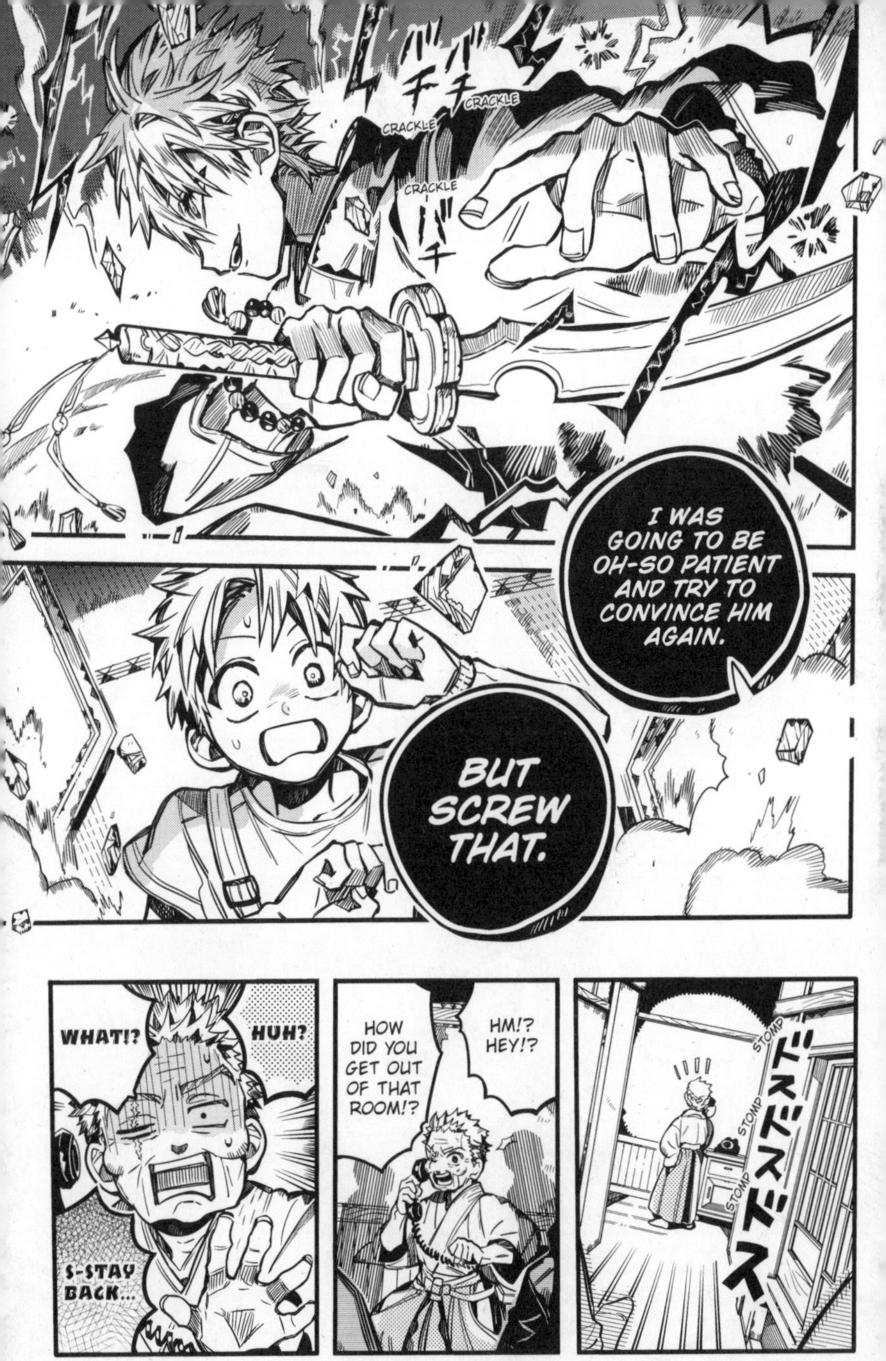
CRACKLE
CRACKLE
CRACKLE
I WAS GOING TO BE OH-SO PATIENT AND TRY TO CONVINCE HIM AGAIN.
BUT SCREW THAT.
STOMP
STOMP
STOMP
HM!? HEY!?
HOW DID YOU GET OUT OF THAT ROOM!?
HUH?
WHAT!?
S-STAY BACK...

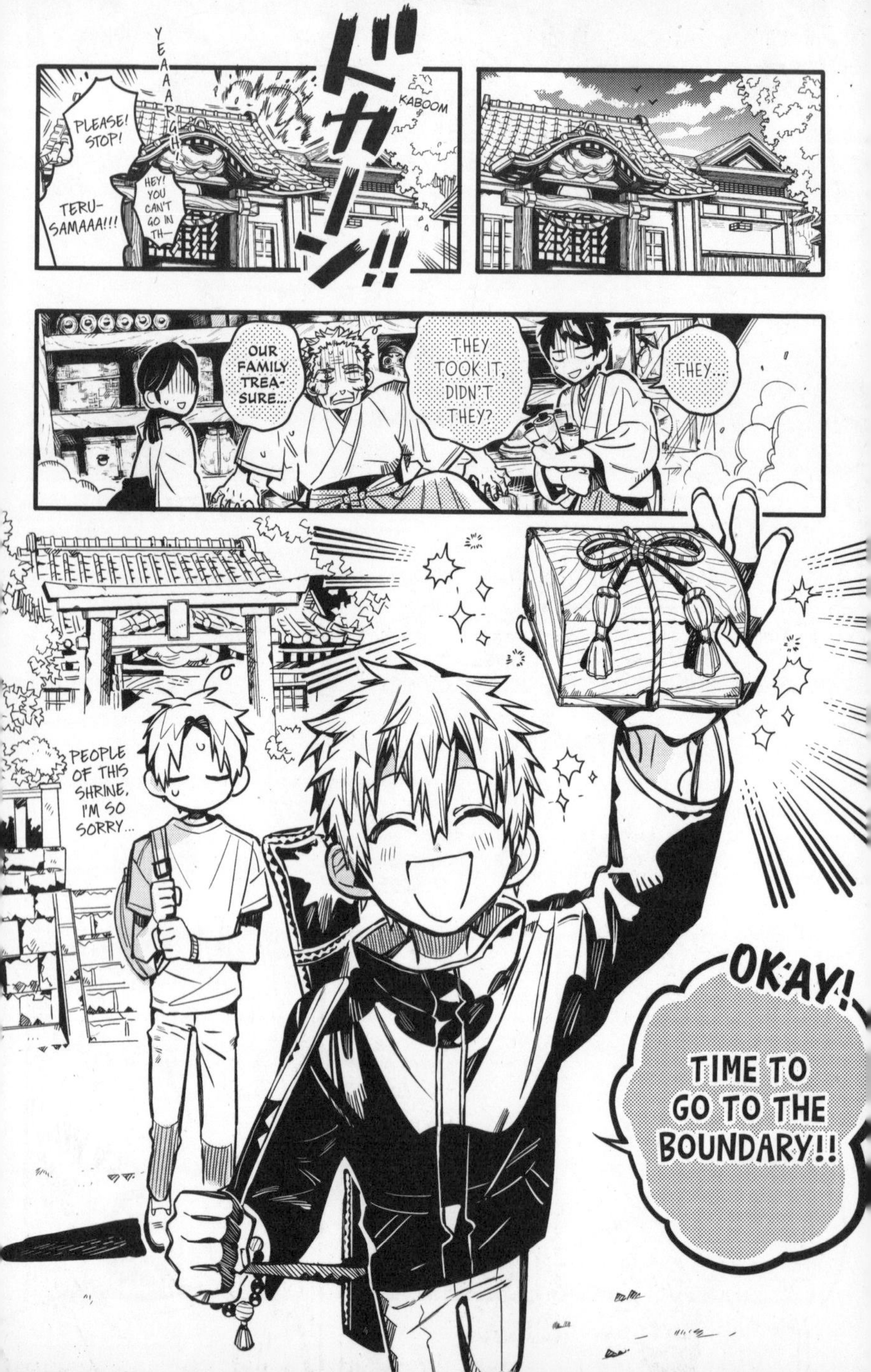
ドカーン!!
KABOOM
YEAAAARGH!
PLEASE! STOP!
HEY! YOU CAN'T GO IN TH—
TERU-SAMAAA!!!
THEY...
THEY TOOK IT, DIDN'T THEY?
OUR FAMILY TREASURE...
OKAY!
TIME TO GO TO THE BOUNDARY!!
PEOPLE OF THIS SHRINE, I'M SO SORRY...

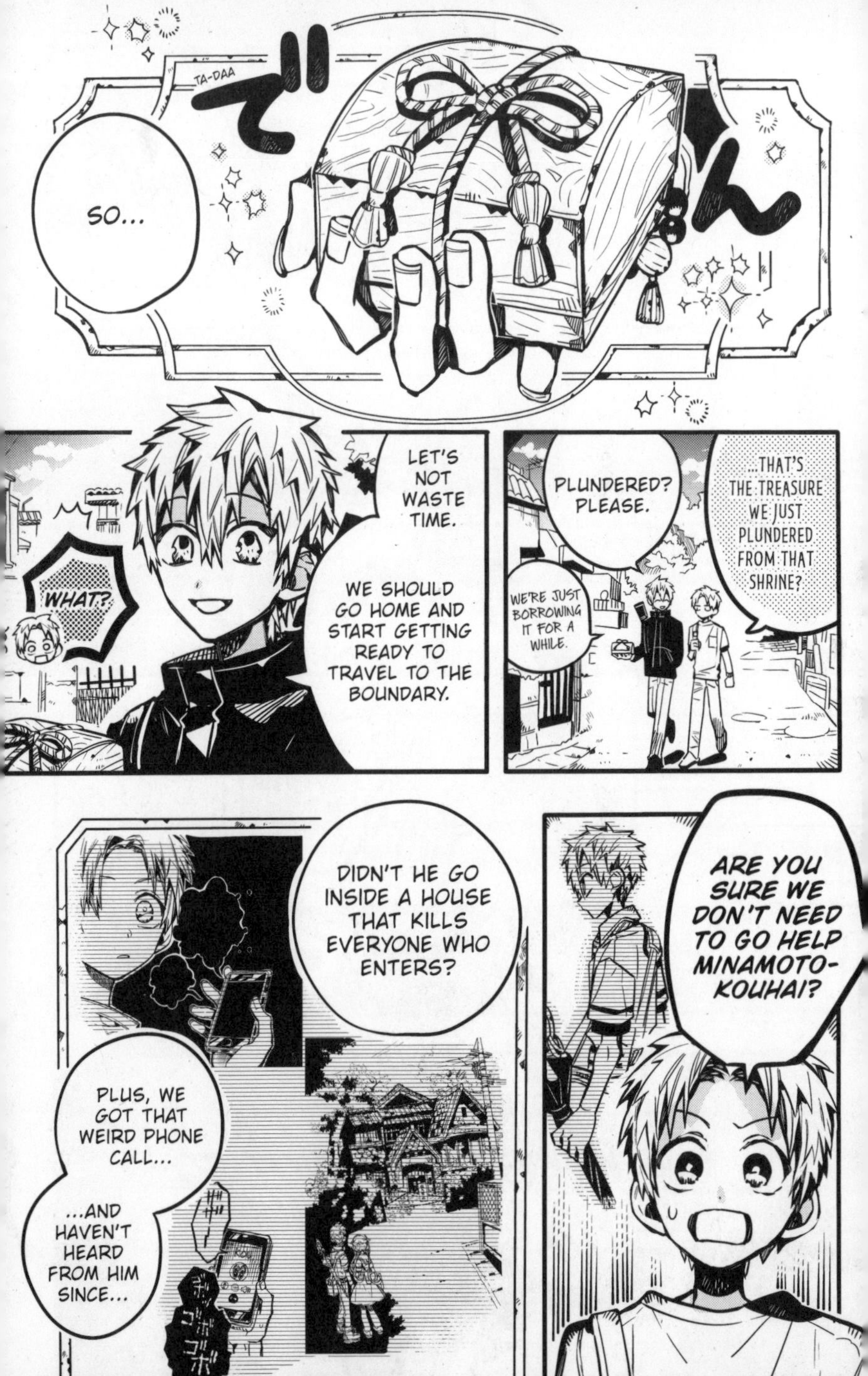
TA-DAA
SO...
...THAT'S THE TREASURE WE JUST PLUNDERED FROM THAT SHRINE?
PLUNDERED? PLEASE.
WE'RE JUST BORROWING IT FOR A WHILE.
LET'S NOT WASTE TIME.
WE SHOULD GO HOME AND START GETTING READY TO TRAVEL TO THE BOUNDARY.
WHAT?
ARE YOU SURE WE DON'T NEED TO GO HELP MINAMOTO-KOUHAI?
DIDN'T HE GO INSIDE A HOUSE THAT KILLS EVERYONE WHO ENTERS?
PLUS, WE GOT THAT WEIRD PHONE CALL...
...AND HAVEN'T HEARD FROM HIM SINCE...

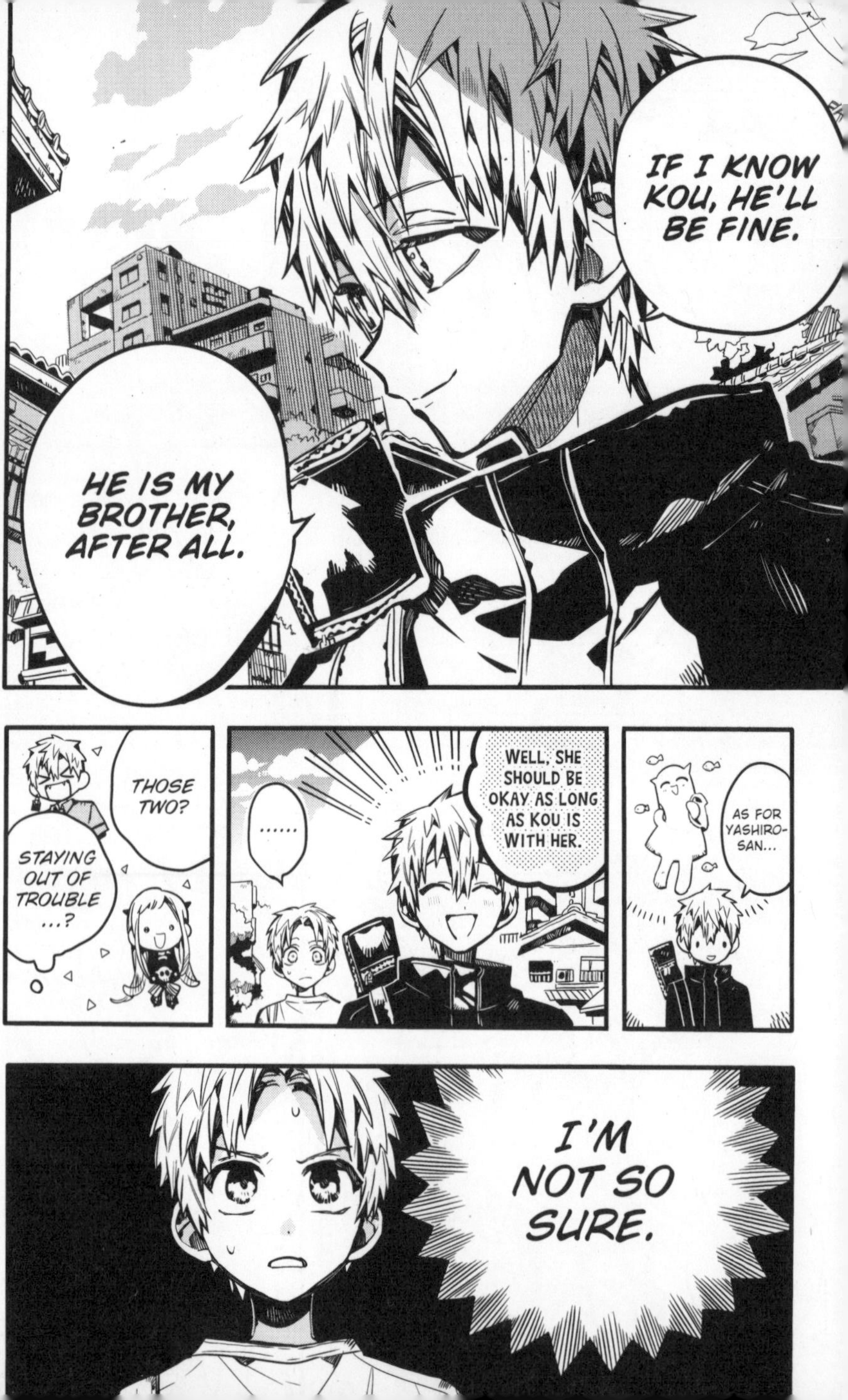
IF I KNOW KOU, HE'LL BE FINE.
HE IS MY BROTHER, AFTER ALL.
AS FOR YASHIRO-SAN...
WELL, SHE SHOULD BE OKAY AS LONG AS KOU IS WITH HER.
......
THOSE TWO?
STAYING OUT OF TROUBLE ...?
I'M NOT SO SURE.

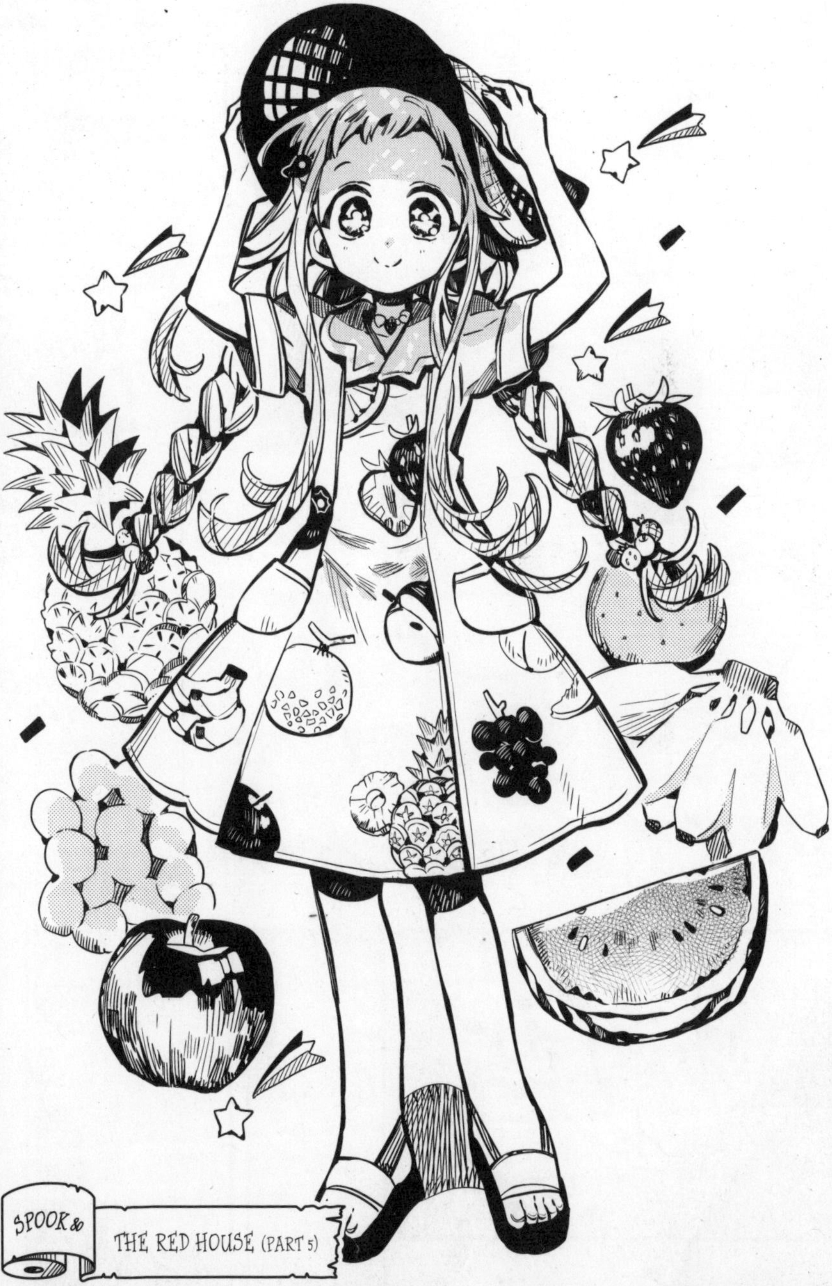

SPOOK 80 THE RED HOUSE (PART 5)

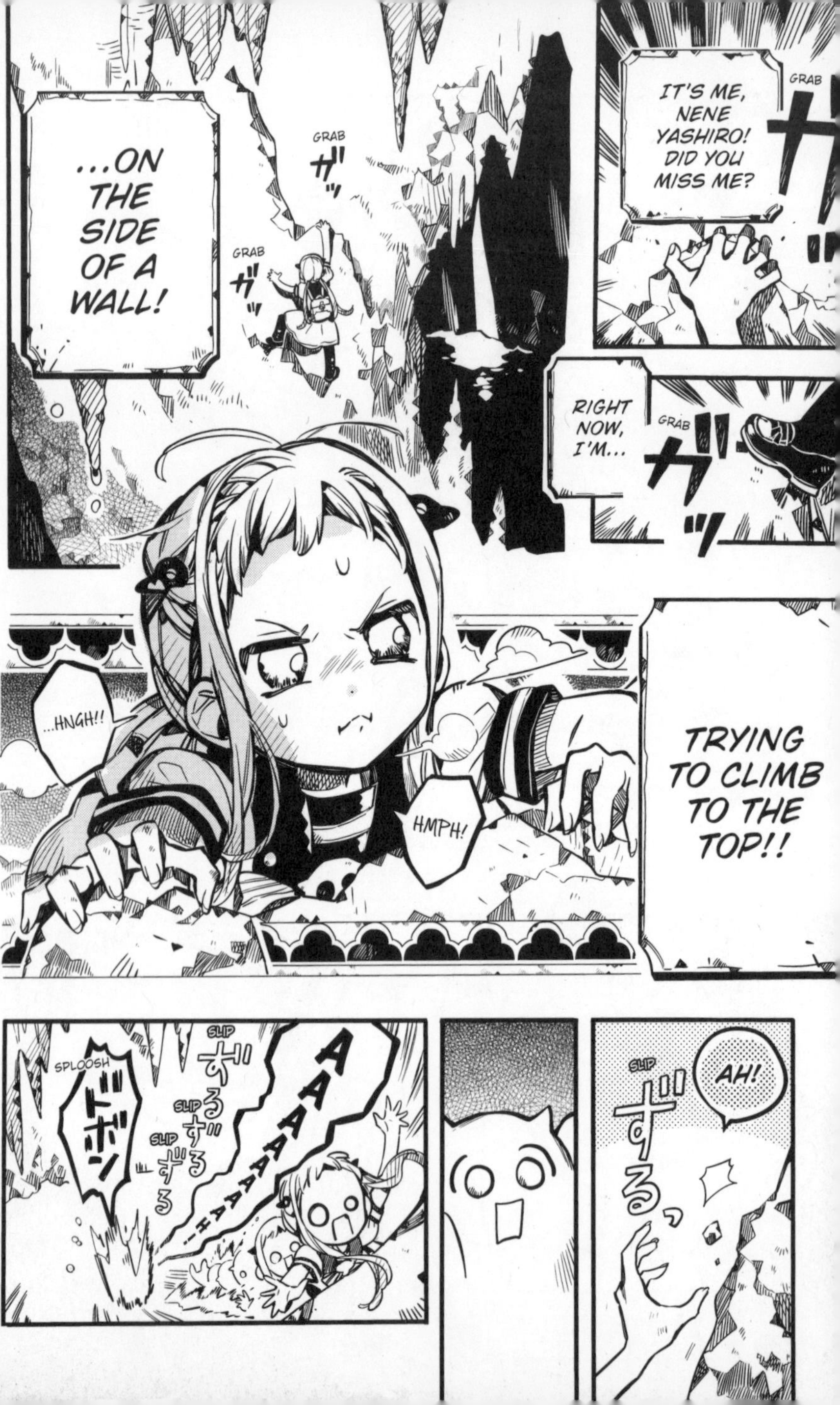

IT'S ME, NENE YASHIRO! DID YOU MISS ME?
GRAB
ガッ
RIGHT NOW, I'M...
GRAB
ガッ
...ON THE SIDE OF A WALL!
GRAB
ガッ
GRAB
ガッ
TRYING TO CLIMB TO THE TOP!!
HMPH!
...HNGH!!
SLIP
ずるっ
AH!
SLIP
ずるっ
SLIP
ずる
SLIP
ずる
AAAAAAAAAH--!
SPLOOSH
ドボン

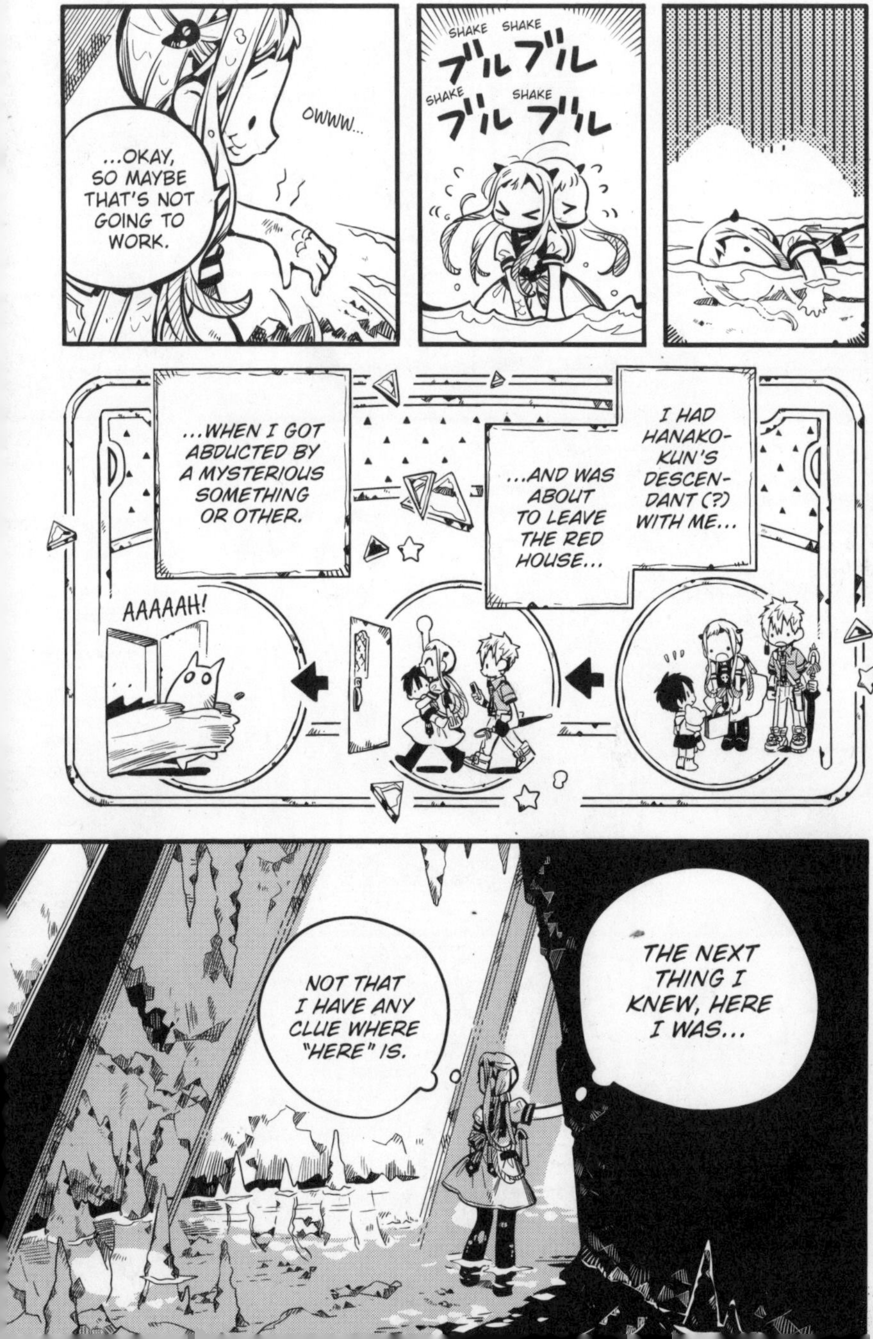
SHAKE SHAKE
ブルブル
SHAKE SHAKE
ブルブル
OWWW...
...OKAY, SO MAYBE THAT'S NOT GOING TO WORK.
I HAD HANAKO-KUN'S DESCENDANT (?) WITH ME...
...AND WAS ABOUT TO LEAVE THE RED HOUSE...
...WHEN I GOT ABDUCTED BY A MYSTERIOUS SOMETHING OR OTHER.
AAAAAH!
THE NEXT THING I KNEW, HERE I WAS...
NOT THAT I HAVE ANY CLUE WHERE "HERE" IS.

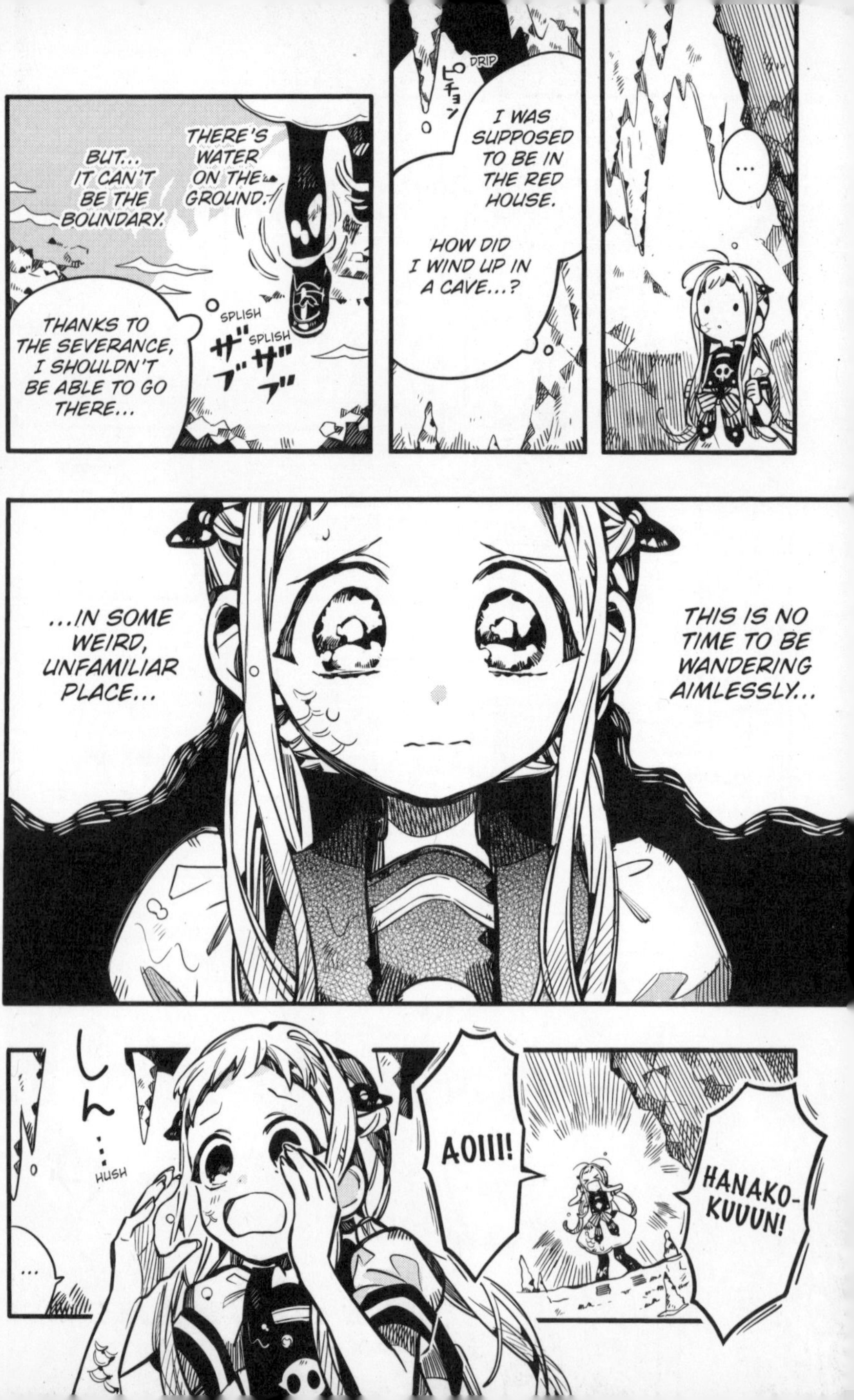

...
ピチョン
DRIP
I WAS SUPPOSED TO BE IN THE RED HOUSE.
HOW DID I WIND UP IN A CAVE...?
THERE'S WATER ON THE GROUND.
BUT... IT CAN'T BE THE BOUNDARY.
SPLISH
ザブ
SPLISH
ザブ
THANKS TO THE SEVERANCE, I SHOULDN'T BE ABLE TO GO THERE...
THIS IS NO TIME TO BE WANDERING AIMLESSLY...
...IN SOME WEIRD, UNFAMILIAR PLACE...
HANAKO-KUUUN!
AOIIII!
しん...
HUSH
...

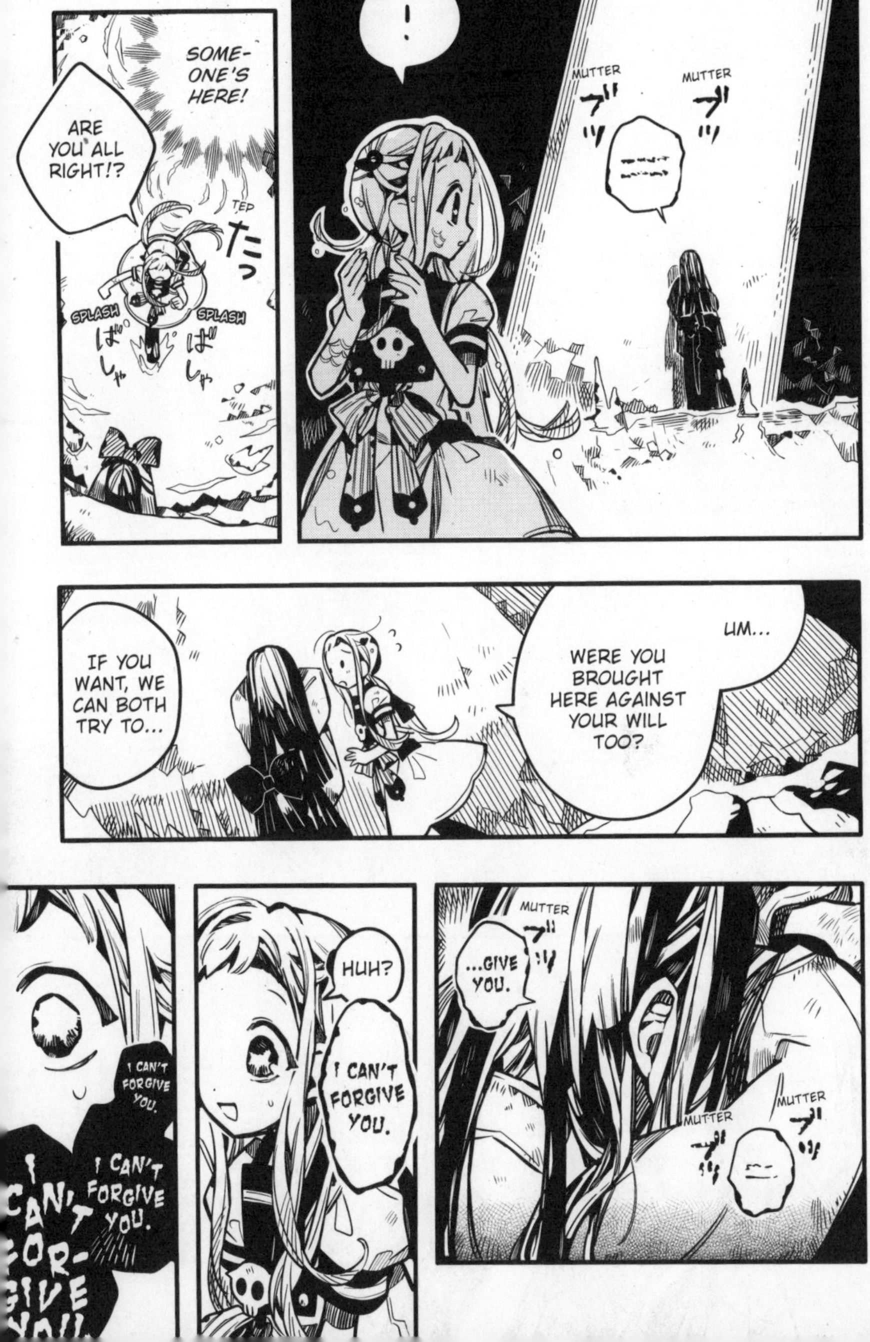
!
MUTTER
ブツ
MUTTER
ブツ
SOME-ONE'S HERE!
ARE YOU ALL RIGHT!?
TEP
たっ
SPLASH
ばしゃ
SPLASH
ばしゃ
UM...
WERE YOU BROUGHT HERE AGAINST YOUR WILL TOO?
IF YOU WANT, WE CAN BOTH TRY TO...
MUTTER
ブツ
...GIVE YOU.
MUTTER
ブツ
MUTTER
ブツ
HUH?
I CAN'T FORGIVE YOU.
I CAN'T FORGIVE YOU.
I CAN'T FORGIVE YOU.
I CAN'T FOR-GIVE

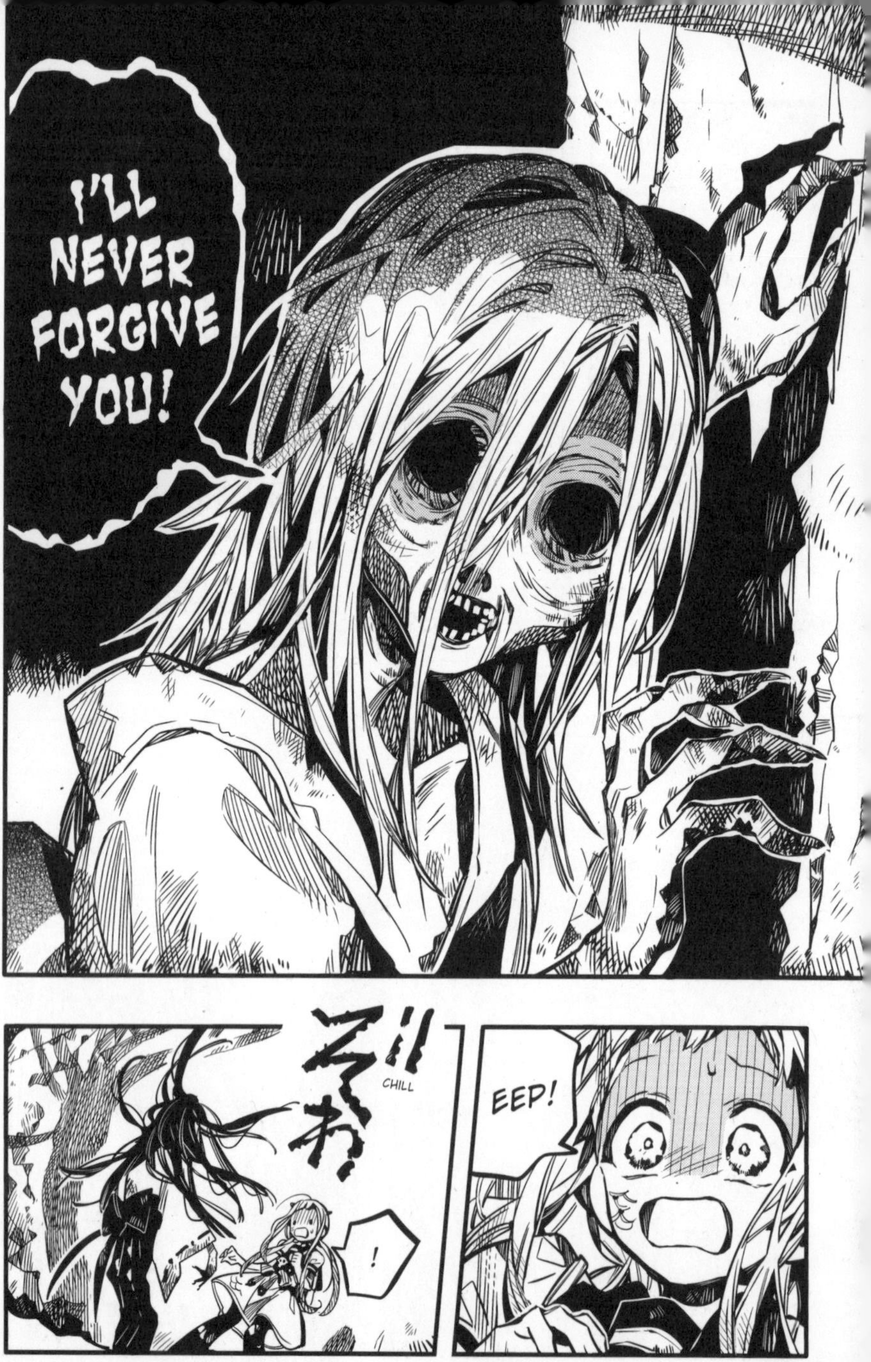
I'LL NEVER FORGIVE YOU!
EEP!
ぞわ
CHILL
!

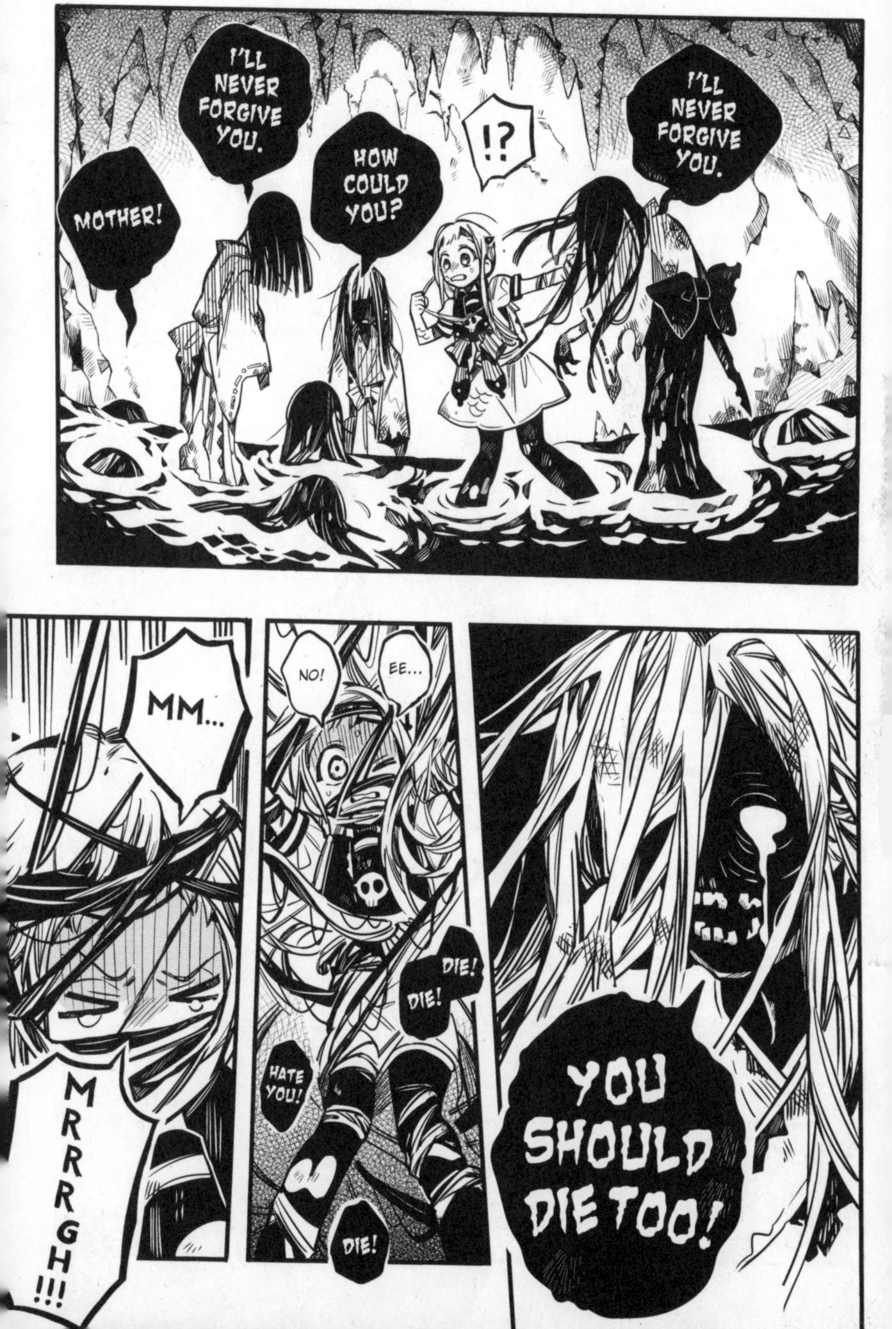
I'LL NEVER FORGIVE YOU.
!?
HOW COULD YOU?
I'LL NEVER FORGIVE YOU.
MOTHER!
YOU SHOULD DIE TOO!
EE...
NO!
DIE!
DIE!
HATE YOU!
DIE!
MM...
MRRRGH!!!

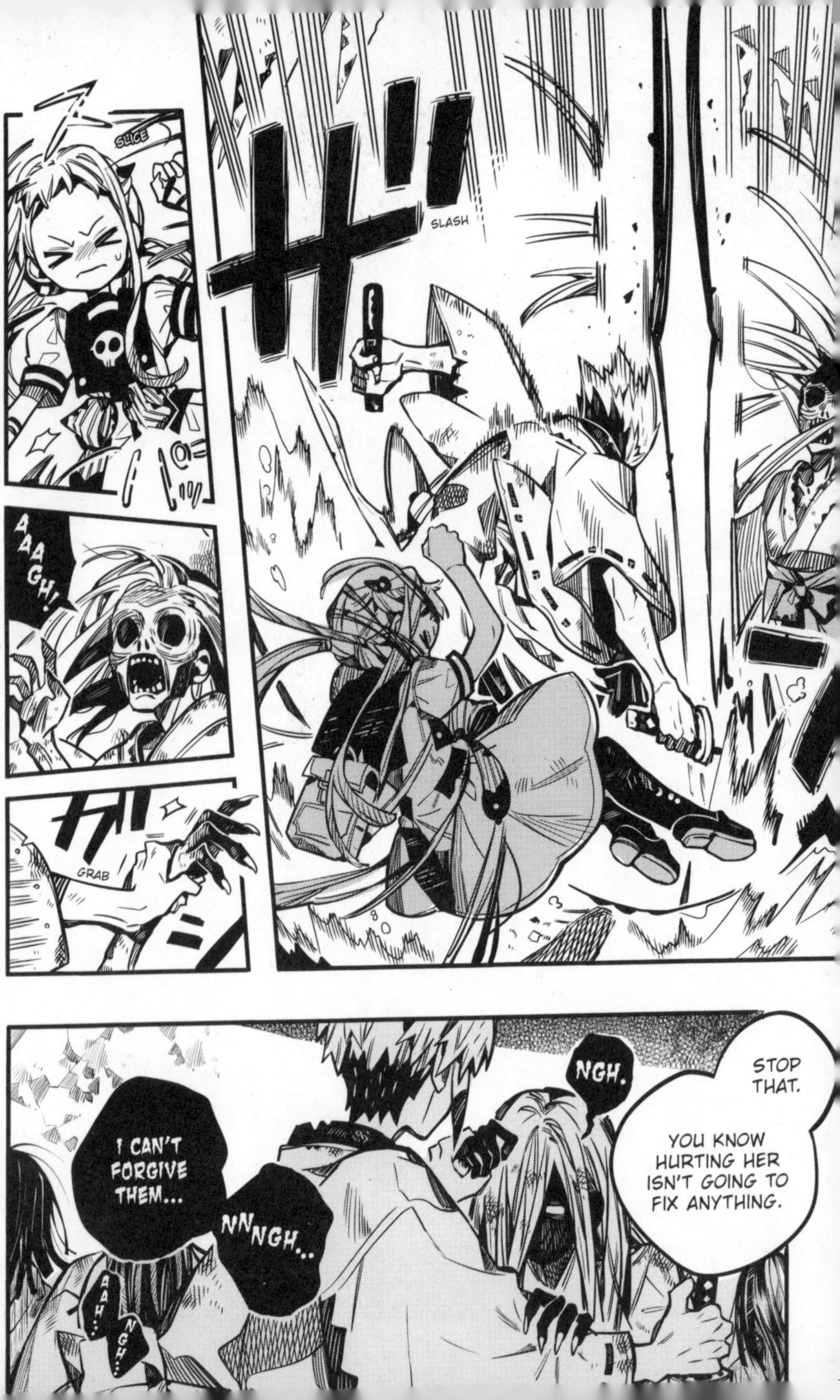
SLASH
SLICE
AAAGH!
GRAB
STOP THAT.
YOU KNOW HURTING HER ISN'T GOING TO FIX ANYTHING.
NGH.
I CAN'T FORGIVE THEM...
NNNGH...
AAH... NGH...

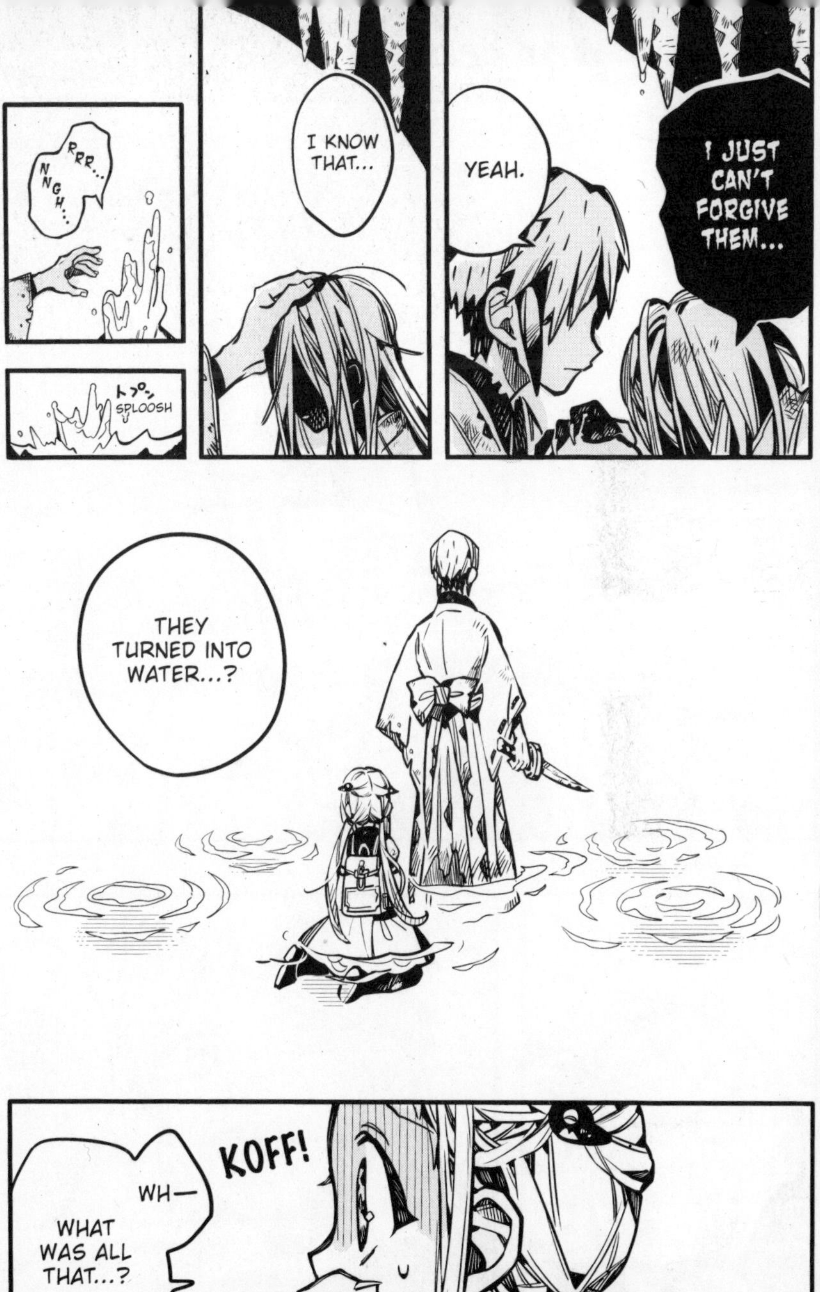

I JUST CAN'T FORGIVE THEM...
YEAH.
I KNOW THAT...
RRR... NNGH...
SPLOOSH
THEY TURNED INTO WATER...?
KOFF!
WH— WHAT WAS ALL THAT...?

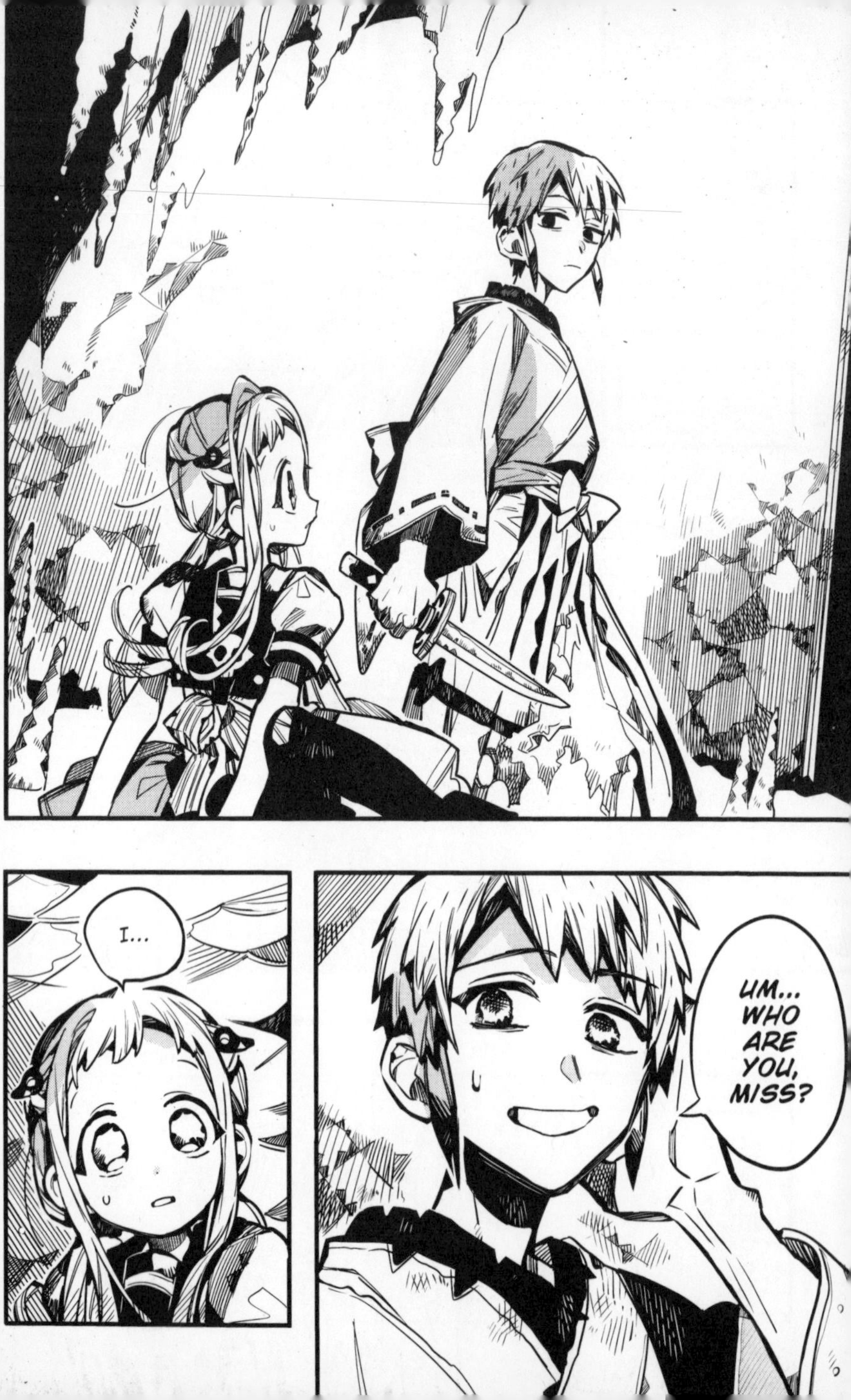
UM... WHO ARE YOU, MISS?
I...

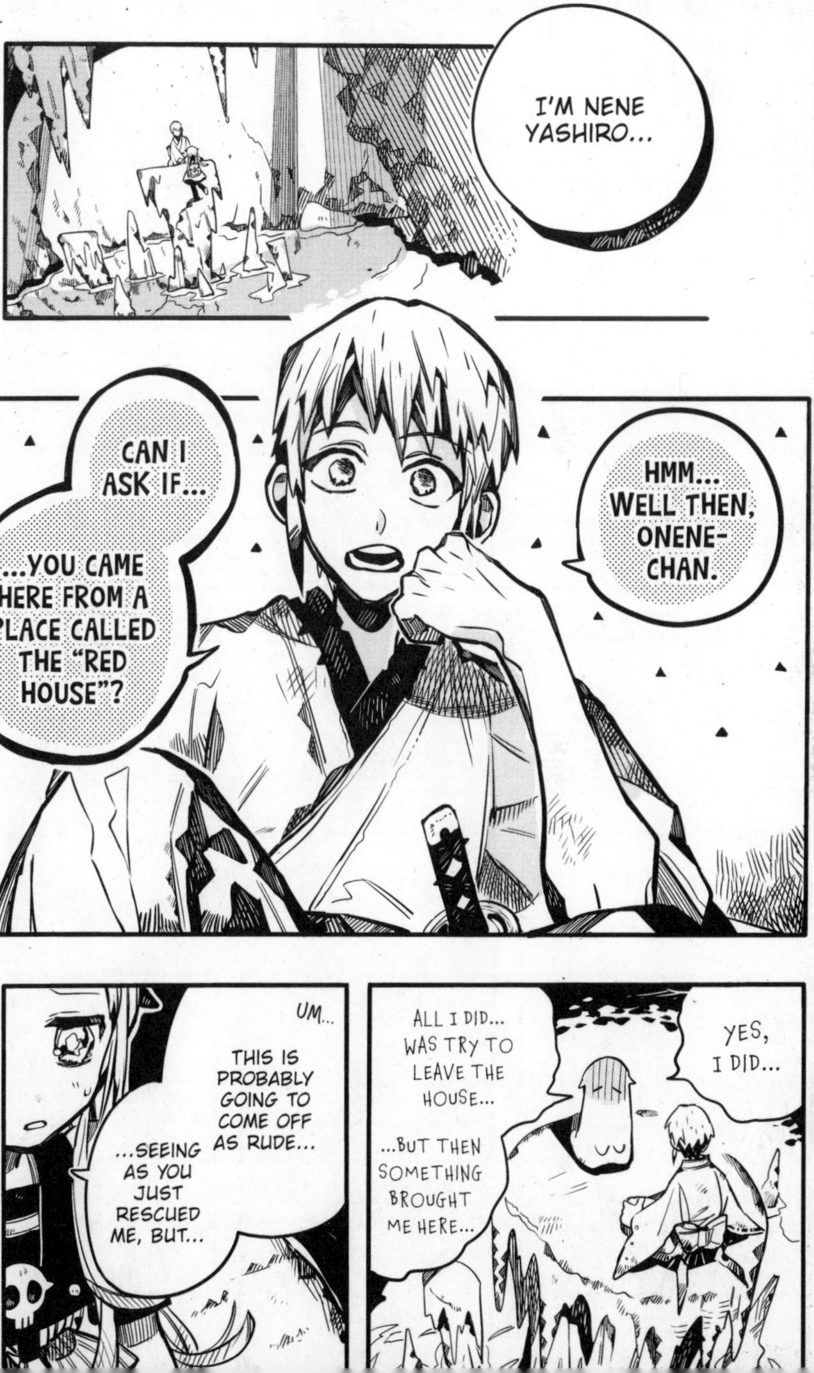
I'M NENE YASHIRO...
HMM... WELL THEN, ONENE-CHAN.
CAN I ASK IF...
...YOU CAME HERE FROM A PLACE CALLED THE "RED HOUSE"?
YES, I DID...
ALL I DID... WAS TRY TO LEAVE THE HOUSE...
...BUT THEN SOMETHING BROUGHT ME HERE...
UM...
THIS IS PROBABLY GOING TO COME OFF AS RUDE...
...SEEING AS YOU JUST RESCUED ME, BUT...

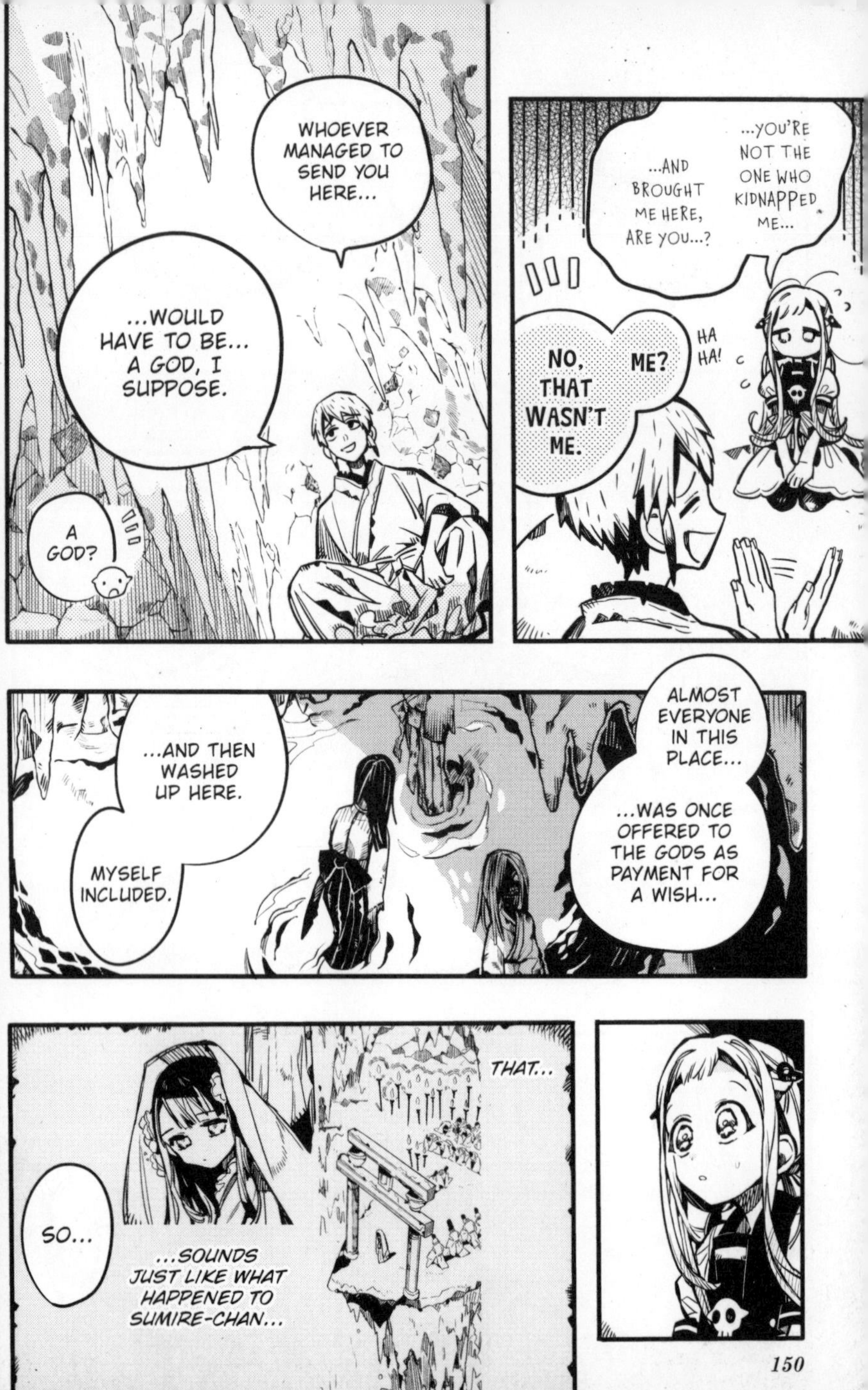
...YOU'RE NOT THE ONE WHO KIDNAPPED ME...
...AND BROUGHT ME HERE, ARE YOU...?
ME?
HA HA!
NO, THAT WASN'T ME.
WHOEVER MANAGED TO SEND YOU HERE...
...WOULD HAVE TO BE... A GOD, I SUPPOSE.
A GOD?
ALMOST EVERYONE IN THIS PLACE...
...WAS ONCE OFFERED TO THE GODS AS PAYMENT FOR A WISH...
...AND THEN WASHED UP HERE.
MYSELF INCLUDED.
THAT...
...SOUNDS JUST LIKE WHAT HAPPENED TO SUMIRE-CHAN...
SO...

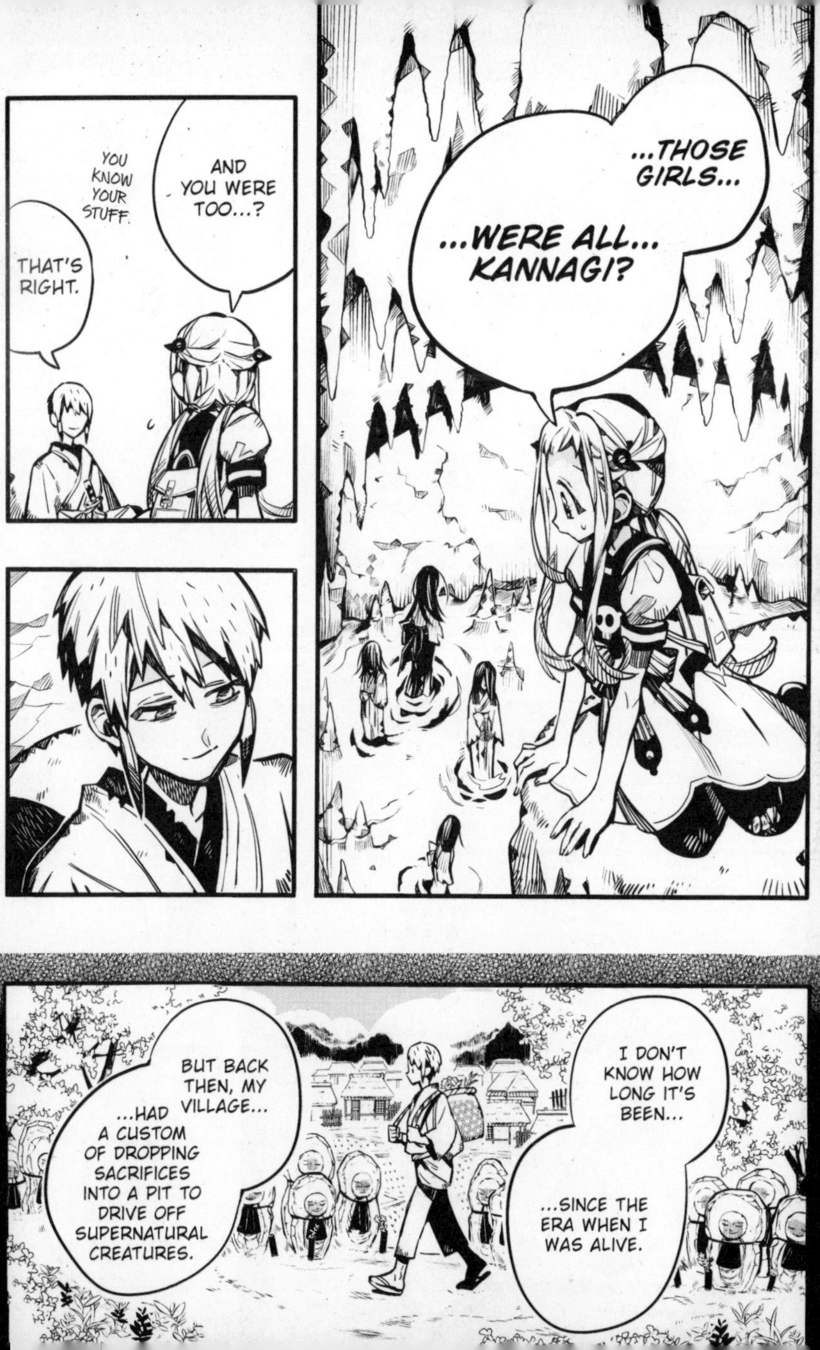
...THOSE GIRLS...
...WERE ALL... KANNAGI?
AND YOU WERE TOO...?
YOU KNOW YOUR STUFF.
THAT'S RIGHT.
I DON'T KNOW HOW LONG IT'S BEEN...
...SINCE THE ERA WHEN I WAS ALIVE.
BUT BACK THEN, MY VILLAGE...
...HAD A CUSTOM OF DROPPING SACRIFICES INTO A PIT TO DRIVE OFF SUPERNATURAL CREATURES.

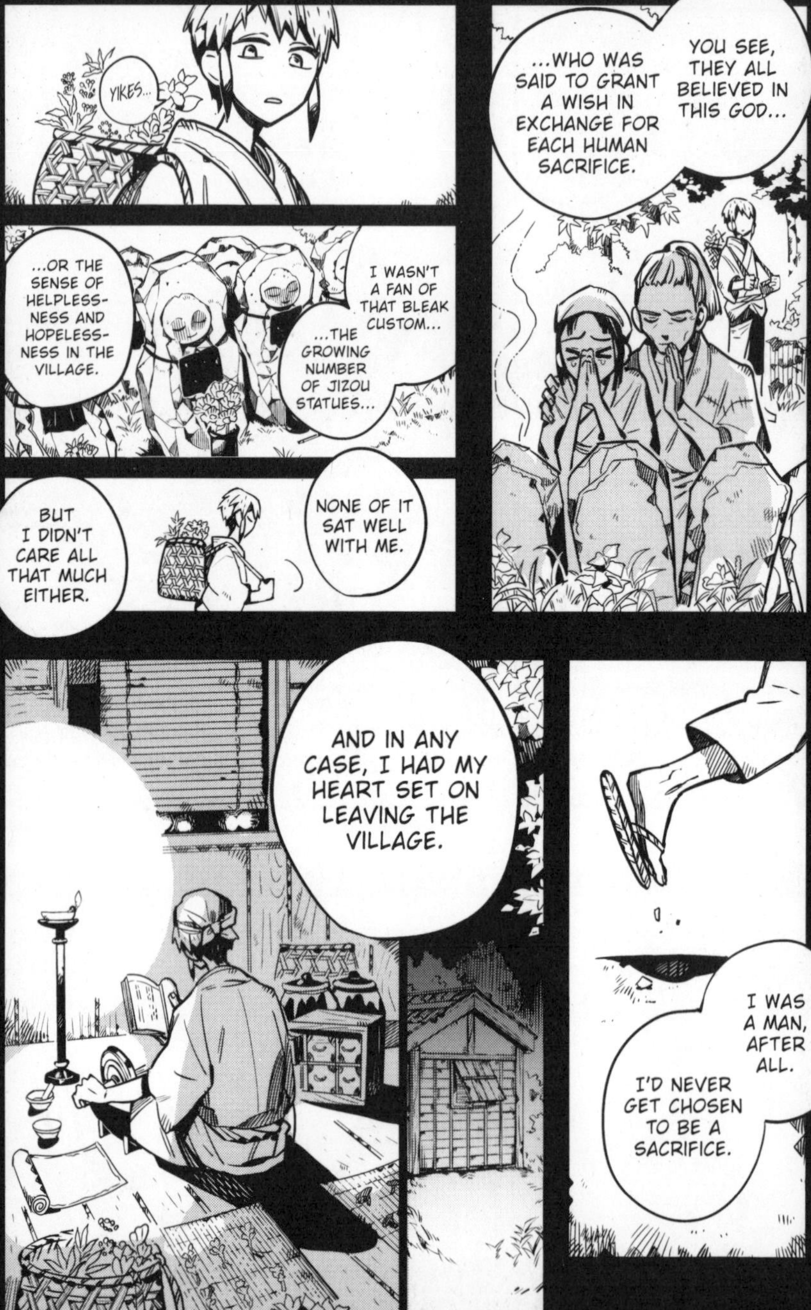
YOU SEE, THEY ALL BELIEVED IN THIS GOD...
...WHO WAS SAID TO GRANT A WISH IN EXCHANGE FOR EACH HUMAN SACRIFICE.
YIKES...
I WASN'T A FAN OF THAT BLEAK CUSTOM...
...THE GROWING NUMBER OF JIZOU STATUES...
...OR THE SENSE OF HELPLESSNESS AND HOPELESSNESS IN THE VILLAGE.
NONE OF IT SAT WELL WITH ME.
BUT I DIDN'T CARE ALL THAT MUCH EITHER.
I WAS A MAN, AFTER ALL.
I'D NEVER GET CHOSEN TO BE A SACRIFICE.
AND IN ANY CASE, I HAD MY HEART SET ON LEAVING THE VILLAGE.

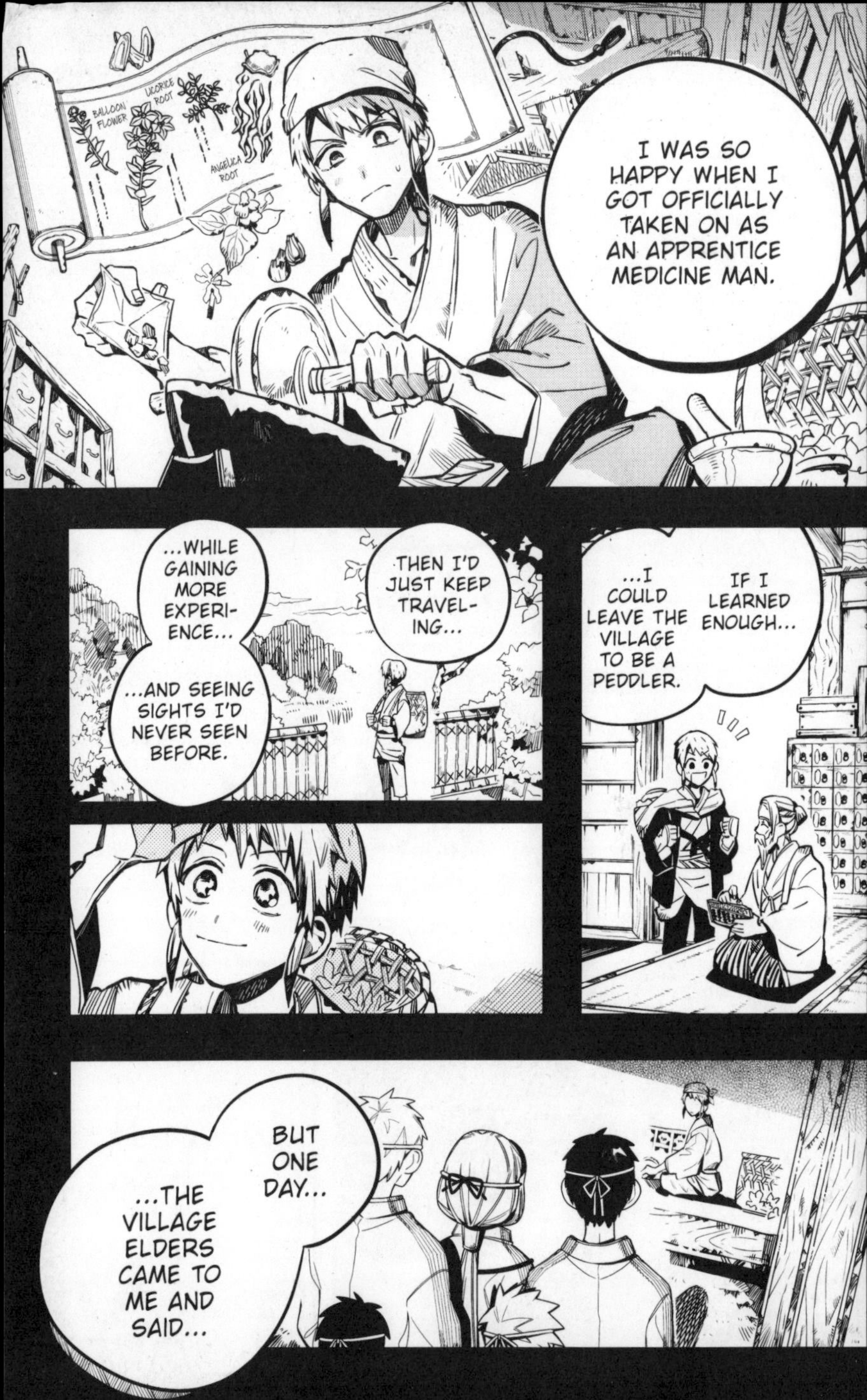

BALLOON FLOWER
LICORICE ROOT
ANGELICA ROOT
I WAS SO HAPPY WHEN I GOT OFFICIALLY TAKEN ON AS AN APPRENTICE MEDICINE MAN.
IF I LEARNED ENOUGH...
...I COULD LEAVE THE VILLAGE TO BE A PEDDLER.
THEN I'D JUST KEEP TRAVEL-ING...
...WHILE GAINING MORE EXPERI-ENCE...
...AND SEEING SIGHTS I'D NEVER SEEN BEFORE.
BUT ONE DAY...
...THE VILLAGE ELDERS CAME TO ME AND SAID...

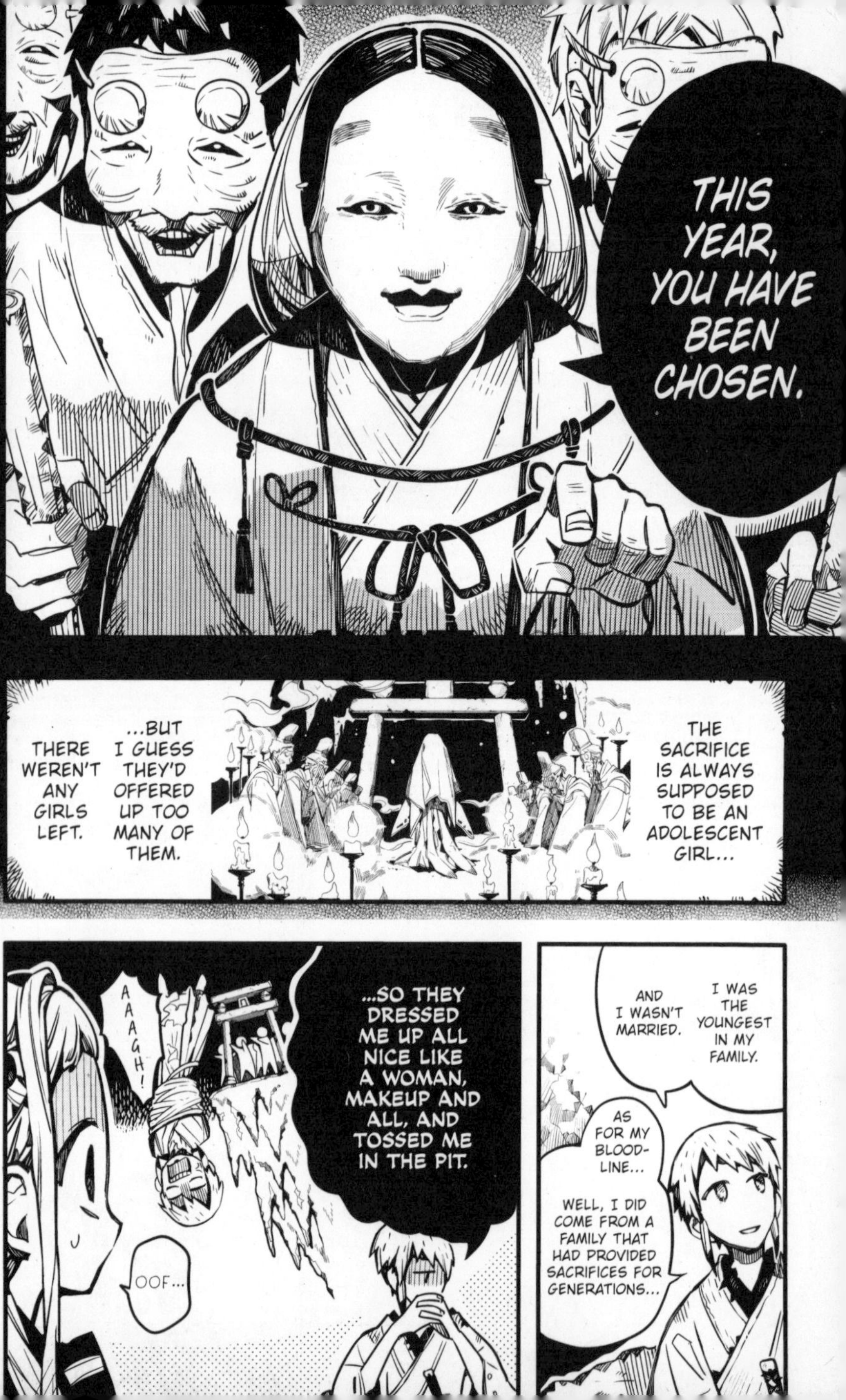
THIS YEAR, YOU HAVE BEEN CHOSEN.
THE SACRIFICE IS ALWAYS SUPPOSED TO BE AN ADOLESCENT GIRL...
...BUT I GUESS THEY'D OFFERED UP TOO MANY OF THEM.
THERE WEREN'T ANY GIRLS LEFT.
I WAS THE YOUNGEST IN MY FAMILY.
AND I WASN'T MARRIED.
AS FOR MY BLOOD-LINE...
WELL, I DID COME FROM A FAMILY THAT HAD PROVIDED SACRIFICES FOR GENERATIONS...
...SO THEY DRESSED ME UP ALL NICE LIKE A WOMAN, MAKEUP AND ALL, AND TOSSED ME IN THE PIT.
AAAGH!
OOF...

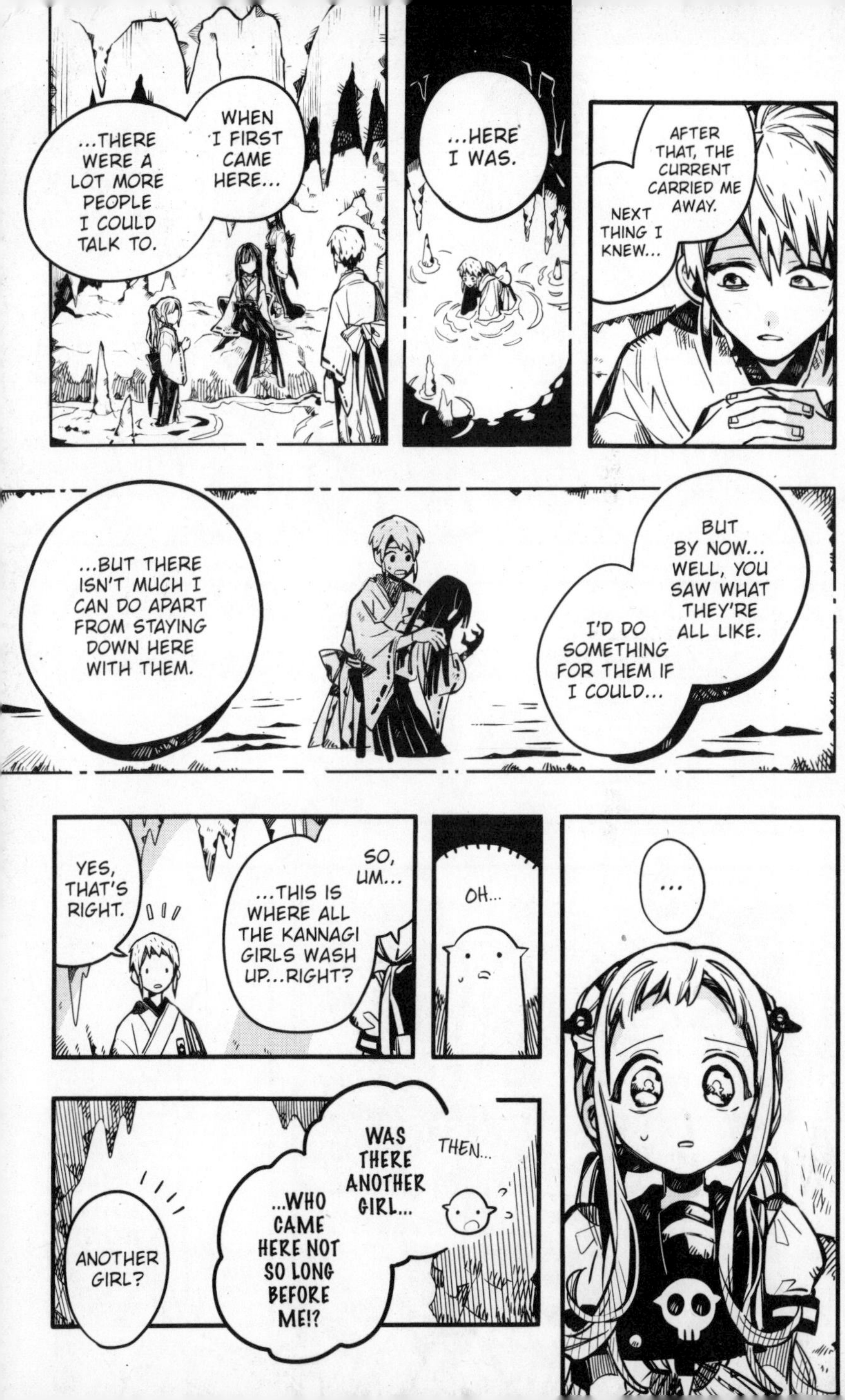
AFTER THAT, THE CURRENT CARRIED ME AWAY.
NEXT THING I KNEW...
...HERE I WAS.
WHEN I FIRST CAME HERE...
...THERE WERE A LOT MORE PEOPLE I COULD TALK TO.
BUT BY NOW... WELL, YOU SAW WHAT THEY'RE ALL LIKE.
I'D DO SOMETHING FOR THEM IF I COULD...
...BUT THERE ISN'T MUCH I CAN DO APART FROM STAYING DOWN HERE WITH THEM.
...
OH...
SO, UM...
...THIS IS WHERE ALL THE KANNAGI GIRLS WASH UP...RIGHT?
YES, THAT'S RIGHT.
THEN...
WAS THERE ANOTHER GIRL...
...WHO CAME HERE NOT SO LONG BEFORE ME!?
ANOTHER GIRL?

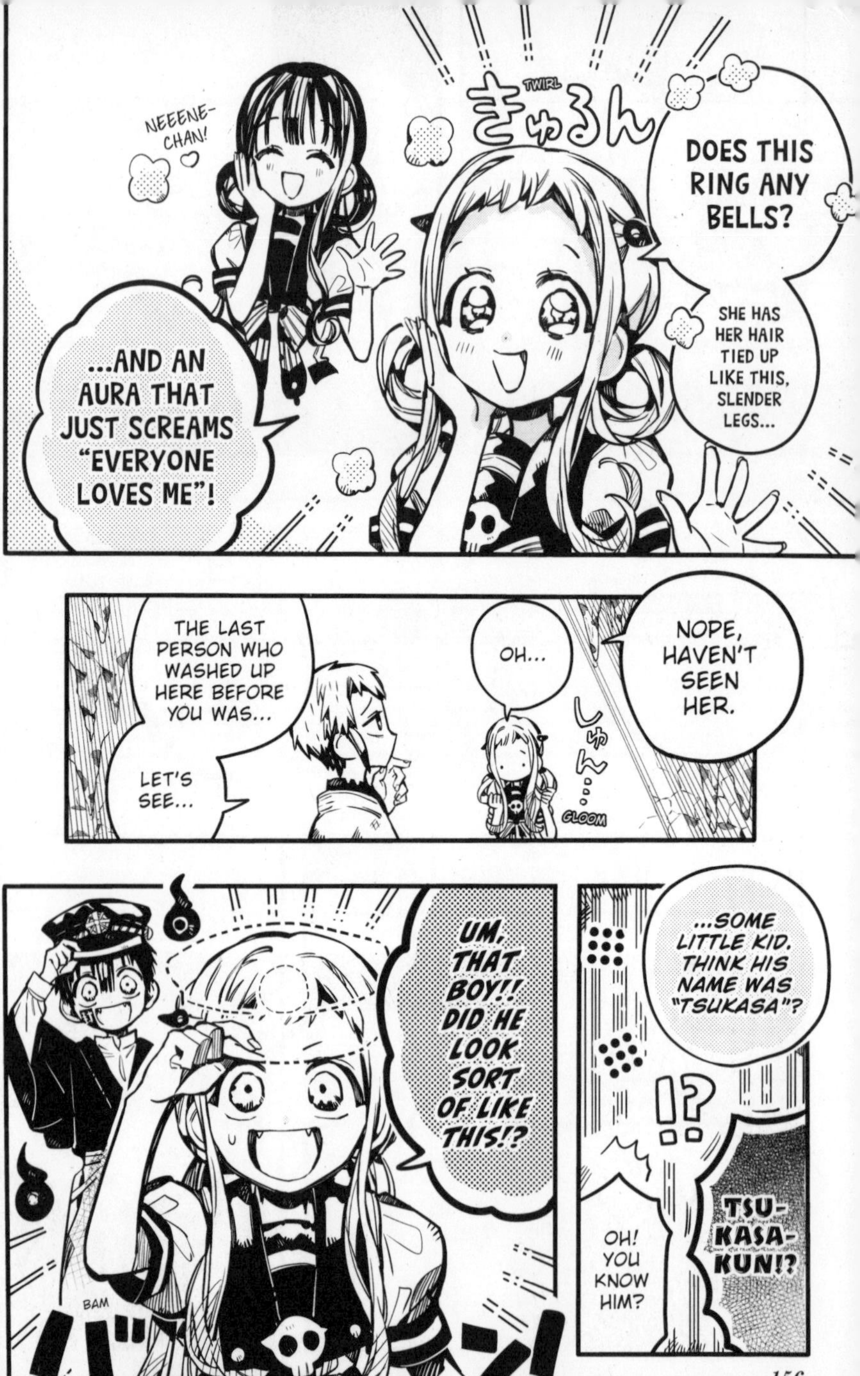
TWIRL
きゅるん
DOES THIS RING ANY BELLS?
SHE HAS HER HAIR TIED UP LIKE THIS, SLENDER LEGS...
...AND AN AURA THAT JUST SCREAMS "EVERYONE LOVES ME"!
NEEENE-CHAN!
NOPE, HAVEN'T SEEN HER.
OH...
しゅん。。。
GLOOM
THE LAST PERSON WHO WASHED UP HERE BEFORE YOU WAS...
LET'S SEE...
...SOME LITTLE KID. THINK HIS NAME WAS "TSUKASA"?
!?
TSU-KASA-KUN!?
OH! YOU KNOW HIM?
UM, THAT BOY!! DID HE LOOK SORT OF LIKE THIS!?
BAM
バーン!

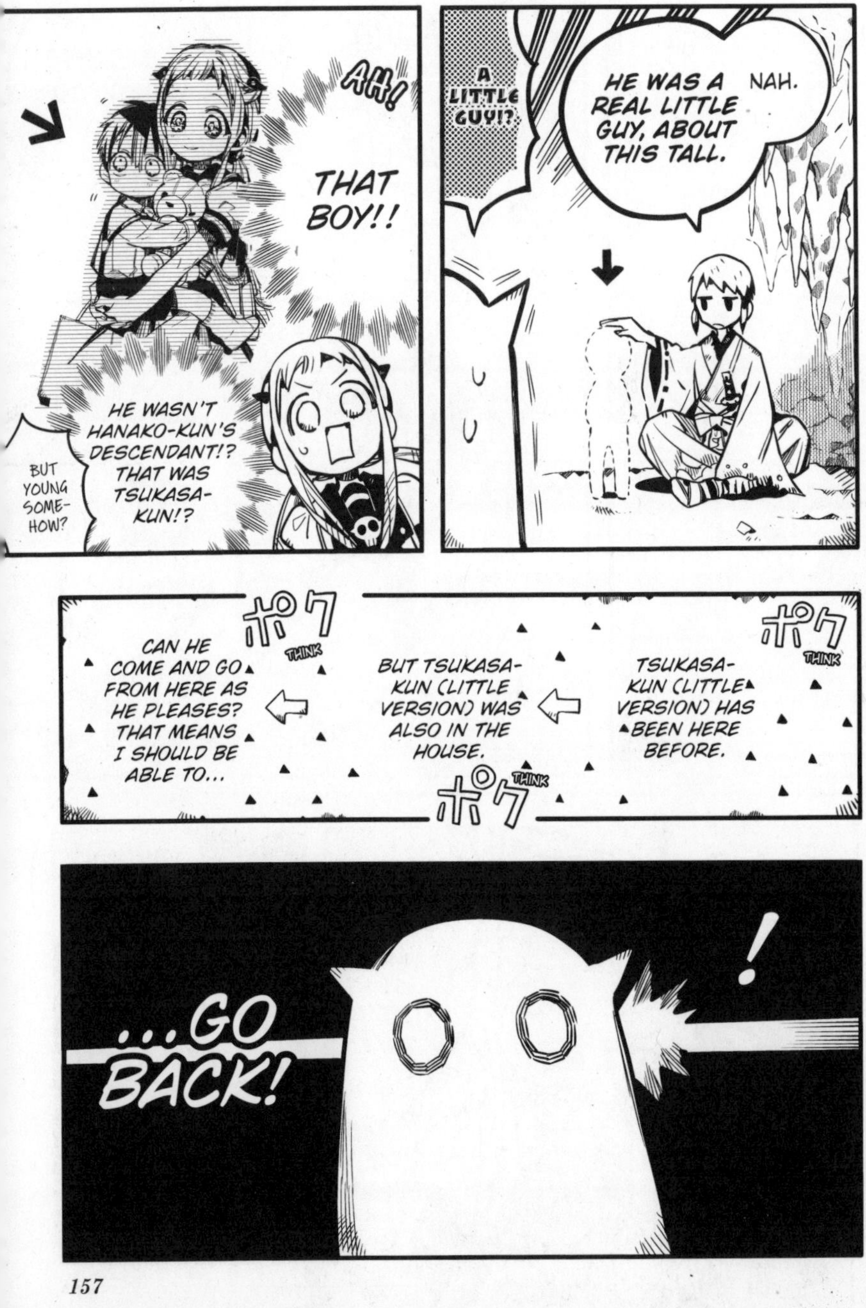
NAH.
HE WAS A REAL LITTLE GUY, ABOUT THIS TALL.
A LITTLE GUY!?
AH!
THAT BOY!!
HE WASN'T HANAKO-KUN'S DESCENDANT!? THAT WAS TSUKASA-KUN!?
BUT YOUNG SOMEHOW?
ポク
THINK
TSUKASA-KUN (LITTLE VERSION) HAS BEEN HERE BEFORE.
ポク
THINK
BUT TSUKASA-KUN (LITTLE VERSION) WAS ALSO IN THE HOUSE.
ポク
THINK
CAN HE COME AND GO FROM HERE AS HE PLEASES? THAT MEANS I SHOULD BE ABLE TO...
!
...GO BACK!

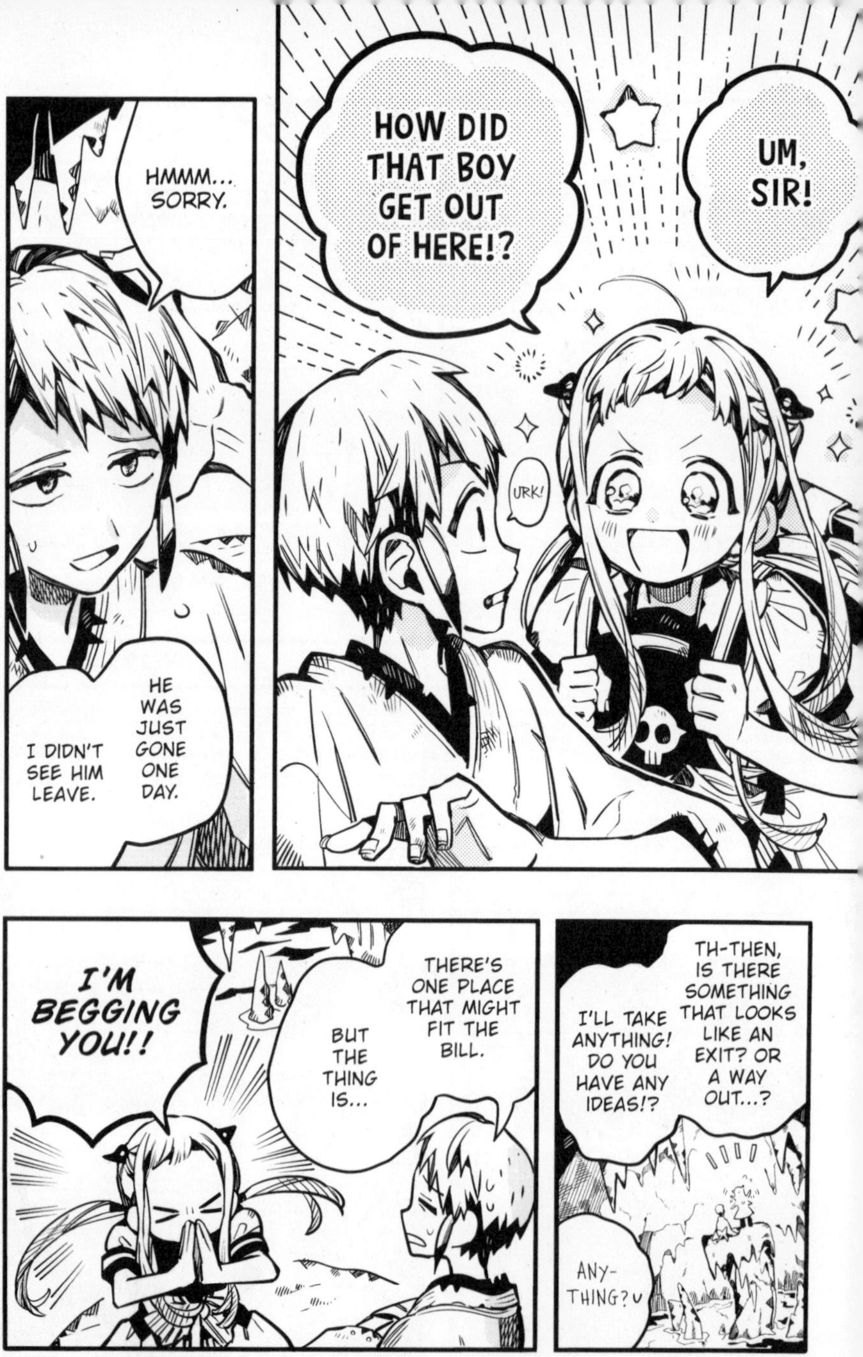
UM, SIR!
HOW DID THAT BOY GET OUT OF HERE!?
URK!
HMMM... SORRY.
HE WAS JUST GONE ONE DAY.
I DIDN'T SEE HIM LEAVE.
TH-THEN, IS THERE SOMETHING THAT LOOKS LIKE AN EXIT? OR A WAY OUT...?
I'LL TAKE ANYTHING! DO YOU HAVE ANY IDEAS!?
ANY-THING?
THERE'S ONE PLACE THAT MIGHT FIT THE BILL.
BUT THE THING IS...
I'M BEGGING YOU!!

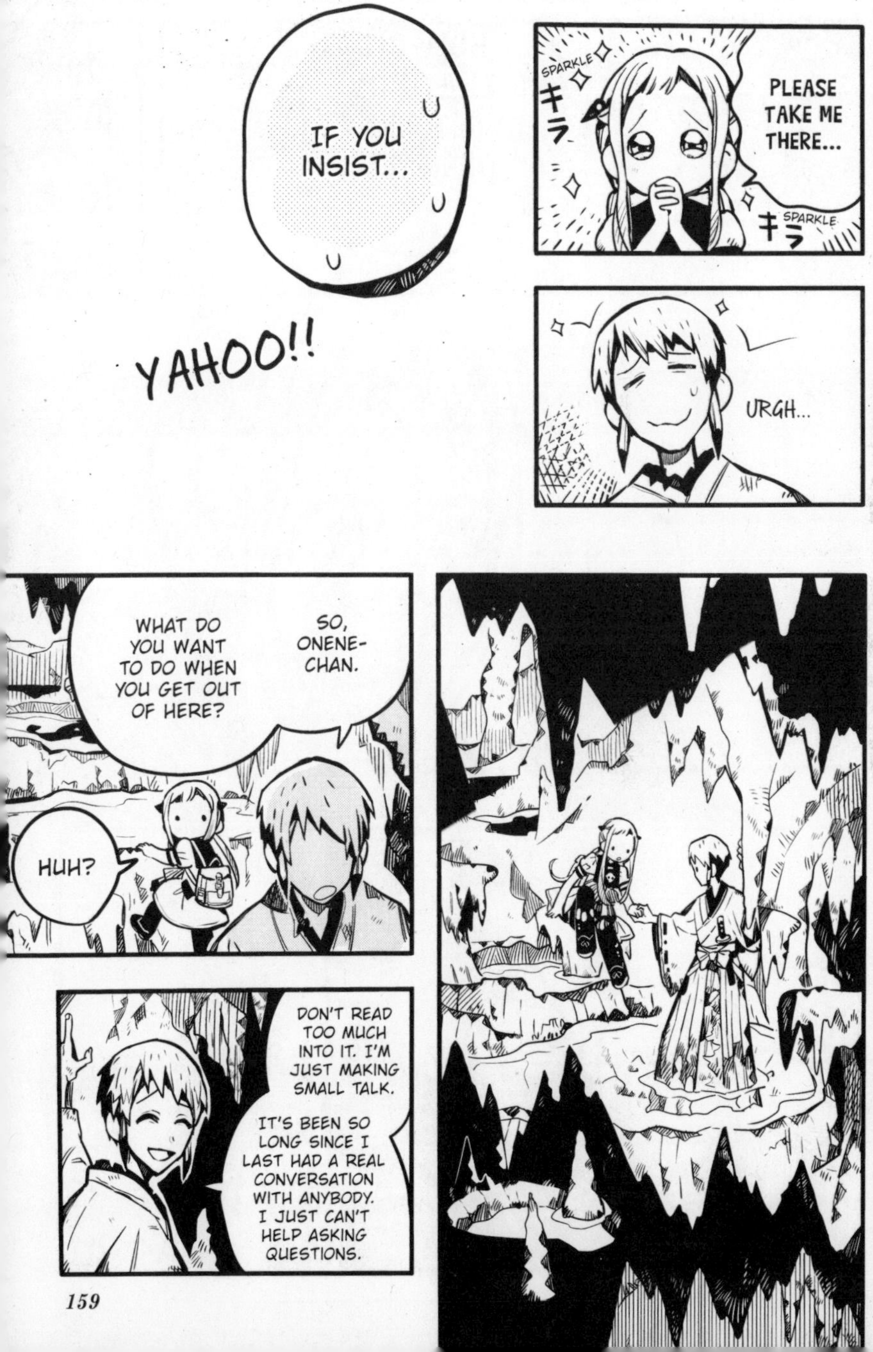
SPARKLE
キラ
PLEASE TAKE ME THERE...
キラ
SPARKLE
URGH...
IF YOU INSIST...
YAHOO!!
SO, ONENE-CHAN.
WHAT DO YOU WANT TO DO WHEN YOU GET OUT OF HERE?
HUH?
DON'T READ TOO MUCH INTO IT. I'M JUST MAKING SMALL TALK.
IT'S BEEN SO LONG SINCE I LAST HAD A REAL CONVERSATION WITH ANYBODY. I JUST CAN'T HELP ASKING QUESTIONS.

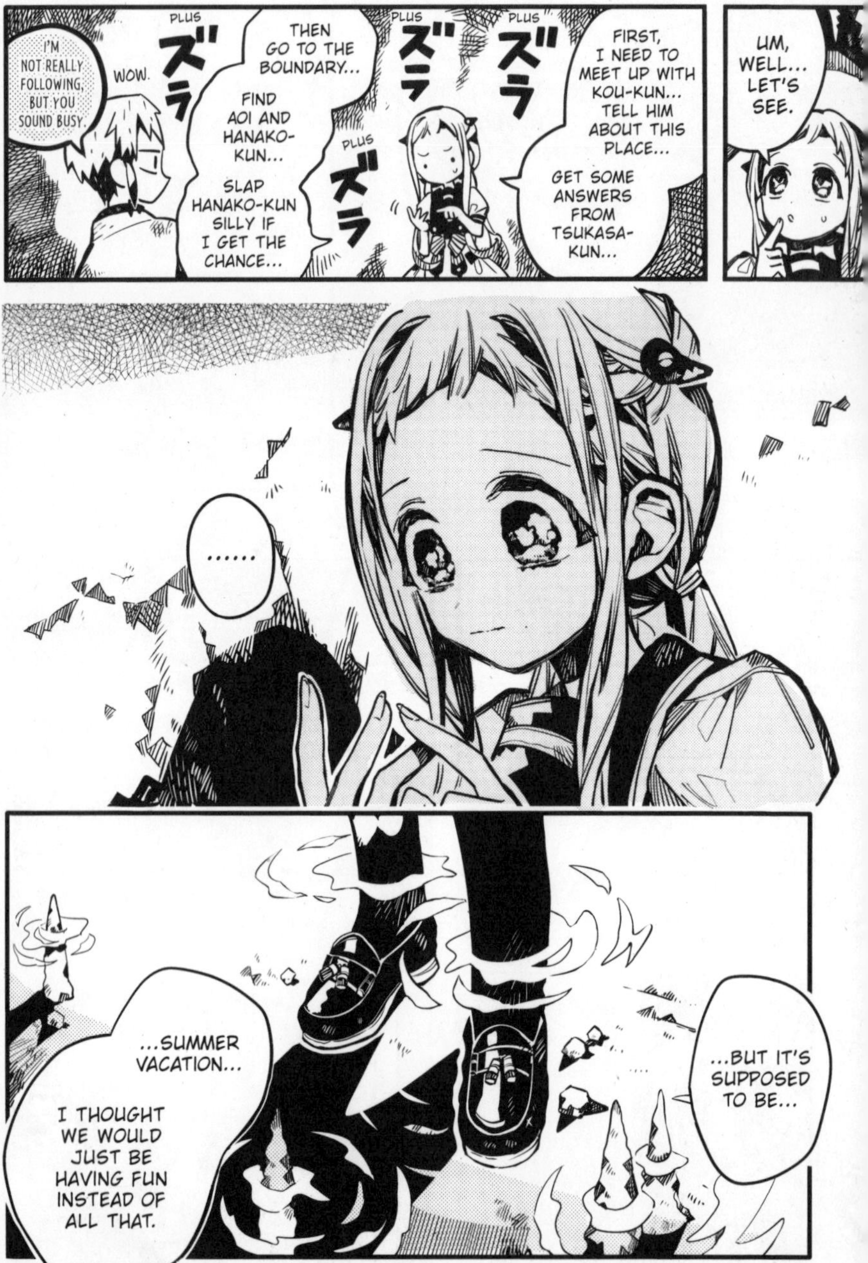
UM, WELL... LET'S SEE.
FIRST, I NEED TO MEET UP WITH KOU-KUN... TELL HIM ABOUT THIS PLACE...
GET SOME ANSWERS FROM TSUKASA-KUN...
PLUS ズラ
PLUS ズラ
THEN GO TO THE BOUNDARY...
FIND AOI AND HANAKO-KUN...
SLAP HANAKO-KUN SILLY IF I GET THE CHANCE...
PLUS ズラ
PLUS ズラ
WOW.
I'M NOT REALLY FOLLOWING, BUT YOU SOUND BUSY.
......
...BUT IT'S SUPPOSED TO BE...
...SUMMER VACATION...
I THOUGHT WE WOULD JUST BE HAVING FUN INSTEAD OF ALL THAT.

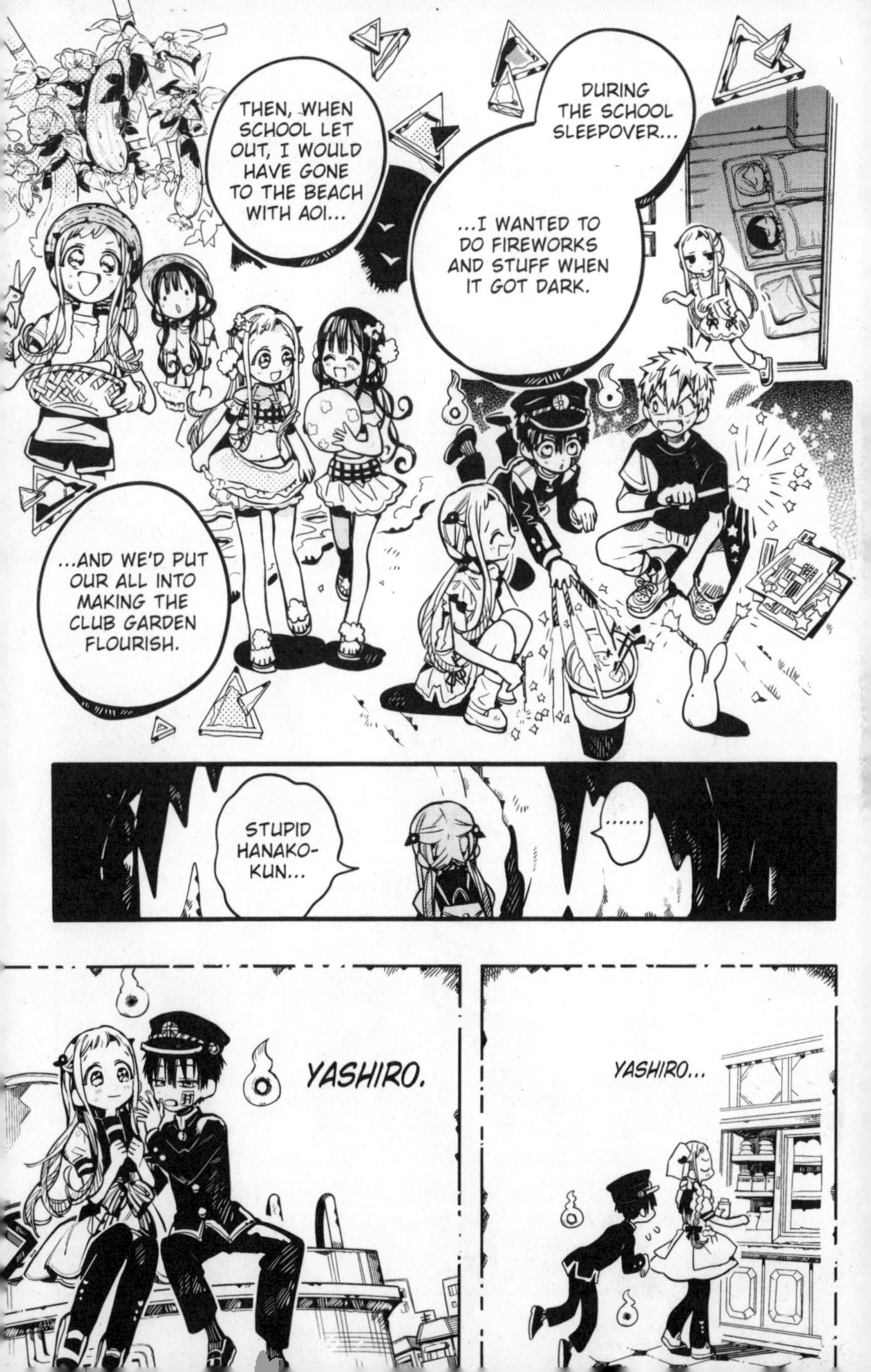
DURING THE SCHOOL SLEEPOVER...
...I WANTED TO DO FIREWORKS AND STUFF WHEN IT GOT DARK.
THEN, WHEN SCHOOL LET OUT, I WOULD HAVE GONE TO THE BEACH WITH AOI...
...AND WE'D PUT OUR ALL INTO MAKING THE CLUB GARDEN FLOURISH.
......
STUPID HANAKO-KUN...
YASHIRO...
YASHIRO.

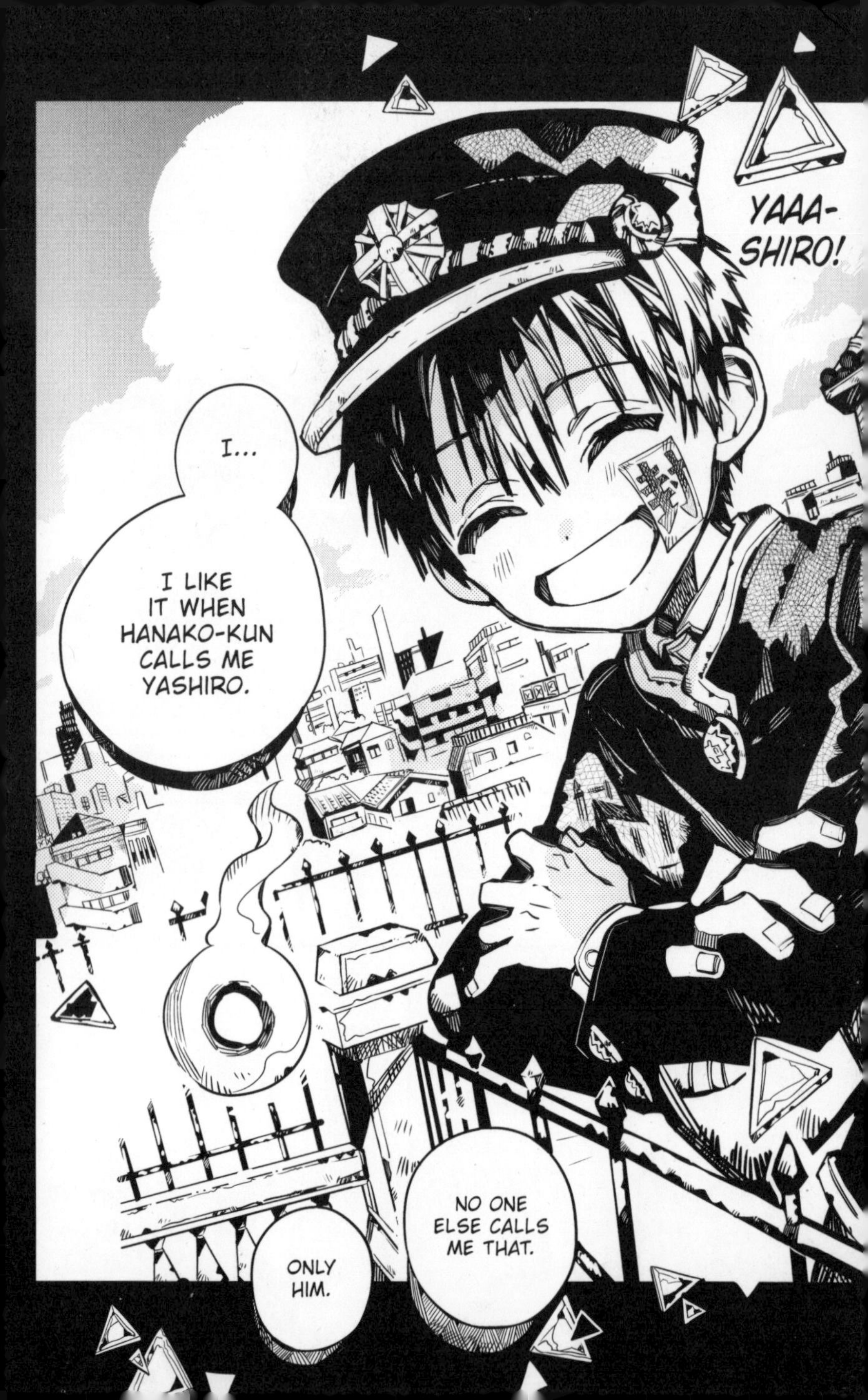
YAAA-SHIRO!
I...
I LIKE IT WHEN HANAKO-KUN CALLS ME YASHIRO.
NO ONE ELSE CALLS ME THAT.
ONLY HIM.

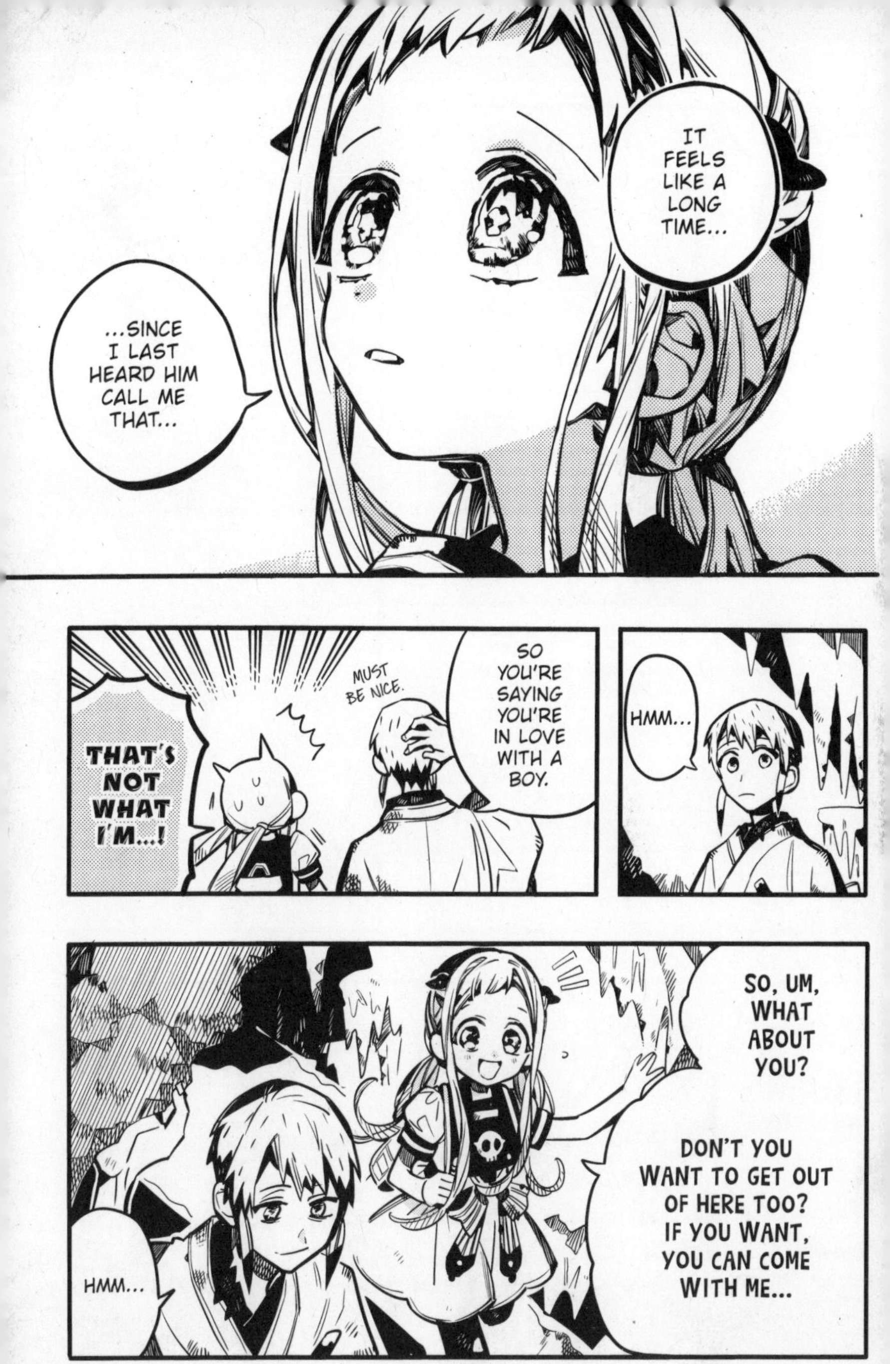
IT FEELS LIKE A LONG TIME...
...SINCE I LAST HEARD HIM CALL ME THAT...
HMM...
SO YOU'RE SAYING YOU'RE IN LOVE WITH A BOY.
MUST BE NICE.
THAT'S NOT WHAT I'M...!
SO, UM, WHAT ABOUT YOU?
DON'T YOU WANT TO GET OUT OF HERE TOO? IF YOU WANT, YOU CAN COME WITH ME...
HMM...

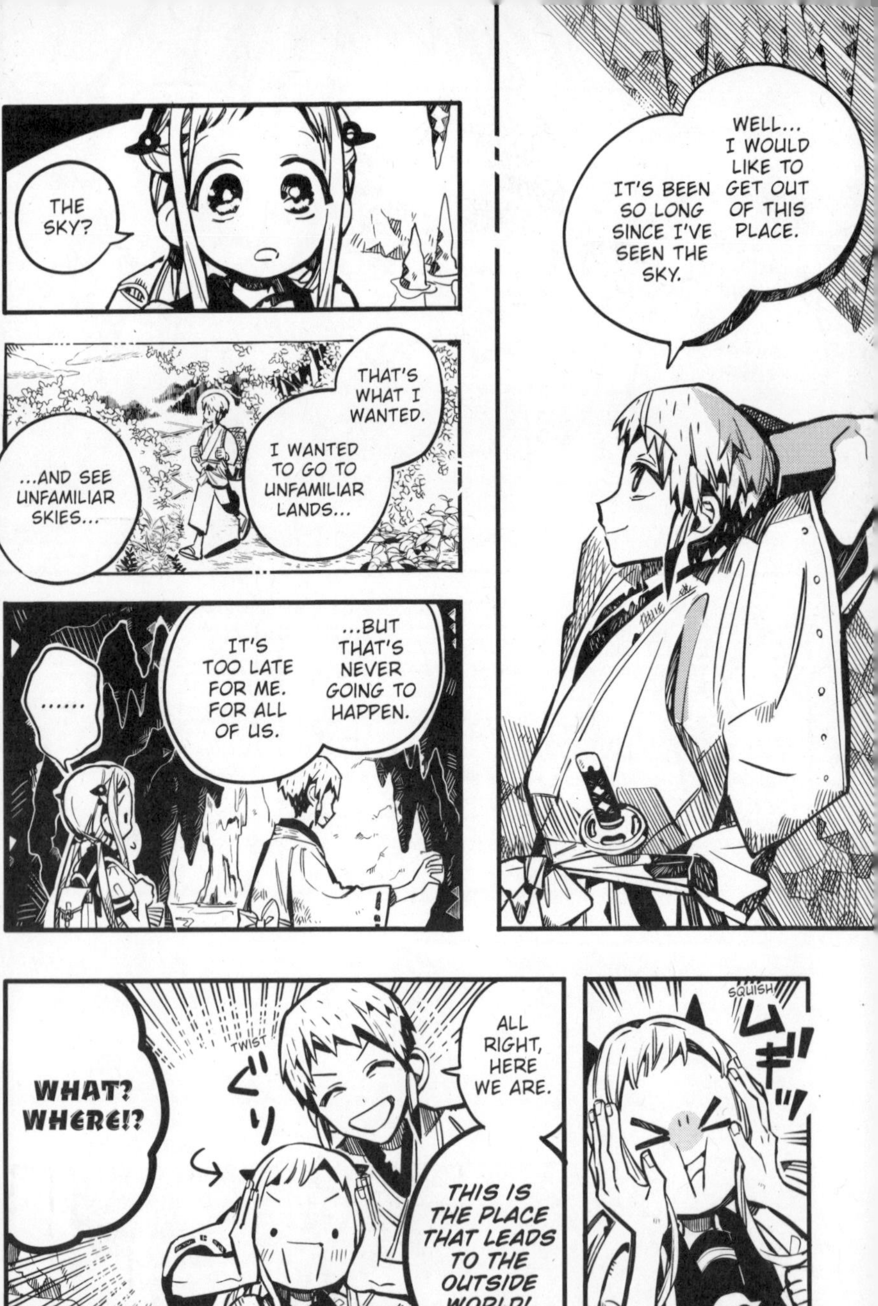
WELL... I WOULD LIKE TO GET OUT OF THIS PLACE.
IT'S BEEN SO LONG SINCE I'VE SEEN THE SKY.
THE SKY?
THAT'S WHAT I WANTED.
I WANTED TO GO TO UNFAMILIAR LANDS...
...AND SEE UNFAMILIAR SKIES...
...BUT THAT'S NEVER GOING TO HAPPEN.
IT'S TOO LATE FOR ME. FOR ALL OF US.
......
SQUISH
ムギッ
ALL RIGHT, HERE WE ARE.
TWIST
ぐり
THIS IS THE PLACE THAT LEADS TO THE OUTSIDE WORLD!
WHAT? WHERE!?

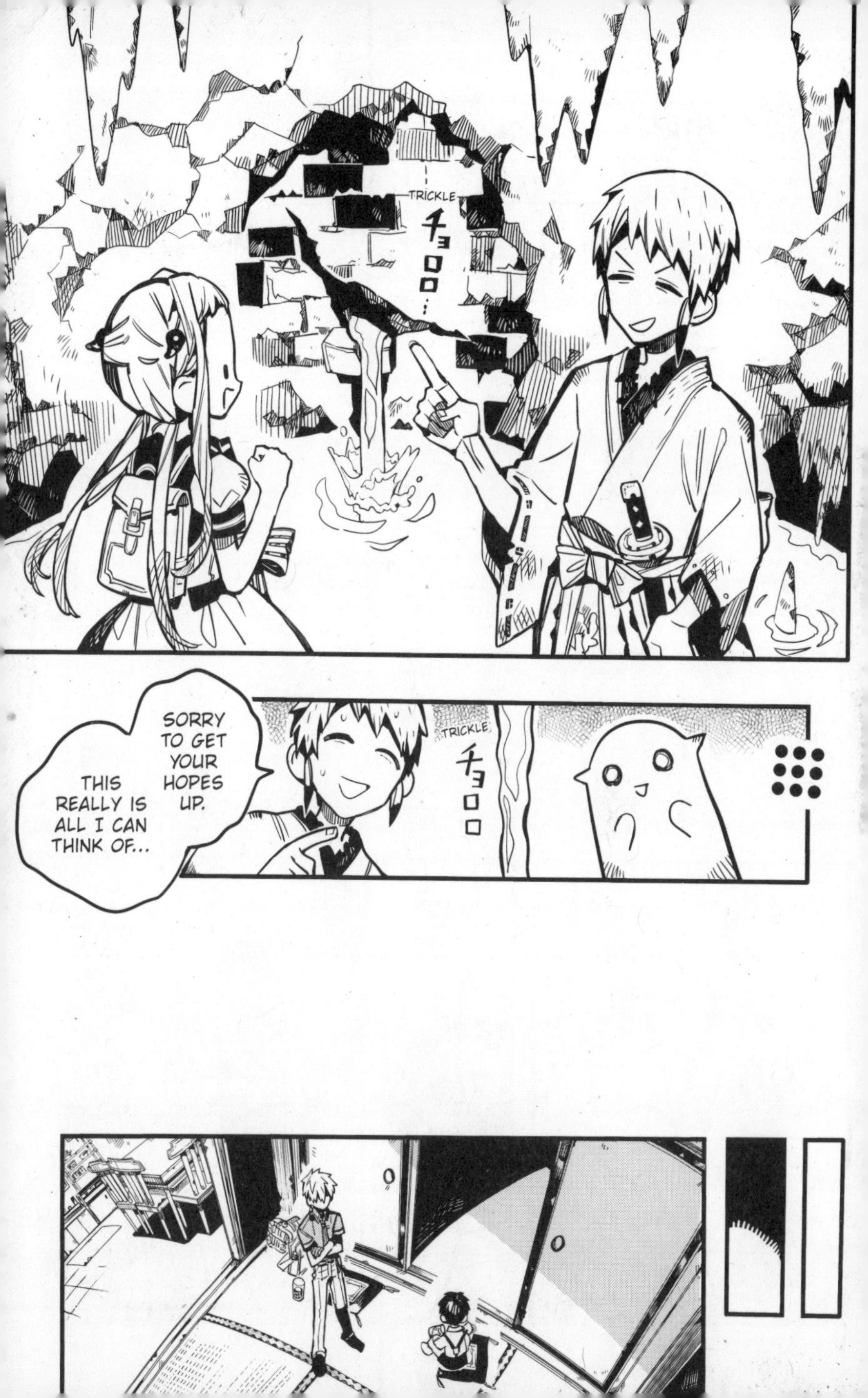
TRICKLE
チョロロ…
TRICKLE
チョロロ
SORRY TO GET YOUR HOPES UP.
THIS REALLY IS ALL I CAN THINK OF…

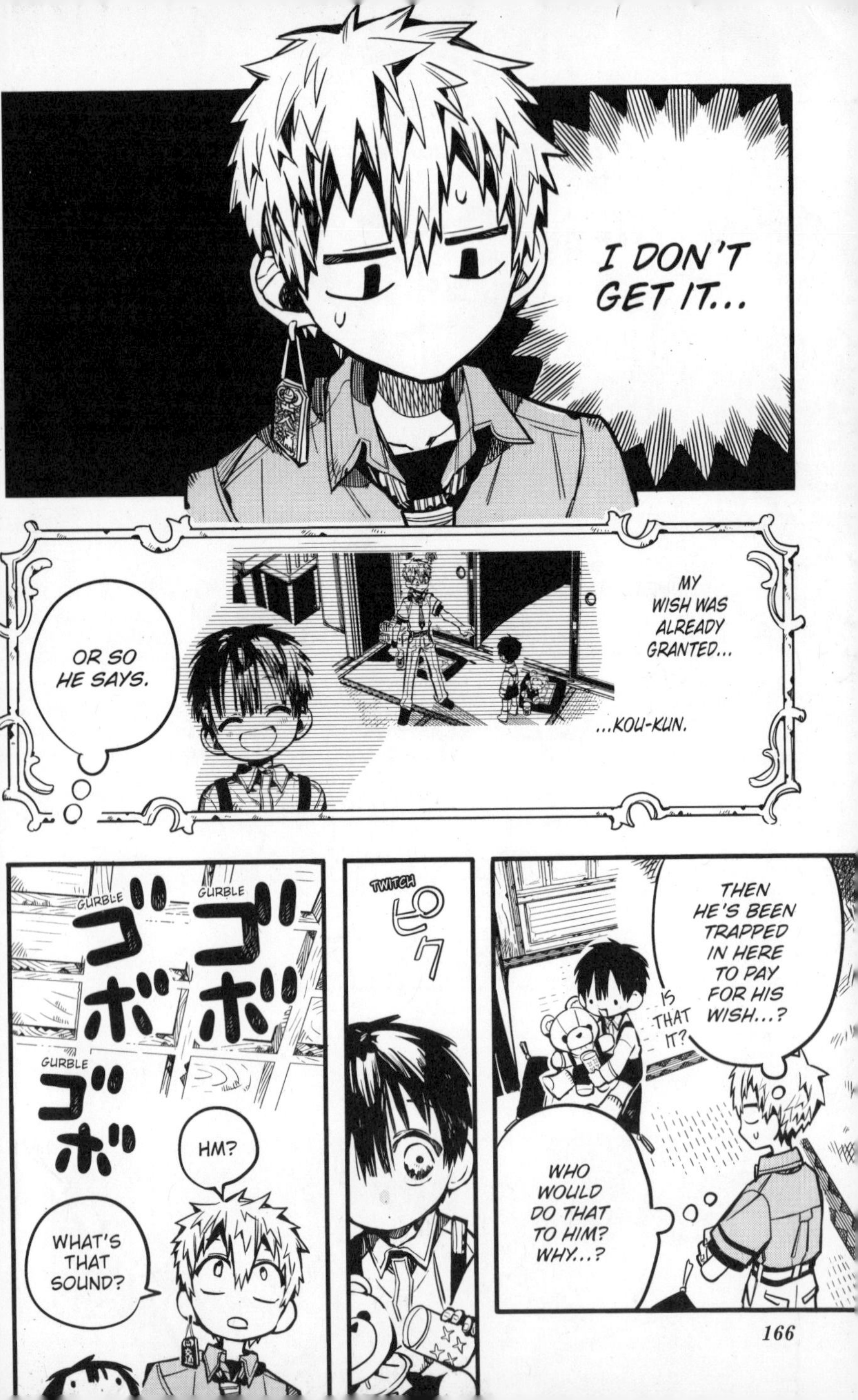
I DON'T GET IT...
MY WISH WAS ALREADY GRANTED...
...KOU-KUN.
OR SO HE SAYS.
THEN HE'S BEEN TRAPPED IN HERE TO PAY FOR HIS WISH...?
IS THAT IT?
WHO WOULD DO THAT TO HIM? WHY...?
TWITCH
ピク
GURBLE
ゴボ
GURBLE
ゴボ
GURBLE
ゴボ
HM?
WHAT'S THAT SOUND?

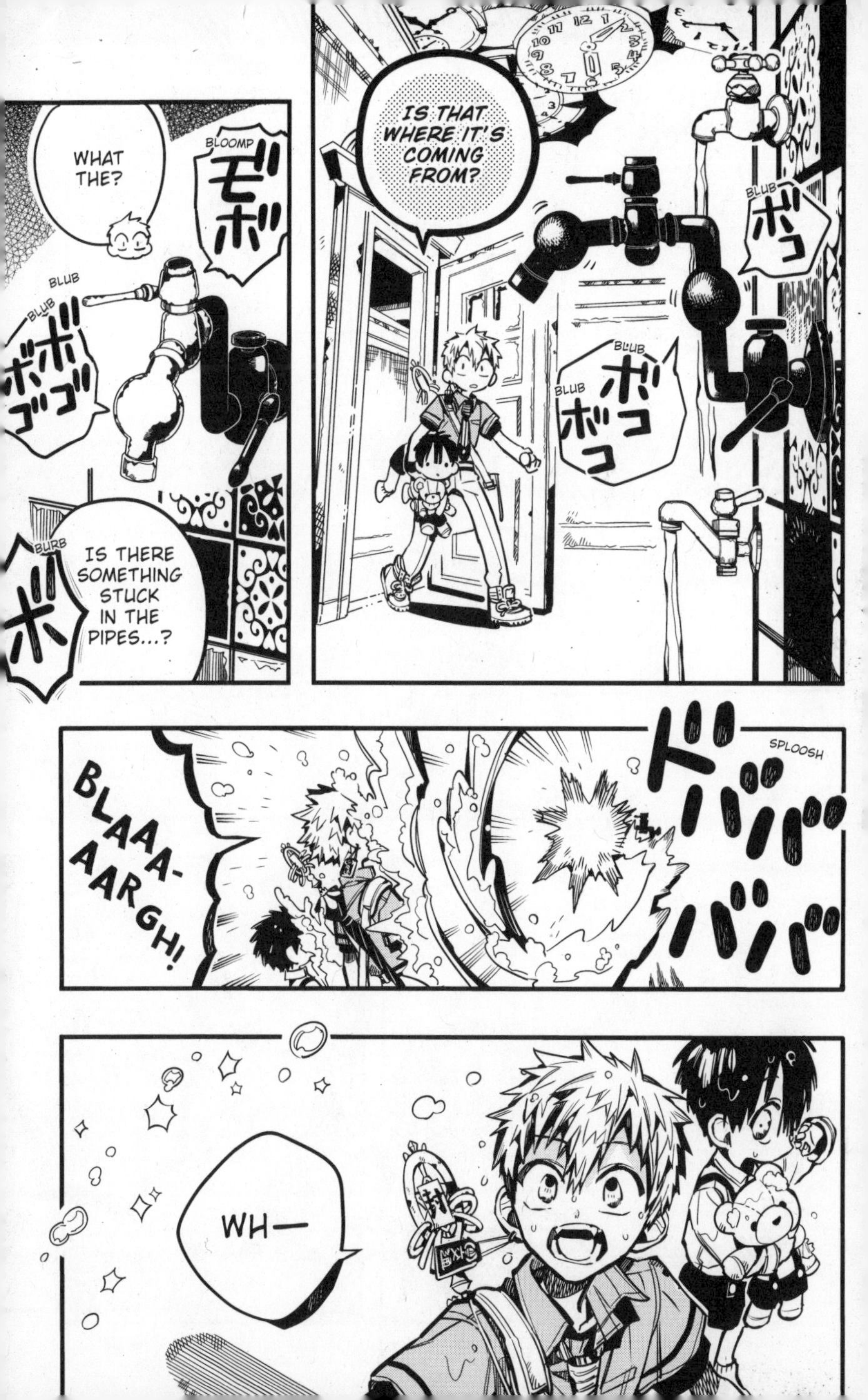
IS THAT WHERE IT'S COMING FROM?
BLUB
ボコ
BLUB BLUB
ボコボコ
WHAT THE?
BLOOMP
モボ
BLUB BLUB
ボボゴゴ
BURB
ボ
IS THERE SOMETHING STUCK IN THE PIPES...?
SPLOOSH
ドババババ
BLAAAA-AARGH!
WH—

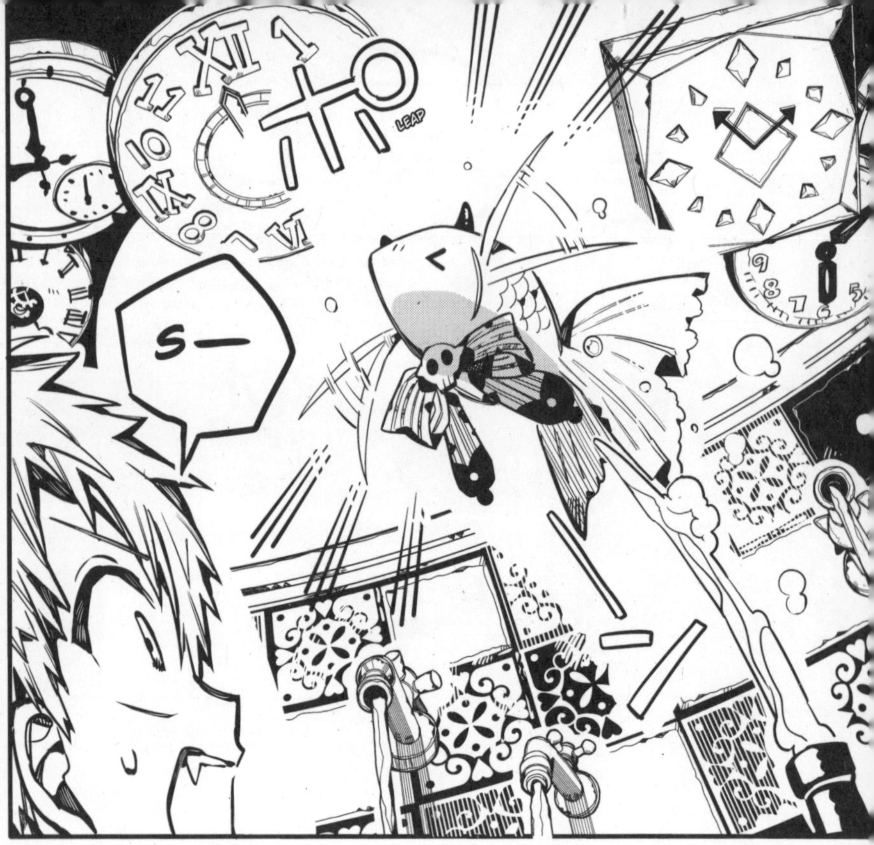
LEAP
S—
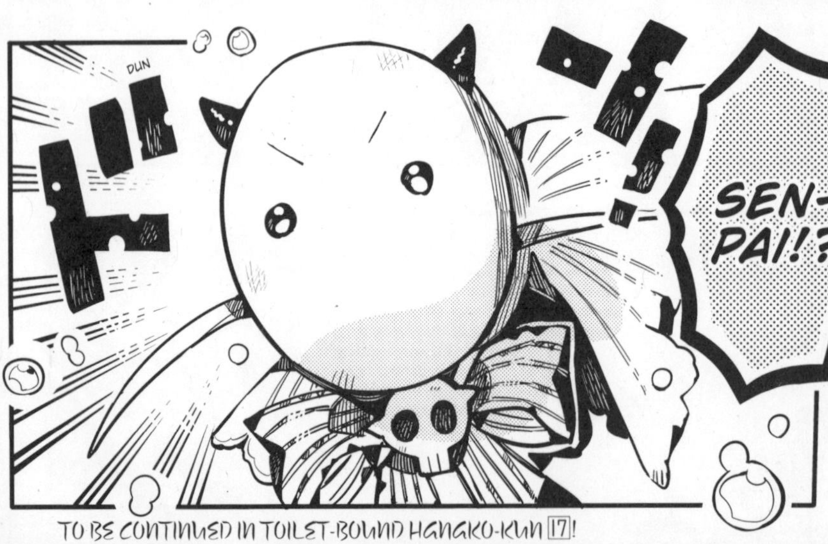
SEN-PAI!?
DUN

TO BE CONTINUED IN TOILET-BOUND HANAKO-KUN 17!

TRANSLATION NOTES

Common Honorifics

no honorific: Indicates familiarity or closeness; if used without permission or reason, addressing someone in this manner would constitute an insult.

-san: The Japanese equivalent of Mr./Mrs./Miss. If a situation calls for politeness, this is the fail-safe honorific.

-sama: Conveys great respect; may also indicate that the social status of the speaker is lower than that of the addressee.

-kun: Used most often when referring to boys, this indicates affection or familiarity. Occasionally used by older men among their peers, but it may also be used by anyone referring to a person of lower standing.

-chan: An affectionate honorific indicating familiarity used mostly in reference to girls; also used in reference to cute persons or animals of either gender.

-senpai: A suffix used to address upperclassmen or more experienced coworkers.

-kouhai: The inverse of senpai, used to address those who are younger or less experienced.

-sensei: A respectful term for teachers, artists, or high-level professionals.

Page 79

"Year of the Earth Pig" is part of the sexagenary cycle, a repeating cycle of sixty named years that was a traditional Chinese calendar system also used by Japan and other East Asian regions. Each year combines one of the twelve Chinese zodiac signs with one of the five classical Chinese elements (wood, fire, earth, metal, and water). While neither China nor Japan still officially uses this system, it continues to be used in some methods of fortune-telling.

Page 123

While doors in traditional Japanese-style houses are not particularly sturdy, shoji screens are just made of rice paper on a thin wooden lattice and are prone to even accidental damage, which is why Akane is particularly confused about not being able to scratch them.

Page 149

In feudal Japan, it was common for a man addressing a woman or girl to add an O to the beginning of her name as a way of showing respect.

Page 152

The bodhisattva Jizou is widely known as a protector of children in Japanese Buddhism, which is why statues of him are created to commemorate the death of a child; see Volume 13's and 14's translation notes for more detail.

RELAY INTERVIEW

——How does that person feel about me?——
Everyone wants to know the answer, and
now you can! We've asked the *Hanako-kun*
cast their favorite and least-favorite things
about one of their fellow characters in
a relay-style interview.

RELAY INTERVIEW

FROM → TO

HANAKO-KUN → YASHIRO

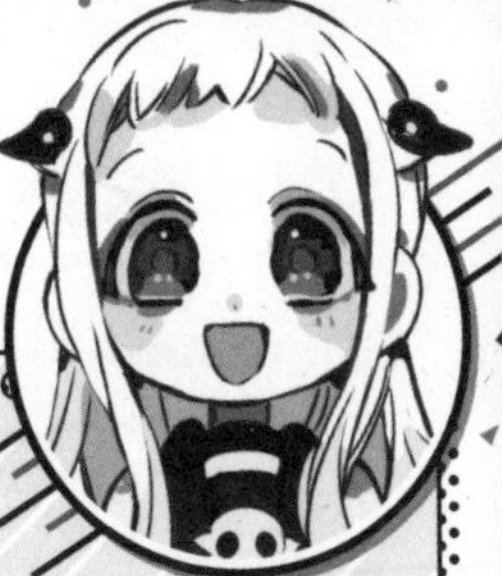

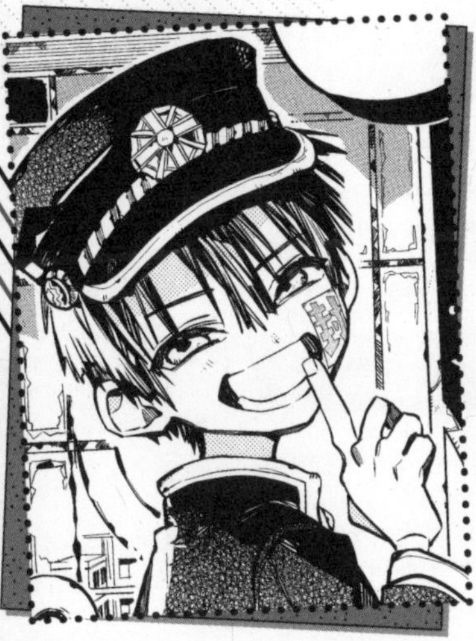

•I LIKE THIS ABOUT HER!

"Her hair, maybe."
It's nice, I guess? Pretty long.

•I'M NOT SO SURE ABOUT THIS...

"Her weakness for hot guys."
I wish she would only have eyes for me...

FROM → TO

NENE YASHIRO → AOI

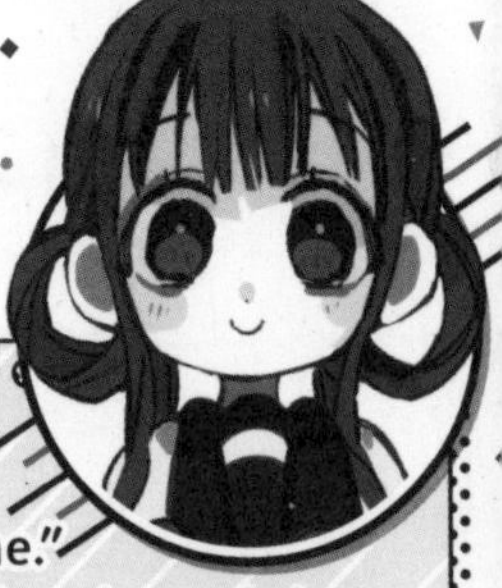

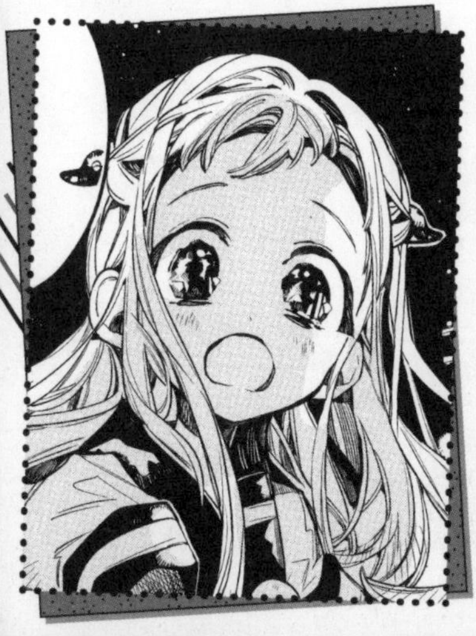

•I LIKE THIS ABOUT HER!

"She opens up to me."
Sometimes I think I'm the only one she's really warmed up to. I might just be a little happy about that.

•I'M NOT SO SURE ABOUT THIS...

"She's extremely guarded."
Still, Aoi has a hard time saying what's really on her mind...and sometimes I feel like I'm the only one sharing. That's not fair!

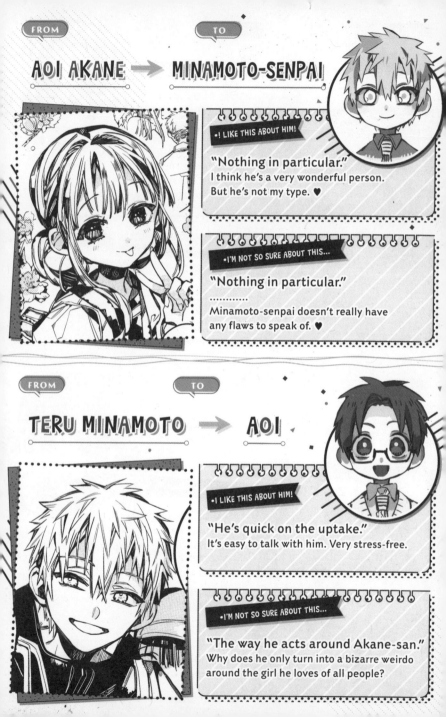

FROM

TO

AOI AKANE → MINAMOTO-SENPAI

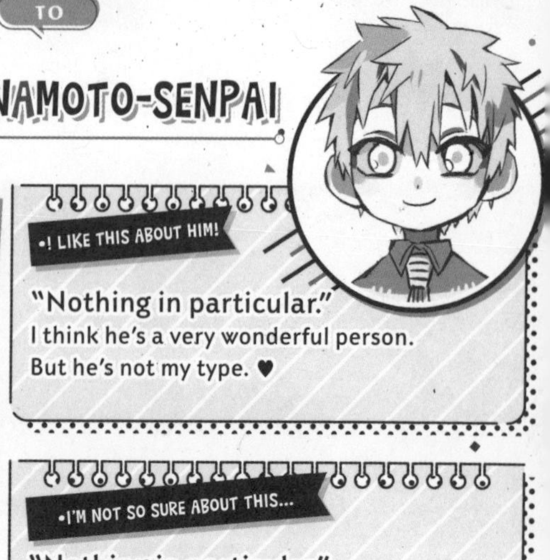

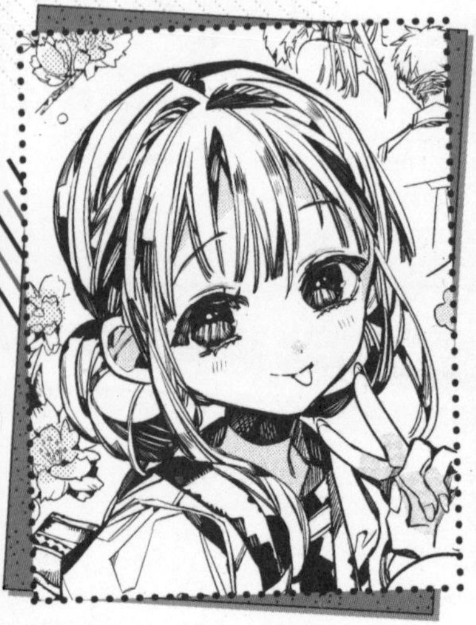

•I LIKE THIS ABOUT HIM!

"Nothing in particular."
I think he's a very wonderful person.
But he's not my type. ♥

•I'M NOT SO SURE ABOUT THIS...

"Nothing in particular."
....
Minamoto-senpai doesn't really have
any flaws to speak of. ♥

FROM

TO

TERU MINAMOTO → AOI

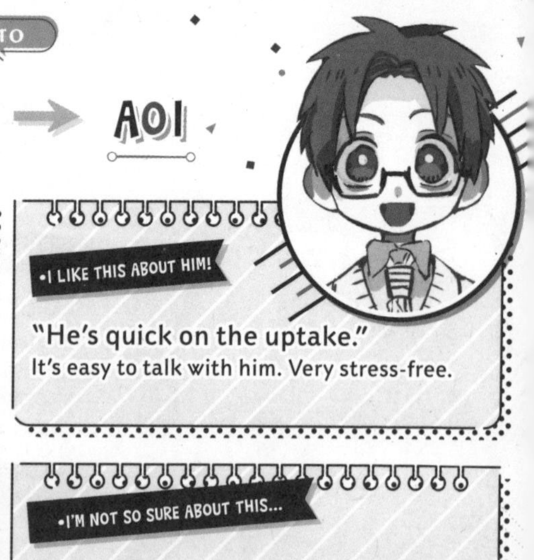

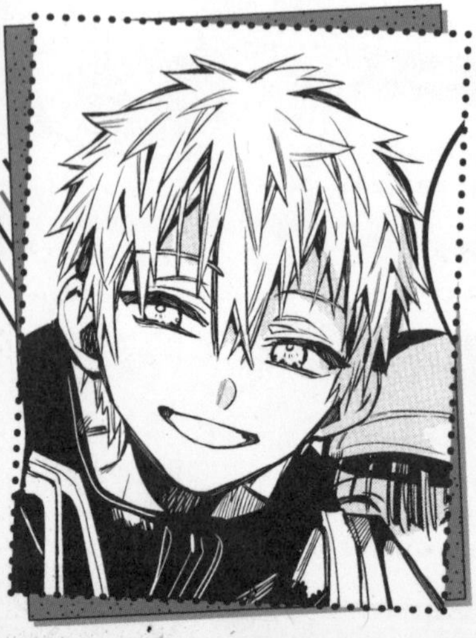

•I LIKE THIS ABOUT HIM!

"He's quick on the uptake."
It's easy to talk with him. Very stress-free.

•I'M NOT SO SURE ABOUT THIS...

"The way he acts around Akane-san."
Why does he only turn into a bizarre weirdo
around the girl he loves of all people?

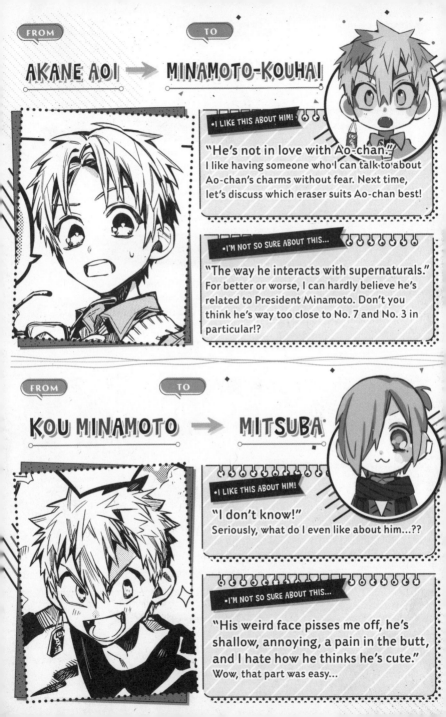

FROM

TO

AKANE AOI → MINAMOTO-KOUHAI

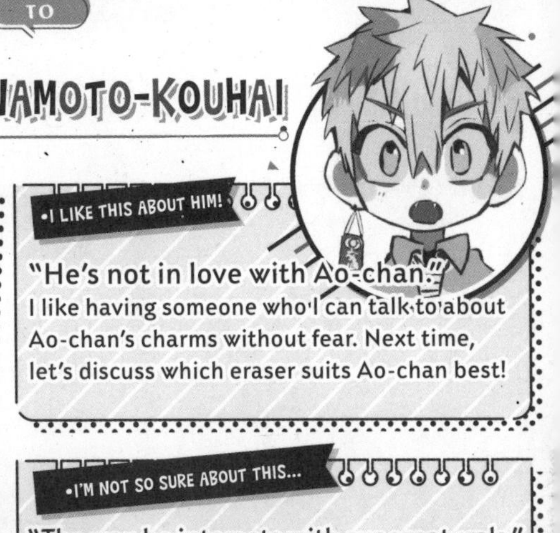

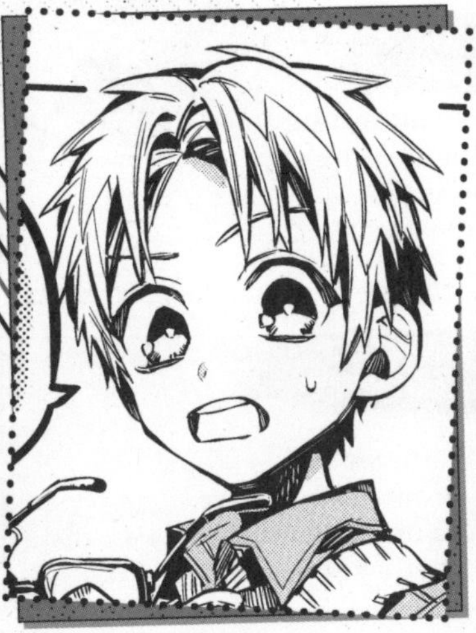

•I LIKE THIS ABOUT HIM!

"He's not in love with Ao-chan."
I like having someone who I can talk to about Ao-chan's charms without fear. Next time, let's discuss which eraser suits Ao-chan best!

•I'M NOT SO SURE ABOUT THIS...

"The way he interacts with supernaturals."
For better or worse, I can hardly believe he's related to President Minamoto. Don't you think he's way too close to No. 7 and No. 3 in particular!?

FROM

TO

KOU MINAMOTO → MITSUBA

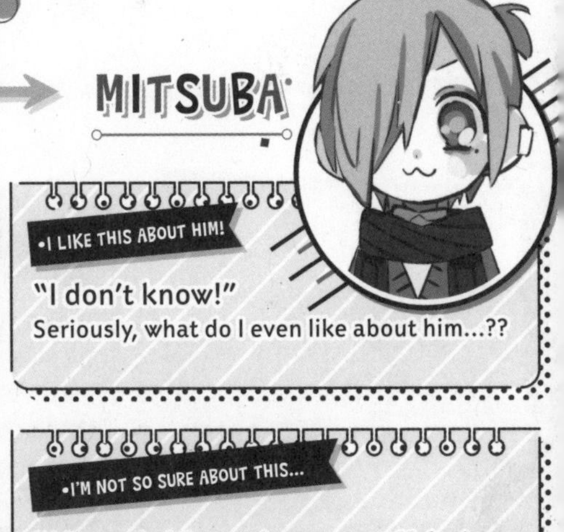

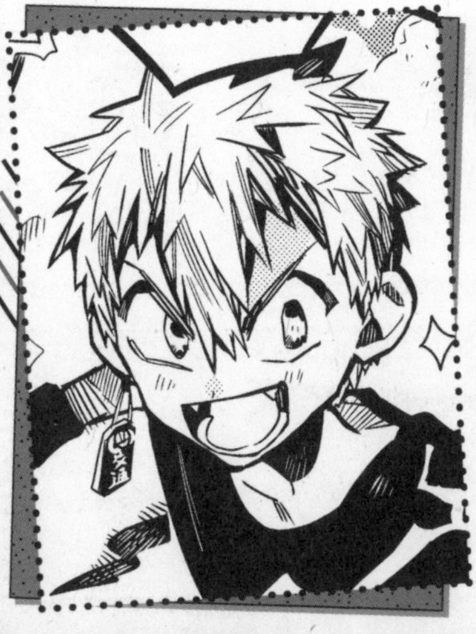

•I LIKE THIS ABOUT HIM!

"I don't know!"
Seriously, what do I even like about him...??

•I'M NOT SO SURE ABOUT THIS...

"His weird face pisses me off, he's shallow, annoying, a pain in the butt, and I hate how he thinks he's cute."
Wow, that part was easy...

FROM → TO

MITSUBA → AIR-SENPAI

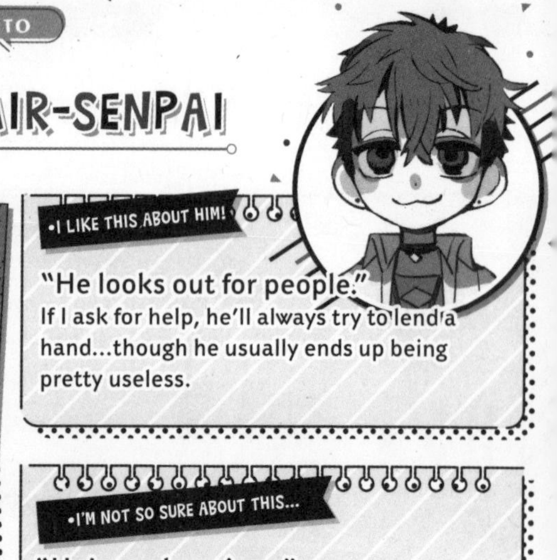

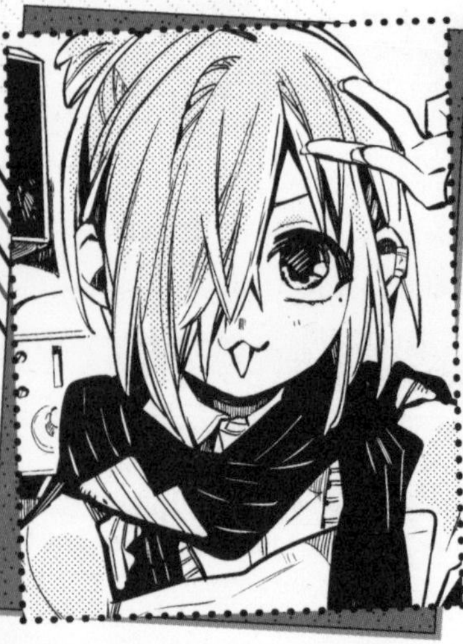

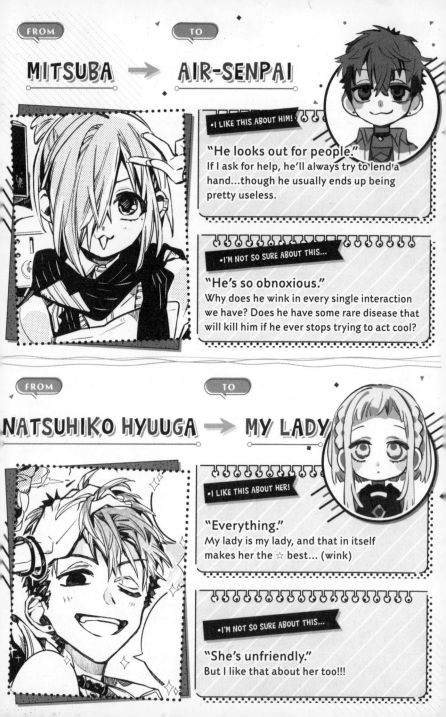

•I LIKE THIS ABOUT HIM!

"He looks out for people."
If I ask for help, he'll always try to lend a hand...though he usually ends up being pretty useless.

•I'M NOT SO SURE ABOUT THIS...

"He's so obnoxious."
Why does he wink in every single interaction we have? Does he have some rare disease that will kill him if he ever stops trying to act cool?

FROM → TO

NATSUHIKO HYUUGA → MY LADY

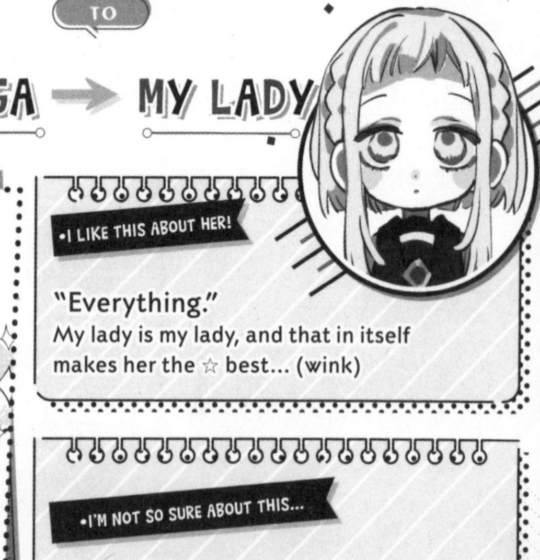

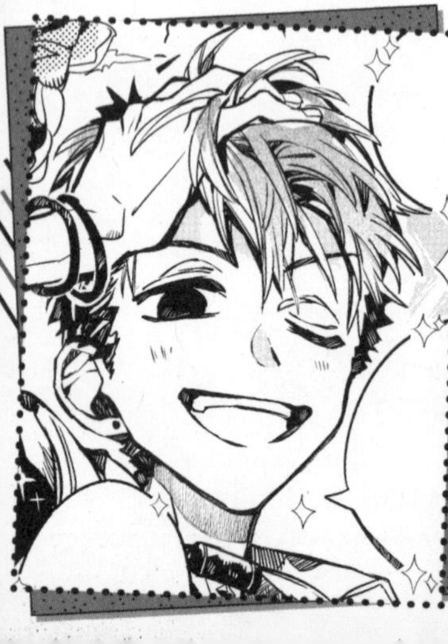

•I LIKE THIS ABOUT HER!

"Everything."
My lady is my lady, and that in itself makes her the ☆ best... (wink)

•I'M NOT SO SURE ABOUT THIS...

"She's unfriendly."
But I like that about her too!!!

FROM TO

SAKURA NANAMINE → TSUKASA

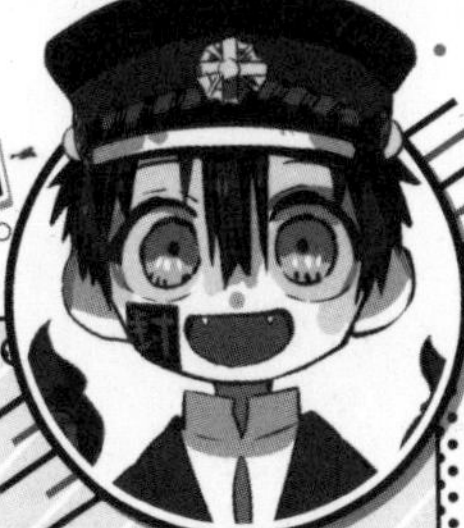

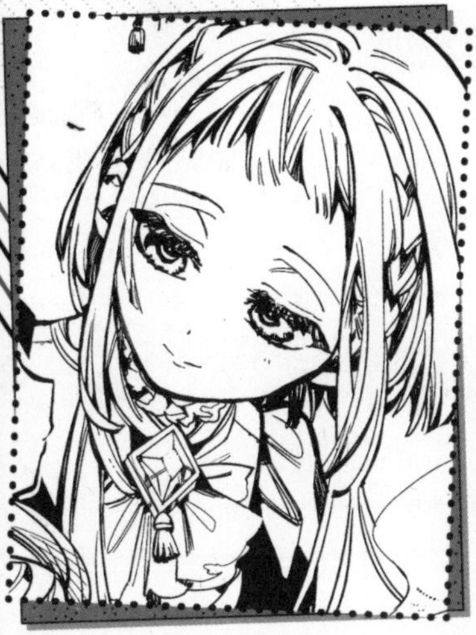

•I LIKE THIS ABOUT HIM!

"His naivete."
He's such an innocent boy. He is cruel sometimes, but he can be kind in his own way.

•I'M NOT SO SURE ABOUT THIS...

"He's too animalistic."
Please stop trying to put everything you see in your mouth...

FROM TO

TSUKASA → AMANE

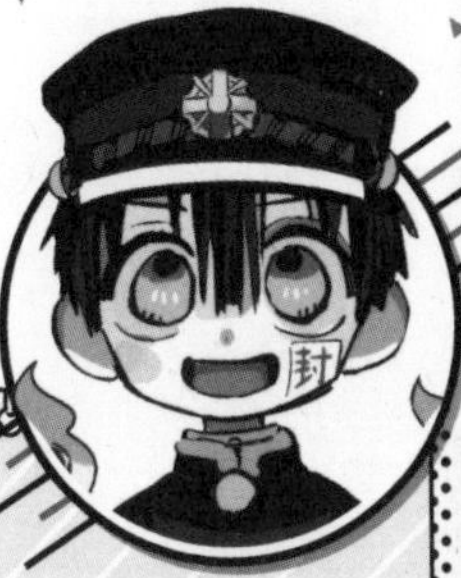

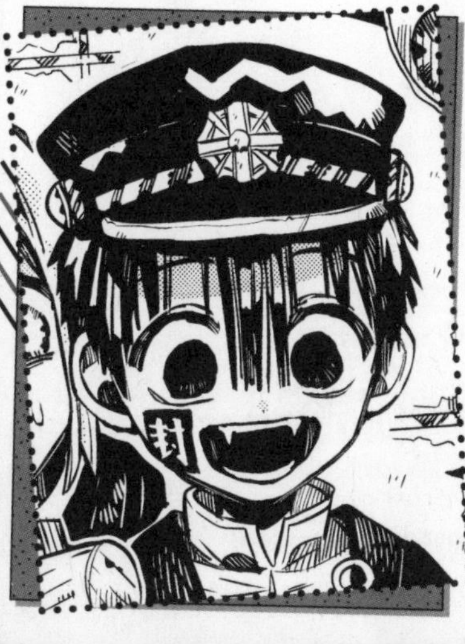

•I LIKE THIS ABOUT HIM!

"Amane."
He's pretty Amane-ish.

•I'M NOT SO SURE ABOUT THIS...

"Amane."
He's pretty Amane-ish...

FUN TIMES WITH KUNISHIGE-KUN

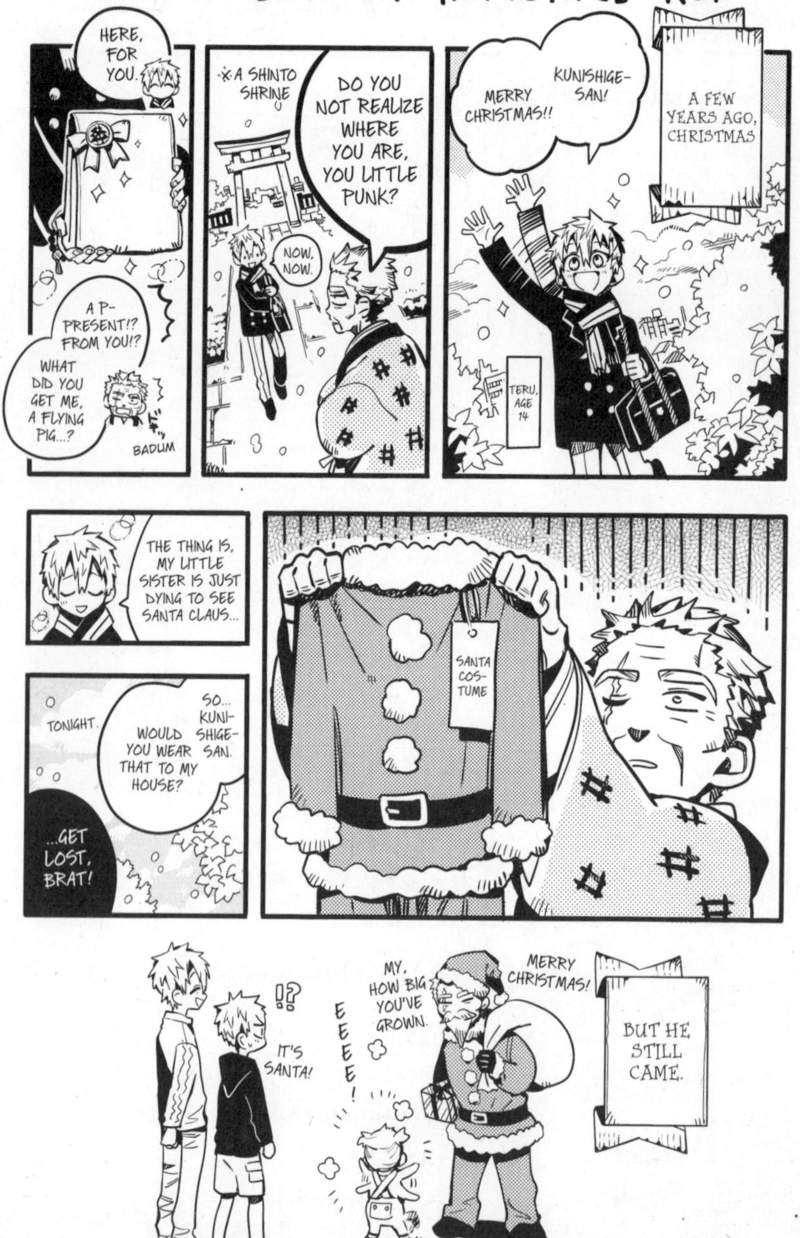
A FEW YEARS AGO, CHRISTMAS
KUNISHIGE-SAN! MERRY CHRISTMAS!!
TERU, AGE 14
DO YOU NOT REALIZE WHERE YOU ARE, YOU LITTLE PUNK?
※A SHINTO SHRINE
NOW, NOW.
HERE, FOR YOU.
A P-PRESENT!? FROM YOU!?
WHAT DID YOU GET ME, A FLYING PIG...?
BADUM
SANTA COSTUME
THE THING IS, MY LITTLE SISTER IS JUST DYING TO SEE SANTA CLAUS...
SO... KUNISHIGE-SAN. WOULD YOU WEAR THAT TO MY HOUSE?
TONIGHT.
...GET LOST, BRAT!
BUT HE STILL CAME.
MERRY CHRISTMAS!
MY, HOW BIG YOU'VE GROWN.
EEEEE!
!?
IT'S SANTA!

FUN TIMES WITH MAMA MINAMOTO

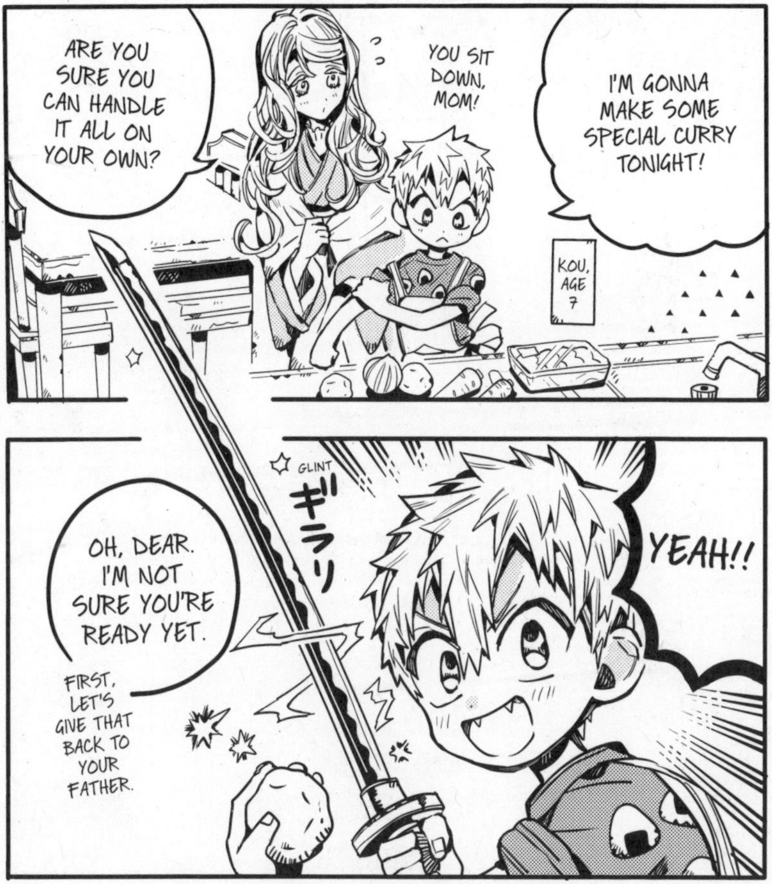

I'M GONNA MAKE SOME SPECIAL CURRY TONIGHT!
KOU, AGE 7
YOU SIT DOWN, MOM!
ARE YOU SURE YOU CAN HANDLE IT ALL ON YOUR OWN?
YEAH!!
GLINT
ギラリ
OH, DEAR. I'M NOT SURE YOU'RE READY YET.
FIRST, LET'S GIVE THAT BACK TO YOUR FATHER.

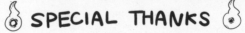

SPECIAL THANKS

EKE-CHAN OMAYU-TAN YUUJI-CHAN

REYU-CHAN KURUMI-CHAN WAKAMIYA-SAN

YUUKI KIYOKAWA-SAN

IMANITY

♡AND YOU♡

Toilet-bound Hanako-Kun 16

AidaIro

Translation: Alethea Nibley and Athena Nibley
Lettering: Phil Christie

JIBAKU SHONEN HANAKO-KUN Volume 16 ©2021 AidaIro / SQUARE ENIX CO., LTD.
First published in Japan in 2021 by SQUARE ENIX CO., LTD. English translation rights arranged with SQUARE ENIX CO., LTD. and Yen Press, LLC through Tuttle-Mori Agency, Inc.

English translation © 2022 by SQUARE ENIX CO., LTD.

Yen Press
150 West 30th Street, 19th Floor
New York, NY 10001

Visit us at yenpress.com • facebook.com/yenpress • twitter.com/yenpress • yenpress.tumblr.com • instagram.com/yenpress

First Yen Press Print Edition: September 2022
Originally published as an ebook in February 2022 by Yen Press.

Edited by Yen Press Editorial: Riley Pearsall, JuYoun Lee
Designed by Yen Press Design: Wendy Chan

Yen Press is an imprint of Yen Press, LLC.
The Yen Press name and logo are trademarks of Yen Press, LLC.

Library of Congress Control Number: 2019953610

ISBN: 978-1-9753-4733-8 (paperback)

10 9 8 7 6 5 4 3 2 1

TPA

Printed in South Korea